Smokin', & Spinnin'

ANDREA B. MILLER

For Mark, thanks for believing in me long before you knew what I was up to. And, your undying support. I love you!

For my girls, you were the driving force behind this project. You will never know how much I love you!

Prologue

I slam my car into park so violently it causes my Honda to shake and jerk. "Son of a bitch!" I exclaim to no one. I am so mad that I cannot breathe. I try desperately to drag air into my lungs as I watch her walking into his house. It is almost midnight. This cannot be happening to me.

As she disappears through the doorway, I shakily reach for my cell phone as all the missing pieces start to fall into place. Brooke was right, but if she knew, who else knew? The phone rings in my ear, bringing me back to reality. It rings once...twice...then three times!

"Damn it, Brooke! Pick up!"

Then suddenly, "What the hell?" Brooke snaps as she answers the phone. I can tell she is aggravated, but I don't give a damn. I gasp, thankful that she did take my call at this time of the night. "Whitney!" Brooke calls out again when I don't respond.

"Were you asleep?" I finally manage to say.

"No, I am going over depositions on a new case. What's the matter?"

I take a deep breath. "You were right!"

Brooke doesn't miss a beat. "I told you those shoes were terrible with that dress. I hope you can take them back!"

I laugh, although this is far from funny. "This isn't about the shoes," I say calmly.

"Well, it's hard for me to keep track sometimes..."

"Him! You were right about him." I cut her rambling off.

There is a disturbing silence before Brooke hisses, "Nooooo!"

"I saw with my own eyes," I say calmly.

I hear Brooke gasp. "What are you going to do? Do you need me to come there?"

With that statement, I realize in an instant that I have only one true best friend in this world. And I know exactly what I must do.

"No!" I say coolly. "I will be in Charlotte tomorrow before the sun goes down..."

Chapter 1

"Mom, I will be fine," I promise. I see the tears begin to sparkle in my mother's eyes. Thankfully, my Dad interjects. "Jillian, she needs to get on the road. She has a long drive ahead of her."

"I know, I know," Mom replies. "Whitney, I just feel like you're running away!"

I laugh out loud. "Well...I guess I am. And I would have left at midnight if it hadn't been for you." There is no need to dance around it. I have got to get the hell out of here. I need some space from this small town, a new start, a new place, and definitely new people.

"What am I supposed to do?" Mom exclaims.

I take her hands. "Mom, all you have to do is call Jessica and tell her to cancel everything. There is still plenty of time."

She nods, then exclaims again, "And what if he calls?"

"I will handle that!" Dad interjects again.

I turn and smile warmly at him. "Oh, he will call. I have blocked his number from my cell phone. So, he will be scrambling sooner or later," I say with a sigh. I know that my dad will take care of it because I have nothing to say.

My dad gently places the last bag in the trunk of my car and shuts it firmly. "That's all, baby girl."

I have everything I need, which are basically the necessities, clothes and cosmetics. I give my dad a huge hug, and his monstrous embrace envelops me. Tears prick my own eyes. I fight them back as only I know how. I never let anyone see me cry, not even that bastard! It is a defense mechanism that my dad burned into my brain from early on. *"Tough, Whitney. Be tough."* I remember my Dad's words. *"Emotion is a sign of weakness."*

I break the embrace with my dad and turn to my mother, who now has tears flowing freely down her cheeks. We embrace as she says sweetly, "I love you, Whitney!"

"Call us, please, as soon as you arrive," Dad says. "And absolutely no texting while driving!"

"Yes, sir, Sgt. Parker," I joke as I stand at mock attention and salute. I have learned to take orders from my military father well.

I jump into my Honda Accord, plug my iPod into the auxiliary cable, and wave goodbye one last time to my parents, who are now embracing each other in the driveway. I sigh. Here goes nothing...I am approximately six hours from Charlotte, North Carolina. My new home. I'm excited yet anxious as I set out on I-95 North out of this sleepy coastal Georgia town.

I press the shuffle button on my iPod, and one of my favorite songs from an '80s hair band comes up. I swear my iPod has a sixth sense. This is a good omen, though. I switch over to the aptly named playlist "'80s Big

Hair." I settle in to travel along with some major rock ballads and try desperately to think of what's ahead and not what I am leaving behind.

The past twelve hours have been pure hell. Within a blink of an eye, I have gone from actively planning my own wedding to packing my bags to get the hell out of Georgia. Thanks to Brooke, I am escaping, and relatively no one knows (or probably cares) where I am headed. I prefer it that way. Everyone in my life, except my parents, of course, have aided and abetted the recent implosion that is my life. I shake my head at my thoughts. Nope, I am leaving that all behind, back in Georgia where it belongs.

As soon as I cross the North Carolina state line, my cell phone begins to ring. The caller ID lets me know that it is my best friend, Brooke, or as I like to call her, my partner in crime.

"Where are ya, babe?" Brooke asks with excitement singing in her voice. She lives in Charlotte; in fact, I will be subletting her apartment since she has recently gotten married and moved out of the city.

"Patience, please!" I say. "I am crossing the state line, won't be long now!" My excitement is equally radiating, or it could be my nerves rattling. I am not sure which.

Truthfully, I have never made a snap decision like this in my life. Maybe that is why my nerves are beginning to overtake the excitement of it all. But I had to get away, move on, and the opportunity to move to Charlotte seemed like the perfect escape even though running from my problems makes me look like a total coward. I don't give a shit what anyone says, though. I am done. I take a deep breath and grip the steering wheel tightly.

Brooke has been begging me for years to move to North Carolina with her, but I wouldn't even consider it. Now is the perfect opportunity to move to Charlotte to get away from the mess in Georgia. I sigh to myself. Brooke is my one true friend. She has worked out all the details to help make this transition a smooth one after all I have been through. My mind drifts again to the last few hours of my life. It has been utter turmoil. I feel the familiar sob catch in my throat. *No! No!* I halt that journey down memory lane. I will not go there. That time of my life is over and done. Those memories are not allowed in North Carolina. I chastise myself again.

The drive is long, tedious, and boring. I am comforted only by the music that wafts through the speakers of my car. Oh, and the comical South of the Border billboards that are every mile it seems. *Jeez!* I arrive in the heart of Charlotte during midafternoon traffic, before sundown, as promised.

It is my goal to get settled in my apartment and start my job search on Monday. I plan to hit the ground running. With this economy, it is harder than ever to find a job, especially right out of college, but I am confident. Failure is absolutely not an option, and neither is moving back to Georgia.

Brooke has given me explicit directions, and I find myself at the apart-ment complex without any problems. I feel a huge sense of relief as I reach the door of apartment 34C. I unlock the door, and Brooke is waiting inside for me!

"Oh my God!" she shrieks as she jumps up from the couch to greet me. She is so over the top, but I do *love* her. She has been my rock. She grabs me in a huge, consuming hug, suffocating me with her thick blonde hair.

"Hi," is all I can manage in return.

Brooke is beautiful—with long, slender legs for days—tenacious, and successful. She totally has her shit together. I, on the other hand, do not. Brooke is close to achieving partner status in her law firm, while

I am just starting my career. *Thanks to you know who.* I am in total awe of Brooke, which makes me feel inadequate too. My thick, mousy brown hair is pulled back in an untidy ponytail, and my river-blue eyes are red and tired from the exhausting drive. And let me not mention the few pounds that I have gained thanks to the recent turn of events in my life. I have got to get myself back in shape, I vow. I hate to feel uncomfortable in my own skin.

"I just can't believe that you're finally here!" Brooke squeals again. She begins to show me around the apartment.

"Brooke, I can't thank you enough for doing this for me," I say.

She rolls her eyes at me. "Whit! Please! You are helping me, remember. I can't handle a mortgage and a lease payment."

I smile. The apartment is small but very comfortable, and I already feel at home. It is a one bedroom, with a huge kitchen with a center island that opens to a great room. The apartment is flawlessly decorated with southern elegance, which is totally Brooke's style.

"OK, I have to get back to the office. I will be over in the morning. Then, Matthew and I will come back into town for dinner tomorrow night."

Matthew is Brooke's husband. A lawyer too, he has moved Brooke out of the city and into the suburbs of Charlotte. Hence, my new digs.

"You call me if you need anything in the meantime. OK?" Brooke jumps up and down with excitement. I laugh at her theatrics. And with that, she is gone with the same flourish.

I sit down on the couch and take out my cell phone to call my parents. I take a deep breath as Mom answers the phone. "I made it!" I exclaim.

"Oh, Whitney! The phone is ringing off the hook. He won't stop calling. She is calling. They all seem to be in a panic."

She gasps for breath as I intercede with a laugh. "Mom! Mom! Please! Everything is OK. Just take the phone off the hook! OK?"

She hesitates. "OK."

I know this is hard for her, but I have got to do what is right for me. "Mom, I have to go, but I will call you soon. I love you!"

I can hear the tears in her voice. "I love you, Whitney!" And the line goes dead.

I haul my belongings in from the underground garage, and suddenly it hits me just how tired I am—not just from the drive, but from no sleep last night and my epic meltdown. I head straight for the shower. I love the bathroom. It is huge. It has a double vanity sink, large walk-in shower, and separate Jacuzzi tub. What the apartment lacks in size, it more than makes up for in amenities. *Oh! I am in heaven.*

I strip off my T-shirt and shorts and then turn on the shower. The hot water is scalding and therapeutic. It rushes over my skin, and I desperately try to wash Georgia off my body and out of my mind. When I emerge from the shower, I realize that I have a new resolve. So, I set out to turn Casa Brooke into Casa Whitney.

It only takes me an hour to accomplish my task. After I unpack, I amble over to the refrigerator. Starving! *Yep, I am going to have to hit the market tomorrow*, I say to myself as I open the door. Shockingly, I find the refrigerator is stocked to the max. *How did she do all that so quickly?* Thanks to Brooke, front and center, I find my favorite bottle of Riesling. *Awesome!* I find a glass, corkscrew, and I'm in business! I smile. Brooke really is too much! But I have never been more thankful for another person in my life.

On top of the counter on the center island is a plain white card bearing my name. I read the note that Brooke has left for me:

Welcome home, Whitney! Circumstances
notwithstanding, I am glad that you are here.
Love, Brooke

I laugh out loud. Always a lawyer, but forever my friend! And I realize Brooke is right again. I am home.

Chapter 2

I am nestled down in Brooke's bed, my new haven, when I hear the door open. Before I can be alarmed, Brooke bounds into the bedroom.

"OMG! Why are you not up?"

I have to remember to get that key back from her.

"Ugh!" I groan loudly. "You have got to call first!"

Brooke sounds back, "Not hardly, this is my damn house, remember! Get up! We have lots to do today!"

I scramble out of the bed and make my way to the bathroom. Thankfully, I showered last night. All I need is a little makeup, a brush through my brown mane to secure it back in a ponytail, and I am good to go.

"All right, let's do it!" I exclaim as I walk into the living room, where Brooke sits patiently reading e-mails on her iPad. She looks up at me warily. "Is that what you are wearing?"

I stand back to look at myself. I have on black yoga pants, a Georgia Southern T-shirt, and my best tennis shoes. "Yes," I exclaim. "What's wrong with what I have on?"

Brooke sarcastically laughs, "You are not going anywhere with me dressed like that."

I feign disgust, roll my eyes, and put my hands on my hips, but I know all arguments with Brooke are futile.

"Whitney!" Brooke exclaims. "You never know when you might meet a gorgeous stranger or your worst enemy. You should always be on top of your game. Not to mention the fact that you are in a new city with new people and experiences, and you need a job. And you only get one chance to make a good first impression.

I roll my eyes at her. "OK, OK...Mom! Thanks for the early morning lecture!" I say sarcastically. "What do you suggest that I wear?"

Brooke bounds up from the couch and back into the bedroom. She calls back to me, "Where are your clothes?"

"In the closet!" I find Brooke rifling through my clothes at rocket speed.

"It looks like the first order of the day is to go shopping. Seriously, Whitney! What has happened to you? You used to be such a fashionista!" she exclaims, looking through my clothes with disgust.

Tears sting my eyes unexpectedly. She knows what happened. I look down.

"Oh shit, Whitney!" Brooke shouts. "I am so sorry. I didn't think."

I shake my head and push back the tears. She is right. I have completely let myself go. "You are right! Let's go shopping!" There is no need to cry about it. It's time to fix it.

Luckily, I am able to find some khaki shorts and a long-sleeve polo button-down to wear from a stash of clothes that Brooke left behind. The outfit is perfect for a day out, and it looks perfect paired with my casual brown flip-flops. Brooke is right. I have to be on top of my game. I exaggeratedly model my new look for her. She nods in approval, adds a few pieces of jewelry, and we are out the door.

The bright Charlotte sunshine blinds my eyes as we make our way through the streets. The great thing about Brooke's apartment is the location. The apartment village lies in the heart of the city, within walking distance of the business district, shopping annex, and historic downtown. I fall in love instantly.

After round one of shopping, we stop for lunch at a small deli called Amelie's.

"So, what is the latest?" Brooke asks outright.

I roll my eyes, signaling that I know full well what she means. I don't want to have this conversation. I turn my head to look out the window, hoping Brooke will stop with her inquisition. She doesn't.

"Have you talked to your mom at all?"

My stomach rolls at that thought. I nod silently.

"Both of them are blowing up my mom's phone. And I have blocked all their numbers from my cell phone," I say without expression. "I don't want to hear any excuses or explanations. I just really don't give a shit anymore! I am sick and tired of hashing and rehashing all this in my mind. The who, what, when, and where of it all is exhausting. He made his choice. He used me, lied to me, and cheated on me. And I can't believe it took me this long to figure it all out. But I am done. I am moving on. End of the discussion."

Brooke eyes me intently. "Good for you!" she exclaims. "I will not mention it or ask another question. I am just so glad that you are here. And in all seriousness"—Brooke reaches across the table to grasp my hand—"you can do a heck of lot better than that bastard!"

I throw my head back and laugh. It feels good. But she is absolutely right!

After lunch, we do a little more shopping. Brooke puts together a few new outfits for me. I seriously love having a personal shopper—it is so easy!

Brooke helps me haul my purchases into the apartment. "Look...I know I said that I wouldn't say anything else, but if you need to talk or decide you want to vent, please tell me. I am here for you. I could stay with you for a few days, if you want me to?"

I shake my head as a sob wells up in my throat. "You know me better than that. But I appreciate your offer!"

Brooke gives me a wink as she leaves the apartment.

Chapter 3

After an action-packed weekend, Monday arrives all too early. I am thankful that I had the weekend to get acclimated to my new surroundings. Brooke has given me a mini tour of Charlotte. *I love it!* Just the apartment village alone is a small city within itself, complete with supermarket, deli, and other small boutiques. Not to mention the bustling nightlife throughout downtown Charlotte.

There is so much to do and take in. I cannot wait to experience it all. I am excited about all the possibilities. But first, I have got to find myself a freaking job, like, yesterday. Until then, I will be relying on my unimpressive savings funded mostly by my unused wedding budget. Brooke is giving me a wonderful deal on her apartment, but I have got to pull my own weight, and moving back to Georgia is *not* an option. I spend the whole day beating on doors, completing employment applications, and responding to newspaper ads. It's a "hurry up and wait" process that drives me insane.

After a hectic first Monday in Charlotte, I meet up with Brooke at a restaurant called Vida for what she calls our inaugural Margarita Monday, our new weeknight ritual. This is one of the many reasons why I love Brooke.

I spy her sitting in a booth in the back. As I slide in, Brooke eagerly says, "Whitney, I've got some news, gal!"

I can see the gleam in her eye. I am concerned because that glow normally means trouble. I frown.

"I have taken on a new client at the firm. It's a temporary employment service. The office manager is super nice, and I have told her all about you. Anyway, she is expecting you tomorrow at eight o'clock a.m. sharp," she says, out of breath but very proud of herself.

"What!" I snap. I am confused. "A temp service? Brooke, I need a real job."

She grunts at me, "Seriously, I know this! But like I said, it is temp-o-rary." She stresses each syllable. "This will at least give you something to do while you wait. Plus, you never know what doors it will open," she adds reassuringly.

I roll my eyes at her, but quickly agree. "OK!" Brooke is right, though. Her words ring in my ears, *"You never know where this might lead."* It is almost an omen. I raise my glass to hers. "Thank you! I think!" And we erupt into a fit of girlish giggles.

* * *

I arrive promptly at the Kelly Services office on the outskirts of Charlotte the following morning. Albeit, I am a little regretful of that last margarita. I have a slight headache but nothing that is unmanageable. I make a mental note that two drinks is my limit, especially on a weeknight.

I am greeted skeptically by a young, blonde-haired, gum-popping receptionist and am quickly ushered into the branch manager's office.

Gail Thomas is a middle-aged woman who is meticulously dressed. Her cropped blonde hair is styled to perfection. Even though I am dressed in a Brooke-approved outfit, her professionalism makes me nervous. She is the definition of professional. She smiles warmly at me and immediately puts me at ease.

"It is very nice to meet you, Whitney," Gail says. "Brooke has told me so much about you and recommends you highly." She smiles again. Another reason why I love Brooke. She continues to rave about my partner in crime, all things that I already know, of course. "Brooke has helped me tremendously, so I am hopeful that I can return the favor."

I smile outwardly to Gail but am frowning inside. *Great! I'm a charity case!*

Gail goes through the temporary service process, various positions that are available, and then hands me a stack of paperwork that I must complete. She asks me a few mock interview questions, mainly about my job experience and my course of study at Georgia Southern University. Luckily, thanks to Brooke, I have bypassed the major interview portion and have jumped immediately into the temporary employee pool. I am filling out the employment forms when I hear an unfamiliar ringtone. I know it is not my cell phone because I always keep it on silent.

I look up to see Gail answer a call on her personal cell phone. I listen inconspicuously to her conversation as I write.

"Jerri! Good morning!" Gail says cheerfully, then listens carefully. "OK, please stop! What are you running over there? A three-ring circus?" After a series of "OKs" and "I sees," Gail reassures Jerri that she will take care of her problem, then hangs up the phone. I look up as she places her cell phone back down on her desk.

Gail meets my gaze and smiles hesitantly. "I apologize for the inter-ruption, but that was my good friend Jerri Andrews. She is the office manager for GCR Racing. Apparently, they have had some issues with their receptionist. She did not show up for work this morning. Would you be interested in filling in until Jerri can hire a replacement?" she says, putting me on the spot.

I am not sure about taking a receptionist position, but at the same time, I don't want to tell Gail no. "Sure," I say confidently, although I am not feeling as positive as I sound. "GCR Racing...What type of business is that?"

Gail is stunned, but replies, "Whitney, are you not familiar with NASCAR?"

I shake my head.

"GCR Racing is a NASCAR race organization that is owned and oper-ated by Garrett Ryan Carter Sr., one of the most legendary drivers in NASCAR." Gail raises her eyebrows at me.

Really? I smile sheepishly from embarrassment. This information means nothing to me since I know nothing about the sport.

Gail looks concerned. "Well, maybe I should send someone else over."

I hold up my hand in defense. "No, I can do it. I am a quick learner and always up for a challenge."

Gail laughs, "This will be a challenge, no doubt."

I raise my eyebrow at her skeptically. *What does she mean by that?*

"Let me give you a quick rundown," she says.

Gail briefly educates me on the world of stock car racing. "NASCAR is big business in Charlotte. A large majority of the race teams are based in and around the Charlotte area."

Gail continues her brief overview, but gives no background on why this job will be challenging. *Hmmm...*I feel a lump rising in my throat from feeling stupid. I despise feeling or being treated as if I am. Or it could be the anticipation of a new job that I know nothing about has me in a panic. But it is nothing that I can't handle.

I manage to mutter, "Will my lack of knowledge of the sport create a problem?"

Gail laughs, "No! It might actually work out better in the long run." She winks at me as she slides the directions to GCR headquarters over to me, a gesture that gives me surety that there is more to this story than what she is disclosing.

I journey out of Charlotte on Interstate 77 North en route to Mooresville, an outlying suburb of the metro area. Approximately forty-five minutes later, I arrive at a huge concrete building with an impressive glass facade. The sign on the building, GCR Racing, lets me know that I have reached the right address. I park my Honda in the expansive lot and make my way to the entrance.

As I walk through the door of the extraordinary building, I am greeted warmly by an elderly security guard. He is dressed very casually in khaki pants and a cobalt-blue polo shirt that sports the GCR Racing logo. His smile puts me at ease as I introduce myself.

"Hi, I am Whitney Parker. I am the new receptionist."

"Why, hello, Miss Parker." He regards me closely in typical elderly fashion. "Mrs. Andrews is expecting you. Please take the elevator to the third floor," he says as he gestures toward the elevator vestibule. I smile and nod my head to thank him.

Before I head over to the elevator, I pause for a moment to look around the lobby. The first floor appears to be some type of a museum and merchandise store. I make a mental note to take a look around when I have the opportunity. I should at least know who I am working for. I am not sure what I was expecting working for a race team, but this place is top-notch.

I stride into the elevator glad that Brooke and I made that shopping trip. Thanks to her, I am smartly dressed in a new and very trendy maxi dress with a bright chevron print, heeled strappy sandals, and my best coordinating jewelry. Accessories can make or break any outfit, and I have hit a home run today, which gives me that extra boost of confidence I so desperately need. I mean, who am I kidding? Accessories are really a girl's best friend, right? Well...now they are, since I hocked the diamond less than seventy-two hours ago. *Jeezus! Enough of that, Whitney.*

I select three on the elevator keypad. As the door begins to close, I hear a slight commotion in the lobby that sounds like a protest.

"*Stop!*"

A young male in his early to midthirties throws his body through the closing doors. Stunned, I glance at the intruder and give him a quick nervous smile, then jump out of his way so he doesn't completely knock me over. He looks back at me with wry amusement although he is out of breath. The stranger gives me a glowing megawatt smile, and his blue eyes dance mischievously.

My heart does a somersault in my chest. *Sweet Jesus!* He is handsome—no...no..."hot" would be a better term to describe him, especially if you like that bad-boy, smoldering kind. Seriously, I haven't met a girl who didn't like that type of guy. He looks a little rough around the edges, literally, as I note the light stubble across his chin and down his jawline. It tells me that he didn't bother to shave this morning. And he is casually dressed in a T-shirt bearing the GCR Racing logo, khaki shorts, and brown leather flip-flops.

Yes, he is...oh-my-God hot!

I shake my head and roll my eyes to rid myself of my wayward thoughts. Then I realize he is regarding me just as carefully. Because I can feel his eyes on me. I shift uncomfortably as I look back up at him. Our eyes meet and lock in a heated stare. My heart flutters in my chest again. I feel like I am going to jump out of my skin. *Damn!*

It feels like an hour has passed since he jumped into the elevator. The silence is unnerving as we continue to make our assessments of one another.

Then suddenly, "Who the hell are you?" the dashing stranger snaps, breaking the hushed anxiety.

Shocked by his arrogance, his outburst takes me by surprise, and I am momentarily lost for words. *Who am I? Oh! Yes...right!*

I stand up straight, square my shoulders toward him, and rebound quickly. "Whitney Parker," is all I can manage, but I do say it firmly, with tenacity. Then, I add just as rudely, "And you are?"

The hot young cad looks back at me, rolls his eyes, and looks confused all at the same time. The elevator door opens with a ping, and he laughs aloud as if I had just told the most hilarious joke. And then he is gone. *What a bastard!*

I step out onto the third floor. I walk into the reception area behind the handsome jerk and am met by mass chaos. The telephone is incessantly ringing. I watch Mr. Pompous Ass disappear into the back as I look around for someone to direct me to Mrs. Andrews's office, but no one even acknowledges my presence. *What the hell?* I wonder vaguely if everyone is as rude as him.

I spy a vacant desk, which I assume to be the receptionist area. I place my bag underneath it and snatch up the phone. "GCR Racing, this is Whitney." Suddenly, I am grateful for countless part-time jobs that have helped me to at least know how to answer the phone properly. Of course, I have no idea who anyone is, so I take a message.

I field a handful of calls and corresponding messages for various people throughout the office. How I will get these notes delivered to the appropriate people is baffling me. I set out to find someone in the office to help me, when an immaculately dressed woman in her midforties approaches me. This must be Jerri. She reminds me very much of Gail, and I can see why they are friends. They look to be cut from the same cloth.

"Whitney?" she asks uncertainly.

I smile appreciatively. *Finally!* "Yes, ma'am."

She looks relieved and makes a haphazard attempt to smooth her hair, which is flawlessly styled and not at all out of place. "I was wondering who was answering the phone. Thank you for jumping right in. It is a little crazy in here this morning," she confesses.

"Yes, ma'am! I can see that." I laugh a little to mask my nervousness.

"I am Jerri Andrews," she says to introduce herself.

I smile knowingly. She offers her hand in introduction, which I grasp and shake firmly, never breaking eye contact.

"Most of us have been in a series of meetings this morning. There were some issues at the race on Sunday, so we are all scrambling. Not to mention the fact that our receptionist has evidently quit." Jerri rolls her eyes in exasperation, which seems a little uncharacteristic for such a professional-looking woman, but she is female. Eye rolling is a standard option for our gender.

Jerri gives me a few simple instructions and promises to get with me after lunch for a more detailed description of my job duties. "Oh! And Whitney...please plan to hang around with us for a few weeks. It is going to be a while before I can start looking for a replacement," she says, strained.

"Sure! I can stay for as long as you need me," I offer.

I can tell Jerri is relieved, but before she can say anything, Mr. Pompous Ass materializes from the back offices. Her face immediately falls. She looks agitated. He strides purposefully back to the elevators without acknowledging either one of us.

Jerri calls out to him, "Four o'clock, Ryan! Don't forget!"

He doesn't dignify her reminder with a response, but he throws up his hand as if to say, "I got this!"

What a jerk! I must have an irritated look on my face because Jerri quickly snaps, "My thoughts exactly!" And we both erupt in laughter.

After our shared moment, I face Jerri to ask, "Who is he?"

She looks at me as if my face just exploded.

"What?" I question.

"Whitney!" Jerri gasps. "That is Ryan Carter, Garrett Carter's son."

I shake my head and raise my eyebrows at her because that information does not help me *at all*.

Jerri looks distraught. "Gail said you were not familiar with NASCAR, but surely you know who Ryan Carter is?"

I give her my best "I have no freaking clue" look with big, innocent eyes. "I'm sorry," I stammer.

She smiles warmly at me. "It's OK. It may actually be a good thing!"

Really! That is the second time I have heard that phrase today. I hope to figure out what it means soon. *Or do I?*

After lunch, the activity within the office seems to calm down considerably. I have had a few minutes to walk around the floor to acquaint myself with the layout and some of the people who take the time to acknowledge me. The ones who do are surprisingly welcoming and polite, but I notice that I am carefully observed. It must be the new-girl syndrome.

I make a mental note to make some work friends fast. I need some inside information on this organization so I can properly do my job. I don't want to continue to be known as the girl who has no idea about stock car racing. I make a vow to learn as much as I can about NASCAR and the GCR Racing organization. I want to make sure that I am doing my job to the best of my abilities. Plus, a little knowledge never hurt anyone.

As promised, Jerri briefly sits down with me to give me some light instructions on my job duties. I like her right away. She reminds me of my mother. She gives me a company directory of employees, which includes office locations, telephone extensions, and job descriptions. This will be extremely helpful.

Then Jerri sighs deeply, "I feel like I need to warn you about Ryan."

Her statement takes me aback. "Oh?"

"Yes," she says, defeated. "He is the reason why we stay in chaos around here. Just last Sunday, he shot his mouth off in a pre-race interview with the Speed Channel about the new NASCAR car dynamics for this season. He was fined fifty thousand dollars for his derogatory statements."

"Oh my God!" I exclaim. That is an insane amount of money!

"Oh no! It gets better!" Jerri says sarcastically. "During the race, Ryan was subsequently fined twenty-five thousand more dollars for his explicit language over his team communications during the race."

"Whoa!"

She nods her head. "And that leaves me to deal with our sponsors, who believe that if he has all this money to blow on these fines each week, then he must not need their corporate contribution."

"Wow!" I say again, still not knowing exactly what to say to her since she has just dumped a wealth of knowledge on me on my very first day of work. Jerri has a lot to deal with. I am not sure whether to run away screaming or stick around to watch this three-ring circus and get paid for it.

* * *

When I arrive home around six o'clock in the evening, I phone Brooke to inform her of my new job status. She screams like a teenager into the phone, "Oh my God!"

My ear is ringing! She oozes with jealously when I tell her that I am working for GCR Racing.

"Shut up! You are not serious!" she says, still in teenager mode. The very first question out of her mouth is, "Did you see Ryan Carter?"

I groan, "How do you know who he is and I don't?"

I can tell by her voice that she is rolling her eyes at me. "Whitney! I have lived in Charlotte for the past three years! NASCAR is big business here!"

I joke, "So I have been told!"

Brooke whines like an impatient child, "Did you see him?"

"Yes!" I exclaim. And Brooke shrieks *again* like a giddy teenager. Then she begins pumping me with information about the infamous Ryan Carter.

According to the gospel of Brooke, Ryan is Garrett Ryan Carter Jr., son of NASCAR legend Garrett Ryan Carter Sr. He is the ultimate bad boy, hothead, and general troublemaker of the stock car racing world, not to mention the only heir to the GCR Racing throne. Brooke goes on and on about Ryan.

"He only dates Victoria Secret supermodels and the like, but he never dates them long."

"Brooke, stop!" I interject. "First of all, how do you know all this information about him?"

I can hear Brooke gasp. "Whitney, he is a major celebrity. He is all over *People* magazine. In fact, he was just featured in the 'Sexiest Man Alive' issue. I mean...have you been living under a rock?"

"Why yes, I have!" I snap and then groan. "Well, secondly, I know why he doesn't keep a girlfriend long."

"Oh?" Brooke responds. "Why is that?"

"Because he is a straight-up jackass!" I exclaim.

"Ugh! Good God Almighty! I don't even care. He is just that hot!" Brooke cries, breathless.

"Brooke, seriously, calm down!" I say flat out.

She guffaws at me. "A million girls would kill for that job!" she shrieks.

"Oh...OK! You don't have to go all *The Devil Wears Prada* on me," I quip. "Because I assure you this is not a dream job. After our episode in the elevator today, I can tell you that he has an insanely huge chip on his shoulder. I mean, he is one arrogant son of a bitch!"

"Elevator!" Brooke screeches again. My eardrum has got to be busted. "What happened in the elevator?" she asks impatiently.

I shake my head and whine into the phone as I give her all the gory details of my first encounter with the one and only Ryan Carter.

Chapter 4

I n the blink of an eye, two hectic weeks have gone by. I am settling into my new home and finding a good stride at work. In those few weeks, I have learned a tremendous amount about the GCR Racing team. I actually know what those initials stand for now. Plus, I am building my knowledge base on NASCAR itself. Thanks to my *NASCAR for Dummies* book that I downloaded into my iPad the day I was hired, I may actually survive this job.

GCR employs three drivers for the Sprint Cup Series. The drivers are Colton Johnson, Garrett Ryan Carter Sr.—who only races in certain events due to semiretirement—and Mr. Pompous Ass himself, Ryan Carter. I have yet to meet Garrett, but I have seen several pictures of him around the office.

I arrive early at the office on Monday. I take a seat at my desk and begin to get organized for the day. It should be a good one. According to the race results, which I now follow, Colton finished in the top ten, while Ryan crashed his car. *Loser!* I actually managed to watch the race broadcast for a few minutes, but didn't get to see Ryan's accident. It was incredibly boring, so I switched it off. The cars go around and around and around, not much action whatsoever. *Complete waste of my time!* I laugh out loud to myself!

"What's so damn funny?" I hear a familiar voice question me.

I look up and into the glowing eyes of Ryan Carter. *Oops! I wasn't aware that I had an audience.*

I gawk and roll my eyes dead at him. *What do I owe this honor?* With my best mocking voice, I say, "Are *you* speaking to *me*?" I point to him, then back to myself for added flourish. My sweet southern sarcasm takes him by surprise. He smugly rolls his eyes in return and is gone.

After our initial encounter, I have seen Ryan only a handful of times aside from today. During those times, I have mostly been ignored, which is fine with me because he isn't worth the time of day either. His arrogance is a tough pill to swallow. Plus, he usually has Annalise nipping at his heels while he is in the office. Annalise is Ryan's public relations manager, although I assume her job description goes further than the office. I can tell by the way she looks at him, not to mention the fact that she is tall, buxom, and blonde. According to Brooke's information and the gossip magazines, this is how he likes his women. Not that I care.

I am sifting through the weekend mail when Jerri approaches my desk with a handful of tasks. Over the past few weeks, she has been liberally adding duties to my job description, which hopefully means she is happy with my work thus far. I love it. It keeps me busy.

There is an early meeting this morning with Ryan's management team, but I have no idea what it is about. Since I am the lowly receptionist, I am not privy to certain details. The phones are quiet for the moment, so I fetch myself a cup of coffee from the break room. On my way back, I stop to chat with my new office friends, Natalie and Josh. Both recent college graduates, Natalie is an intern in the marketing department, while Josh is working his way up through logistics.

We are catching up on the weekend, the race results, and general gossip, when I hear a commotion coming from the boardroom. I quickly retreat back to my desk, taking in some cautious looks from the other employees as I go. I hurriedly take a seat at my desk and watch my computer monitor as if I am working.

I hear the boardroom door open and slam into the opposing wall. *Oh damn!*

Annalise exclaims, "You son of a bitch!"

Oh no! This can't be good. I turn back from my desk to peer down the hall in time to witness Annalise stride purposefully from the boardroom toward me. Quickly, I turn back around and face my computer to avoid making eye contact with her, because frankly, this is just embarrassing for everyone.

As she makes her way down the hallway toward me, I hear her shout back at the boardroom, "I quit!"

Oh Lord! I know now what Gail meant when she said, "three-ring circus." One mystery is solved.

Annalise stops when she approaches my desk. I know she is standing behind me because she is breathing like a dragon on my back. I warily turn to face her. She is glaring at me like she is about to foam at the mouth. *Damn!* Where is a shotgun when you need one? Our eyes meet, which is shocking because she has always been too busy looking down her nose at me to even act like I exist. *Bitch!*

Briefly, I wonder why she's so mad. It must be a lover's snit! I cock my head to the side as my thoughts ramble. Come to think of it, I am not sure why she and Ryan are having issues. They should be a perfect fit for one another. They have an excellent combination of "bitch" and "bastard," which should make an award-winning team. Accidentally, I laugh out loud at my thoughts. Then I automatically put my hand up to my mouth to stifle my giggle. *Too late!*

"What's so damn funny?" Annalise snaps, radiating anger.

Oops! That's twice today. I shake my head and stutter, "I...I'm sorry."

She holds up a thick leather-bound agenda, which I believe she is about to throw at my head. Instead, she takes the book and slams it down hard on my desk. It hits the counter with a loud bang that causes me to jump instinctively.

She eyes me with complete and utter contempt. *What the hell have I done to her!* But then she changes tact with a blink of her long, heavily mascaraed eyelashes and smiles at me with this smug "go to hell" look.

"Good luck, sweetie!" she says before she turns sharply on her heel toward the elevator.

What the hell did she mean by that?

She hits the down arrow, like, a million times. Finally, the elevator door miraculously opens to whisk her away. I continue to stare at the elevator, dazed as I try to process what just happened.

Finally, I let out a huge breath. Wow, that was intense! Thank God she is gone, but what in the world was that all about? I have never seen her, or anyone, for that matter, that mad. *Jeezus!* I quickly attribute it to Ryan. Who else?

Suddenly, I hear Jerri shout from the boardroom, "Whitney!"

I jump up again, still rigid from the encounter with Annalise. I awkwardly make my way into the boardroom. Those present watch me closely as I shift nervously from one heeled foot to the other. In the corner of the room, I spy Ryan, looking gorgeous and smug as usual, talking to two guys in the back corner. He looks up when he realizes I have entered the room.

Ryan laughs as he speaks to Jerri. "Come on, I was only kidding, Jerri!"

Jerri angrily fires back at him. "Were you kidding? Well, I'm not! It actually wasn't a bad idea on your part. She does have a degree in public relations and marketing. And she has been getting this office into shape in the two weeks that she has been here," she cries out in a tantrum.

Oh wow!

"But she doesn't know jack shit about me or NASCAR!" Ryan shouts back.

Oh my God! They are talking about me as if I'm not in the room.

Jerri turns to me, finally acknowledging my presence in the boardroom. "I'm sorry, Whitney. Annalise, as I guess you heard, has just quit. I need you to temporarily fill in this weekend in Michigan for her. Actually, you are going to be Ryan's temporary public relations manager until we secure a replacement," she says carefully, making sure that I am agreeable.

Um...what? "Michigan?" I ask warily, but not really as a question. I am trying to process all these events in my head.

Before Jerri can respond, Ryan interjects and throws his hands up in the air. "Seriously! Michigan, the next race, that Michigan."

Jerri intervenes. "Yes, Whitney, can you handle that?"

This is all happening way too fast. I steal a nervous glance at Ryan. He is livid. I look back to Jerri.

"Wait just a damn minute, Jerri!" Ryan snaps.

And Jerri explodes holding her hand up for him to keep quiet.. "No, *you* wait just a damn minute! This is nobody's fault but your own. I am done letting you call the shots around here, not to mention screw with my staff! Literally!" she says through gritted teeth as she blazes back at him.

I can tell her blood pressure is through the roof. *Good for her!*

"Whitney, please come to my office in an hour. We will go over specifics and what needs to be accomplished this weekend. I need to find Annalise's agenda," Jerri says more calmly.

I am keenly aware that all eyes are on me in the boardroom. I stand up straight and roll my shoulders back. I can do this, by God. I am not about to let anyone, especially Ryan Carter, intimidate me.

"I already have it. She gave it to me on her way out," I say confidently with my newfound resolve, which doesn't give away the fact that she basically threw it at me.

"Great!" Jerri sounds relieved. "Please bring it with you, and I will help you make your travel arrangements for the weekend as soon as we determine a plan of action. That is all for now." She speaks calmly now, but I can tell she is severely stressed. It shows around her eyes. Poor woman! Ryan is getting the best of her. I make a vow to make sure I handle him from here on out.

As she dismisses me, Jerri turns back to Ryan, who jumps up so fast that his chair slams over backward. "Jerri, I'm going to speak to my father about this."

Jerri unravels instantly, which causes me to be paralyzed from leaving the boardroom. "Please do! When you do, be sure to tell him why Annalise is no longer here!" He looks like he is about to explode with rage knowing full well that he won't be able to say one word to his father. "This discussion is over, Ryan!" Jerri finishes.

He moves to exit the boardroom and pauses in front of me to exclaim in my face, "I cannot fucking believe this!"

Without using my brain-to-mouth filter, I respond hastily, "Then I guess you need to learn to keep your damn mouth shut!"

Ryan eyes me with the most chilling look, which sends goose bumps down my spine. But I square my shoulders and return his heated stare. He has no idea what he is in for with me because I am not going to take his shit! I don't care *who* he is! I am not backing down. Then, suddenly, he is gone.

The remainder of the day flies by. Natalie and Josh confirm my suspicions about Annalise at lunch. Apparently, Annalise and Ryan were trying to keep their extracurricular relationship under wraps, but the word around the water cooler is Ryan stalked off with another girl after the race on Sunday, and the shit hit the fan this morning in the management meeting. *Typical!*

According to another source that Josh would not name, Ryan said in front of everyone in the boardroom that I would make a better public relations manager than her. *Sweet Jesus!* No wonder she looked like she was about to murder me, then chop my body into pieces when she left. I laugh to myself because that comment certainly blew up in his face.

Jerri and I finally meet late in the afternoon. She inundates me with information like a rapid-fire gun. I fiercely scribble as many notes as I can, being careful not to forget any major details. She goes over travel details like what hotel I am supposed to stay in and what flight to book.

Jerri also gives me a series of thick documents. "I had these printed for you. Use your downtime to start reviewing them."

I raise an eyebrow in question.

"These are Ryan's sponsorship agreements and his employment contract. There is a wealth of information there that you should know."

I nod my head.

"I have decided that you can just take a late flight into Michigan on Saturday night. Since it is your first weekend at the track, I don't want to overwhelm you."

Then Jerri goes into track events that I need to attend, like the sponsor breakfast, mandatory drivers' meeting, and driver introductions. I am very overwhelmed, to say the least. But I try to keep up with her as best as I can. She also gives me a list of the other management team members who will be at the track, and their contact numbers. This is going to be a very interesting weekend. I don't have a freaking clue about what am I doing, but I am sure as hell not going to let anyone know that, least of all Ryan. *I will show him.*

Jerri looks defeated as we conclude our meeting. "Three," she says simply. I give her a confused look, and she continues, "Annalise is our third public relations manager this year. Just for Ryan."

I raise my eyebrows, considering her confession as a warning.

Jerri continues to explain, "For some reason, this race season, we have had the most problems from Ryan. Back during the off-season, he had a small cameo role in a movie that shot out in Los Angeles, and he came back from that experience with a double dose of attitude, *trés* movie star, if you know what I mean." She laughs. "I don't know if he is burned out or if he is losing his focus or what. It is disheartening because he has so much potential." She sighs and shakes her head. "And no one knows how to handle Ryan. Well, they don't know how to handle him outside of the bedroom, which is where they all wind up!" Suddenly she looks remorseful. "Did I say that out loud?"

And we both laugh. My head is swirling with information, but I vow to myself that I can handle Ryan. *I'm going to show Mr. Pompous Ass that I can do this job.*

My job as public relations manager is basically to arrange scheduled events for sponsors, meet and greets with fans, and televised race interviews throughout the weekend. Since Annalise has already made these arrangements, I will only have to go on Sunday to assist Ryan with these events. The main goal, Jerri says, is to make sure Ryan attends every event that he is scheduled for—oh, and make sure he stays in line, which is a job in itself. So, basically, I am a babysitter, well, a glorified babysitter, for Ryan Carter. *Great!* I think I should request an assistant already!

I have never been to a NASCAR event, so I have no idea of what to expect. I make my travel arrangements for Brooklyn, Michigan, according to Jerri's instructions. I am a ball of nerves as I make my flight and hotel reservations for Saturday and Sunday. I am trying to be as meticulous as I can because I don't need to screw this up before I get there.

I have to cancel Annalise's arrangements and make new ones for myself. I have never been to Michigan, or anywhere else, for that matter, but something tells me I won't be able to do much sightseeing. I have to be at the track with Ryan early Sunday morning for pre-race activities, then stay through the main event, until the checkered flag falls and Ryan returns to Charlotte. Then, a red-eye flight from Detroit will bring me home late Sunday night. This is all too much information to process without alcohol. I look down at my watch. It's after five o'clock. *Praise God!* I have got to get out of here!

Chapter 5

Luckily, today is Margarita Monday! And I am having dinner with Brooke, so hopefully she can help me to hash all this out. I seriously need her advice. I arrive at Rock Bottom Brewery in downtown Charlotte around six o'clock.

Brooke is perfectly dressed and coiffed even this late in the day. It makes me ill. I am frazzled as usual, no doubt thanks to the insane day that I have had.

Brooke signals for the waiter to come over as she says to me, "You look like you need a drink!"

"Thanks!" I snap. "That is a polite way of saying, you look like shit!" The waiter walks up on cue as I say, "I'll have what she is having, but make mine a double!"

The waiter retreats, and Brooke eyes me intently. "What the what?"

"Well..." I say cautiously, "I got a new job today."

"Oh?" Brooke looks at me intently, waiting on me to continue.

I sigh, "You are looking at the new "acting" public relations manager for Ryan Carter."

Brooke's mouth drops wide open, and I raise my eyebrows at her. I have never seen this look of pure shock on her face. *This is one for the record books.*

"Well...actually," I say straight, "it's basically a glorified babysitting job with a fancy title." I continue to bore myself with the details of my new job description. Brooke looks dazed as she continues to stare at me with an openmouthed gape. "Brooke!" I wave my hands at her to break her gaze. "Say something!"

She guffaws. "I would babysit his fine ass any day, no matter what the title!"

I groan loudly, "Oh my God! He's such an ass! Honestly, I don't know how he walks around carrying that incredibly huge chip on his shoulder, like, 'Oh! I'm Ryan Carter. Stop the traffic, please!' What a bastard!" I say in a huff.

The waiter arrives with my margarita, so I discontinue my conversation momentarily. I take a long, glorious sip. The tequila burns down my throat. Ahh! Just exactly what I needed, and to hell with the two-drink minimum tonight! The waiter retreats again, and Brooke doesn't miss a beat.

She eyes me. "Oh, come on! You have to admit that he is sexy as hell!"

I take a sip from my glass and answer warily, "OK! OK! Yes, he is hot, but his personality is a cat of a different color!"

Brooke nods her head and quickly says, "That's just what makes him Ryan Carter."

I roll my eyes again. "Oh! And according to the office gossip, he has, like, a new girl at every track, so he probably has something Ajax won't take off!"

Brooke instantly chokes on her margarita and snorts. "Please, I got something that works way better than Ajax!"

And we erupt in a fit of girlish giggles, clinking our margarita glasses.

Chapter 6

My plane touches down in Detroit around eight o'clock on Saturday night. I have begged Brooke to come with me because, frankly, I am terrified, but she is stuck working on a huge case for her firm. I have never really traveled anywhere, much less alone. I mean...I know I won't technically be alone once I get to the track, but it would have been nice to have a travel companion.

I have to stay at the Detroit Metro Marriott at the airport. I check into my room, which is surprisingly comfy. After a quick shower, I change into my pj's. I pull out my iPad to review tomorrow's activities at the track. A race courier will pick me up in the morning to deliver me to the track in Brooklyn. The track is sixty or so odd miles west of Detroit. I check and double check my schedule to make sure I have everything together. And somewhere in the middle of it all, I fall asleep.

I wake up to intense sunlight flooding my room. Oh no! I sit up in the bed quickly to get my bearings. I fell asleep without setting the alarm. *Shit!* I fumble around for my iPhone. I steal a glance at the time once I get my hands on it. It's 9:00 a.m. I am so late!

I scramble around as I throw on a pair of khaki pants, GCR logo polo shirt, and my Asics tennis shoes. My cell phone starts to ring. I grab it and don't recognize the number.

"Hello!" I say, exasperated.

The voice on the other end sounds just as annoyed. "This is MIS Courier Service, and I have been waiting on you for over an hour. I am instructed to take you to the speedway. Are you ready to go?"

"Yes," I exclaim. "I am sorry, but I overslept. I am on my way down." I can tell the courier is less than thrilled by my confession.

I throw my belongings into my overnight bag and basically run down to the lobby. I find the driver waiting outside by the curb, and I jump into the car. A young black guy, about twenty, rolls his eyes at me as I slide into the backseat.

"I am so sorry!" I profusely apologize, but I can tell my driver is not interested in hearing it. He slams the car into drive, and we pull away from the hotel with rapid speed.

It is a beautiful day, about eighty degrees. The scenery en route to the track is breathtaking as we roll through the Irish Hills of Southeast Michigan. As we drive, I try in vain to work my hair into submission with my brush. I finally give up and secure it back in a ponytail. Then, I apply a few light makeup touches. *There, that will have to do*, I say to myself as I snap my compact closed. Thank God for the drive into Brooklyn, or I would have been a walking hot mess for the rest of the day.

As we make the last curve on Highway 12, I look up, and the Michigan International Speedway looms like the *Titanic* on the horizon. "Wow!" I say audibly.

My driver eyes me in the rearview mirror. "Have you never been to MIS?"

I shake my head. "This is my first NASCAR event ever!"

As we approach the enormous structure, we pass acres and acres of parking areas, fans, and shopping villages that have been erected for the race weekend. There are people everywhere. All of a sudden, I am extremely nervous. I was too busy being late to be anxious, but now the floodgates are open. My heart begins to race as we enter a tunnel.

"Where are we going?" I ask nervously.

"This is the infield tunnel. It takes you into the center of the speed-way, where the drivers, teams, and headquarters are located. It is where you need to go."

I nod my head at him and look down at my phone. I am exactly one hour and thirty minutes late. I wonder vaguely if I should text Jerri to let her know, but then, I don't want her to worry or question my abilities either. I decide against it and put my phone in my pocket.

Sunlight fills the car as we enter the raceway infield area. I try to take a deep breath, but anxiety takes over. "I need to go to the drivers' meeting. Do you know where that is?" I ask the driver, who is a little friendlier now.

"Sure, I will drop you off at the end of the lane that takes you right to the building."

"Great!" I say as the driver puts the car in park. I grab my bag and exit the car, but not before I apologize for my tardiness again.

OK, I say to myself. *Get it together!*

I start down the lane toward the main facility of the racetrack. I make it to the door, and there is absolutely no one even milling around outside. I steal a glance at my phone for the time. I have completely missed the sponsor breakfast, and I am now thirty minutes late for the drivers' meeting. *Damn it!*

I open the door slowly to peer into the building, to make sure that I am, in fact, in the right place. As I look into the meeting hall, I meet the eyes of about a hundred people who turn cautiously to see who has dared enter the mandatory drivers' meeting *late! Oh my God!* Sheer mortification sets in, and I jump through the door like a scared cat.

The moderator of the meeting continues to discuss safety precautions, weather, and pit road regulations. Luckily, there is standing room only, and I am able to disappear behind a group of guys who are standing at the door. My face is flushed with hot embarrassment. I feel like I am going to throw up.

I look around the room to spot Ryan. It is easy to spot him because he is in the second row scowling back at me. My stomach drops through my knees. I mouth to him, "So sorry!" He gives me a cold stare and then turns his attention back to the gentleman who is giving details about pit road speeds and extra safety measures that have been put into place since the new track configuration. It is like Greek to me. I have no idea what this man is talking about or if it applies to me.

As soon as the moderator answers a few questions from drivers, the meeting is adjourned. Everyone quickly disperses and lines up to head out the door. I stand by the door to wait for Ryan. I don't make eye contact with anyone because I am just so embarrassed by this point. *Jeezus!*

Ryan strides past me with only a look of sheer disgust. I don't even get a "Hey," "Bye," "Kiss my ass," or anything from him. *Bastard!* I throw my overnight bag over my shoulder and fall in line behind him and the other drivers.

As we walk, I hear Ryan say, "That will be my new fucking babysitter!"

Ugh! I don't miss a beat and say just loud enough for him to hear me, "When you stop acting like a child, you won't need a babysitter, will you?"

Ryan angles his head back in acknowledgment of my statement, but doesn't say anything.

"Yes, I do hope you heard me," I mutter under my breath. I keep up the pace as we walk swiftly and quietly through the infield area. It is a zoo.

As we enter the driver introduction platform, I notice a few members of security who fall into line with us—and thankfully, just at the right time. A throng of fans descend on Ryan. *Sweet Jesus!* They are all clamoring for his attention, autograph, and photographs. I get pushed around in the crowd, but I stand my ground and follow Ryan's lead.

This is madness, but I can tell Ryan loves it. As the fans push and shove us to get his attention, Ryan takes his time and care with each one. I notice as we continue to push through the crowd that he turns back and steals a quick glance at me, but I am not sure why. The look on his face is very out of character for him. It's almost as though he is concerned for me. As our eyes lock, I feel my pulse quicken. It puts me at ease, though, it is fleeting.

Ryan sails through driver introductions effortlessly. The crowd goes wild when he is presented to the audience and saunters across the stage. I fall back into line with him as we walk to a last-minute fan meet and greet in the Nationwide hospitality tent. He continues to ignore me. I have no choice, but to follow Ryan's lead because I have absolutely no idea where to go or what to do.

We enter the Nationwide suite, and Ryan stops abruptly in his tracks. "What the fuck is he doing in here?" he exclaims, turning back to face me with fevered rage across his face.

What now?

"Who?" I ask, because I don't immediately see who he is referring to.

"Colton!" Ryan snaps.

I look across the room and spy Colton Johnson, another dashing stock car driver, who is Ryan's teammate. I guess good looks are a prerequisite for NASCAR drivers.

"Oh, the meet and greet was with the entire team since it is a shared sponsorship," I say matter-of-factly, like I have been handling this for years.

Ryan immediately jerks me out of my confidence. "We need to get a few things straight!" He explodes into a fit of rage as the entire tent turns to witness his meltdown. "Colton and I may be teammates, but that is it. I don't do press with him. I don't do interviews with him. Are we clear?"

Whoa! This is news to me! I am so embarrassed that I don't even have a sassy comeback. And I keep my mouth shut to avoid any further mortification.

"Yes," I mutter quietly. "I am sorry, Ryan!" I add an apology in hopes he will calm down. My face must be seven shades of purple, and I suddenly can't breathe. Ryan must notice my vulnerability because he doesn't miss a beat.

"This is exactly why I was against you taking this position, not to mention the fact that you were over an hour late this morning! But that's fine because if I have anything to say about it, this will be your *first* and your *last* race."

He accents those last words with utter contempt for me. Tears spring to my eyes. I look down so he can't see them.

Ryan turns on his heel and vacates the Nationwide venue without even meeting the contest winner. I am so upset and embarrassed that I am livid. I cannot even think straight. I walk over to where Colton is talking with the fan to apologize.

Colton smiles at me sympathetically on my approach. I begin to pro-fusely apologize for Ryan's behavior and for my errors. Colton imme-diately puts me at ease.

"Whitney, that is typical Ryan Carter. There is no need for you to apologize!"

I smile at him and let out a huge breath that I didn't know that I was holding. I hold out my hand to him. "We haven't officially met, but as you know now, I am Whitney Parker."

Colton smiles a gorgeous smile that lights up his green eyes, and he extends his hand to firmly grip mine. "The pleasure is all mine," he says smoothly.

He is beautiful. He has the most vibrant olive skin, which lets me know that he must have some Italian heritage. I want to reach out and caress his face. *Cool it, Whitney!* Colton is the kind of handsome that Ryan could be if he didn't act like such an ass. The total package. *Why do all these drivers have to be so freaking hot?*

Colton leads me out of the tent. "We had better head back to pit road. It will be time for opening ceremonies soon." I gladly take his lead. Colton guides me through the infield area, into the pit area. He gives me a brief tour of his pit box and shows me where I should sit over Ryan's pit. "Ryan qualified behind me, so he is further down the lane." Colton turns my body to face the back as he points out the #62 flag that represents Ryan's race team.

"Huh?" I exclaim with my best southern drawl.

Colton laughs, "Each driver has to qualify their car before each race. The starting race lineup is determined by who has the fastest car. We line up based on those results. And your buddy is almost at the back. I think he is thirty-first or so." Colton laughs with a tsk-tsk.

I don't give a shit about Ryan right now. I am enjoying this time with Colton. He is actually taking the time to show me around and to get me acclimated to this new world in which I am now gainfully employed. It is amazing how nice he is. He is the polar opposite of Ryan, not at all arrogant. However, I do suspect that he has those tendencies. I am sure in this sport, it is a requirement.

I turn back to smile at Colton. "I really appreciate you taking the time to do this because I would have been clueless. Honestly, I walked into all this blindly, and I should have known better or have been better prepared."

Colton smiles again. "Listen, you will be fine. Ryan's a jerk. Plus, the only way to learn is to actually get out and do it. Next week, you will be a professional."

I laugh out loud. "It doesn't look like there will be a next week for me, according to Mr. Carter. Speaking of which, I better get back over there now!" I say to Colton as I roll my eyes.

As I turn to go, my iPhone falls out of my front pocket. Colton leans over to retrieve it from the ground. Before he returns it to me, I notice that he swipes into the home screen and quickly taps something into it with his thumbs.

I open my mouth to ask him what he is doing, but I am interrupted by the sound of my name: "Whitney!"

I turn back to see who is calling me. It's Ryan. My face immediately falls. It is evident that he is pissed off *again*. Great!

I turn to Colton as Ryan strides up to us. "Gotta go!" I turn to leave, and Ryan blocks my path.

"What the fuck!" Ryan explodes again. "Where the hell have you been?"

I don't even dignify his question with an answer. As I stride away from Ryan, I hear Colton call out to me, "See you after the race, Whitney!" And he playfully tosses my phone back to me.

What? I am momentarily confused as I reach out to grab it, and then it hits me. Colton is trying to aggravate Ryan by making him think we have something planned after the checkered flag falls. I laugh out loud. I do really like Colton.

Ryan calls after me again, "Whitney!"

I continue to ignore him as I waltz into the pit area and scale the ladder up into the pit box like I have been doing it for years. I look down at Ryan, who is regarding me intently, roll my eyes, and take a seat.

As it gets closer to race time, several other team members join me on top of the pit box that overlooks pit road. "Whitney, I assume? An older gentleman in his midfifties reaches out to introduce himself.

I nod my head. "Yes, sir."

"I am Ben, Ryan's road manager. I hear he is giving you a rough time so far."

I smile. "Yes, sir, but it isn't anything I can't handle."

Ben laughs heartily. "Well, from what I hear, you are already giving him a run for his money!"

I laugh out loud at his confession. "I guess we will see about that!"

Ben starts to speak again, but is interrupted by the beginning of the opening ceremonies. He motions for me to stand up with him. The national anthem is sung by a well-known country music artist. Then another person takes the stage, who exclaims, "Gentlemen, start your engines!"

With that command, forty-something race car engines roar to life. It is like a shotgun to my heart. Really, it scares the shit out of me, and I jump instinctively. It is so loud.

Ben laughs, but quickly retreats. "I should have warned you about that!"

I take a deep breath as I try to regain my composure. I can't even manage a word as the blood sears through my veins. I feel like I have literally been shot. My face flushes from embarrassment again.

Ben hands me a radio with a headset. "Here...take this. You can listen to communications between Ryan's spotter and crew chief." I must have a look of ambiguity on my face because Ben begins to explain. "Ryan's spotter, Mike, helps him from the tower up there." He points to a large building over the front straightaway. "Mike helps Ryan to see through his blind spots."

I nod my head as I take in the information.

"Bobby, Ryan's crew chief"—he points out a man standing below in the pit area who looks to be in his fifties, too—"he oversees Ryan's car and any adjustments or repairs that need to be made to it during the race. Throughout the race, Ryan will have to bring the car into pit for gas and new tires. And sometimes any other adjustments the car may need. So, you can hear what is going on between these three major components." Ben smiles as he completes my mini NASCAR lesson.

When I finally catch my breath, I take the headset, place it over my ears, and adjust the volume. The radio crackles to life, and I can hear Ryan going through a serious of checks with his crew chief, Bobby, as forty-four cars make their way down pit road and onto the track. As the green flag falls, the cars roar to life again. I can feel a slight anxiety build up in my chest, or maybe it is nervousness. Whatever this feeling is, it is foreign to me.

The laps go quickly as the cars speed around the track at upward of 195 miles per hour. Watching the race in person is a hell of a lot different than watching it on television. This is actually exciting, watching the cars sweep into the curves and fire down long straightaways. The speeds alone are thrilling. I listen as Bobby calls the lap speeds out to Ryan. Into the last corner, Ryan accelerated to 210 miles per hour. *Wow!*

Halfway through the race, Ryan radios into Bobby. "There is a problem with the car since the last pit stop," he says anxiously.

"What?" Bobby spouts back.

"The car is good through the straightaways, but it is really tight in the corners. I am having a hard time holding it down."

I look down into the pit area to watch Bobby as he responds, "Well... fight it until a caution comes up or until the next stop! We can't lose track position."

Ryan comes unglued. "What? The next caution will be courtesy of me slamming into the wall!"

I watch as Bobby throws his hands in the air. "Well...I guess you are going to have to work for it today. I will make a track bar adjustment when you come in! Stop whining and concentrate, Goddamn it!"

I wince at Bobby's harsh expletive. It must have taken Ryan by surprise, too, because he doesn't say another word.

The track conditions are excellent, as is the weather. The laps start to count down. I keep waiting for an accident as the stock cars battle for position. The cars go three, sometimes four, wide through the back straightway. After the last pit stop, Ryan has not complained about the car being tight; however, he has been unable to get good track position thanks to an accident mid field. I can tell from his actions on the track that he is trying desperately to gain positions. Ryan chases the eighth-place car into turn four in an attempt to gain another position, but he eventually runs out of racetrack. He manages to pull his car across the finish line and take the checkered flag in ninth position.

The whole team is excited since this is Ryan's highest finish all season. Ben jumps up from his seat. "'Bout damn time!"

I laugh as I follow him down off the pit box. I walk over to the garage where Ryan pulls his car in. The whole team rushes over to congratulate him. I watch from the side as he takes off his helmet and racing gloves inside the car. Several reporters are clamoring for a comment on his season's best finish. This is where my job comes in. I step over to Ryan as he climbs out of the car. Immediately, I can tell he is pissed.

"Whitney! Deal with them! I don't have a comment!"

"Ryan!" I exclaim. "What is wrong? That was a great finish!"

Ryan turns back to me. "Do what I fucking said!" And he stalks away. *Sweet Jesus!*

I turn back to the reporters, who thrust microphones into my flushed face. "I am sorry, but Ryan does not want to be interviewed at this time." I apologize profusely. *Third time today!* I am getting good at this. It seems as though expressing regret is going to be at the top of my job description.

The reporters retreat, and I realize that I am alone in the garage except for a few random crew members who are milling around. All of a sudden, it hits me: "Damn! My bag!" I must have left it on the pit box. I walk back over to pit road to retrieve it. I have to get back to the airport so I don't miss my flight home.

I am still upset about the day with Ryan. Being late was my fault, but I cannot handle him being so angry and rude with me. It makes me nauseous. I retrieve my bag just as they are about to roll the pit box away.

Bobby, Ryan's crew chief, comes out from behind the box as I begin to walk away. "Whitney?"

I turn to acknowledge him as he stretches out his hand for introductions. I nod. "Yes, sir."

"Bobby," he says gruffly. "Next week you are welcome to leave your belongings in the hauler. Annalise had a locker where she stored her stuff that you can have now."

I wince at her name. "Hauler?"

Bobby laughs. Here we go again. "Ahh...I had forgotten that they said you knew nothing about NASCAR."

They?

I nod sheepishly, trying to conceal my embarrassment as Bobby explains, "The hauler is a tractor-trailer rig that we take to the track each week. It hauls Ryan's stock cars, engines, parts, tools, and so forth. The cars are stored in the top portion, and we use the bottom portion as...sort of a command center during each race."

I nod again and say politely, "Thank you!"

Bobby must sense my humiliation. He adds with a slight pat on my back, "You will catch on quick! Don't worry! Oh! And don't take any of Ryan's shit. That is the first thing you need to learn." Bobby chuckles and shakes his head as he walks away. *Nice!*

I take my phone out to note the time. I have about three hours until my flight leaves. I have to find Ryan to sort this all out before Monday. My best guess is that he is in his luxury motor coach, which I learned about from Sam, Ryan's driver, during the race. I walk over to where the buses are lined up, but I am in the middle of a sea of forty-five or more team buses that all seem to look alike.

I walk a couple of rows over and catch a glimpse of Sam, who sat with us on the pit box. "Hi, Sam," I say. "Is Ryan inside?"

"I believe so, Miss Whitney," he responds. "I just got back here."

I don't understand why everyone is so nice except for Ryan. It doesn't make any sense to me.

I knock firmly on the bus door. A few seconds pass, and no one answers. I knock firmly again and am almost knocked off my feet when Ryan swings the door open. I step back, stunned. Ryan's expression changes from suspicious to sheer contempt.

"What the hell do you want?"

I roll my eyes. "I need to talk to you for a second."

"About what?" he snaps.

"I'm really sorry for being late."

Ryan shakes his head at me with disgust.

"I...I..." I stammer, but before I can complete my sentence, a half-dressed blonde emerges from the bus.

"Ryan," she whines.

Ryan turns to acknowledge her and says over his shoulder to me, "Go home, Whitney!" as he slams the door in my completely mortified face.

Chapter 7

Despite tossing and turning throughout the night, I am up and dressed for work by six in the morning. I cannot stop reliving every single embarrassing exchange with Ryan yesterday at the track. I was completely and utterly humiliated in the Nationwide suite. Not to mention the horrifying confrontation on Ryan's bus with him and the random blonde bachelorette. The more I think about it, the madder I get. *God bless America!*

I arrive at work very early. It is a little before seven when I take a seat at my desk. Even though Ryan scored a top-ten finish at Michigan, I know the shit will hit the fan sometime today. Especially if he dares to show his face in here, it will be hard for me to keep my cool. But Monday is his day off, so maybe he will stay away for both of our sakes.

I plan to tell Jerri about how he treated me. *Or should I?* I second-guess myself. There is nothing she can do about it anyway. I'm a big girl. I need to put my big-girl panties on and deal with it. Or him, I should say...not it. I'm going to suck it up and be better prepared for next week and do my freaking job. He is not going to get to me. I repeat, he is not going to get to me.

I begin organizing myself for the day with a checklist of things that need to be accomplished. I begin to hear other employees mill around the office, and I know it is getting close to eight o'clock. I am grateful that I am already at my desk with my coffee so I don't have to make small talk this morning. I am not in the mood.

Around 9:00 a.m., Jerri sticks her head in my office. "Good morning," she says sheepishly. She already knows.

"Hi!" I say in return, as chipper as I can muster.

"That bad, eh?" Jerri raises her eyebrows at me.

I laugh. "How do you know what happened?"

She laughs too. "I have several sources that reported to me last night. Oh, and not to mention the Nationwide exec who burned my ears over Ryan's behavior at the meet and greet. My ear is still hot from that telephone call!"

"Am I fired?" I ask her warily.

Jerri sighs and shakes her head. "No! Whitney, this is typical behavior for him this season. And I just don't understand why. But, we have to deal with this, this morning. We are having a meeting at ten to recap the race and work damage control. It looks like it's becoming our MO on Monday." She shakes her head again. "Seriously, I want to get Garrett involved, but I don't want to complain to him either."

I interject. "We can handle Ryan. So...let's not get him involved just yet." I reassure Jerri and myself too.

I laugh thinking about my errant thoughts from earlier. They mirrored Jerri's exactly but on a different level.

"Don't worry!" I exclaim. "We got this!"

Jerri smiles warmly at me.

"Will Ryan be at the meeting?" I ask nervously.

"No," she says. "He doesn't know about it, so hopefully he won't randomly show up. I need for us to work together on damage control without his interference."

I sigh, relieved. *Praise the Lord!*

The morning seems to be flying by even though I have this nervous cloud of dread over my head. Shortly before l0:00 a.m., my iPhone sounds off, reminding me of the meeting. I gather "the book"—my agenda—and a few requests from sponsors for next week's race, then begin to head out the door.

As I walk out the door of my office, an incoming text alert stops me in my tracks. I turn back to my desk to grab my phone. It's a text message from "the one and only Colton Johnson." I throw my head back and laugh. So, that is what he was doing with my phone on Sunday. He was programming his number into my contacts. I had completely forgotten about that because I was too preoccupied with my rage for Ryan.

Hope you like?

I am confused. I type back:

??Like what??

As soon as I hit send, a slight knock on my door causes me to look up, and a deliveryman enters carrying two obscenely large vases of pale pink roses. *Oh my God!*

The look on my face signals the deliveryman to ask me, "Whitney Parker?"

I nod, unable to speak. *Hmmm, maybe?*

I quickly sign for the delivery. There is no card, but I already know who they are from. I fire off a text to Colton.

Like??!! I love! You have made my day! Thank you!

Colton responds.

You are very welcome. After what you went through yesterday, you deserve it.

I continue our conversation.

You don't know the half. I am going to have to have a drink tonight to calm my still-shot nerves. lol

---

Colton responds instantly.

Drink? Sounds good. May I join u?

My heart leaps into my chest as I read his words. Holy shit! Is he serious?

Sure. I have a weekly standing appointment with a friend downtown. You are welcome to join us. Colton types:

> Okay. Text me details later.

I can barely type.

> Will do.

Colton confirms:

> Looking forward to it.

Oh sweet Jesus! I am sweating. How did all this happen in, like, the last five minutes? Oh no! Now I have to break this news to Brooke. She will flip her shit. I switch over to her contact information to text her.

> When and where are we drinking tonight?

Brooke responds quickly.

> Anywhere. It's been a day already. Brewery?

I confirm:

> Fine. I can be there by 6.

Brooke replies:

Perfect.

I type my next message hesitantly.

OK. I will have a plus one tonight.

Brooke questions simply:

Who?

I try to divert her.

Friend from office.

Brooke snaps at me with her text.

Don't be flip, Whitney. Who?

I respond hastily yet simply.

Colton Johnson.

I brace myself for Brooke's response as I stare at my phone in anticipation. As I watch my phone intently, I hear a slight cough of interruption coming from my doorway. Startled by the disruption, I drop my cell phone onto my desk. I look up at Jerri, who is not happy with me. She stares at me with a questionable look as she eyes me, then the embarrassing display of floral arrangements that now adorn my office. Jerri looks back at me with her eyebrows raised and a confused look on her face. I am not sure if she is unhappy about the flowers or the fact that I am late for the meeting because I am preoccupied with my personal cell phone.

"Whitney! We are waiting on you," Jerri says as my cell phone starts to ring. *Shit!*

"Jerri, I am sorry."

She turns on her heel and out of my office.

I look down at my phone, which is now vibrating. It is Brooke. She is calling instead of texting. This cannot be good. I hit ignore on my phone, which immediately diverts her call to my voice mail, which will piss her off even more.

I fire off a quick message to her.

Late for meeting. Call you back soon.

I drop the phone back onto my desk and flee my office to catch up with Jerri. I arrive in the boardroom and take a seat by her. It is a few minutes after ten, and no Ryan. I let out a huge sigh of relief as I sink down into a chair at the boardroom table. *Thank you, Jesus!*

Jerri starts promptly. "OK, we need to get down to business." She begins to recap the race and the issues at hand. We start with the Nationwide fiasco, and I hear the boardroom door open as Jerri continues to speak. I don't look back, but I know immediately who it is. My stomach rolls with nausea.

Shit! He is here.

The door slams shut just as Ryan shouts, "That was all Whitney's fault! Let her clean up the mess!"

Bastard!

I whip my head around to where Ryan is standing. Of course, he looks all smug and arrogant as hell standing in the back of the room. I stand up in fury, and my face is flaming red. He is not going to embarrass me again, not today.

"Oh! I am so sorry that I didn't know that I needed to schedule exclusive engagements for you. You threw down the temper tantrum, not me. So, please tell me how this all my fault?" I finish flabbergasted. My face must be purple by now with the combination of rage and embarrassment. *Damn him!*

Ryan doesn't miss a beat. "Because you don't know shit about me or about NASCAR, which is why you have *no* business being my public relations manager!" he shouts back at me.

"It was your bright idea!" I yell back. We are now in a full-blown screaming match.

We continue to argue as if no one else is in the room. "Fine!" Ryan roars like a bratty teenager. "When you and Jerri get done running me down, I have a few issues with you from yesterday that need to be addressed as well!"

Jerri gapes at us, shocked, much like a mother breaking up a fight between siblings. She castigates Ryan, then me, and hushes us both. "Take a seat now! Both of you!"

I scowl at him. *How old are we?* He smiles mockingly back at me. *You bastard!*

Jerri lightly taps my arm, which signals me to take my seat as well. Ryan sits quietly in the back of the room as Jerri begins to tell me what steps we need to take for damage control. I fiercely scribble notes as she fires away again.

"And Whitney!" I can tell she's aggravated. "Language! For God's sake, please remind the guys about their language over team communications. We were hit with another twenty-five-thousand-dollar fine for Bobby's rant yesterday. It has got to stop!"

I nod nervously, taken aback by her tone. "Yes ma'am."

She finishes with more instructions for me and begins to adjourn the meeting without giving Ryan a chance to complain about me. But Ryan immediately interjects.

"This meeting is far from over! It appears that Whitney believes she works for Colton instead of me." I flush and look down. "She spent over an hour walking around the infield with him. She was not present with me for an interview that I gave which was not even approved. If she had been there, I would have known. Plus, not to mention whatever they did after the race." He raises his eyebrows in a "You know what I mean" look. "I believe that is a direct violation of company policy!"

Ryan's comments fly all over me like a heat rash. *You would know!* "That is a lie, Ryan Carter, and you know it! You embarrassed the hell out of me at that Nationwide event!" I let my rage fly. "Yes, I am learning, and I am doing the best that I can. But there is no excuse for your unprofessional behavior yesterday. I don't care who you are. And, yes, I am the one that will have to clean up your mess!" I am out of breath.

"That's your fucking job!" he slams me back, and I wince.

"And your job is to keep the sponsors and fans happy. They pay the bills!" I retort. "If I need to schedule a simultaneous meet and greet from now on, I will! So get over yourself and act like a professional adult."

"Good luck with that!" Ryan exclaims. "Until you learn to do things my way, you'll be back in here doing damage control week after week!"

This is like arguing with a stop sign. I'm not winning here!

"Oh!" Ryan gloats like he has had an eureka moment. "I almost completely forgot. Whitney, did you mention to Jerri that on Sunday you were almost two hours late and that you didn't even make it to the sponsor breakfast? And walked into the mandatory drivers' meeting *late*, embarrassing us all!"

Jerri turns to me with a look of unbelief on her face. My face falls as I try to explain.

"Yes, Jerri. I was late. I am sorry. My alarm didn't go off," I lie with a half-truth.

Jerri gives me a disappointed look as Ryan sounds off again. "Sounds like grounds for termination to me!"

I put my hands on my forehead. *Would you please shut the hell up!*

I try a different approach. *Breathe, Whitney. Breathe. I cannot lose this job.* I move away from Jerri and walk toward Ryan. As hard as it is, I put my anger aside to think clearly.

"Look, Ryan, I am new to all this. All I need is some direction. You could have handled that situation entirely differently, but you chose to humiliate me."

The look on Ryan's face softens for a moment, but it is fleeting. "Yes, I could have, but I bet your ass you won't make that mistake again."

I gasp. I throw Ryan's agenda down on the boardroom table. I can't take this. I cannot fight with someone who doesn't fight fair.

I turn sharply on my heel toward the boardroom exit. I need air. I have to get out of this room for a few minutes. I fling open the door, and it hits the opposing wall with a bang. Several of the other employees in the boardroom jump at the impact. As it sounds out, I have an immediate flashback of Annalise's demise. I stalk back to my office.

I walk past a group of employees who are quickly scattering back to their desks after eavesdropping, no doubt. As I walk past the last row of cubicles, I witness two women exchange money over the top of their working spaces. Abruptly, I stop, then walk back to the women.

"What the hell was that for?"

"I...um..." a middle-aged woman stammers, surprised by my outburst. She shakes her head and looks down. "I'm sorry, but there was a bet in the office to see how long you would last," she mutters apologetically.

"Oh really!" I say matter-of-factly. I am even madder now. "Well give her her money back because I'm far from done here!" I instruct the ladies, and they nod guiltily.

After that slight detour, I continue to my office in a huff. I cannot believe this. My own coworkers actually made a bet against me to see how long I would last. That is complete bullshit. Oh, I will show them. I wear out the carpet in my office, pacing and ranting to myself. *Lord, please forgive me, but that motherfucking son of a bitch!* I quickly remember myself. I'm not going to do this. He is not going to run me. I'm going to do my job, and by God, he is going to do his.

Jerri cautiously sticks her head into my office. "I'm so sorry, Whitney," she offers, dejected.

"It's OK, Jerri. It's not your fault. I just need a few minutes to regroup and get my thoughts straight, is all."

Jerri looks confused. "What do you mean? You're not quitting?"

"Hell no!" I respond suddenly, without thought. Then remorsefully I add in my best southern drawl, "I'm sorry, Jerri, but no, I'm not. He ain't running me outta of here."

I make a few more laps around my office as I quickly devise a plan in my head.

"May I have your permission to speak to him freely?" I ask Jerri. "I believe I can handle this now."

Jerri smirks. "By all means. I am out of options and open for suggestions."

I look down at my desk for support for my plan. I spy Ryan's employment contracts and sponsorship commitments, and instantly my plan is established.

I say with grand authority, "I'm ready, Jerri! Let's do this!"

Chapter 8

I take a deep breath, grab the stack of bulky documents off my desk, and head back into the boardroom. With Jerri flanking me to the right, I feel strong, although my heart is about to burst out of my chest. She and I stride purposefully through the boardroom door.

I look Ryan squarely in the eye as I slam the contracts on the mahogany table in front of him. *Damn! That felt good!* Ryan tries to cover up his surprise that I have returned to the boardroom, but fails miserably. He gapes at me with a "deer caught in the headlights" expression, then quickly changes to his trademark smirk. I laugh to myself. Whitney 1. Ryan 0.

"What's this?" Ryan says coolly.

I am now keenly aware that every eye in the boardroom is on me. I've made my scene. Now I had damn well follow through. I steal a quick glance at Jerri. She is my backbone. She gives me a slight nod as if giving me permission to proceed. I drag in a hasty breath and square my shoulders to him. *Here goes...*

"Ryan." I look him directly in his radiant blue eyes. The glow in them causes me to falter. "When...Jerri asked me to take over the position of public relations manager for you, temporarily, I took the liberty of reviewing your employment contract as well as your sponsorship agreements."

Ryan raises his eyebrows with light amusement. "And...?"

"It seems that you have gotten a tad bit confused about your job description," I say matter-of-factly.

"And how's that?" Ryan cracks.

"I would like to remind you that you only have two jobs to do." I hold up two fingers to accentuate my statement. I start my list. "Number one, drive your race car." There is an audible gasp in the room, but my eyes do not leave his. His trademark smirk has been replaced by a lost look. I have embarrassed him, maybe. "And number two, abide by your sponsorship agreements."

My blood pressure accelerates as I continue my rant. "It is my job to make sure that number two is accomplished. Therefore, you stick to number one, and I will make sure job number two is done correctly. And I can do my job a helluva lot better if you will act like an adult, for God's sake!" I add to hasten my point. "Frankly, *we*..." I hesitate to look around the room for backup, but of course, no one will meet me gaze. "*We* are all sick and tired of your arrogant, condescending bullshit!"

Ryan shifts in his chair like he is about to say something, but remains silent. He looks as though steam is about to unload from his ears. Whitney 2. Ryan 0.

"According to these contracts, Ryan, you have directly violated some aspect of each one of your commitments and responsibilities. Why your sponsors, let alone your management, put up with this behavior is beyond me."

Ryan jumps up from his chair, then slams his fist down on the table. "Because I am Ryan *fucking* Carter, that's why."

I cringe, recoil, and then reload. "Well, Ryan *fucking* Carter, you need to get your shit together, or you won't have a race car to drive at all!" I shout. "Every single one of your sponsors has a right to pull the rug out from under you right this very second because you are too damned concerned with that incredibly large chip on your shoulder."

A few snickers go up from the other employees who are witnessing my meltdown in the boardroom. I continue to ignore these outbursts because Ryan and I are deadlocked in a heated stare. Our intense standoff is broken by the sound of a small, one-person round of applause. We both turn to search the back of the boardroom to find our enthusiast.

As I look, I catch a glance at Jerri. Her face is deathly pale with a shocked look of horror. A man in what appears to be his midfifties glides effortlessly over to Jerri and me. He is dressed simply in jeans, plain white T-shirt, and work boots.

Jerri calmly whispers, "Garrett!"

Oh no! Oh shit! It's Ryan's dad, the owner of GCR Racing. My face drops, no doubt mirroring Jerri's look of horror, I'm sure of it. I don't take my eyes off Mr. Carter, but I can hear the pleasure in Ryan's voice when he makes a throaty, mocking "hmmmm" sound. The opposing team is finally on the scoreboard.

I take a step back, defeated. What have I done? How long has he been standing there? I continue to watch the exchange between Garrett and Jerri. He greets her fondly. She smiles and nods, although her face is still horribly pale.

Garrett turns his attention back to me. "Well, Miss..." He trails off, realizing he doesn't know my name.

"Pa-Parker," I stammer. Without even looking at Ryan, I know he is enjoying this. *Bastard!*

"That was quite a speech, Miss Parker," he continues. "I'm Garrett Carter, by the way."

I smile and nod as I shakily take his proffered hand. I'm not sure what to say. Clearly I have said enough, so I stay silent.

Garrett turns back to face his wayward son. "Now, Ryan...as Miss Parker so eloquently put it"—he motions to me with a sideways glance—"you really *do* need to get your shit together."

Ryan's face falls flat in a shocked line. By his expression, I can tell that he assumed his dad was on his team. After an official review, the opposing team's point has been revoked.

Garrett continues, "Ryan, I came in here today to speak to Jerri about you, especially since you skipped our morning breakfast."

Ryan doesn't look at Garrett. Instead he looks out the window of the boardroom.

"But to my surprise, Miss Parker has said enough for all of us. I believe she got right to the point."

My face burns with embarrassment.

Ryan slowly turns his chair back around. His gaze shifts between me and Garrett. Seven shades of red flash over his face as he listens stoically to the warning his father carefully lays out.

"Listen, and listen good, son. If I experience any more problems from you, whether it is from this office/staff, on the track, off the track, and/or from any of our sponsors, I will fire your ass!" Another audible gasp goes up. "You got that, son!"

Oh my God! This is not happening! I am mortified as Garrett continues to reprimand Ryan.

"Because frankly, son, *I* have had enough!" He pauses a moment for Ryan's response, but doesn't get one. "Are we clear?"

Ryan doesn't miss a beat and mutters, "Crystal," through gritted teeth.

Garrett immediately castigates him. "Don't start with your damned smart mouth! Are we clear, son?"

"Yes, sir," he says with his mouth in a firm line.

"Well then...good. I'm glad we understand one another. Now, I have some work to attend to, and I am sure the rest of you do, as well. Let's get to it."

Jerri replies a soft, "Yes, sir!" for the group as Ryan slams his chair back and walks hastily out of the office, not making eye contact with anyone.

I let out a huge breath that I didn't even realize I was holding. I look around to find a chair to steady myself. I feel like I am about to fall over.

As the other employees escape the boardroom and make their way back to their desks, Garrett turns to me with a straightforward command as he gestures toward the exit. "Miss Parker, walk with me!"

Damn! He is going to fire me after all!

Chapter 9

I follow Garrett out into the hallway, and we make our way toward the exit. He calls for the down elevator, which opens quickly, and we enter in silence. I have a huge lump in my throat and a feeling of dread in my stomach. I feel nauseous. The elevator doors close as Garrett inputs a special code into the keypad to reach the B level, which I assume stands for the basement.

As the elevator begins its descent, Garrett turns to me. "I was quite impressed with your speech?"

What?

"I don't believe anyone has every spoken to my son that way before. Well…except for his mother maybe!" He laughs.

A gush of air escapes my lungs. "So, I'm not fired?" I mutter, sounding relieved.

Garrett laughs heartily. "No, on the contrary, Miss Parker, I would like you to become Ryan's permanent public relations manager."

I am shocked. I gape at Garrett, not sure of what to say. I start to stammer, "I...uh...Thank you, Mr. Carter."

"Please, call me Garrett." He smiles as the elevator door opens.

We walk into a vast open area that looks like a museum. The floor is pure white polished marble. There are stock cars and glass trophy cases placed strategically throughout the space. Racing photographs and mementos decorate the walls, all in tribute and celebration to the legendary career of Garrett Ryan Carter Sr.

Garrett speaks as I survey the room in amazement. "Jerri said that you were new to stock car racing, so I thought I would give you some insight to me and my organization," he explains as he waves his hand toward his collection.

"Wow, this is incredible!" I say in awe.

"Everything on this floor is in its original state and from my personal collection. We have reproductions on the main level for our fans and visitors."

I nod and automatically understand why.

"That is the reason there is a special code for this level and only certain people have access to this floor," he further explains.

As Garrett speaks, I take a moment to look him over. He is ruggedly handsome. I know now where Ryan gets his looks from. Garrett has the same fierce blue eyes that dance with a devilish gleam. Only, he does not have the overexerted arrogance to go along with it. His beautifully sculptured jawline mirrors Ryan's perfectly. And although their hair colors do not match, the hairline is the same.

As we begin our tour, Garrett talks comfortably about his humble beginnings in racing, building his first car with his father, NASCAR great Garrison Carter, and training his son to become a driver. "I have been very fortunate in the fact that I love what I do and that I also happen to be good at it." He smiles fondly at the memories. "It also helps that my son loves the sport as much as I do and is as good, if not better, than me." He winks at me. The way he speaks of Ryan is heartwarming. It almost makes Ryan seem like a normal person.

Since Garrett is being so open, I dig for more information. "Forgive me for the stupid question, but how did you become a NASCAR driver?"

Garrett smiles and gestures for me to follow him over to another corner of the display room. "This is my father, Garrison Carter." He motions toward several dated photographs on the wall.

I smile and nod as I examine the photographs, another handsome Carter. Those roots also run deep.

Garrett speaks slowly and hesitantly. "My father was a very difficult man, but a hard worker and great provider for our family. Whenever he had free time, he spent it obsessing over his homemade stock car that he raced locally on a dirt track not too far from here." He takes a deep breath. "I was mesmerized by him. I wanted to be with him every second, so I spent as much time with him as I could, which meant being with him in our garage, working on his car."

Garrett continues with ease, "He was a hard man, and in order to please him, I paid attention to learn as much as I could about this sport that he was so transfixed by. The more I learned, the more praise I received from him, which was little at best. But I wanted to please him, and that is what it took." He sighs deeply at his recollections, and I watch him intently, completely enthralled in his story. "Which I guess will explain why I am so forgiving and lenient with Ryan. That is something that I struggle with. I want to make sure Ryan knows how important he is to me above all this because I always felt second-rate with my own father."

Garrett's revelation makes me want to cry. He senses my reaction and gestures for us to keep moving through the tour.

We approach a large display case in the back of the showroom that boasts ten large silver trophies. Garrett falls in line behind me. "I still can't believe those. It all seems surreal after the fact."

I have no idea what the awards are for, so I ask, "What do these trophies represent?"

Garrett eyes me warily. "Those trophies represent ten NASCAR championships that I have won throughout my career. I have won more championships than any other driver in the history of stock car racing."

I flush, embarrassed at my ignorance.

Garrett recognizes my embarrassment and helps me to understand. "Each week, drivers accumulate points based on how they run in the race, how they finish, and laps led, et cetera. After the last race, points are tallied, and the driver with the most points wins the season championship. Since I am semiretired now, my goal is to get Ryan in the best position possible to continue this legacy."

"How many championships has Ryan won so far?" I ask naïvely.

Garrett chuckles. "Zero!" He shakes his head. "Ryan has a very different racing style than mine. I am more patient, whereas Ryan is very spontaneous, or hasty, if you will, with his actions, which leads to more accidents and car problems. I am trying to teach him to be more patient, persistent, and consistent on the track, but I haven't gotten very far with that yet." He sighs.

"Good luck with that," I interject, but am instantly remorseful of my quick outburst.

Garrett doesn't acknowledge my rant as he continues, "Ryan has every ability to be as good if not better than I have been in my career. Don't get me wrong, he has a long way to go, but I see a great deal of myself in him, especially at his age. His mother says I can't really give him a hard time because I was the same way at his age. Then again, she has no room to talk either because Ryan has an extra dose of hardheadedness that comes directly from her."

I watch as Garrett's eyes light up and sparkle at the mention of Ryan's mother. He laughs quietly. He is such a sweet man, and it is very evident how much he loves his family. Why can't Ryan be like this?

I laugh. "Yes, sir. I know too well. We don't exactly see eye to eye on a lot of things."

"I know, or, well...so I have heard," Garrett admits. "There are several people who keep me informed of goings-on around here, even though Jerri likes to keep me out of it. Honestly, I have never seen anyone handle Ryan like that." Garrett laughs and shakes his head. "I believe that you will be good for him. He needs someone to give him a good ration of shit every day. He has wonderful potential and far more opportunities than I ever had. It is finally time for him to come into his own because one day soon, this will all belong to him," Garrett says as he gestures around to his accomplishments.

Chapter 10

It is a little after noon when I make it back to my desk. After the heated boardroom bout with Ryan and a walk down memory lane with Garrett, I am finally able to sit down at my desk to start preparing for Sonoma. I can't even grasp the fact that I will be flying across the continental United States in less than a week.

Jerri wants me to attend only Sunday's race again this week but says I will be ready for a full weekend by Kentucky. I have got to take this one race at a time, especially if I want to keep this job. I am going to have to stay one step ahead of Ryan and show him that I can do this job and do it well. I wonder how he will take the news that I am his new permanent public relations manager. Hmmm…I am glad that I don't have to deliver that information to him.

I look around my office to get my bearings. The beautiful pink floral arrangements make me smile and remember the conversation that I was having with Colton before all hell broke loose. Then, all of sudden I remember—Brooke! Crap! I have to deal with her. She has got to be seventy shades of pissed by now.

I shuffle some papers on my desk and find my iPhone buried underneath a stack of Ryan's sponsorship agreements. I am scared to look at it. There is only the one voice mail from Brooke, which I am hesitant to listen to, but I hit play anyway. Brooke's voice booms through the speaker.

"Whitney Elaine Parker!" I pull the phone away from my ear. *Jeezus!* "I know you declined my call and deliberately sent it to voice mail. How in the hell do you spring this on me over text? Colton Johnson. Oh my God! Who, what, when, where, and how! Come off the details!" I laugh out loud as her message ends.

I tap the call log and select Brooke's cell phone. The phone dials, and in about half a ring, Brooke is on the line.

"Where the *hell* have you been?" Brooke exclaims.

I am still enraged, and I take it out on her. "Listen here, I have just been through World War Three in this office, with *him*, not to mention the fact that I just about got fired by his father. So, I would appreciate it if you would cut me some damn slack right now."

Brooke gasps, shocked by my outburst. "OK...OK...But you can't spring some news like bringing Colton Johnson with you for drinks tonight over text and then leave me hanging!"

I groan. "I will explain everything later."

Brooke whines, "How? You won't be able to talk in front of Colton."

She is right. I stop a moment to think. "I will meet you at six and tell him to be there at seven. Is that good?"

"That works," Brooke says. "See you soon."

I hang up the phone with Brooke and look around to make sure no one is watching me or that Jerri is not lurking around. I don't want her to catch me on my personal cell phone again. The coast is clear. I switch over to my message app.

I select Colton's previous message. I type:

> We are meeting at the Rock Bottom Brewery downtown at 7. If you are still interested, that is...

I wait for a response with my heart in my throat. Within a few moments, my phone buzzes in response.

> Yes, very. See you there.

My heart flutters.

> Okay.

This has been one hell of a day, and it ain't over yet.

Chapter 11

I arrive at the brewery in downtown Charlotte promptly at six o'clock. Brooke is waiting for me in a booth in the back. She eyes me intently as I slide in.

"First of all, you look like hell!" she exclaims.

"I had a wonderful day. Thank you so much for asking!" I say sarcastically back to her.

Brooke smirks at me. "Go to the bathroom and get yourself together before he gets here. I will get a round of drinks coming."

I sigh loudly, and my shoulders fall. I don't know if I even have the energy after the day I have had. I rest my arm on the table and put my head in my hand.

"Whitney, here," Brooke calls out to me and produces her makeup bag from her purse. "Go! It will make you feel better."

She is right again. I nod my head and stand up to walk to the bathroom. I turn back sharply to Brooke. "No tequila. Not tonight. I have to keep my head on straight."

Brooke gives me a wink. "Smart girl!"

After twenty minutes in the bathroom, I am able to make myself somewhat presentable by touching up my makeup and brushing through my brown hair. Even it looks tired. I sigh and head back to the table.

Brooke lights up when she sees me. "Much better!"

"Thanks, Mom!" I mumble sarcastically as I slide back into the booth. There is a glass of white wine waiting in front of me. I down almost half of it in one swallow.

Brooke eyes me intently. "Come on, spill it! You only have ten, maybe fifteen, minutes tops before he gets here! Go!"

I know what she is waiting for, so I dump all the gory details of the last twenty-four hours before Colton arrives. I hold up my hand. "First of all...don't get all giddy about this. Nothing, I repeat nothing, can happen."

Brooke frowns at me. I roll my eyes at her.

"Do you need a reminder that I have just gotten out of a long, agonizing relationship, which I am to blame for." Brooke tries to interrupt me, but I don't give her a moment to cut in. "Yes, my fault! Stupid, and I don't even know what other adjectives, best describe my current situation. I am not going back there. I am no longer know that girl! So, I am not about to get involved with another man, especially one that I have to work with. I have let one man control me and run my life. It ain't going to happen again!"

Brooke looks at me wild-eyed. "Are you sure that you didn't hit the tequila before you left the office?"

I laugh out loud. "Sorry, I didn't mean to whip out my soapbox!"

Brooke laughs in return. "Oh, that's fine! Just put the soapbox *up* and tell me about the day's events at Peyton Place!"

I finish off my first glass of wine as I begin to recap the day for Brooke.

Brooke whistles out at the conclusion of my story. "What a son of a bitch!"

"I told you!" I retort. "See? Good looks will not cover a multitude of sins." I click my tongue at her. Before she can comment, an incoming message alert on my phone catches both of our attentions.

"Is it him?" Brooke asks warily.

I look down at my phone. It is him. It's Colton.

Are you here?

It seems like the restaurant has gone completely silent. I look back up at Brooke and nod my head as I type my response.

Yes, booth in the back.

My phone rings out again, signaling his response.

Walking in.

I put my phone back down in my purse, take a deep breath, and look up at Brooke. "He is on his way." Brooke has the power seat, of course, which looks out over the restaurant. I watch her as she looks for his arrival. "Tell me when you see him." She simply nods.

I take another hasty sip of wine to finish off my second glass. As I swallow the clear substance, I hear Brooke mutter under her breath, "Here he comes."

My heart skips a beat, and I am immediately anxious. I look up, and the gorgeous Colton Johnson is standing beside our table with his breathtaking megawatt smile.

Dressed like a businessman, his style catches me off guard, but it is flattering for him. He has on khaki dress slacks, a patterned button-down shirt, and a navy-blue blazer. He looks like he just punched out at the law firm, not the garage. But, oh, he is so very handsome.

I smile at Colton nervously and hurriedly make an awkward introduction to Brooke, who I can tell is as equally smitten as I am. Colton slides into the booth next to me, and I inch over to make room for him.

"Ladies, it looks like I am behind a round," Colton says, eyeing our empty wineglasses.

His statement immediately puts me at ease. Brooke and I both laugh. Then, our evening with Colton Johnson begins.

After what seems like hours of talking about racing, Colton sighs and looks over to me. "I have thoroughly enjoyed my evening with you ladies." Even though he includes Brooke in that statement, his eyes never leave mine.

I shift uncomfortably in my seat. *My oh my!*

"I have an early day tomorrow. My flight leaves for Sonoma at six in the morning," Colton confesses.

I nod knowingly. Most of the drivers are leaving in the morning to begin qualifying for Sunday's race, including Ryan.

"Do you mind walking me out, Whitney?" Colton asks.

I flush scarlet and steal a glance at Brooke, who is wide-eyed. "Sure."

I slide out of the booth behind Colton, nod to Brooke, and hold up one finger, signaling that I will be right back, but I know she wouldn't think of leaving just yet. I follow Colton across the restaurant to the entrance. As we reach the door, he grabs my hand and ushers me out into the street.

My breath catches in my throat. His touch is intense, and I can't look at him. We walk briefly down the street. There is a chill in the night air, and briefly I feel uneasy, as if I am being watched. I chalk it up to nerves.

Colton approaches a sleek white Chevrolet Corvette and walks around to the passenger side. "Get in," he says softly as he opens the car door. I look at him, confused, but before I can say anything, Colton says, "Just for a minute." I nod as I slide down into the seat.

I cannot breathe. I am so nervous. What could he possibly want with me? I try in vain to act cool and break the tension as he slides into the driver's side. "I love your car."

Colton smiles. "Just one of the perks of driving a Chevrolet stock car."

I am shocked. "GM gave you this car?"

"Yes, General Motors awarded it to me after I won Rookie of the Year a few years back."

I nod, impressed but clueless. I will have to Google that one. Colton twists his body to face mine, then reaches out and grabs my right hand, which forces my body to face his. I look at him suddenly very shy.

"Whitney..." Colton says as he slowly threads his fingers through mine, "I don't think this is a secret, but I really like you."

I gasp. *What?*

My emotions must show on my face because Colton laughs softly. "I do. And I want to know more about you."

I feel a huge lump rising in my throat. I stutter, shaking my head, "Wh-Why?"

Colton shrugs his shoulders, but his eyes never leave mine. "Isn't it obvious?"

I shift in the seat and feel myself starting to sweat. "Wouldn't that be a conflict since we work together?"

Colton raises his eyebrows at me and only nods his head.

"I see," I say and turn to look at the window. I don't know what to say to him. Yes, his offer is tempting, but I can't jeopardize a job that I have just gotten, because that would mean a direct failure, which leads me straight back to Georgia. Do not pass go; do not collect $200.

I turn back to look at the gorgeous Colton Johnson. The look on his face is one of concern. "What are you thinking?"

I swallow the lump in my throat. "Colton, I...I...don't know what to say or what to think." A look of disappointment now washes over his face. I continue to explain, "Look, I really like you, too, but I have just moved here, this is my first job, and I don't want to do anything to jeopardize it. Garrett gave me the PR position today, and I don't want to give him any reason to take it away."

"Really?" Colton asks. "Why didn't you say something earlier? Congratulations!"

I laugh. "I am not sure congratulations should be in order yet! It has been a day!" Colton laughs too. I shift my weight again in the seat. "Could you just give me some time? I know that sounds *so* cliché. But I want...I need to do my job and to get a grasp of this sport so that I can be successful. Moving back to Georgia is not an option for me."

Colton smiles warmly at me and immediately puts me at ease. "I am not sure why you are so hesitant to return to Georgia, but you seem to be a very determined and headstrong girl, Whitney. Take all the time you need."

And with that statement, Colton leans across the center console of the car and lightly presses his lips to mine. My body tingles. His lips are soft and taste divine. I want to lean into his kiss and place my hands on his face, but he pulls back, leaving me bereft.

Colton looks at me with a sly smile and whispers, "Good night."

Chapter 12

This tumultuous week has dragged on and on. Between the showdown with Ryan in the boardroom on Monday morning, dinner with Colton on Monday night, and preparing for Sonoma, I am worn out, and it is only Wednesday. My flight leaves Saturday morning for the land of wine and spas. I shake my head. This would be any girl's dream destination, but nope. I am headed to the desert for a NASCAR race. *I am one lucky girl*, I think sarcastically.

I stare blankly at my computer screen. I have read the last clause of Ryan's sponsorship with Coca-Cola about three times now, and still I have no clue what it says. I prop my elbows up on my desk to support my head in my hands. *Focus, Whitney, focus.* This is my mantra. I have to be better prepared for Sunday's race in California. I will be damned if I'm going to let him embarrass me again this weekend. Embarrass! Oh hell no! It was complete and utter humiliation. I shudder as I remember Ryan reprimanding me like a child in front of God and everybody. The thought of it still makes me nauseous. *Bastard!*

The office is deathly quiet. All afternoon, I have been poring over the upcoming race schedule, sponsorship commitments, and my own reliable copy of *NASCAR for Dummies* that is safely stored on my iPad. I know it's late, but I have no idea what time it is. I steal a glance at the clock on my computer monitor, 9:45p.m. *Damn!* I cover my face with my hands and groan loudly.

"Is it that bad?" a familiar voice questions me from the doorway. *Gasp!*

I spin my desk chair around so fast that I almost fall out of it. I manage to jump to my feet so I don't go headfirst into the floor. My heart is racing. I feel like I have just plummeted off the Matterhorn Bobsleds at Disneyland. *It's Ryan. Holy freaking shit! What in the hell is he doing in here?*

Ryan is leaning on the entrance to my office, all smoldering with that arrogant-ass smirk on his face. He is dressed very casually in jeans and a GCR Racing polo shirt. It is cobalt blue, my favorite color. I can tell he is very amused by my reaction.

"You scared the shit out of me!" I snap at him. "Don't ever do that to me again!"

"Good! I should have. You shouldn't be up here this late, alone," he says, emphasizing the last word with his sculptured smartass mouth.

I shake my head at my own thoughts. Catching my breath, I raise an eyebrow at him and ask internally, *Why would you care?*

"What the hell are you doing up here so late anyway? Security leaves at eight o'clock," Ryan questions me as he casually takes a seat in the leather chair in front of my desk.

"I..." I stammer. I open my mouth to speak, then close it again because I can't come up with a lie quick enough. My brain won't function, but I don't want him to know what I'm doing. I don't want him to know that he got the upper hand on me Sunday. "Ummm..." I fumble again, but manage to say, "Jerri had a couple things that she needed finished before the morning."

Ryan rolls his eyes at me. "Sure she did! Come on, let's go!"

"Go?" I snap. "I'm not done with what I am working on."

Ryan is beginning to show aggravation as he stands back up, pleading for me to leave. "Whitney! You are not working on the A-bomb!" He leans over my desk, peering at me as he rests his hands on my desk. "It's late! Let's go!" he demands.

Let's? Since when is there an us?

Ryan gives me a stern look. "I want to make sure you get to your car safely."

Seriously, stop! What's with the chivalry?

I deliberately roll my eyes at him and groan loudly, mainly because I know he is right. I sit back down at my desk to try to get myself together. I am mentally and physically exhausted. I log off of my computer, grab my bag and iPhone, and bend over to slide my black high heels back onto my bare feet.

I can feel his eyes on me even though my back is to him. I turn back to face him. Ryan is watching me with intent amusement, and I flush when our eyes meet. He is making me nervous.

"What!" I quip sharply to throw him off my discomposure.

He shakes his head at me. "Just waiting on you, Miss Parker." And then he follows that statement with that smug grin of his.

"What are you doing here anyway?" I snap at Ryan. "Shouldn't you be halfway to California by now?"

Ryan laughs. "Road courses are not my thing, so I am in no rush to get out there."

I snort, "Typical!"

I stand up, roll my eyes again, and stride past him in a huff. He laughs at me as he follows me to the elevators. I reach the elevator doors before him and quickly touch the down button, desperate to get away from him, because, frankly, I am uncomfortable. Plus, I am not his biggest fan these days.

Ryan hesitates as he falls in line behind me. A wave of concern washes across his face and he quickly changes pace. "Come on...let's go this way." He grabs my arm, redirecting me toward another door, aptly marked "stairs." There must be an after-hours exit.

When Ryan removes the lead on my arm, I notice a burning sensation that has lit up my whole body. *What the hell is that?* It must be nerves because I am not sure what his intentions are. His current behavior is something I have yet to witness. He must be bipolar.

I follow Ryan slowly down several flights of stairs, when he calls back to me, "Have you eaten?"

Why? I think.

"Uhh, no," I mutter and realize suddenly that I am, in fact, starving. My lunch is long gone.

We reach the bottom floor. He opens the back door of the building and leads me outside. Only we aren't in the parking lot. We are behind the building, facing a small path through a wooded area. My heart skips a beat. *Oh shit! This is it. He is gonna kill me! He is gonna kill me and hide my body in the woods.*

I take a few steps back cautiously. Ryan must notice the concerned look on my face because he says, "Relax, Whitney, damn! I'm not a rapist." I raise my eyebrows at him as he rolls his eyes and gestures toward a small clearing in the woods. "This path leads to my house. My mom brought over dinner tonight, and there is more than I can eat."

I notice that what he says is not an invitation, it's more like a command. He starts down the path, and I put my hand up, signaling him to stop. "Wait just a damn minute. It's dark, I can't see, *and* I have on high heels," I whine. "I do not walk through the woods in the daylight, much less in the dark."

He groans, and I can tell he is losing his patience with me. In frustration, Ryan bends down and sweeps me off my feet, cradling my body in his arms.

His swift gesture takes me by surprise. "Ryan!" I gasp. I instantly lose my breath as my arms instinctively wrap around his neck for support. Our eyes lock for a moment in the dark. My stomach does a backflip. I quickly move my arms down to his shoulders. By the look on his face, I think I may have surprised him with my intimate touch. But why would it? He is accustomed to girls falling all over themselves at his feet. I desperately try to regain my composure, but fail miserably.

My chest is burning, making it impossible to get any air back into my lungs. My blood is blazing through my veins. Ryan must sense my discomfort because he shakes his head and looks away.

"Are you always this stubborn?" Ryan tries to change the subject. I guess he must be as uncomfortable as I am.

I laugh nervously. "Yep, I gotta degree in that too!" I tease, referencing our first standoff in the boardroom. Ryan lets out a throaty laugh, and the atmosphere between us considerably lightens.

Ryan strides effortlessly with me in his arms through the dark path and into a cleared cutover. He sets me down gently to the grass, and I can just make out the lights from a house that sits on top of the hill. How in the world will I be able to walk that far in these shoes, I wonder.

"This way." Ryan touches my arm again softly and leads me over to a golf cart that is parked within a couple feet of us.

I break the uncomfortable silence and ask him again, "Seriously, shouldn't you be in Sonoma already?"

Ryan shakes his head. "Honestly, that race isn't worth the jet lag!"

I sit down beside him in the golf cart, and we take off quickly, with a jolt, up the hill to Ryan's home. There is a chill in the night air, but I don't know if it's the weather or prelude of things to come.

Ryan pulls the golf cart into a huge three-car garage occupied by only two vehicles. In one bay is a pristine white Chevrolet Silverado truck. It looks like an adult version of a little boy's Tonka truck. It is raised up from its normal frame and has huge tires with flashy chrome wheels. In the next bay, closest to the house, is a sleek black custom Chevrolet Camaro. The paint sparkles under the fluorescent lights in the garage. I want to run my finger down the side, but I don't dare. As I walk past the gleaming car, I can make out Ryan's signature and his number, 62, in script just past the driver's side door.

"Wow!" I say audibly, but don't realize it until Ryan responds arrogantly.

"You like that?"

It looks like sex on a stick but I don't tell him that. He doesn't need any more fuel for his smug fire. "It's nice," is all I can manage.

I follow Ryan a few steps up from the garage into a modern ranch-style house. There is a wonderful aroma wafting throughout the interior. It doesn't look like your typical bachelor pad. It is immaculately decorated and shockingly clean. He must have a housekeeper. We proceed down a hallway that is lined with various family and racing photos much like the ones in his dad's museum. I slow to admire a few, hoping that they will give me an insight to Ryan. Surely he can't be a pompous ass all the time.

Ryan quietly rounds the corner, and I follow him into a large kitchen that is open to a great room boasting a large flat-screen television and fireplace. He walks over to the counter where a bubbling Crock-pot sits.

I break the silence. "Whatever is in there smells heavenly."

Ryan turns back to me, props himself up against the counter, and smiles a gorgeous megawatt smile that I haven't seen since that fateful day in the elevator. It takes my breath away.

"My mom is an awesome cook." He seems relaxed, and even his arrogance has evaporated.

I watch Ryan intently as he turns back to the Crock-pot, lifts the lid to stir the contents, and switches the dial to off. He opens a cabinet and pulls out two plates.

"Can I help you do something?" I offer in hopes to quell the weirdness.

"I got this." He denies my help, but then asks, "What would you like to drink?"

"What are my options?" I say flirtingly. *Whitney Elaine Parker! What are you doing?* I scold myself. Most likely, I know, I am trying to break the awkwardness, but this is definitely not the way to do it. I chastise myself again.

"Let's see," Ryan says as he peers into the fridge. "I have sweetened tea, water, and Bud Light." Ryan seems to mirror my flirtation as he turns back to me with an eyebrow raised waiting for my response.

Not good, Whitney!

"Bud Light," I say, even though I know I shouldn't drink because I have to drive home shortly. However, I do need something to calm my nerves and take the edge off. Being with Ryan in this setting is intimidating to say the least. He is acting like a completely different person. It's actually hard to swallow. How can someone be such an ass, then flip the switch to...? *How is he acting? Nice? Hospitable?* I shake my head at my thoughts because I am clueless.

"Whitney!" Ryan exclaims, breaking me from reverie.

I jump instinctively as Ryan narrows his eyes at me, then continues to set the table for us. With his back to me, he says, "I don't want you at the office that late anymore. Do you understand me?"

I really don't understand. "What's the big deal?"

Ryan stops what he is doing and turns to face me. "Security leaves at eight p.m., and there have been a few incidents in the past with obsessed fans and paparazzi and such."

Whoa! What kind of incidents?

"Do you understand me, Whitney?"

I nod my head in agreement but am suddenly a little freaked out too. Warning duly noted.

Ryan watches me carefully as he motions for me to take a seat at the barstool under the center island in the middle of the kitchen. He raises an eyebrow at me. "What is it?" Suddenly, I am very aware that he is watching my every move. He sets a plate of steaming roast beef with vegetables on the granite countertop in front of me.

"Nothing...it..." I shift on the barstool. "The way you're acting is different, which is taking some readjustment on my part," I mutter.

He raises his eyebrows but says nothing. We sit in silence as we both eat. I take a bite of this classic southern dish, and it tastes as divine as it smells. I realize it has been a while since I have had home cooking. It makes me long for my mother.

"Is something wrong, Whitney?" Ryan asks again, breaking me from my reverie. He is very in tune to my mood, which makes me shift uncomfortably again in my seat.

"No, I'm sorry." I feel the need to apologize because he has had to ask me this question twice. "This is just really good. It makes me miss my mother."

He gives me a sympathetic smile and puts down his fork. "Why did you move to Charlotte?" His question is unsettling. I have a hard time admitting it to myself much less to him.

I shrug ambiguously as I put my own fork down on my plate. Suddenly, I have lost my appetite. "I just wanted a new start after college, new place, new people, I guess," I lie, and Ryan immediately calls me on it.

"Sounds like bullshit to me. What, or should I say who, were you running away from?"

His statement surprises me. *How could he know?*

"Since when have you become Dr. Phil?" I snap. *I am not having this conversation with you of all people.* Unwelcome tears spring to my eyes, and I instinctively look down to avoid his inquisition. I fight back the tears. I look back up at him directly and raise my eyebrows ambiguously, giving nothing away But, I falter. I can't maintain eye contact with him, because this moment is way too intense. I roll my eyes and look away.

I can feel his eyes on me, and it burns me internally. It is a feeling that I have never felt nor can describe. *It is time for me to get the hell out of here.*

I stand up in defense to clear my plate, but Ryan jumps up and blocks my move, taking my plate from me. I don't make eye contact with him. I follow him to the sink and prepare to make my exit.

"Thank you for dinner," I say with all southern politeness. "I probably wouldn't have eaten otherwise." I finish.

Ryan turns back from the sink and says over his shoulder, "I figured as much."

Instead of bolting for the door, I mistakenly ask, "Is this your way of apologizing?"

Ryan abruptly stops what he is doing looks back at me sharply. "Apologize?" he exclaims. "What the hell would I apologize for?"

I quickly snap back at him, "For acting like a complete ass and humiliating me in Michigan, not to mention the fiasco in the office this week!"

Ryan drops the utensils in his hand into the stainless steel sink, and it makes a loud clanging noise almost like the ring of a bell that signals the start of a boxing match. And the look on his face tells me we are, in fact, about to go another round. He shuts off the water faucet, grabs a dish towel to dry his hands, and slowly turns back to face me. *Let's get ready to rumble!*

"First of all," Ryan begins, holding up two fingers, "there are two things *you* need to get straight. Number one, I don't apologize! Period. Not ever! Not for anything!" *Oh no! Here we go again... Mr. Shit Ass has returned.*

I cringe and close my eyes.

"And number two, if you are going to continue to work with me in this sport, you need to get *your* shit together."

Oh hell!

"And *NASCAR for Dummies* ain't gonna help you!" he finishes with a flourish, catching his breath.

How in the heck does he know about that? I roll my eyes directly at him.

"Now...humiliation, you say?" Ryan fires away. "Let's talk humiliation. Why don't you try being the one and only son of legendary NASCAR driver Garrett Ryan Carter Sr." He takes a ragged breath. "Everything I do is under constant scrutiny of media and the NASCAR organization. Nothing I do is good enough. I am constantly in his shadow. If I win, the question is, how did your dad help you to win? If I lose, how is your dad going to handle your finish today? What would your dad have done differently? When are you going to win a championship, Ryan? Do you know that your dad had already won two championships at your age? And on and on and on. I am so sick of the bullshit! And this season has been the worst by far."

Ryan is furious but also dismayed. He runs his hands through his sandy brown hair, exasperated at his own tirade. I want to reach out and run my hands through it to comfort him. *Damn it! No, you don't!* I chastise myself.

"Well...it's probably your fault because you are trying to be a NASCAR driver turned Hollywood celebrity. You need to a make a choice! If you can't cut it in your dad's world, maybe Hollywood would be the right call for you! You certainly have the attitude for it!" I exclaim.

Ryan gives me another cold stare and mutters through gritted teeth, "Go to hell!"

Ooh! I hit a nerve!

I flush and look down at my feet because that phrase hurt. Thank God there isn't anyone here to witness this one. I quickly regain my composure from the anger that is welling up inside me.

"Why do you have to be such an arrogant son of a bitch?" I don't hold anything back. My tone and choice of words evoke a range of emotions across his beautiful face.

Ryan raises an eyebrow at me. "Arrogance is my best form of defense. Haven't you figured that out already?"

Huh? Defense against what?

The dumbfounded look on my face causes him to change tact immediately. Ryan himself has a defeated look on his face that makes me think that he slipped and said too much. I don't understand his emotions, but he doesn't give me the opportunity to think it through.

"Well...let's see!" Ryan starts. "As you so eloquently put it in the boardroom, my job is to drive the race car. I don't like to get caught up in the day-to-day bullshit that involves running a race team. It's not my thing. My focus is driving my car to win races and to win championships. Everything else should fall into place. However, lately, my support team is failing me, which is why I have to come into the office to make sure everyone is doing their job. And I don't like it. It makes me ill and, as you say, arrogant."

I open my mouth to speak, but Ryan lifts his hand, signaling me to stop. "I am not about to apologize to you, or anyone else, for that matter, for the way I am. I am who I am. That is why I am a hell of a race car driver. And, yes, I need an excellent support team at all times to guide me with the little things like sponsorship commitments, appearances, and such. All I know is driving the car, so I need someone that I don't have to babysit. Got it?"

I don't respond, but I don't break eye contact with him either.

"Look, Whitney," Ryan explains, a little calmer, "you don't understand this. But I was born into this...into this sport. It is in my blood. Stock car racing is all I know. I need someone who understands that. I need someone on my team that has grown up in NASCAR and that can relate to how it operates. I don't need someone that has never even watched a damned race on television. Do you understand?"

He finally gives me an opportunity to respond. Words finally come to me with his last statement. "Oh! You also need someone that is fuckable, too, right? Don't forget that requirement! And I guess I don't fit that bill either."

Ryan furrows his brow. "Annalise?"

I nod.

"Not that it is any of your damn business, but that was my mistake."

I rebound again. "Mistake? Hell, from what I hear, you have made several of those since the new season started."

Ryan paces the kitchen floor. "Yes, I crossed the line with her, only because I knew it wasn't working out."

What!

"I have to have someone who I can trust to guide me each weekend to get me through the extracurricular activities that accompany my sport. I don't have the time or the luxury to wrap my head around those things. I only want to drive my car. And I just haven't found that right person this season. I thought Annalise would be a good fit."

I snort at Ryan as he continues his explanation while rolling his eyes at me.

"Her family roots run deep in NASCAR, and we had a good working relationship until I crossed the line and complicated things. In the end, I knew she couldn't be trusted."

Why? I wonder.

Ryan runs his hands through his brown hair again. "I don't know how to explain this to you. You just can't understand this, Whitney, because you don't know me or my sport!"

I take my eyes off his and look down. I don't want him to see the hurt look wash across my face, but I am too late. I am sincerely trying to do my best, but I don't think that will ever be good enough for him, no matter how much I learn.

Ryan immediately stops his tirade. "Damn it, Whitney! Don't look at me like that. God! You make me feel like such an ass."

"You are!" I shout back, crestfallen. Tears spring to my eyes again, but I push them back before they can fall. Even though Ryan is a complete bastard, I have a hard time when people don't like me, especially for no reason. "I really am trying. Just give me a chance."

Ryan sighs, dejected himself. "This sport is not something to try. Yes, there are things that you can learn, but you have to feel it here"—Ryan points to his heart—"and be addicted to the adrenaline rush that pulses through your veins every week to really know this sport."

Sadly, I finally realize what point he is trying to get across to me. I don't know what those feelings are like because I have never experienced them.

I look up at Ryan. "You're absolutely right. I don't understand. But if you give me some time and guide me, help me to understand, I know I will get it. I am *not* going to give up, no matter how much you *hate* me."

Ryan looks up at me, shocked. "I don't hate you, Whitney."

"Could have fooled me," I say sadly and shrug my shoulders.

Ryan growls low in his throat, no doubt frustrated by me. It is so hot. *No, it's not. Asshole alert, Whitney!* Then, suddenly I realize that I like pissing him off.

"I am not the heartless bastard that you make me out to be. And I don't hate you." Ryan sighs loudly as if defeated. "Come on."

He turns to me and takes the beer from my hand that I didn't even realize I was still holding. I think he is about to usher me out the door, but instead he intimately grabs my hand and interlocks his fingers with mine. His touch is like a lighted match that explodes from the tips of my fingers throughout my body. I almost have to gasp from the sensation. *Hmmm...I wonder if that is what an adrenaline rush feels like.* I look up at Ryan, and he has a surprised look on his face. *Did he feel that too?* He quickly drops my hand. Then several shades of what looks to be regret wash over his beautiful face. He appears to be conflicted somehow, but I am not sure.

Ryan walks into the great room, and I follow behind him. I can barely make out soft music that flows throughout the space, but I like what I can hear. "Who is this?" I ask as I point to the open air.

Ryan looks up like he is tuning his ears in to the soft music. "It's... Adam, I think?"

Adam!

"Maroon 5," he says in answer to my unspoken question.

"You say that like you know him," I say.

Ryan shoots me a look that basically says, "No shit," and instantly I know that they must be friends. I listen closely as Adam sings sultrily about secrets, a song that I have never heard before, but which now speaks volumes about my life. I make a mental note to download it onto my iPod.

Ryan gives me another confused look, then motions for me to sit down on the sofa as he makes his way over to the ginormous home theater system. Immediately, his demeanor changes to excited, like he just had the most brilliant idea. I almost want to giggle at his expression.

"This will be an unusual way to get an insight into my sport, but at least it'll be fun." He opens a cabinet under the television and produces two game controllers. He tosses one at me. "Here, sit on the far right side of couch."

I reach out to grab the controller from the air and slide down to the end of the couch. Ryan walks over purposefully and leans into where I am sitting. He runs his hand down inside of the couch arm. We are in extremely close proximity. I can feel the fire rekindle in my chest and ignite throughout my body. *What the hell is he doing?* I can feel his hot breath on my neck, and I can smell his scent. It's an invigorating mix. He presses a small lever, and the couch transforms suddenly into a recliner. A footrest pops out from below and immediately reclines my body backward.

"Sweet!" I tease. *Stop it, Whitney!*

The beer must have worn off because my nerves are back with a vengeance thanks to this nerve-racking close encounter. He turns on the television with a series of remotes, and the screen comes to life. Then he switches on the game console, and *NASCAR Unleashed* brightens the screen.

"A video game? Ryan, you're not serious," I say in horror.

Ryan laughs and takes a seat at the opposite end of the couch. "Yep! This is as real as it gets besides being in the car. It is amazing the technology of these things nowadays. I can log in and race people all over the world. And what's funny is that they don't even know that it's me. It is almost as good as the real thing." He laughs to himself.

Ryan purposefully chooses the track that he will be racing at on Sunday. Then he gives me a series of instructions on how to operate my car by using the controller. We are all set to battle on the Xbox. I am horrible at it, of course, but he is a champion in virtual reality too. Ryan was right! It does give me a good insight into what it's like in the car and on the track.

Ryan coaches me through the track specifics of the Sonoma speedway. He talks incessantly about the road course track, qualifying times, and pit regulations. My brain is piled high with information that I can't even begin to process. I need my iPad to take notes.

Ryan is in his element, although I have crashed my car for the third time and given up. I set my controller down and continue to watch what he is doing. I lay my head back and curl up on the comfortable brown leather sofa. I can barely keep my eyes open as he continues to pump me with information about the track, pit stops, and other drivers.

"Whitney? Are you getting all this?" he questions me quickly, but returns his attention back to the virtual track.

I nod quietly as I struggle in vain to take in all of the specifics, but my mind begins to drift. My efforts to stay awake give way to the overwhelming exhaustion that has engulfed my body.

Chapter 13

I am warm and strangely comfortable. My eyes slowly open, and I am slightly disoriented, but only for a moment. It takes me only a second to reconcile that I have fallen asleep on Ryan's sofa. I sit up and look around the great room. The television is still on, but muted and tuned to ESPN's *SportsCenter*. And asleep on the opposite end of the couch is the one and only Ryan Carter.

I shift from my contented position on the couch and realize that I have been covered up with a blanket. *Wow! That was thoughtful.* I am shocked! I stand up to gather my faculties. I walk over to the kitchen to find my iPhone and my bag. *What time is it?* A steady rain is falling, and the cloud cover makes it impossible for me to even estimate what time it may be.

I find my belongings and glance at my phone. Then, all hell breaks loose!

"*Ryan!*" I scream.

He awakes, jumps up and off the couch like he has been attacked. "What the fuck, Whitney?" he yells back, out of breath.

"It's almost nine a.m.!" My whole body shakes. "I am so freaking late for work!" I pace the kitchen floor in a full-blown anxiety attack. "What am I going to do?" I wail with my head in my hands.

Ryan is watching my meltdown with wry, sleepy amusement as he stumbles back to the couch. "What time is it?" he says as he yawns sleepily.

I completely ignore him as I pick up my phone and stare at it, hoping that it has some unforeseen powers to turn back the clock. I notice two missed calls. *Oh shit!* Both of the missed calls are from the office, and I start to hyperventilate. Fanning my face, I can't breathe. I check my voice mail icon, one new voice mail.

I continue to pace the floor as I press the play button to listen to the voice mail. "Hi, Whitney! It's Jerri. I noticed your car in the parking lot but can't seem to find you in the building. I know you were here late last night, so I was worried. Call me, please."

"No, no, no!" I cry out. "This is not happening!" I sit down on the couch beside Ryan, who still looks half asleep, but amused from my morning meltdown.

This is so unprofessional and possibly career ending. I put my head in my hands and run down my laundry list of problems in my head. Let's see...my car is still in the parking lot at the office. *How the hell will I explain that?* How am I going to get back to the building? I can't walk from Ryan's house. And he damn sure isn't going to drop me off. There is no time for me to go back into Charlotte to my apartment. I haven't had a shower. My hair looks like hell. And Oh! My! God! I have no clothes. I'm going to have to take the walk of shame into my office wearing the same clothes I had on yesterday. *Please God. This is not happening.*

112

Ryan calmly says, "Just call Jerri and tell her you overslept. She knows you have been working late hours."

I snap my head back in his direction. *Wait! How does he know that?*

"We will figure out the rest," he says as if he already knows my list of crises.

We! Then it hits me like a ton of bricks. Everyone at the office is going to think I slept with Ryan! *Oh dear God!*

I try my hardest to get control before I call Jerri. I count to ten slowly in my head and take a deep breath. "Jerri, hi, I'm soo very sorry, but I overslept! No, ma'am! I..." I steal a look at Ryan, who bids me to continue. "I stayed with a friend last night. She picked me up from the office. Yes, ma'am! She is going to drop me back off in a few minutes. Yes, ma'am. No, ma'am, I am fine. Again, I am sorry, but I am on my way. Yes, ma'am, thank you." I hang up, mortified. I am a terrible liar. "Ryan! Why didn't you wake me up?"

He shrugs at me with a yawn. "You looked...I don't know...I could tell you were exhausted, and you seemed peaceful. So, I didn't want to disturb you," he fumbles. *What?*

I begin to pace the floor again. "Yeah, well, I don't look peaceful now, do I?" I snap.

"Whitney, you have *got* to calm down!" Ryan pleads with me, stressing his point. "Do you need coffee or something?"

Yes! It appears that I need a new brain. Thank you very much!

Ryan is right, though. I do need to calm down. I don't want him to see me like this. Southern girls are famous for their hissy fits, but most of us throw them internally to maintain our strong, solid façade.

I let out a huge breath. Coffee would be a start. "Yes, thank you!" I gladly accept his offer.

"I'll go fix a pot, a strong one!" He smirks as he strides his sexy smart-ass into the kitchen.

"This is not funny, Ryan *fucking* Carter!" I shout, following him into the kitchen in exasperation.

Ryan laughs and sets out my plan of action. "Go take a shower in my bathroom. It's down the hall, to the right. Take a shirt from my closet. There should be several in there that you could wear with those slacks. Then you should be good to go." He commands with full authority.

Then another load of bricks hits me from behind. He is so calm because he has done this before. I am so freaking stupid. How did I let this happen?

Begrudgingly, I head down the hall to Ryan's room. I open the door to find another atypical room that is immaculately decorated. The bed is even made.

"What the what?" I murmur to myself as I pass through to his bathroom. It is fabulous, with wall-to-wall limestone and granite countertops. It looks like it has never been used. Mr. Arrogance must be OCD as well.

I emerge from Ryan's oasis in record time. It's a shame that I didn't have more time in there. His shower with those double spray heads was magnificent. It did wonders to calm my nerves. I take a towel from the rack outside of the shower. As I wrap myself in it, I can smell

Ryan. His smell completely paralyzes my body causing my muscles to clench down deep. *What is that about?*

I walk to the bathroom counter to find a steaming cup of coffee waiting for me. *When did he come in here? Did he see me naked in the shower?* I shake my head. *Bad thoughts, Whitney!* The coffee is scorching hot. The first sip burns my tongue, but it is made just the way I take it. *Good guess?*

I open the door to Ryan's bedroom and stick my head out to make sure that he is nowhere in sight. Confident that I am alone, I pad across the bedroom, still naked except for the towel that I am wrapped up in, to find Ryan's closet. The first door I try opens up a labyrinth that should not belong to any man. It is another phenomenon. His closet is huge. The man has more clothes than I do. They are all arranged by type, style, and color. I run my hands over his neatly pressed clothes that look like they came straight from the dry cleaner. Ryan's wonderful smell rises from the material. It is now forever burned on my brain. *Sweet Jesus!*

I find a plain white button-down shirt, which I secretly love, from what looks like the casual section. *It is a shame for a man to have that many clothes*, I think as I shrug it on his shirt and head back into the bathroom. I manage to brush my hair into compliance. I am tempted to search the cabinets for a straightening iron. I know there is one here. But then again, I don't want to know whatever else I might find in those cabinets either.

Thankfully, I find some makeup in my bag. I look myself over in the large mirror of Ryan's bathroom. This isn't my best, but it is far better than I had expected. I take a deep breath to calm myself before I have to face Ryan again.

I walk back into the kitchen with my empty cup of coffee. Ryan is sitting at the counter with his own cup. He works me over with his intense blue eyes, and it makes me uncomfortable.

Ryan says smugly, "You had to pick my favorite shirt, didn't you?"

I smile sarcastically in return. "You may not get it back either." I wink. *Whitney! Stop!*

"I'm glad to see that you calmed down." Ryan rolls his eyes at me and takes my cup from hand to refill my glorious concoction. I watch him with anticipation as he adds milk and cream. I realize I am holding my breath just watching him do this mundane task.

"Thank you!" I say too loudly but appreciatively. "It's just how I take it!"

Ryan hands the cup back to me and smiles wryly. He turns back to the counter and opens a cabinet drawer. "Here!" He slides a set of car keys across the counter to me.

"What's this?" I say, confused.

He replies calmly, "The keys to the Camaro." I almost choke on my sip of coffee.

"Excuse me...what?" I exclaim with a laugh. I shake my head and speak again before he can respond. "I am not driving your car to the office!"

Ryan snaps at my hardheadedness "Yes, you are, unless you want me to drive you back to the office on the golf cart!"

I guffaw at him. He knows that isn't an option.

"The car was just delivered to me yesterday, and only my business manager knows about it," Ryan says, deadpan.

Dumbfounded, I look at him.

"I will get it later. Just leave the keys in it."

I am in shock. "Uhh...I...OK," I stutter.

Ryan raises his eyebrows at me and ushers me down the hallway to the garage. He opens the back door and presses a small white button on the wall. The garage door opens slowly and quietly. The rain is still falling outside. I pause and watch Ryan as he crosses the garage floor over to the Camaro. He turns back to me with a weird, almost angry look on his face.

"And just so you know, I haven't even driven the damn thing yet. And Whitney, so help me God, I will lose it if you get as much as a scratch on it!"

I raise my eyebrows at him because I have no doubts.

"I cannot believe I am even doing this." He shakes his head at me while he opens the door to the car.

I smile broadly, pleased with myself. *Sweet!* Too bad I don't have farther to drive. I walk to the beautiful piece of machinery and gently place my bag in the passenger seat. Ryan takes my coffee cup from me.

"Hey! I wasn't done with that!"

"You are now!" Ryan says authoritatively. I frown. I guess he is a control freak about his vehicles too.

I walk around to the other side of the vehicle. Ryan opens the driver's door for me, and I slide in. I run my hands around the steering wheel as I take in the new car smell. This car is phenomenal.

Ryan gives me some basic instructions as if I have never driven a car before. I nod amenable even though I am annoyed.

"I have been driving since I was fifteen. I think I can handle this," I say as a matter of fact.

"It's custom," he says proudly. "It has a Z06, LS7, V-8 engine."

I raise my eyebrows at him. "What?"

"It is the same motor setup that is in a Corvette. It was custom built just for me." He beams with his trademark arrogance.

I laugh mockingly, antagonizing him.

"Just be easy with the pedal, Whitney."

"Hmmm..." I mutter while taking in all that worthless information, and before my brain can stop my mouth, I say, "Why don't *you* have a Corvette?"

The look on Ryan's face is priceless, as I recall the cool state-of-the-art interior of Colton's car. It is smooth just like him. Ryan opens his mouth to speak, then closes it again. He looks conflicted or maybe even angry. I am not sure which. But I am sure that he is wondering who I know that has a Corvette. He only shakes his head and doesn't say a word.

"Just be careful. The roads are wet. And this car can get away from you quickly," Ryan warns as he moves to shut the door.

"Wait!" I stop him from closing the door. "How do I get back to the office?"

"Whitney, get serious!" he shouts at me.

"What? Until yesterday, I had no clue that you even lived behind the office." I smile sweetly at him and say sarcastically, "So, yes, I need to know how to get back to the office parking lot, pretty please."

Ryan hesitates.

"Surely, you don't want me to drive through the path?"

Ryan runs his hands through his hair in exasperation, but then begins to laugh at me. "Whitney, what in the hell am I going to do with you?"

Chapter 14

My plane lands in San Francisco with ease. I quickly exit the airport to find the courier who waits to take me into Sonoma Valley. I am in the land of vineyards and spas, which would be any gal's dream vacation, but no. I am here on business, and for a NASCAR race at that. *Yay for me*, I think sarcastically.

I laugh at my own thoughts as I slide into the car with the courier, who is less than friendly. I take out my cell phone to check in with Brooke. No answer.

I arrive at a quaint little boutique hotel about twenty minutes from the track. When I reach the check-in, a young guy who I suspect is gay gives me the once-over. I smile as I give him my name, "Whitney Parker."

He responds coolly as he types away into his computer, "I don't have a reservation for that name."

I take a step back. *Damn!* I forgot to change the name from Annalise's reservation to mine. After the week I have had, I probably can't even spell my own name.

"I am so sorry, but I meant to go through the proper channels to change the name on this reservation," I say. The attendant raises his eyebrows at me. "Miss Martin no longer works for GCR Racing. I am her replacement."

My explanations are in vain because Mr. Rules and Regulations, who is not convinced, lays out a sermon on the proper procedure on changing reservations. Finally, after I produce my driver's license, my GCR identification, race weekend corporate credentials, and the company credit card, he grudgingly changes the name on the reservation.

"Will you be taking over the complete itinerary for Miss Martin?" he asks.

Ummm, yes! I scream to myself. *She no longer works for GCR.*

I fight my sarcastic tongue and mutter a polite, "Yes!" What itinerary could she possibly have outside of the track? I shake my head. When it comes to her, there is no telling whatsoever.

As I arrive in my room, my cell phone begins to ring. I fumble with my bags, then finally drop them to the floor to retrieve my iPhone from my purse. It's Brooke!

"Hi!" I say, out of breath, and collapse onto the fluffy bed.

"Did you make it?" Brooke asks.

"Yes. I just had to go through an act of Congress to get checked in, but I am here." Just as I complete my sentence, there is a loud knock on my room door. "Just a sec, someone is at the door."

I lay the phone down on the bed and bound over to the door. I open it and am almost knocked over by a room service attendant with a rolling cart. I stand back, stunned. *What the hell?* The cart is filled with a bucket containing a bottle of chilled champagne, a tray of chocolate-covered strawberries, and a vase of pale pink roses. I stand shocked in disbelief. *Colton?* The attendant politely shoves a white folder at me with Annalise's name on it. My stomach rolls with nausea as I read her name. It's not for me.

After he retreats, I remember—Brooke! I amble back to the bed and sweep up the phone to my ear. "You there?" I exclaim.

"Yes!" she responds, irritated.

"A waiter just brought in a whole spread of champagne, flowers, and chocolate-covered strawberries.

Brooke gasps, "From who? Colton?"

I take a moment to think. My stomach rolls again remembering my own display of pale pink roses from Colton. No, couldn't be, or could it?

"I don't know...Wait...The waiter handed me a folder. No, it's not for me..." Then I remember it is still in my hand. I am so confused. I open the folder, and several papers fall out. "Damn it! I just dropped everything. Hang on."

I kneel down to find Annalise's itinerary spread out on the floor of my hotel room. I browse the documents. Most of them are hotel accommodations, but then I hit the jackpot, a letter from the concierge.

Dear Miss Martin,

It is our pleasure to accommodate you and your guest during your stay with us. If you have any further needs, please contact me directly. Also, please find the attached documented itinerary for your spa and dining appointments.

Sincerely,

Hotel Concierge

"Whitney! Whitney!" I can hear Brooke whining through my cell phone. I snatch it up.

"Annalise. She must have ordered all this shit!"

Brooke gasps again. "Who for? Ryan?"

I am flabbergasted. She must have forgotten about all this. "I don't know..." I flip over to the next page and read the remaining itinerary. "Brooke! She has booked a couples massage for six tonight, too, then a late dinner for two at nine p.m. at the Vine." I sit down on the bed, stunned.

I am trying to gather my thoughts, and Brooke begins laughing in my ear.

"What is so funny?" I hiss.

"This is your perfect opportunity to get back at Ryan."

"What?" I snap.

"Yes, you should text him and ask him what you should do with all that stuff. Or...Or tell him it is a shame that you are enjoying those extravagances all alone."

"Are you crazy?" I shout. "Why?"

"Play a joke on him, get him back!" Brooke whines.

"How is this a joke? I'm sorry, but I don't get it!"

Brooke sighs loudly into the phone. "It's not really a joke, but just have some fun with him. It will rattle his cage since they were together, make him think!"

"I don't even have his cell phone number, Brooke," I confess.

"What?" she says in disbelief.

"Well, I guess I have not needed it, and who even knew I was allowed to have that top secret information!"

Brooke laughs out loud. "Who could you call to get it? Jerri?"

"No! I can't do that!" I whine back. "She will know something is up, and you know I'm a terrible liar."

"Just do it!" Brooke cries. "Call her, and call me back." Brooke hangs up on me so there is no further discussion.

I fall back onto the bed in exasperation. That damn Brooke. She can talk me into anything. What in the world am I going to say to Jerri? What can I come up with? Then it hits me...Ryan will probably be pissed, but then again, what's new? I grab my phone, select Jerri's name from my contacts, and press send.

The phone rings a few times, and I believe it's going into her voice mail, but suddenly Jerri answers. "Hi, Whitney! Everything OK?"

I take a deep breath. Here goes nothing. "Jerri, I had a few issues at check-in and then a problem with an event tomorrow?"

"Oh?" Jerri replies, concerned.

"There is absolutely nothing to worry about," I say, trying to reassure her and myself. "I had forgotten to change the name on the reservation from Annalise's to mine, but that is all handled now. However, when I got to my room, there were flowers, champagne, and chocolate-covered strawberries."

Jerri gasps, "Are you kidding me?"

"Uhhh, no, ma'am," I respond. "There is more...Apparently she had a couples massage booked and dinner reservations for two later tonight. I am not sure who the intended second person was, but I do know that she used the company credit card to book these appointments. Should I cancel them?"

"Yes, please!" Jerri sounds exasperated and pissed off all in one tone. "I am glad that you called me because I have just come across some other unapproved charges on her company card. I guess it is a good thing she's gone now because it would only have been a matter of time. Please...just cancel them all now."

"It will be my pleasure to handle that!" I say matter-of-factly.

"Thank you so much, Whitney. You don't know how grateful I am to have someone as professional as you are," Jerri adds.

Well damn. Why did she have to go say that? Now, I feel like shit for what I am about to do.

"There is just one more thing," I mutter. I have to make this sound good and as vague as possible. "One of our sponsors would like to change a meet and greet to a question-and-answer session in the morning. Are you agreeable with this last-minute change?" I hold my breath, hoping that Jerri gives me the correct response.

"Sure, that is fine with me, but Whitney, you really need to confirm that with Ryan. You know how he is."

I let out my breath. *Score!* "OK, sure, I will be glad to do that, but I don't have his cell phone number, and I am not due at the track until the morning…"

"Whitney! I am so sorry, but I thought you had his number. Honestly, I don't know where my brain is."

I laugh. "Seriously, I haven't needed it until now. Plus, the less I talk to him the better."

Jerri erupts into laughter. I grab the hotel notepad and pen off the nightstand and jot down Ryan's magical cell phone number.

"Thanks, Jerri. See you on Monday!" I hang up quickly.

I take another deep breath. I need a drink. I grab the champagne from the bucket. I dial Brooke's number again. She answers quickly just as I bust the top on the bubbly.

"Seriously? Did you just pop open the champagne?"

"Damn right I did. If I am letting you talk me into doing this, then I need alcohol. Besides, I am definitely not letting it go to waste either."

Brooke shrieks, "Did you get his number?"

"Got it!" I respond as I pile up in the middle of the luxe hotel bed. "Call me on the hotel number that I am texting to you now. We can talk while I text Ryan."

"Gotcha!" Brooke hangs up again.

Shortly the hotel phone buzzes, and I grab it up. "OK," I say. "Here goes the first text."

"Wait!" Brooke interjects. "What are you going to say?"

"Hush! I will read it!" I say, then read each text aloud to Brooke as I send them.

My first text reads:

> Thanks for the warm welcome to Sonoma.

Ryan's response is automatic.

> Who is this?

I type hastily, giving the play-by-play to Brooke.

> It's Whitney.

Another quick response.

> What are you talking about?

I type:

> Well…the embarrassing display of flowers, cham-
> pagne, and strawberries that were just delivered
> to my hotel room. Were those not from you?

I laugh as I read my text aloud and take a hasty sip of the champagne.

"You are too much!" Brooke laughs. "This is way better than some of the stupid pranks we pulled in high school!"

Another message comes through from Ryan.

> Hell No!

"Oh no! He is getting pissed, Brooke," I say after I read his latest response. I fire another message. I need to end this quick.

> OK, guess I have a secret admirer then.

Ryan is quiet. There is no response.

Brooke says, "Nothing?"

"Nope." I am stuck on what to say next.

"Say something about the massage and dinner," Brooke prompts.

Before I can think about what to type, Ryan sends another message.

> Why are you at the hotel? You are sup-
> posed to be at the track.

"What?" I screech.

"What did he say?" Brooke cries out.

"He is crazy. Jerri said that I did not have to go until Sunday."

Coolly, I text him back.

> Sorry, I don't have to be there until the am. I
> guess I am on my way to a massage appoint-
> ment and dinner. See you tomorrow.

Brooke laughs as I read it aloud to her. "That will make him think!" I laugh, but an incoming text alert startles me. "Wait, Brooke, here is another message."

> I don't give a shit what Jerri told you. You work
> for ME. Get your ass over here now.

"Damn it, Brooke!" I exclaim. "Shit! He is officially pissed now. I knew it. I knew this was going to happen."

"Oh boo! Let him be pissed," Brooke says.

"Yeah, you don't have to work for him, so that is very easy for you to say! We were in a much better place this week too," I shout.

"What?" Brooke exclaims. "What did you mean by that?"

Oops! I said too much! I have failed to mention my night with Ryan to her, for obvious reasons. I finish off my glass of champagne and take a deep breath. "Well...yes, let's see...he hasn't cussed me out since Monday, but then again, I haven't seen him either."

Brooke is silent. I am not a good liar, and Brooke is an excellent lawyer whose job is to determine when people are lying. Another message comes through from Ryan.

I expect you here in thirty minutes.

"Ugh! Great. Just great. Brooke, I gotta go," I slam the phone down on the receiver. I take a breath and pick it back up again. I dial 0 for the front desk and pray that the same guy who checked me in doesn't answer. Luckily a girl answers. "I need a car or shuttle or cab to the race track. I need to be there quickly."

The young girl on the line is very helpful. "Yes, ma'am. All of our shuttles are out, but I will have a cab waiting for you."

"Thanks!" I say quickly as I slam the phone down again.

I jump up and walk into the bathroom and look in the mirror. Damn Brooke. I have about five hours' worth of airplane on my body, not to mention exhaustion and jet lag, and he wants me to come to the track now. I run a brush through my hair, touch up my makeup, and I am out the door, but not before pouring myself another glass of champagne in a hotel paper cup. The small amount of bubbly that I have already drank has gone straight to my head. I am sure drinking on the job is against company policy, but I am going to need this in order to deal with Ryan.

The twenty-minute ride to the Infineon Raceway is probably the longest of my life. The night air in the desert is cold. I wish I had a jacket or sweatshirt or something, and the impending confrontation with Ryan only makes it worse. When I arrive at the track, I make my way over to the GCR hauler. The first person I see is Bobby.

"Hey Whitney, we weren't expecting you until tomorrow!"

I laugh. "I wasn't expecting me either, but I have been summoned by the higher-ups!" I say with mock enthusiasm, putting quotes around "higher" with my fingers.

Bobby laughs a deep, jolly laugh that eases my trepidation. "Ahhh... well, good luck with that. He is in an especially foul mood tonight!"

Great! And I am the one to blame for it.

"What's wrong?" I say as if I don't know, as if I wasn't the root cause of it all.

Bobby sighs. "First of all, he missed his damn flight last night!"

Oh shit!

"Which made him late for qualifying, which means he will have to start at the rear of the field tomorrow!" Bobby groans with disgust.

I nod, wild-eyed, taking all this information in. *Damn! It is my fault after all!*

"He says he wants to go over the schedule tomorrow since there were some last-minute changes," I lie. "I hope it doesn't make the situation worse."

"Well...good luck!" Bobby exclaims. "He's on his bus changing clothes, two rows over, last bus." He motions as he directs me.

"Gotcha! If I don't return in, oh...say twenty minutes, you might better call the squad," I say as I head out to find Ryan.

Bobby laughs again. "Whitney, you are good for us! I like having you around."

I stop dead in my tracks. I turn back to face Bobby, taken aback by his comments. He smiles at me, nods, and then goes back to work.

I find Ryan's million-dollar luxury coach, take a deep breath, and knock firmly on the door. What seems like hours pass, and the door finally swings open. My breath hitches in my throat, and my heart literally stops. Ryan is standing on the top step wearing only his jeans, which haven't been buttoned. His chest is bare, and the outline of his muscles is breathtaking. I never knew race car drivers were so fit. Ryan notices my gawk, rolls his eyes at me, and retreats back inside, leaving the door open. I scramble up the stairs and into the bus behind him about twenty shades of red. He sits down on the couch in the living area and pulls on his shirt.

After a beat, he looks me over, and I shift, uncomfortable, from one foot to the other. The second "cup" of champagne was a very bad idea. It is hard for me to focus on his face.

Ryan narrows his eyes at me. "Have you been drinking?"

I roll my eyes at him and accidently slur, "No!" *Oh well!*

Ryan brushes off my vague speech and doesn't acknowledge my lie either. "What the hell were those text messages about? Were you making that shit up?"

I blink at his inquiry. "No, I, uh...I was just trying to piss you off." I look down at my hands.

"Well...you succeeded!" he snaps as he pulls on his dark brown loafers.

"No, I was just surprised that Annalise had orchestrated all that. I had no idea that is what you people do on a race weekend." Ryan raises his head sharply to me. "I mean, it must have been serious between the two of you."

He laughs in mocked disgust. "Far from it!"

"I wasn't lying about all that stuff. When I checked in, there was all this extravagance. I was taken aback. Then, they gave me the itinerary that was addressed to Annalise. It listed the appointment time for the massage and then the dinner reservation," I try to explain.

"And you are sure it was for two?"

I nod my head and sash back, "Yes! The last time I checked, a couples massage isn't for one." Ryan's mouth falls in a firm line, and I'm not sure which issue he is angry about—what I did, my attitude, or Annalise's plans.

"And you're sure the delivery wasn't for you?" he questions again.

"Uh, yes! The itinerary was clearly addressed to her. Besides, who would send something like that to my hotel room?" I say, brushing off his insistence.

Ryan isn't convinced. He narrows his eyes at me and cocks his head to one side. "It wouldn't be hard to guess."

What the hell does that mean?

Before I can respond, Ryan starts again, "Well, the joke's on you because I never leave this track. I stay here on this bus all weekend long so I can focus on everything that is happening at the track and with the race."

My mouth busts wide open as well the lid to pandoras box, as I unload a huge question that was better left unsaid. "So, who was all that for?"

Ryan raises his eyebrows at me. "Now that would be the million-dollar question of the day, wouldn't it?" He stands up and tucks the hem of his shirt into his jeans, grabs a ball cap bearing the GCR logo, takes a glance in the mirror, then heads toward the door. "But...the pieces of the puzzle are starting to fall together!" Ryan says, deadpan.

What is he talking about?

"Where are you going?" I exclaim in exasperation.

"Out!" he shouts to me over his shoulder.

"No shit! Why did you have me come out here?" I call out to him.

He turns back to me. "To piss *you* off! Whitney, don't try to screw with me like that again because in the end, I always win!" And he slams the door in my face. *Great!*

With that statement, I stumble back on his anger and sit down on his couch. I never once thought that all those plans wouldn't have been for Ryan. But thinking back on what he said last night at his house, that Annalise couldn't be trusted, maybe he suspected that she was seeing someone else. Was she seeing someone else behind his back? If so, then I just confirmed it for him. I flash back to the memory of my own flowers, they were identical to the ones in my hotel room. *It's just a coincidence*, I tell myself brushing off my suspicions. There are too many questions and what ifs! I stand up and make a mental list of them to go over with Brooke when I get back to my hotel room. This is getting good...

Chapter 15

The wheels of the airplane's landing gear softly skid across the runway, jerking me back to reality. I am thankful to be back in Charlotte on solid ground after another nonstop weekend of traveling. My whole body aches. I have no idea what time it is or what time zone my body is on. I only know that I want be in my bed asleep. The stewardess gives the all-clear sign as we taxi into the gate. I pull out my iPhone and quickly switch it back on. It takes a few minutes to regenerate, but it remains silent. No messages or e-mails.

I quickly text a message to Brooke to let her know that I have landed safely. As I hit send, my thoughts darken. Besides my mother, she is the only person who would care. Big sigh! I have hardly spoken to my mother since I left home, especially after I was given the public relations position. I know she is hurt that I left so abruptly. Hell, if it hadn't been for her, I would have been known as the next runaway bride.

I switch over to e-mails and type a quick one to my mom.

Mom,

I am sorry that I haven't been able to talk to you much lately. I am fine. Really. I love my new job. And as you can see, I am working almost seven days a week. I have just landed back in Charlotte after spending the weekend in California. I will talk to you again soon. I just wanted you to know that I love you and I miss you.

Whit

As I press send, a single tear rolls down my cheek. I quickly wipe it away and then glance around to make sure that no one noticed. *Jeezus! Get a grip, Whitney!* It must be the jet lag.

Ryan was right. The road course was definitely not worth it. I laugh as I recall his comments over team communications at the start of the race, *"Y'all get comfortable. This is going to be boring!"* Thankfully, Bobby quipped back with somewhat decent language, *"Stop your damn whining! Get up on the wheel and get after it!"* I laugh. I am beginning to enjoy my job despite the asshole I have for a boss.

I sailed through Sonoma with much more confidence, and to our team's surprise, Ryan finished in the top ten again, which is a coup for him because not only does he hate road courses but he had to start in the back. I can agree with him on the road course. Sonoma was so boring. With speeds reaching between only eighty and a hundred miles per hour, the one hundred and ten laps were the longest of my life. The track action this weekend was completely opposite from last Sunday in Michigan.

Aside from the Saturday-night riffraff, Ryan and I were able to get through the race without another incident, thankfully. He was all business, but much more receptive of me. Well...he did completely ignore me the entire time, that is fine too. He wasn't rude, then again, I didn't give him any reason to humiliate me either. And there was no mention of our dinner and subsequent morning after, but I'd ruined that all-too-brief interlude with my Saturday-night stunt, which I am still surprised about. Brooke and I talked it to death when I got back to my hotel, but still couldn't make heads or tails about what Annalise was up to. I bet Ryan gets to the bottom of it, though. I laugh out loud to myself.

All in all, it is a step in the right direction, but one fact remained the same at both races—new track, new girl, or should I say girls! Ryan stalked off with one on each arm after his post-race interviews yesterday. I shake my head at that memory and groan. *Bastard!*

The captain says his farewells over the airplane speaker, and we are given permission to exit the cabin. I reach up and take my carry-on bag from the overhead compartment. I realize that his dismissal is more than clearance to depart; it is also a wrap-up for my insane weekend. But now that Sonoma is over, next up is Kentucky. There is no time to recuperate or recover. I have to keep moving!

Chapter 16

nother week has gone by in a dazed blur. I am still getting the hang of my job and learning about this sport, which makes my days go by quickly. It seems like there is not enough time in the day for what I need to get accomplished. I double check my itinerary and forward a copy to Jerri via email and hit my office door buzzing at five o'clock on the dot. I have to get home to pack for the track. I leave early tomorrow traveling by plane to Kentucky. Ever since I have been given the title of PR manager, I have been on a traveling whirlwind. In twenty-eight years, I have never been out of my home state of Georgia, and in the last few weeks, I have flown to Michigan, California, and now Kentucky. It's exciting.

I get to my apartment in record time to set out on the task at hand. I make a hasty to-do list to double-check that all my *shit* is in order. I laugh at myself. This weekend, Jerri has allowed me to travel on Friday so I can attend qualifying and other events that are scheduled throughout the weekend. I am super excited that she has trusted me to attend all of these events. I must be doing something right.

Aside from the track, I have not seen nor heard from Ryan in over two weeks, since I was at his home. He has been all business at the track and has made no mention of our dinner. This is good, I have to admit!

We shouldn't blur the lines between professional and personal lives. Besides, he was probably just lonely that night anyway. No doubt he has a new girl shacked up in his bed every night. *Bastard!*

I take a quick shower to wash my body and my long brown locks. I know I won't have time to maintain my hair over the weekend, so I take extra time with it tonight and then use my hair dryer to blow it out. Once that task is complete, I snap on my straightening iron for later. I shuffle to my closet to find a shirt to wear around the apartment, and the first thing I spy is Ryan's shirt hanging amongst my clothes. I flush at the memory, and a delicious heat spreads throughout my body.

I pull it off the hanger and shrug it on. After two weeks, it still smells like him. His scent, it's divine. My mind immediately retreats to the night at his home. My blood roars throughout my veins as I recall the way Ryan carried me in his arms through the wooded path and intimately grasped my fingers in his kitchen. I shudder as the heat pulses through my body. I laugh at my reaction before an internal light bulb goes off! *That's it!* That was the whole purpose of that night. He wanted to get to me, to get under my skin. *Well now!* I have finally figured out his MO. Well, he may have gotten under my skin, but neither he nor anyone else will ever know it, I assure myself. But right now, in the privacy of my own home, he can writhe under my skin all he wants.

Yes, he is hot. I will admit it that. He is arrogant too. But, that night in his home, I saw a different side to Ryan Carter, a side that I liked. He was kind, considerate, and finally somewhat understanding of me. But I still don't understand him. I know he has a lot riding on his shoulders, but that is no excuse for how he acts. I shake my head. I will probably never understand.

I pull on a pair of cotton boxer shorts under Ryan's shirt and sashay around the apartment checking off my list. I open a fresh bottle of white wine, pour myself a tall glass, and set up my iPod in the dock. I shuffle the music, and it begins cranking out some vintage Gloria Estefan. Somehow, I believe my music device has the ability to read my moods. The music is perfect for my frame of mind, not to mention energizing for my body tonight.

"One, two, three, four...Come on, baby, say you love me!" I love this music. "Five, six, seven times!" Singing out loud, I fold the final piece of clothing into my suitcase, zip it up with a flourish, and stand it up by my apartment door. *Check!*

I turn back toward my bedroom and am stopped dead in my tracks by a firm knock at my door. *Who could that be?* Completely bewildered, I rush back to the door and rip it open in haste.

It's Ryan! Shit!

Suddenly, I am insanely aware of how underdressed I am. I flush with embarrassment and look down. I have on his shirt with no bra, boxer shorts that barely cover my ass, and my brown hair is wild from the blow-dryer. He, of course, is sexy as hell leaning on my doorway with jeans, T-shirt, and that smug look of arrogance on his face.

"I guess I'm not going to get that shirt back," he says conceitedly.

I laugh nervously like a schoolgirl and cross my arms over my chest. *Whitney, get control!* I scold myself. "Nope," is all I offer in an attempt to control my giddiness. *What the hell is wrong with me?*

Ryan walks past me, into my apartment, uninvited.

"Please come in," I say with my best sarcasm.

He briefly looks around my apartment, then asks, "What are you doing?"

"I...uh...just got out of the shower, and I'm packing," I mutter as if he should know. I walk into the kitchen and grab my glass of wine. "I think the real question is what *are* you doing here! Oh wait...never mind that...How in the hell do you know where I live?" I question firmly, waving my glass for embellishment.

He shrugs ambiguously and sits down on my couch. "A buddy of mine lives in this building," he says unconvincingly.

"Oh bullshit!" I exclaim. "You're a terrible liar." Ryan blinks rapidly at me as a mouth the word "stalker."

"How do you do that?" he snaps at me.

"Do, what?" I snap back.

"See right through me," he mutters.

Whoa! Where is he going with this? My iPod turns traitorous on me, and Gloria Estefan's "Here We Are" starts to play through the speakers. I turn toward the dock and roll my eyes. *Damn it, Gloria! This is not the time!*

This conversation has turned majorly uncomfortable. I change tact and use sarcasm as *my* best form of defense. "Well...let's see. Number one, seeing through people is one of my many God-given talents. And number two, arrogant people like yourself are usually transparent."

Ryan looks dumbfounded and at a loss for words. Then he regains his composure, shakes his head with a slight smile, and says, "Touché!" and we both laugh nervously.

"Can I get you something to drink? Then, maybe you can tell me why you're *really* here?" I open my refrigerator. "Let's see. I have—"

Ryan interrupts. "I'll take a beer if you have it."

I turn back to him and frown. "Aren't you driving?"

"Just one then," he quips.

As I pull out a bottle of Bud Light, he approaches me from behind, resting his hand on the refrigerator door. "Are you always looking out for me?"

I take a deep breath, conscious of his closeness. "Apparently, baby-sitting the stock car driver slash part-time movie star, is my job," I tensely whisper. I hand the beer over to him and walk quickly around the island in the center of my kitchen, which is clearly a defensive move on my part to create some space between us.

Ryan takes a swig of beer and watches me intently as I gracefully leap up and sit on the countertop. I take a sip of my wine, mimicking his move, all the while hoping that it holds some magical powers to calm my nerves. It doesn't. I try to change the subject instead.

"Look...about Sonoma, I really didn't mean to make you mad. I was just trying to have a little fun with you since you always seem so uptight. Plus, Brooke aided and abetted."

"Who's Brooke?" Ryan asks, cocking his head to one side.

"She is my best friend. This is her apartment. I'm subleasing it from her."

He nods. "So that's how you got here."

I cock my head to one side, mirroring his action again, but I am now confused about his statement. He seems bizarrely interested in my background and has completely sidestepped my Sonoma apology. *Strange!*

I sigh, "So, what *are* you doing here?"

He leans against the other end of the counter and looks despondent. That's different. *What happened to my arrogant bastard?*

"I told you...I have a friend that lives in this building," he says as he looks at me dead in the eye. But I still know that he is lying. I laugh.

"OK, well...that is your lie, and you can tell it any way you want to," I say flippantly.

Ryan shakes his head and throws up his hands in defeat. "Jesus Christ, Whitney! I don't know myself! I have been driving around this building for a solid hour!" he shouts. "I...I just wanted to see you."

His sudden outburst shocks me, and I mutter, "Why?" in a surprised whisper. I take another sip of wine, which now does seem to have magical powers of courage, so I let it fly before he can respond. "Lemme see if I can help you sort this all out. Were you lonely? No girl to shack up with tonight, or did you think it was finally time to fuck over the new employee?"

He winces as if I slapped him and slams his fist onto the counter. I jump. *Oops! Too harsh? Yes, maybe.*

"Damn it, Whitney!" he retorts and runs his hands through his hair. "I liked spending time with you the other night, but I just felt like I needed to create some distance between us. I know how it looks but...but this time it's different." *What the hell?*

I'm intrigued. I raise an eyebrow and open my mouth to snap back, "What is different?"

Then, Ryan harshly cuts me off. "Don't start with your damned smart mouth!"

I giggle out loud, but Ryan is not amused. "You sound just like Garrett," I say, recalling our episode in the boardroom.

Ryan shakes his head and rolls his eyes knowingly. I humor him.

"What's different about this...or me, should I say?"

He throws his hands in the air in exasperation. "I don't know!" Ryan starts pacing around the kitchen island. "Maybe it was the way you handed my ass to me on a platter that morning in the boardroom, or the fact that I can't intimidate you because you are not threatened by who I am or what I do because you're so new to all this," he rambles and waves his right hand in the air for effect.

Ryan stops his pace in front of me and positions himself between my long, freshly shaven legs. *Oh no!* I pull them up in defense, but he places his hands on my thighs to stop my movement. My body explodes with intense feeling as my breathing stops. I look at him in anticipation. *Damn!*

I watch his mouth closely as he says, "Or maybe it's how I can't stop thinking about you and wondering why you ran away from Georgia."

I shake my head and look away from him. Ryan's ramblings have become a revelation, and suddenly he has gone from arrogant to vulnerable. It's a lot to take. I force the tears back that begin to well up in my eyes. I don't know if it's our close proximity or the wine, but I am feeling disoriented. I can't process the events that are unfolding in my apartment.

"So, I am a mystery to be solved? Is that it?" I say quietly.

"No," Ryan quickly retorts.

I take a deep breath, swallow, and say firmly, "I am *not* having this conversation with you, Ryan."

He looks at me warily. I try to get away from him, but he pins my legs to the counter with his firm hands. "Why?" he whispers.

"Why do you even care?" I add in rebuttal.

Ryan stresses the phrase again in frustration. "I don't know! I-I... just want to know, Whitney! For the life of me, I've never given a shit about anything or anybody but racing. So this is all new to me."

I don't know what to say. I try to speak, but I hesitate as he looks at me deeply with those piercing blue eyes. It's unnerving.

Then, he slowly runs his strong hands up either side of my thighs. "What drove you so far from home?"

"I-I..." His intimate touch makes me stutter. I say it fast. "Same old sad story, an innocent girl gets her heart broken by an arrogant bastard like you!"

Ryan doesn't respond with words. He firmly but softly runs his hands up my thighs, around to my behind, and connects them together.

He uses his newfound grip to pull me in close to him. I look down, embarrassed from the personal contact.

Ryan whispers, "Don't do that...Don't categorize me with whoever the hell he is." He lifts my face up so I am forced to look him in his beautiful blue eyes. "I wanna make you forget about him." His words make me go weak as my stomach drops out of my body through my feet. *Holy shit!*

Ryan leans in to press his lips to mine, but I pull back. *Way to go, Whitney! Way to ruin a perfect romantic moment!* The shocked look on his face lets me know that rejection is not an emotion he knows well.

"You can't be serious!" I say a little too high-pitched. "We are not even friends." I throw my hands up in the air, "You are not even cordial to me!"

"Cordial?" Ryan says testing my word choice. "I can show you cordial!" I roll my eyes and laugh nervously, still not believing that Ryan is in my apartment.

Ryan runs his hands through his air and the gesture seems to change his mood. He gives me a disappointed look and says, "I am dead serious."

I let out a long breath. "I can't do this!"

"Why?" Ryan hits me right back with his words. I look away.

"First of all," I begin, "how do you go from hating someone to showing up unannounced in their home acting all romantic as hell?"

Ryan shakes his head at my statement. "I don't hate you. I told you that before."

I roll my eyes in return. "Oh, please! A few weeks ago, you would have run me over with your race car if you had the chance."

Ryan laughs, "Now...that is probably true, but I do like a good challenge, Miss Parker."

I eye him cautiously. "Well, it ain't happening! Not tonight. I need this job. And I am not going to end up like the infamous Annalise."

The mention of her name—or my rejection, I am not sure which—sends several shades of red across Ryan's beautiful face. His demeanor changes instantly. I move to jump down from the counter again, but he holds me firmly in place with his hands on my thighs.

"Colton?" Ryan asks. "Is that why?"

I snap my head back and lock eyes with him.

"You're seeing him, aren't you?"

I laugh nervously. "Oh! So...this is why you're here. This is what this is all about...Colton!" I shout mockingly at him.

"Well...are you with him?" Ryan looks at me with a quiet fury in his eyes.

I raise my eyebrows at him. "Jealous much?"

Ryan looks angry as he waits for my answer.

"I...uh...no... that is none of your business!" I move to jump down from the counter, but Ryan is back at my side within a blink of an eye, halting my escape for the third time.

My breath catches in my throat as Ryan reaches up to gently caress my face. "OK...so if you're not with him, what's the problem?"

I shake my head nervously. "The problem? *Which one?* For one, you are practically my boss. We cannot be involved."

Ryan looks annoyed, but retorts, "Well, if I am your boss, then I can do whatever the hell I want to!"

His statement scares me. I can feel myself start to sweat. "Is that a threat?" I say warily.

Ryan shoots me a "get real" look that eases my fear. Then he says, "I could never hurt you, Whitney."

I shake my head as I feel tears spring to my eyes. Ryan has come out of nowhere, literally, with these professions of what...? Love? Hell no! Lust? I am still not convinced. Is this just a game he is playing? I am completely and utterly confused. I look down at his hands, which are gently placed on my thighs. I glance back up into his fierce blue eyes and say, "It's not *if* you will hurt me; it's how bad."

Ryan looks pained by my statement but doesn't relent. He moves his hands from my thighs to my cheeks to intimately caress my face again.

His touch burns and resonates throughout my body. I feel my blood roaring through my veins, much like the gunning motors of the stock cars at the track. I close my eyes. This moment is far too intense for eye contact. In an instant, I realize that the only other time I feel this way is when I am at the track during the race, with him. Over the last few weeks, I have found that factor of adrenaline and addiction at the track. Much like Ryan tried to explain to me in his home that night, I just didn't understand what those emotions were. And in this moment, now I know. In my entire life, I have never felt this way about anyone or anything. It is a revelation on my part. I have the love of NASCAR, this sport, in my blood. And now, I must admit that I want Ryan in my blood, too. I open my eyes.

Ryan searches my face for some clue as to what I am thinking. His breath is hot on my face, and his scent overtakes all my senses. I know where this is leading. I don't want to be another cliché at the office. I don't want to be another notch in his belt. Can I even handle this? Do I even have the power to stop him? Do I want to stop him? *Too many questions.*

Ryan leans in and presses his lips to mine, and my hands instantly go into his hair, reciprocating his desire. He reacts by pulling me into a tight embrace.

I protest and pull back from his tender kiss. "Ryan, please don't," I whisper. "I can't risk my job. I can't go back to Georgia."

He looks at me cautiously. "Whitney, don't make this complicated."

"Complicated?" I laugh. "I think we trumped complicated thirty minutes ago."

He nervously says, "True story."

"But technically, you are my boss, remember?" I plead with him, hoping he will stop so I don't have to make this decision.

Ryan huffs, "Last time I checked, you were bossing me around!"

I laugh. "No, I'm just your fucking babysitter, remember!" I say sarcastically.

Ryan shakes his head while a look of deep regret washes over his face. *What is that about?* His mood swings are making me nuts.

Then suddenly our light moment turns serious again as Ryan pleads with me, "I have never wanted anyone as much as I want you. You are not like any of the others."

I shake my head at the thought of "others," celebrities and supermodels. I definitely don't fit that bill. *So, why me?* I look down, fighting back more tears. His words are sincere. I believe him, but I am torn because I know this is wrong. And I know it has a high probability of ending badly. My entire life has been spent making the best choices to make everyone else happy, but right now, I couldn't give a shit less what is right. I am lost in this moment. It feels so right, and all I want right now is... for Ryan to make love to me.

Ryan can tell by my actions that I am in deep thought. He softly says, "Don't overthink this."

With my tears successfully fought, I look at him with anticipation and don't offer another protest. With that, he pulls me in close to him, wraps my legs around his back, and gently lifts me off my kitchen counter. I am breathless from his dramatic, intimate gesture. For once in my life, I want to enjoy whatever is about to happen. I don't know if Ryan wants one hour or one night from me. I don't care, and to hell with the aftermath. I will deal with the consequences later. I wrap my arms around his neck and bury my face in his shoulder as he carries me down the hall to my bedroom.

Ryan enters my bedroom and attempts to lay me down on top of the bed, not bothering with the duvet. I keep my legs wrapped around him tightly, which forces him down onto the bed with me, letting him know that I want him too. I run my hands through his hair, and the dam breaks. Ryan kisses me with intense passion that leads to a desperate need. He is right. There is something about us. I felt it from that moment he jumped into the elevator with me. I was attracted to him then, but this desperate need for another person is different for me too. Suddenly, I want to be as close to him as I can be.

Our clothes fly off, and our bodies began to move together. I no longer want to stop him. I want this passion to swallow me up, then drown me in the pleasure that I feel with Ryan. I want to totally experience this intense connection and not think about the repercussions of my actions for once in my life.

Ryan rises up, pulls back slowly, and looks me in the eye. "Are you sure, Whitney?"

I nod.

"I don't want you to do anything that you don't want to do. I want you so bad, but I will wait if I have to."

I nod again, pained by his confession. Then I whisper, "Stop talking. I want you. I need you." I flush with embarrassment at my words. This is so unlike me to be direct, especially in this setting.

With those words, Ryan gently enters my body, wrapping my legs around his back. "God almighty!" he exclaims with raw emotion as he starts to move.

Our bodies pick up an enticing and strangely choreographed rhythm, like they were made for each other. I am lost. There is no first-time awkwardness. I feel my body building and escalating until it explodes gloriously into a million pieces. My body convulses with pleasure as he releases into me and buries his head in my neck.

We lay together, sticky and sweaty. I am wrapped tightly around his body, not wanting there to be an inch that separates us. What's done is done. I know whatever the aftermath is, I will deal with it, but I am not going to think about that now. Ryan shifts under me, and I raise my head to him.

"Am I hurting you?"

He smiles shyly back at me and whispers, "No," then pulls me in closer so that I am lying across his body, tightly in his arms. I fight and fight, but I am overwhelmed by these events. I reluctantly drift off to sleep draped over *the* Ryan Carter.

* * *

I am awakened by Ryan's movements. He shifts slightly and gently rolls me over to the side, and I feel him leave the bed. I look up, struggling for my eyes to adjust to the darkness, and watch as he moves slowly to gather his clothes and begins to dress. Dread pools in my stomach and makes me nauseous. He got what he came for, and now he is leaving. *Oh God! This is so awkward!*

I sit up in the bed quickly and unexpectedly, taking him by surprise. I grasp the sheet around my naked body even though the room is dark.

He smiles. "I didn't want to wake you, but I am going to get something to eat."

"You're leaving?" I ask sleepily.

He moves swiftly back to my side and smiles that beautiful, glorious smile. "What I meant to say was...I am going to get us something to eat." I feel a thousand pounds of relief release from stomach. He leans in and kisses me tenderly. "I will be right back," Ryan whispers against my lips.

It must be at least midnight, if not later. I have no idea where he has gone to get food, but I suspect it is the late-night deli located in the apartment village. While he is gone, I shower again. I emerge from the shower minus the sweat and stickiness, but am amazed that I can still smell his scent on my skin. I find some suitable pajamas and steal a glance in my bathroom mirror. My hair is now even wilder than before! *Gah!*

Luckily, my straightening iron is still on and is smoking hot. I position myself on the counter in between the double vanity sinks and set out to tame my hair. I separate it into sections and begin to straighten each strand into submission. With every strand, I remember a different moment: his sincerity, his words, his hands all over my body, his breath on my neck.

I am lost in what I am doing dreaming about what just happened. I never knew I could have that type of physical connection with another person, especially one I despised up until a few hours ago. The electricity and the rush of being with Ryan is something I have never experienced.

Then my thoughts drift wayward to the consequences of what I have done. It was so worth it. I bat the negative thoughts away. *I am rather enjoying my sexual instant replay, thank you very much!*

I am almost done with my hair when I spy Ryan standing in the doorway of the bathroom watching me intently. I smile nervously, relieved to see him. How long has he been there? I wonder.

He walks into the bathroom and softly says, "You are so beautiful." He turns me around on the counter so that I am facing him. "Every single inch of you."

I am stunned at his statement. Mr. Pompous Ass has a romantic side. I lean in and kiss him affectionately.

Ryan pulls back from my kiss, leaving me bereft. "Come on. I'm starving." He lifts me off my perch and into his arms. "What is it with you and counters?" he asks jokingly.

I laugh, "What is it with your need to carry me everywhere?"

Ryan rolls his eyes at me and automatically sets me down to the floor. We walk hand in hand to the living room, where he has set up a small pseudo picnic on my coffee table. Suddenly, I realize I am starving, too.

Ryan has, in fact, gone down to the deli, which is one of my favorite places to eat. He has brought back a variety of things like chicken salad, cheeses, and fresh-baked croissants. It all tastes heavenly.

While we eat, we talk. Ryan incessantly quizzes me about Georgia. I know what he wants to know about, but I delay on that subject. He continues to ask me questions about my family and my life growing up as if he is desperate to know me better. It's heartwarming but confusing still. My head is swimming from what has transpired in the last few hours.

"Tell me..." Ryan trails off.

I shake my head. "Why? Why can't you just let it go?"

Ryan shrugs at me. "I want to understand you, is all. You seem so strong. I mean no one has *ever* spoken to me the way you did that day in the boardroom, not even my own mother. But at the same time, or at times, I mean, you seem troubled. And that is hard for me to take."

Hard for you? Ha! I lived it.

I sigh, "A mystery...there's that word again."

"No!" Ryan immediately cuts me off. "That is your word, not mine! Isn't obvious to you by now that I care?"

I snort. "I have never been one to confuse sex with care or concern."

Ryan rolls his eyes at my statement, but I can tell he is losing his patience with me.

"OK." I acquiesce. "Look...it really isn't a big deal. I'm trying to move past it all. That is why I don't like to discuss it. But...I was engaged."

Ryan's eyes light up, surprised.

"Yes...and about two weeks before the wedding, I caught the bastard with the bitch formerly known as my best friend."

"Damn!" Ryan exclaims as he whistles through his teeth. I raise my eyebrows at his outburst and open my mouth to speak, but he stops me before I can say another word. "Whatever you are going to say, don't! I will be damned if you are going to compare me to him. I mean, you don't even know me!"

I laugh out loud. "I know enough!"

The look on Ryan's face begs me to continue, although I know I have already said too much. Conflicted, I begin again, "I just didn't see it coming, you know? And what makes me the maddest is that I am smarter than that. All the signs were there. Brooke even tried to warn me, but I refused to believe it. I was angry at myself for being so... so stupid!"

Ryan watches me intently as I go on. I can now see the strain of concern on his face. It makes my confession easier.

"I mean, I let this asshole drag me around for years. I put my own career on hold, waiting on him to finish college and get his shit straight." I point an aggravated stare to Ryan. "And then I find about them."

My face burns as anger wells up inside my body, an emotion that I refuse to relive again. And I quickly remember myself.

"Why am I telling you all this?" It makes my stomach roll with nausea to think that I have divulged this information. I push my croissant back in disgust.

"I think you are being way too hard on yourself, Whitney."

I laugh in mock abhorrence. "You don't get it. I am from a small town, very small. And I would say, oh...about seventy-five percent of the people in the area knew what was going on, even my freaking wedding planner. The best part about it was I just ran away. I blocked their cell numbers from my phone and didn't look back. I didn't have the energy or the courage to deal with it."

Ryan's eyes widen in shock either at my outburst or confession, but I am not sure which. I put my head down in my hands.

"I was completely and utterly humiliated. I don't take well to those emotions, as you already know. But here I am spilling my guts to you, and embarrassment is setting in all over again." I pause. I can tell Ryan is conflicted because he sits still but doesn't say a word, no doubt at a loss.

"How long ago did this happen?" he finally says after a brief but too long pause.

I sigh deeply. "Let's see, about...five weeks ago."

I watch Ryan intently for his response. His face falls as he says quietly, "Oh wow."

"I would have run away in the middle of the night if it hadn't been for my parents."

Ryan nods as if he understands. Then, he shakes his head. "I didn't realize..."

I shrug my shoulders. "We don't exactly 'talk.' Besides, I wouldn't have discussed it, *ever*, had you not dragged it out of me."

Ryan eyes me warily like he has crossed some arbitrary line into Reboundsville. I continue to explain.

"The funny thing is that I was so over it, you know. I guess I had been over him, over our relationship, for a while now. I just didn't know it. Because when I found out, my internal light bulb went off, and I was done."

Ryan continues to sit in silence. It makes my skin crawl. *What is he thinking?*

"What's that old saying? Fool me once, shame on you; fool me twice, shame on me? Well...I have let one asshole run me over, and I will be damned if I am ever going to let that happen again," I exclaim as I stand up in defense.

"What do you mean by that?" Ryan snaps in reference to the asshole comment.

"You know full well what I mean, Ryan," I retort.

I can see a look of hurt flash across his face as he says in a gritted whisper, "Stop it, Whitney. That is not fair."

I sigh. "It's six of one, and a half dozen of the other." I add quickly, "Although, I am starting to alter my opinion of you, especially after the last few hours." I smile wryly as I take the last bite of chicken salad from the plastic container. "Please don't make me regret it."

Ryan looks at me intently, like he is trying to figure me out while processing all the information I have just dumped on him. Then, he abruptly stands up and begins to clear our makeshift picnic. Before I can stand to help him, he is by my side again. He leans down and picks me up off the floor.

"Where are we going?" I question him even though I already know the answer.

"I am going to work on completely changing your opinion of me!"

I throw my head back and laugh as he carries me back into the bedroom.

Chapter 17

I bound through airport security and step into my gate at Charlotte Douglas International Airport just as the attendant is giving the last boarding call for Louisville, Kentucky. I am getting good at this. I settle into my seat on the US Airways Express jet and think to myself, what a difference a few weeks make. I have never been far from the Georgia coastline, but within the last few weeks, I have become a seasoned traveler.

And then there's Ryan. The same statement applies to him too. We have gone from wanting to strangle each other to making sweet love in my apartment. Well, all over my apartment is a better assessment. I smile as I remember our last round in my kitchen this morning as Ryan attempted to leave to make his own flight. It all happened so fast that now, sitting here on this plane bound for Kentucky, it doesn't seem real. I shake my head at my thoughts because I still am mystified about the details.

I am broken from my reverie as the flight attendant goes through safety checks. As the plane begins to taxi down the runway, a pool of dread falls like lead into my stomach, and the graveness of my situation rolls over me like a black cloud. A lump wells up in my throat. *What have I done?*

Well, let's see...Number one, I have violated company policy. Violated? No, I am sure there is a far worse term than "violated" to describe what Ryan and I did last night. My job is toast if anyone finds out. Number two, I have slept with the boss's son, which directly coincides with number one, I know. It also qualifies for direct disappointment with Jerri. I don't want to let her down. And number three, I am completely and utterly mortified at my behavior. This is so unlike me. I cannot believe I have crossed so many lines. This is bad.

A series of chills run down my spine as the plane ascends into the sky. I can't think about all this now. I take my iPod out and secure my earbuds. Maybe some good music will drown out all these thoughts. I select songs on my iPod touch, then press shuffle. This should be good. She always has a sense of humor. The prelude begins as Sade sultrily warbles the jazzy words to "No Ordinary Love." Yeah, well, no shit, Sade. I make a mental note to download some new music onto my iPod. I lay my head back and continue to listen as she sings to me the words that directly apply to my tryst with Ryan.

Shortly before noon, my plane touches down in Louisville. The track this week is actually in Sparta, Kentucky, which is only about an hour away from my present location. A courier is waiting for me in the airport arrivals, and we take off on Interstate 71 North with minimal chitchat. Instantly, I love Kentucky. The scenery is breathtaking as we journey into the little town of Sparta. Since the track is in a somewhat remote area, I am staying in a little bed-and-breakfast right across the state line of Indiana, but I won't get to check in until Ryan's qualifying and press events are over tonight.

My nerves start to build as we approach the track. I can see it looming in the distance. I realize that after last night, I don't know how to do this job professionally anymore. I mean, we definitely crossed that line last night. How in the heck am I supposed to act with him? *Professional, Whitney. That is how you act.* But will the new feelings I have for Ryan show on my face? What if it is something I cannot hide? I know I can't them hide from Brooke at all. She will be on to me in a flash. I am tormenting myself with this internal dialogue, and it is making me nauseous.

When we arrive to the infield area of the track, I take a deep breath to steel myself. I can do this. I will do this. I am dressed casually today in khaki pants and a Team GCR polo shirt and comfortable tennis shoes. My hair is down and loosely flowing over my shoulders, though I have secured a hair band around my wrist just in case it gets unmanageable. I set out to find Ryan's hauler in the mass of vehicles in the infield area.

After qualifying his #62 Chevrolet today, he has a fan experience in the Bluegrass Club here at the track, which consists of a small question-and-answer session with a few invited guests of the track owners. This event was added at the last minute, and I desperately hope he doesn't give me hell for it!

Finally, I find the hauler, where the crew members and Ben are all huddled together around Ryan. Ryan is dressed in his cobalt-blue fire suit, but it isn't completely zipped up. The top of his jumpsuit is resting on his hips, revealing a plain white T-shirt that he wears underneath. *My Goodness!* The mere sight of him stops me dead in my tracks. He is gorgeous. I vaguely wonder if I will ever get tired of looking at him. Immediately, my presence causes the group of guys to disperse. I smile sheepishly, still not used to being the only female on this team of guys.

There is a noticeable tension within the team that I automatically attribute to my arrival. All of a sudden, the paranoia sets in. *Do they know already?*

Bobby, Ryan's crew chief, greets me fondly and sets me at ease. "Hey Whitney, there are a few issues with Ryan's car this morning, but I think we may have successfully worked them out."

I can feel Ryan's eyes on me, but I don't acknowledge him. I maintain eye contact with Bobby as he continues to speak.

"Problem is...we won't know until he takes the track to qualify."

I nod my head. "Is there anything you need or that I can do to help?"

Bobby smiles at me and turns his gaze to Ryan. "Just keep hothead over there in line!"

I groan louding, feigning disinterest and Bobby laughs out loud at me. Finally, I steal a glance at Ryan, who raises his eyebrows at the both of us and walks away. No doubt he's less than amused by my exchange with Bobby. My stomach rolls with nausea as I watch him head over to the garage area.

So, this is how it is going to be. This is how it has to be. I walk to the back of the hauler and find a place to put my bag up. I didn't realize how uncomfortable this was going to be. *That's what you get for not thinking at all, Whitney*, I chastise myself. I have to find Ryan, and we have to talk. Obviously, we cannot work like this. I am already paranoid and anxious. I set out to find Ryan and get this straight. Last night cannot happen again. There are too many factors at stake.

I find Ryan in the garage just as he is zipping up his fire suit. I watch as he gracefully slides his long, slender body down into the #62 Chevrolet race car. I know now is not the time for this conversation, so it will have to wait. Just before he pulls on his helmet, he notices me in the garage. He acknowledges my presence by signaling for me to come over to him. His demeanor has changed noticeably. He seems happy to see me.

I walk over to Ryan's Chevrolet. "Good luck," I say softly.

He cocks his head to one side, looking at me inquisitively. "What's wrong?"

I shake my head and look away.

"Whitney!" Ryan calls for my attention.

I shake my head again. "I can't do this," I say. "I cannot lose my job. I didn't realize how uncomfortable this would be in the light of day."

Ryan looks taken aback. "I have to get on the track, but we will talk about this later," he says firmly.

"No." I disagree with him because there is nothing to talk about. "I made a mistake. We have to put it behind us and move forward as if nothing happened." I sigh, "Just do your job, and I will do mine." And I walk away as Ryan guns the motor of his race car.

I walk back to the hauler to watch qualifying on the monitor. Ryan takes the track effortlessly. He pulls his car onto the mile-and-a-half tri-oval and takes two laps to build speed. The time starts on the third lap. Ryan enters the first corner, holds the car down on the line, and accelerates as he exits the second turn. Then he fires down the back straightaway. His time must be good because Bobby is excited and talking animatedly into his headset. All this NASCAR jargon still has me confused. Evidently, based on Ryan's performance on the track and Bobby's attitude, the car is fixed. I continue to watch the monitor as he clears the third and fourth turns and slides across the start/finish line.

Ryan clocks in a time of 29.962, with a top speed of 180.338 miles per hour. *Wow!* The crew is excited and boisterous at Ryan's qualifying time. His time lands him close to the pole position, but there are several more cars that have yet to qualify, and it will be this afternoon before the starting lineup is determined officially. According to Bobby, the car is "right on," and all the adjustments that were made prior to qualifying were successful.

I, too, am excited, but still reeling from the events of the last twenty-four hours. Ryan bounds back into the hauler like an excited teenager to receive a series of "atta boys" and slaps on the back. He doesn't acknowledge me. After the excitement has died down in the hauler, I walk over to remind him about his afternoon event.

"You have an hour before you have to be at the Bluegrass Club. You have time to take a shower and change if you like. I will meet you over there," I say.

"Where are the questions so that I can review them?" Ryan snaps at me with a hard look.

I don't understand. "What questions?" I ask softly, trying hard not to incite a riot.

The expression on his beautiful face immediately changes from annoyance to pure, volatile rage. He looks as though he is grinding even his back teeth. It is actually comical to watch how mad he gets at me at times, but now is not one of those moments. *Oh boy! Here it comes...*

Chapter 18

Finally, I arrive at the bed-and-breakfast right across the Kentucky-Indiana line in Switzerland County. It is quaint, quiet, and away from the track craziness. I remove my track credentials before I check in at the front desk, but I am still wearing my GCR team shirt, so I am not sure what autonomy that might grant me. It isn't too late, but I am exhausted from the travel and lack of sleep from the night before. I have a fleeting thought to just collapse on the bed, but I am scared that I will fall asleep. I remember what happened the last time I did that, and it is another mistake that I don't want to repeat.

After Ryan ripped me a new one before the Bluegrass Club meet and greet, I sincerely hope that not providing him with a copy of possible questions for the event will be my only screw-up this weekend. I cringe recalling his words to me, "What the fuck, Whitney?"

Sheesh! I can only deal with one weekend dose of humiliation, thank you very much. But another lesson was learned: always make sure the bastard is overly prepared! No, excuse me, make that two lessons learned, the one aforementioned and the second: no matter what personal lines Ryan and I have crossed, I still have a job to do, and he will let me know, with the quickness, when I do it wrong. *Ugh!*

I kick off and actually sling my Asics across the room. It feels good. I pull out the contents of my overnight bag to find my pajamas and cosmetic bag. On the way to the bathroom, I am interrupted by an incoming text message alert. I groan as I retreat back to find my phone, but am relieved to see Brooke's name across the home screen. Her message reads:

Where are you?

I sigh as I sit down on the bed to respond to her message.

Kentucky.

Her response is instant.

I swear I cannot keep up with you anymore.

I laugh out loud.

Yea, me either. lol

Brooke sends another message.

I haven't seen you in weeks. Drinks on Monday?

She is right. I hadn't realized that I have not seen her in a while. I want to see her, but there is no way. I have to prepare for Daytona because I fly out next Wednesday.

Can't Monday! Sorry! The race this week is Saturday night, so I will be off on Sunday. I need help with clothes for Daytona. Can you bring me some options? I will call you Sunday morning.

I sigh regretfully as I await her response. I know she will be disappointed, but maybe we can spend some time together on my day off.

Deal! See you Sunday! Love!

I smile.

Love! Love!

I put down my phone and make my way back to the bathroom. The shower is small, but the pressure and the heat of the water more than make up for it. I wish the water would melt my body and I could just wash away down the drain. How easy would that be?

I emerge from the shower and wrap myself in a towel. Suddenly, I am cold. There is a draft in the room. I find a plush robe hanging behind the bathroom door. I pull my towel tight to secure it and then pull the robe on over my towel. But it doesn't help matters. I am chilled down to the bone—most likely because of what I have done and the dark cloud of regret that is hanging over my head.

I sigh, dejected, as I look at myself in the mirror. I am so disappointed in myself that I can't even bear my own reflection in the mirror. *Seriously, how did all this happen?* I shake my head and walk back into the bedroom. Maybe I just need to go to bed.

I walk back into the room and stop dead in my tracks. I shriek. Ryan is laying across my hotel bed. He sits up straight and holds his finger against my lips, directing me to be quiet.

"Good God!" I say, breathless, holding my hands against my chest. "How did you get in here?"

Ryan stands up and grabs me determinedly without answering my question. My heart flutters, and I am frightened, but only until Ryan kisses me desperately and says, "Do you want to forget about what happened in your apartment last night?"

I know I don't. I silently shake my head.

"Then don't ever walk away from me again!" He searches my face with a pained look of uncertainty. *Could he be questioning all this, too?* Then, he reaches up to softly caresses my face, and I know there is nothing more to talk about.

Chapter 19

I sit in the pit box over pit road as forty-two race cars descend onto Kentucky Motor Speedway's tri-oval track. Ryan has an excellent starting position, about two rows back from the pole, which I hope he can maintain. The weather is clear, and a warm ninety degrees, but the threat of an evening thunderstorm has pushed up the starting time one hour. There are about sixty thousand fans in attendance for this Saturday-night race, my third NASCAR race and my first one at night. Saturday-night races have their advantages, one being a rare Sunday off. Since I have accepted the position as Ryan's public relations manager, I work seven days a week. I don't mind it, though, because I am developing a new love for this sport. And despite Ryan, I love my job.

The green flag falls. Here we go! My pulse quickens, and the adrenaline begins to flow and roar through my veins. I love this feeling. Ryan was right. It is very addictive. I settle into my seat alongside Ben to watch the next four hundred miles unfold and set my radio frequency to listen to Ryan's communications between him, Bobby, and Mike.

"Y'all ready up there!" Ryan's voice squawks over the radio. "Let's see what's she's got tonight!"

Ben shoots me a confused look, then says, "He's in a good mood! What's up with that?"

I shrug my shoulders ambiguously and give my best "I have no clue" to Ben as I hear Bobby begin to give Ryan a lecture. "Ryan, the car is good, buddy. Don't push it. Take it easy. Maintain your line. Keep your nose clean." Ryan doesn't respond.

Mike adds, "We can do this tonight, Ryan. Just let me guide you through it."

Ryan only says, "Ten-four," in confirmation.

Ryan seems to take his pre-race lecture to heart. The laps start to tick away as he maintains his starting position. After a series of pit stops due to caution flags, Ryan picks up a few spots. He is now up to fourth position. The crew is pumped. Because of the lightening fast pit stop, Ryan has advanced.

Ben lets out a yell, "Woo-hoo!"

Surprised, I look over at him, and he raises his hand up to me. I give him a dumbfounded look, but then instantly realize that he wants to give me a high five. I get it now! I hit his hand as he laughs at my response.

Ben pulls me into a sideways embrace. "You're getting it, Whitney!" He is right. I can do this. I can play with the boys!

As Ryan departs pit road, I hear him mutter, "Way to go, guys!"

The sun begins to set, and the lights come on. This is so exciting.

Bobby reiterates his starting lecture to Ryan. "Be patient. You can do this!"

I mutter a silent prayer to myself, *Come on...Come on.* A win tonight would be phenomenal for Ryan, just the motivation he needs to win a championship. Within the last few weeks, he has been finishing consistently, which is what this team needs.

My mind drifts back to our "talk" last night after he broke into my hotel room.

"Ryan, I am sorry, but this is all overwhelming," I say in desperation as we lay together in the bed. "I mean, literally, I cannot wrap my head around what has happened between us in the last twenty-four hours." I pause, waiting for a response from him.

"Whitney...I don't know what you want me to say. Yes, this is complicated. No, I don't have any answers."

Great! That is no help to me at all.

I sigh, "I just need to know..."

"Know what?" Ryan says softly.

"Was this...last night, I mean...was it a one-time thing for you? If so, you don't have to feel sorry for me or dance around my feelings. Just say it!"

Ryan lifts his body, props himself up on his shoulder, and looks at me questioningly. "Would I be here with you now if I thought it was?" I take a deep breath as he continues. "Whitney, I told you last night that this is different for me. I don't know how to explain it, but I have never had feelings like this for anyone. Yes, I have had relationships, here and there, but I have never wanted anyone like I want you."

"And what if you decide you were wrong about your feelings? Where does that leave me besides unemployed?" I say, dejected because I know this can only end one way, badly. And I cannot, nor will not, go back to Georgia.

"Whitney, I have wanted you since the day I jumped into that elevator and laid my eyes on you."

I am shocked but my heart swells though it is clouded with self-doubt. I nod my head silently.

"You don't believe me, do you?"

I look back up into his fierce blue eyes and shake my head. "I figured you were just telling me what I wanted to hear."

Ryan looks hurt. "I am here with you tonight, aren't I? I have risked someone finding out so I could be here with you. I could tell you were upset today in the garage. I wanted to make sure that you were OK. I want to explore this... these feelings that I have for you. But we have to go about it the right way."

"And just how do we do that exactly?" I snap sharply.

"Whitney! Whitney!" I am broken from my reverie as Ben shouts my name. "Are you awake?" He looks at me warily. "Ryan is up to third place with ten laps to go!"

I immediately focus my attention back to the monitor. *How long have I been daydreaming?*

Ryan has a shot to win this. I watch the monitor carefully and listen intently to the radio transmissions. Ryan is noticeably silent as Mike gives the command through each turn.

"Maintain. The number-eighteen car is trying to pass you on the right. Hold tight. Push. He backed off. He ain't as fast as you."

Ryan's car roars down the backstretch. Some of the cars behind him go three wide desperately trying to advance position with the laps winding down. Ryan is running bumper to bumper with another driver for second place.

Bobby's voice booms through my headset. "Ryan, he has the fastest car on the track. If you can pass him, you are gonna have to fight him off the rest of the way. Be patient. If you can't pass, just maintain. This would be our best finish so far this season. Just hang on, buddy."

Ryan doesn't respond. He maintains position by successfully blocking pass attempts from other competing race cars with Mike's help. There are only five more laps remaining. I am so nervous that I start chewing my nails. Ben is very quiet but is tapping his foot. He is anxious too.

Ryan falls in line behind the #24 car as they push out of turn four to take the white flag, which signals one more lap remaining. Ryan gets a run on the Ford stock car of Greg Kyle, but has to drop back through the turn. Both cars fire down the speedway through the backstretch nose to nose. I jump up from my seat. This is too much.

Ryan falls back in line again as they negotiate turn three and go into turn four. Before they complete turn four, I hear Mike shout, "Ryan, you're too close! Back off!"

But it's too late. Ryan runs up on Greg and taps his right-rear quarter panel, sending the #24 Ford into the wall out of turn four. The car of Greg Kyle slams the wall hard and creates a six-car mix-up in the aftermath.

I gasp, "Oh my God!"

Ryan comes out clear and roars his car down the front stretch in pursuit of the first-place car. It is a photographic finish as the car in first place crosses the finish line just .06 seconds ahead of Ryan.

Damn! I let out a huge breath as I watch Ben scale down the pit box, into pit road. The team is ecstatic even though Ryan scored second place instead of first. What a finish!

Before Ryan can pull his car back into the garage, his crew, reporters, and paparazzi alike descend upon him, clamoring for congratulations and comments on the race. I jump protectively in between Ryan's car and the mob.

"OK...OK, everyone, please step back. Give Ryan a moment to get out of the car, and he will be glad to answer questions." I stick my head in the window of Ryan's car. "Are you OK?"

He beams at me. "That was fucking awesome!"

I smile. "Uhh...it's awesome for now, until the driver that you wrecked comes over to kick your ass!"

Ryan gives me a "yeah right" look and laughs as he slides out of his #62 Chevrolet. "Shit happens!"

The reporters scramble at the sight of Ryan and shout rounds of questions. I interject, "One at the time, please! Ryan will answer all your questions!" The reporters take heed and begin to act more graciously.

"What happened with Greg, Ryan?"

"I guess he checked up into the corner. It all happened so fast."

I laugh to myself. *Bullshit!* I stand to the side as Ryan continues his post-race interviews. In the middle of the interrogations, my cell phone begins to ring. I am not sure how I even hear it, but I take it out of my back pocket. The number is unfamiliar, so I step away from the chaos to answer it.

"Whitney," a recognizable voice calls out sternly to me. "Garrett Carter. May I please speak to my son?"

My heart skips a beat. *How does Garrett have my cell phone number?*

"I...um...Hi...Yes, sir! Just one moment, Mr. Carter." I walk over to the crowd that has gathered around Ryan. I push through and gain his attention, holding the phone down closely beside me. I raise my hand to the reporters as Ryan watches me warily and completes his sentence. As soon as he finishes, I interject. "That is all. Ryan has an important call to take. Thank you all very much!"

The reporters groan, but quickly disperse. Ryan raises his eyebrows at me as I hand him my cell phone. I mouth "Garrett" to him. He grabs the phone and walks away. I can tell he is speaking animatedly with his father and wonder what it is about, but I cannot tell with his back to me.

With his gorgeous megawatt smile, Ryan turns back to face me. I watch him as he speaks to his father. Ryan is beaming from ear to ear. Whew! I was worried there for a moment by the sternness in Garrett's voice.

Ryan walks toward me, then suddenly stops. I hear him say, "Hold on, Dad."

I watch him as he pulls the phone from his ear and reads the display. He continues walking to me, and his demeanor automatically changes. The look on his face is frightening. My heart flutters.

He holds the phone back up to his ear. "Dad, I gotta go!"

What is wrong?

Ryan takes the phone from his ear again and hastily hits the end button. Then, in one quick movement, he tosses the phone at me. I act fast, but I am unable to catch the phone before it hits me square in the chest.

"You have an important text message, Whitney!"

I jump and look at him, confused. Ryan gives me another angry look and walks away.

I follow behind Ryan as best as I can, but he is pissed. I steal a quick glance at my phone. I swipe the home screen and select "messages." There is a new message from Colton Johnson. *Shit!*

It's been two weeks. Can I see you?

Oh my...Damn! I try in vain to catch up with Ryan, calling out to him. "Ryan," I shriek for the third time, and he finally turns around. His face is about fifty shades of red. "Look, I can explain..." I plead with him. I look around to make sure that we don't have an audience. Ryan remains quiet, no doubt too angry to speak. It makes me nervous. I shift from one foot to the other. "Is there somewhere we can discuss this?"

"This"—he waves his hands in the air as we stand in the dark rows where the buses in the infield are parked—"is as good as it gets."

I look down at my feet not knowing what to say at all.

Ryan explodes. "At least I know you haven't seen that motherfucker in two weeks!"

I look back up at him like he has slapped me. "It wasn't like that, Ryan!"

"No?" he retorts. "Then how about you tell me what it *was* like? You said you weren't seeing him!"

"Ryan!" I exclaim, flustered. "Can we please get out of here? What if there is someone listening?"

Ryan grabs me by the arms and pulls me in between two buses. "There!" he shouts. "Go!"

"Colton...he asked me out. Well, we actually went out for drinks before, but it was not a date or anything."

Ryan raises his eyebrow at me in disbelief.

"I swear!" Colton wanted me to go out with him again, but I told him that I would not risk my job. We had to work together, and it was against GCR policy for us to be involved," I say, out of breath. "I asked him to give me some time, but I didn't mean anything by that. I just needed an out." I look at him intently, praying to God that he believes me.

Ryan rolls his eyes and turns to walk away.

I shout at him, "Ryan, don't you dare walk away from me!"

He looks over his shoulder, stops briefly only to say, "Go home, Whitney!" and continues to walk away.

For once, I want to cry, but the tears won't come. *Shocker!* I feel like someone has struck me in the back with a two-by-four as I stand in the middle of the buses. I hear a rumble of thunder that lets me know the predicted thunderstorm is beginning to roll in. I look down at my watch. I don't have the time or luxury to continue this discussion with Ryan. I have to get to the airport, so I don't follow after him. I just let him go.

I watch, defeated, as Ryan disappears into the sea of motor coaches. All I can think is, *Damn it! Damn Colton! Damn Ryan! Damn it all!* I want to throw down and kick and scream like a toddler.

Another round of thunder breaks me from my internal temper tantrum. I have got to get out of here. I stalk back to the hauler, praying all the way that I can make it to the airport in time and that my flight is not delayed by this weather. As I enter the hauler, my phone prompts me again with an incoming message alert, Colton again.

___

???

___

I roll my eyes at the message, but I don't respond. I look up from my phone to find Bobby watching me intently from the counter. It appears he is jotting some notes in his race log, and I have disturbed him.

"I...um...I am sorry if I interrupted you. I just need to get my bag."

Bobby smiles and nods. "That was a hell of a race, wasn't it?"

I nod enthusiastically. It really was. "The best so far," I say to Bobby. "Well, of course, it is only my third one." I laugh. "I have never seen anything like that. It's so..." I wave my hands in front of me, desperately seeking the right word, and Bobby finishes my sentence for me.

"It's a rush."

"Yes!" I exclaim, and I point my finger at Bobby. He laughs at me.

"You know, Whitney...I have been trying to process these last few weeks and make heads or tails of Ryan's recent turnaround."

I nod, verifying that I am following the conversation.

"And the only common variable that I can come up with is you!"

What! I snap my head back to attention. My eyes widen. "I don't know what you mean, Bobby."

He continues, "Ryan's first top-ten finish of the season was the first weekend that you were at the track as his PR manager after Annalise left."

My blood boils at the sound of her name. *Bitch!* I look at Bobby with shocked surprise. I am not sure what he is getting at.

"I may be old, Whitney," Bobby says, "but I am far from stupid. I have witnessed some noticeable changes in Ryan in the past few weeks, all for the good. And for all intents and purposes, I hope he maintains it."

I mutter under my breath, "I'm not so sure."

Bobby laughs, "He is a stubborn old bastard, just like his daddy. He will come around, though."

I blush and look down at the metal floor. Suddenly, I am scared. Does he know? If Bobby knows, then who else knows?

I look back up. "Bobby...I..."

He interjects by throwing up his hands. "I am not sure what you're doing, if you're doing anything at all, but whatever it is, it's keeping Ryan in the top ten. And frankly, I don't give a shit. Just keep him from smoking and spinning. That is all I give a damn about." I jump at Bobby's expletive outburst.

I smile nervously, but at the same time, I feel the need to reach out and hug him. I take Bobby by surprise as I reach out and grab this big old bear of a man by the neck and pull him into an embrace. Even though I can tell he is surprised, he wraps his arms around me in return. Instantly, I feel better.

I just make it to the airport. My flight is barely given clearance as the thunderstorms roll in behind me. I stow my bag in the overhead compartment just as the flight attendant calls for all electronic devices to be turned off. You know, that is not a bad idea. I am going to turn off this cell phone and not turn it back on until Monday morning. No calls, no texts, and no e-mails. It will all wait until Monday because *finally* I have a day off. Praise the Lord!

All of a sudden, Brooke comes to mind. *Shit!* I told her that I would spend tomorrow with her since I have not seen her in a week. I fire off a quick text to her.

Long nite in Kentuck! Plane delayed. Exhausted.
Call you tomorrow when I wake up.

I hate to lie, but I need some time to myself tomorrow. I press send. I have been across the United States in three weeks, and I need some rest. I switch my phone to off and feel like a thousand pounds have been lifted off my shoulders. Who knew one little device could harbor such emotions of anxiety and stress?

I try in vain to get comfortable, thankful that the plane ride this weekend is a short one. I fail. The airplane reaches a cruising altitude, and I switch on my iPod. I decide to select a playlist. I don't want to leave a shuffle selection up to fate, especially after the night I had.

I select the John Mayer playlist. This is safe, maybe? "Back to You" begins to pipe through my ears. I swear. I cannot win with this device either. The remainder of the flight epitomizes that song. No matter what I do, my thoughts come back to Ryan. Our argument tonight, the late night at his home, the night he showed up unannounced at my apartment, it has all happened so fast. I guess now it is over just as fast. But, it is probably for the best. I sigh as I try not to think about that.

But my thoughts don't relent. They make me angry instead. I am upset that Ryan would not listen to my explanation. I told him the truth about Colton, and I have done nothing wrong. He can be mad all he wants, but now I am mad because he's acting like a child.

But, why would he get so mad? Why would he care, unless he is jealous? Wait a minute...I mean, surely not. He has a new girl every week at the track. This is just a passing fling for him. I shift in my seat, uncomfortable.

In the midst of all that has happened, I have not had a chance to think myself. Actually, I did not think at all when I jumped into bed with Ryan, where it might lead or how long it might last. *He will eventually move on, Whitney,* I scold myself. And I am right, it is only a matter of time.

Chapter 20

I finally reach my apartment shortly after midnight. I am so exhausted from the weekend and my internal conflict that I am nauseous. I throw my bag down in the kitchen and lock the door behind me. I peel my clothes off down the hallway and leave a trail into the bedroom. I am not getting a shower because I am too exhausted to stand up. I pull on an old Georgia Southern T-shirt and clean underwear. If you can't take a shower, clean underwear is always the next best alternative.

I walk into the bathroom and remember that Brooke gave me a supply of Ambien to help with the jet lag that I experienced from Sonoma. I think I might need one now. I am so exhausted that I shouldn't have a problem sleeping, but I want to make sure. I don't want to spend the night tossing and turning and thinking about him. So, I grab the bottle and shake one out, then take a sip of water out of the faucet to wash it down. *There!* I have the day off tomorrow, and I plan to enjoy it. I barely make it to the bed before I am out like a light and glorious sleep befriends me.

A slight pounding noise breaks me from my deep, drug-induced sleep, but I am too blissfully serene to care. I roll over and hug my cool pillow as I succumb to the wonders of modern medicine again.

* * *

After what seems like years, my eyes flutter open. I feel rested, but I am in a state of not being able to wake up, not to mention slightly disoriented. A loud pounding noise breaks me from my present state. *What is that?* I toss and turn, trying to regain my blissful slumber, but the hammering continues. I sit up in my bed warily. It takes me a beat to realize that someone is knocking on my door.

I struggle to my feet and pad down the hallway in a daze as the knocking turns to pounding. What in the world? Still dazed, I open the door.

"Jesus Christ, Whitney!" Ryan shouts at me, infuriated. I wince as he pushes me back inside and closes the door behind him. The door clicks, and Ryan booms again, "Where in the hell have you been?"

It takes me a few minutes to process his words because I am still stoned from the Ambien.

"Whitney!"

I shake my head. "What?" I shout. "Where do you think I have been? What does it look like?" I look down at myself and realize that I need more clothes on.

Ryan walks over to the island in my kitchen to put down his cell phone and keys. "What is wrong with you? Whitney, did you take something?" he asks, turning back to me.

I give him my devilish grin. "Ambien!"

He rolls his eyes at me. "How long have you been asleep?"

"I don't know...What time is it?" I fumble.

"Whitney, it is nearly three o'clock in the afternoon!"

Holy shit! That is some good stuff right there.

"Oh! I don't know...a couple, twelve hours, maybe fourteen." I raise my eyebrows at him innocently, knowing full well that I am about to incite another riot.

"Jesus, Whitney! No wonder you haven't answered my calls or messages! And I have been pounding on your door since nine a.m.! What if someone saw or recognized me?"

I am mad now. Ryan has barged into my house again, unannounced, and woken me up from my glorious sleep. "Don't you dare start with me! I am—was—exhausted. You pissed me off, and I wanted to be left alone! So, I turned my phone off."

Speaking of my phone, where in the world is it? I start looking around at my bags that are scattered around on the floor, lying right where I left them early this morning. I lean down to grab my carryon bag, and I can feel Ryan's eyes on me.

"What are you looking for?" Ryan asks, aggravated.

"My damn phone!" I reply, mirroring his tone.

I quickly find my iPhone and press the on button until it lights up. I steal a quick glance at Ryan, who is watching me intently. I walk over, place my phone on the island beside his, and roll my eyes at him all at the same time. He reaches out abruptly and pulls me into his arms.

Ryan runs his hand around my neck and up into my hair. Instantly, I go weak at the knees. "You made me mad too, but I was worried about you!"

Oh my!

Ryan searches my face. "You need to wake up. Do you need something to drink?" he says, but he does not turn me loose. He leans over to press his lips against mine. I place my hand across his chest and press firmly to stop him.

I can feel his pectoral muscles against the palm of my hand, and my breath hitches in my throat. No matter how mad at am I am, I cannot resist him, but I'm going to try. "I am still pissed at you! So don't think you can waltz in here, sweep me off my feet, and everything is fine."

I pull back from him, but Ryan holds me firmly in place. Slowly he smiles. "I want to be so angry with you, but for the life of me, all I can think about is making love to you."

I blush. And then I go weak in the knees again. *Damn!* How does he have this power over me? And like him, I can't stay mad at him either. I shake my head and look down, not knowing what to say. Ryan gently places his hand under my chin and pulls my face up to meet his.

As he leans in to kiss me, a series of loud cell phone message alerts come through. It sounds like a chorus of electronic tones signaling new e-mails, voicemails and text messages. I look up at Ryan and then over to my phone. He pulls my face back to him. He leans into my body again, but this time holds me in a tighter embrace. He presses his soft lips to mine. I run my hands up into his brown hair and sigh against his kiss.

Then, all of a sudden, our embrace is interrupted by another loud knock on my door. We both jump back. *Shit!* My apartment is like Grand freaking Central Station today. I leap out of Ryan's embrace and rush over to the door.

"What the hell?" Ryan exclaims as I go to look out the peephole.

I have a deep pool of dread in my stomach because I already know who it is. I look through the peephole and confirm my suspicions. It is Brooke and Matt. *Double shit!* I turn back to Ryan and shoo him away.

"Who is it?" Ryan whispers.

"Brooke," I hiss.

"Whitney!" Brooke shouts from outside of the door.

I jump again. I turn back to Ryan and mouth, "Go, go! To my bedroom! Just hide!"

Ryan turns sharply on his heel and disappears just as I hear Brooke fumbling for her keys. I snatch open the door.

"Whitney!" Brooke exclaims. "Where the hell have you been?"

I jump back at her outburst. What is with these people? *Jeezus.*

"Where does it look like I've been?" I throw my hands down at my clothes—or lack thereof.

Brooke barges through the door, and Matthew follows behind her like a whipped dog. She is carrying a garment bag that looks to be packed full of clothes. Suddenly, I remember what we were going to do today. She was bringing me clothes to try on for Daytona week. *Crap!* I watch as Brooke tosses the bag onto the coffee table.

"What are y'all doing here?" I say.

"Whitney, I have been trying to call you all day, and I panicked when I couldn't reach you!"

"Why? Didn't you receive my text message?" I question her, recalling the last message I sent to Brooke before the plane departed.

"No!" she exclaims.

"I sent you a text before my plane took off. It was delayed, I was exhausted, and I just wanted to sleep today. I turned off my phone," I say, exasperated.

Brooke raises her eyebrows at me, and I can tell she is pissed.

"Please let me get some clothes on!" I turn on my heel to the bedroom, praying that she doesn't follow me. She doesn't. Ryan is sitting on the edge of my bed when I enter the room. As soon as I enter, he charges me. The power of his embrace forces us into the wall with an audible thud. His lean hands encircle my body, and his lips find mine within an instant. He captivates me. I have lost all control to him. I don't even care that Brooke and Matthew are a few feet away.

Brooke's voice breaks me from my trance. "Whitney?"

I groan softly against Ryan's lips and pull away. "Be right there!" He raises his eyebrows at me, and I shush him by putting my index finger up against his mouth. I mouth, "I'll be right back!"

I pull on some lounge pants and toddle back into the kitchen, where Brooke stands, peeved. She has a cell phone in her hand.

"Whose is this?" she asks.

My heart falls to the floor. It's Ryan's cell phone. I give her a strange look and say, "It's my work cell."

"But I thought you were using your own cell phone for work," she quickly retorts.

OK, here we go with the inquisition. "No...I mean yes...I have my personal one and a work phone, but I don't use it."

Brooke gives me a hard stare. She knows I am lying. I am a terrible liar! I walk over and attempt to take the phone from her. She pulls it back abruptly.

"If you don't use it, then why does it have a password?"

Oh Damn! I did not see that one coming. She is starting to tick me off now. "Give me the freaking phone!" I shout a little too loud.

Brooke takes a step back, stunned by my tone. "What's the pass code, Whitney?" she retorts. I have challenged her now and my odds of winning are not great.

I finally lose it. "What the hell is your problem? Did you not have enough depositions or cross-examinations this week, Brooke? Or did you just feel the need to come over here and give me hell on my only day off?"

Matthew snickers in the background as I continue my rant.

"I mean, this is my only day off in weeks, and you barge in here and start questioning me about a damn cell phone?" I pause. I can see a look of hurt on Brooke's face, but it is fleeting. She throws the cell phone at my head, which I barely catch before it smacks me in the face.

"Come on, Matthew." And she walks out the door. I roll my eyes at her immaturity. Matthew does as he is told and follows suit out the door, giving me a small wave and nod of the head.

As the door slams, I slide down onto the couch. I put my head in my arms. No, No, No! I can feel Ryan approach from the hall. I don't look up at him. I feel sick about the way I acted, but I had to get her out of the apartment. And she pushed me too far.

Ryan sits down beside me. "I take it she doesn't know?"

I shake my head silently. He runs his hand around my neck and up into my hair. It takes my breath every time he does that. I look up into his eyes.

"Let's get out of here," he says softly as he pulls me up from the couch.

I nod. Sounds like the best idea I have heard all day. Well...since I have been awake, that is!

"Get dressed and meet me downstairs," Ryan commands, then kisses me swiftly.

As he leaves the apartment, I race back to my bedroom. I don't know where we are going, but I couldn't care less at this point. Actually, that's not really true. I would have preferred it if he had just stayed here and we just went to my bedroom.

Now insanely awake, I throw on some navy-blue Capri pants, a white blouse, and some cute flip-flops. I run a brush through my long hair and whip it up into a ponytail. I grab some light makeup, touch up my face, and add a little lip gloss. I know we are not going "out" in public, but I at least want to look nice for him.

I spritz on some perfume, grab my phone and keys, and I'm out the door. I scale the stairs effortlessly and walk out into the street. I look at the cars parked on the curb, expecting to see Ryan's sleek black Camaro, but it is his big white Chevrolet truck that I find parallel parked almost at the end of the block.

I look around to make sure no one is watching. I am clear. I bound up to Ryan's life-size Tonka truck. Before I can pull the door handle, it swings open from inside, and I am met by Ryan's gorgeous face and megawatt smile. My insides flutter. I grab hold of the door handle, step up on the rail, and hoist myself up into the truck with Ryan.

"Ready?" he asks. I only nod and smile in an attempt to not give my anxiousness away. Ryan pulls his truck out and onto the road, and we meander through the streets of downtown Charlotte.

"Where are we going?" I ask, but feel confident in the fact that we are going to his house. There isn't any other place we can go.

"I had planned to take you to the lake today," Ryan says as he makes a left turn, following the I-77 signs, "but since you didn't bother to answer your damn phone, you shot those plans to hell and back."

"Hold on! When I left Kentucky last night, you had basically cussed me out during the little temper tantrum that you threw down, then walked away without giving me the opportunity to explain." I shrug. "I assumed we were done."

Ryan laughs wholeheartedly. "Whitney, I am far from done with you!" And with statement, he reaches out and hooks his hand around my upper thigh to pull me across the bench seat so that I am sitting shoulder to shoulder with him. Our bodies touch, and the delicious heat radiates throughout my body, causing my face to flush.

Every inch of my body aches for him. I take a deep breath to calm my giddiness. I look up at Ryan to find him watching me just as intently with a pained look of emotion on his face that I cannot read. I can't tell if its concern for him, for me, or for the both of us. Finally, Ryan smiles at me, breaking the sexual tension, and kisses me quickly before turning his eyes back to the road.

Ryan takes the on-ramp to the interstate cautiously. It makes me laugh out loud.

"What's funny?"

"You. I guess I expected you to drive with a heavier foot."

Ryan looks at me attentively. "Normally, I do, but not with you in the truck, though."

Oh!

"Besides, I wouldn't want to scare you!"

I roll my eyes, but am shocked by his endearment. "I don't scare easily. You should know that by now!"

"Yeah, well...we will see about that!"

I know he has something up his sleeve. Ryan picks up his speed as we head out of Charlotte.

"So, the lake?" I ask.

He nods. "I have a house up on Lake Norman. I thought we could spend the day up there, but—" I hold up my hand to stop him from saying anything further, but he continues. "You are going to have to settle for dinner at my house instead."

Ryan wraps his left arm around my body and pulls me in closer to him. I snuggle into his warm embrace and smile. Wherever he is, is where I wanna be.

Chapter 21

"Help! I need help!" I say audibly, but only to myself. I cannot think or concentrate because the phone is incessantly ringing, and the office chatter is above acceptable levels. Not to mention the recurring thoughts of last night with Ryan. I am overwhelmed to say the least.

This week is the big Saturday-night race at Daytona International Speedway in Daytona Beach, Florida. My plane leaves in the morning, and I am nowhere near ready. Ryan's schedule is jam-packed with events, and requests are still coming to me via e-mail, text, calls, and fax. I want to scream. I prop my elbows up on my desk and put my head in my hands. *Think, Whitney, think.* But all I can think about is Sunday afternoon and evening with Ryan.

After my argument with Brooke, I gladly accompanied Ryan to his home for dinner. It's not like we can go anywhere in public, but I love being there with him. We are in our own bubble, away from the craziness that is his life, well, my life, too, now. He is accustomed to it. *Me...not so much!*

Since our professional relationship has taken a personal detour, I am obsessed with making sure that I complete all my job responsibilities to the letter. I don't want to give him any cause to be upset with me. Fearful that I am trying to include too many events in the week, I fire off a text to Ryan.

I need help.

His response is quick, and I instantly regret that I sent it. I should have sorted this all out myself. I am a big girl.

With what!?

My heart flutters.

I'm stressed. Requests keep coming in, and your schedule is already slammed. I don't want to say no, but I don't want you cuss me out AGAIN either.

Another instant response leads to a frustrating conversation with Ryan.

Are you serious?

Yessss.

Just do the best you can Whitney.

That is not helping me.

I trust you.

Well that's a first, thanks, but that doesn't help. Can you come into the office?

No, plane leaves in a few hours. You can handle.

I slam my phone down on my desk. *Damn!* I am not making any progress today. I look at my phone for the time. It's almost noon. Maybe lunch will help. I make my way to the break room. The whole office is abuzz, and the excitement of the employees is on my last nerve. I am way too overwhelmed to be enthusiastic. I am so ready to get on the plane and get the hell out of here, then figure it all out as I go.

I walk through the break room door and spy Josh at one of the tables. I lay my sandwich down and groan loudly.

"What is that for?" Josh asks.

"You people are on my nerves!" I erupt. Then, consciously, I look around to make sure no one is offended by my comments.

Josh eyes me warily. "First of all, 'you people' includes you now. Second of all, Daytona races are the biggest of the year. Daytona is the Mecca or Holy Grail of NASCAR. And thirdly, Garrett will be driving on Saturday too. It is really exciting."

I groan loudly again. "Not you too." I lay my head down in my hands on the table.

Josh humors me. "What seems to be the problem?" I look up at him. "It's just too much! Ryan's schedule is already full, but requests keep coming in, and I don't know what to do because whatever I do, I am sure it will be wrong."

Josh snorts, "Aw, now, I'm sure lover boy will be glad to help you sort it all out."

A look of sheer mortification falls over my face. *How could he know?* Josh raises an inquisitive eyebrow at my reaction. I quickly remember myself, then shoot Josh a "get real" look, and he erupts in laughter. Crisis averted. *Whew!*

Josh and I talk about the race. He gives me a historical background on the Daytona International Speedway, which is very interesting. I like the fact that the very first NASCAR races were raced, in fact, on the beach. Now, that had to be something. Josh also adds that the entire staff of GCR Racing has been given tickets to the race by Garrett, which explains the mass hysteria.

I make my way back to my office to devise a plan to get through the rest of the day. I look down at my phone on my desk. I didn't realize I'd left it lying on my desk. I quickly pick it up to see if I have missed any calls or messages. Four missed calls and two new text messages. *Damn!*

I select the call log. Ryan has called four times, but has left no voice mails. *What the heck does he want?* I switch over to text. There's one text from Jerri that tells me the final travel itinerary for my trip is ready. The second text is from Ryan! I am disappointed that I have no messages or calls from Brooke. I know she is still pissed at me, but if I get too close to her, she will know. I want to tell her so badly, but I can't risk it. I have to distance myself from her until we figure this all out.

I pull up Ryan's text to read it.

Come over to the house. I will go over the schedule with you.

I almost drop the phone! *What? Oh no, no, no!* I text him back.

I thought you had an afternoon plane.

I am seriously confused. Ryan responds.

I can take a later flight. Tell Jerri you are leaving to pack.

I note the time on my phone. It's only one o'clock. I pause. I can't do that. I know I will technically still be working, but I can't leave this office before five o'clock. He always puts me in an awkward position. *Damn him!* Jerri will know I'm up to something. I am a terrible liar. If I go there who knows where that might lead. Oh, I know where it will lead, all right, because work is the last thing on his mind. I don't need that distraction right now. I should make him come here.

I type out my response.

I can't. Please come here.

He responds instantly and stubbornly.

No.

Bastard! I guess I will figure it out on my own. I don't need him. I can handle this. I type out my final response.

Fine. I will handle myself.

I wait for another response. I don't get one. Another standoff. Well, I better get back to it. Time is ticking. I sit back down to my computer to finalize my daily itinerary. Pre-race activities begin Wednesday in Daytona and go heavily until the start of the Pepsi 400 on Saturday night. I need to make sure I am organized each day. I don't need or want another misstep with Ryan. I want him to be confident in my abilities to do this job.

I'm finally getting into the groove of it all and actually loving it. Each week, my job is a means to an end, an exciting end. I love how each week culminates with a race. I am thriving on it, not to mention developing a love for the sport. I remember Ryan desperately trying to explain the adrenaline rush and how stock car racing can get embedded in your veins. I thought it was all bullshit. But I know better now!

I am fiercely typing out Friday's schedule when a voice calls out to me from the doorway of my office, "Looks like you figured it out!"

Ah, that will be Ryan! I turn around slowly in my chair to face him, and there he stands, my smug bastard dressed casually in a white knit polo shirt and neatly pressed khaki shorts, leaning against my door.

"So, did you really need my help or just want to see me?"

I groan loudly and roll my eyes directly at Mr. Arrogance.

"Forget it, Ryan! I got this!" I say flippantly.

"Do you now?" he quips.

"I made some executive decisions, which I am sure you will chastise me publicly for if you don't like them."

Ryan takes a look back out into the hallway, then steps into my office, conscious of outside ears. "Whit..." he says sultrily.

Whit? When did that start?

"I have other ways to handle you now."

"Ryan!" I gasp, praying no one is within earshot of that comment. He laughs at my horror. I shake my head and roll my eyes at the same time at him.

Ryan takes a seat at my desk, and I eye him intently. *Damn, he is so hot.* I shake my head. *No! Don't go there.* Ryan laughs at me.

"What's so funny?"

"The expression on your face completely gives you away. It's comical that I can tell exactly what you're thinking about!"

I groan. "OK, would you please go so I can finish what I am working on?"

"OK...well then...since you don't need me now"—Ryan winks at me— "I'm headed to the beach."

Confused, I ask, "I thought you were not leaving until later?"

"I changed my plans, but since you declined my offer, I guess I will be on my way." He cocks his head coyly to one side.

Ryan stands, walks toward the door, and turns back to face me. "See you at the beach, *Whit*!" Then a wry smile comes over his face, and he completely changes his tone and tack. "I'll expect my complete itineraries before I get on the plane, so you better get to it! I know I will have to make several changes." He says this in a loud, obnoxious tone, no doubt so others in the office can hear his arrogance. He pounds the casing of the door with his fists, gives me a wink, and is gone.

Bastard!

Chapter 22

I arrive in Florida by noon the following day. It is early July, which means the weather is *hot* and humid. Thankfully, I have packed a lot of light dresses. The entire team is booked at the Plaza except, of course, for Ryan, Garrett, and Colton. They will be staying on their buses in the infield of the racetrack. That's got to suck. Then again, their buses cost well over a million bucks each. Still, they are missing the beach view.

As I cross the lobby to the elevators, I notice that the Plaza is equipped with a full-service spa. I am envious. I wish I could make time for a massage. No such luck, though. I barely have enough time to put my bags in the room before I have to meet the other team managers and security members. GCR has hired a few extra security personnel for Garrett and Ryan. It is my job to oversee them. I have to meet them in the lobby for a briefing soon.

I steal a quick look at the clock on my iPhone. I have enough time for a quick shower to wash off the plane germs and freshen up. I hang up my clothes and jump into a cool shower in an attempt to wash off some of the humidity, which I know is futile since I will be going right back outside.

I change into a strapless cobalt-blue maxi dress, which matches the color of Ryan's car, and flat sandals. We will be doing a lot of walking, so flats are my friend. I throw on the accessories Brooke chose for me, which includes a gorgeous, beaded necklace. I am thankful that she brought these clothes over on Sunday before our big blowout. I miss her.

My hair is another story. This Florida humidity is killing it. I pull it back in a frizzy bun. Several wispy layers that refuse to be confounded by my hair tie fall softly around my face. I secure my sunglasses on top of my head and stop to look in the mirror before I walk out the door. I don't recognize my refelction. Due to my hectic work and life these days, I have lost a considerable amount of weight, which I don't mind at all. But I look different; I actually look happy. There is color in my cheeks and a sparkle in my eye. *Hmmm. I wonder why?* I smile smugly at myself in the mirror. I am officially excited. *Let's do this!* I almost want to skip into the lobby. *Get control, Whitney,* I chastise myself.

As the elevator doors slide open, I scan the vast lobby for the security team that Jerri hired for the week. The owner, Maxwell Scott, is not hard to miss. I recognize him from his company profile picture on the Scott Security Services website. Maxwell stands about six-five, weighs about 250 pounds, and has a slick bald head, very marine-ish. I like him instantly.

Maxwell and his team of three are dressed professionally in black pants and black shirts with "Security" written in white across the back. I approach the group that looks like an elite Navy SEAL team with a laugh. My giggle causes the group to turn around, as my approach surprises them.

Maxwell eyes me intently; then I can see a glint of recognition wash over his face. "Miss Whitney?"

I smile, nod, and offer my hand in introduction. "Maxwell."

He returns my smile and takes my hand. "Max, please call me Max!"

We talk as we begin walking out of the hotel lobby, "Thank you for taking on this contract with such short notice. Jerri was adamant about having extra security for the team since we have so many pre-race activities throughout the beach."

Max nods. "I completely understand. I have secured the two black Cadillac Escalades from the local dealer in town. They are waiting outside." He pauses, then ushers me toward the waiting SUVs. "The vehicles are registered under my name for privacy, but the owner knows they are for GCR Racing transportation," he says as we walk through the hotel lobby and out into the Florida sunshine.

"Great!" I exclaim as he opens the back door and I clamber into the bucket seat on the passenger side in the second row. Max speaks briefly into the wire in his ear, no doubt syncing up with the two team members in the other Escalade. He puts the the vehicle in drive and we set out to the track to retrieve Garrett, Ryan, and Colton for our first pre-race event.

On our way to the speedway, Max and I talk briefly about the week ahead. "Did you receive a copy of the itinerary that I faxed to your office?" I question Max.

"Yes, I did. Other than a few logistical questions, I am good to go."

"Good." I nod my head at him, pleased at his competence. "All four guys will be with us for the duration of the week, is that correct?"

"Yes, ma'am!"

"Great! Jerri was adamant also that we have two security team members with Garrett at all times, then one for Colton and one for Ryan."

Max nods in agreement. "Don't worry, ma'am. We will handle everything."

I sit back in my seat and feel at ease knowing that we have contracted with the right security company.

We ride in silence for the remainder of the trip. I take out my iPhone. The picture on my home screen is one of Brooke and me taken by Matthew the night after I arrived in Charlotte. I smile. So much has happened since then. I switch over to text to send her a quick message. I hate fighting with her. She is the only person I have left in my life, and I don't want to screw that up too. I type.

> In Daytona. Hot! Thank you for the
> clothes. I am sorry. I miss you! <3.

I hesitate over the send button, but only for a moment. I was wrong. I hit send. When I look back up, I am shrouded in darkness as go through the infield tunnel.

The guys are all at the track, but the first event of the race week is a live question-and-answer session down at the Daytona Beach Pavilion. Then, Garrett has arranged a team dinner at the Cellar. By the time we enter the infield, I am giddy. The adrenaline is already pumping, and it is only Wednesday.

We arrive to find the guys huddled together at Garrett's hauler. I laugh because I can't believe they are all ready to go. They are like a bunch of women, usually, never on time. Max brings the Cadillac to a stop. I slide out of the first Escalade with help from the other security team member. Max stays behind the wheel. As I scramble out of the SUV, my iPhone prompts me with a new message. I look down quickly. It is Brooke. My whole body relaxes when I read the message from her.

Me too! <3.

I smile flamboyantly because I am overjoyed that our little tiff is over. I toss my phone over my shoulder into the Escalade. The guys abruptly stop their conversation and pause to gawk at me. *What in the world?* I look myself over quickly to make sure a boob hasn't popped out of my dress or I've had some other wardrobe malfunction. That was uncomfortable. *Jeezus!*

Garrett, Colton, and Ryan walk over to our transportation. I notice that Ryan hangs back from the crowd. Garrett greets me formally with a knowing smile, "Miss Parker." Colton smiles grandly at me behind Garrett's back so that only I can see him. I nod to them both and smile in return as he and Colton scramble into the second Escalade, which leaves me to ride alone with Ryan in the first one with Max.

Ryan raises his eyebrows to me as I follow him into the Escalade and sit in the bucket seat beside his. Thank God there is a noticeable space between us. I steal a glance at Max in the driver's seat and start to make a hasty introduction. "Ryan, this—"

Before I can finish, Ryan booms, *"Maxwell!"* and they bump fists. Clearly they know one another.

"OK, I guess you two have met?" I question them both.

"We were in military school together," Ryan admits.

"What?" I exclaim.

Max interjects. "Yes, until his ass got kicked out!"

I laugh out loud.

"Well, at least I didn't get kicked out of the marines!" Ryan hurls an insult at him.

"Technicality!" Max exclaims. I shake my head in amusement as they talk animatedly to catch up.

Chapter 23

We make it to the pavilion area, but the traffic is gridlocked. I am nervous now. Ryan immediately sets me at ease. "Did you get everything worked out?"

"What?" I ask, momentarily dumbfounded by him.

"The schedule, Whitney?"

"I...uh, yes, I did," I fumble. "Oh, I did have another late request come through, from the Make-A-Wish Foundation, but I have it all worked out."

Ryan nods his head. "When do we go to the hospital?"

"We aren't going to the hospital," I respond.

"Why?" Ryan asks quickly. "You didn't turn them down, did you?"

"No, of course not, I spoke with Jake's parents. Oh! His name is Jake. He is ten years old and has non-Hodgkin's lymphoma. He has been doing remarkably well this week, so his doctors and parents agreed that he could attend the race." I smile, pleased with the fact that I was able to work all that out for this precious little boy.

Dumbfounded, Ryan looks at me like I am speaking French. "Really?" Ryan asks curiously. "You arranged for them to get tickets and pit passes?"

"No...Jake and his parents are going to attend the race as your personal guests, and Jake is going to sit with me over pit road. His parents will be sitting in the spectator's pit box."

Ryan's mouth immediately drops open in astonishment. "Are you serious?" he finally manages to ask. His reaction makes me nervous.

"Is that OK? I mean..." I try to explain. "If you are not comfortable with that, I can make other arrangements. I thought this would be more memorable than you just visiting him in the hospital."

"No, Whitney! That is...is awesome! I can't believe you organized something like that. Annalise sure as hell never would have."

I roll my eyes at the sheer mention of her name. "Whatever..." I grumble.

"You know," Ryan laughs, "you are even more beautiful when you are mad!"

I gasp audibly and turn my eyes sharply to him, then to the front seat, where Max and his partner are talking between themselves. Thank God they didn't hear that.

I turn back to Ryan, who continues, "Why do you think I try to piss you off so much?"

I open my mouth to speak, then close it again. Ryan laughs.

"Speechless?" Then he mouths with great enthusiasm, "*Wow!*"

I roll my eyes at him again, but am overtaken by the strong urge to laugh out loud.

We maintain radio silence while we sit in beach traffic. I steal a few glances at Ryan. It is taking all my restraint to not crawl into his arms. I wonder if he feels the same way. I shake my head at my thoughts. I can't go there, at least not now. I have a job to do.

When we arrive at the pavilion, I have no more time for obscure thoughts. The scene at the beach is complete madness, not to mention paparazzi gone wild. The security team does an excellent job getting us inside the venue through a rear entrance. I climb out of the Escalade as security clears a path for Ryan up to the stage. I try to follow behind him, but Ryan ushers me ahead of him, leading me through the crowd with his hand on the small of my back. *Will I ever get enough of his touch?* The answer is automatic. No.

The question-and-answer session with Team GCR goes incredibly smooth and fast, no doubt because I am enthralled with the guys and how they interact with their fans. Not to mention the fact, I get to learn too. I need to have my own question-and-answer session with Ryan. Maybe I don't need that downloaded version of *Nascar for Dummies*, after all. I laugh at myself and my wayward thoughts. I am in deep, deep trouble.

Chapter 24

Finally, I reach my hotel and crash onto the bed fully clothed. After only one day of events, I am exhausted, not to mention a little drunk. No...scratch that, a lot drunk. The team dinner was the most nerve-racking event so far. I am in constant fear that my feelings for Ryan will show on my face. So, I unfortunately tried to alleviate those fears with wine. The third glass backfired on me. My only saving grace was being seated at opposite ends of the table from Ryan, which allowed me to interact with other members of the GCR team.

I can't even think about that now. My head is spinning. I shift in the bed and throw my leg over the side. My toes find the floor and momentarily stop the room from spinning. Tomorrow is going to be hell. *Jeezus!*

I am about to fall asleep, when I hear a series of soft clicks and what sounds like my hotel door opening. My heart leaps into my throat. I am alarmed, but due to severe exhausted and intoxication, I cannot move. Before I can catch my breath, I feel a familiar hand on my upper back caressing my bare skin. The breath that I was holding escapes my lungs with a relieving sigh.

I raise my head to turn my cheek toward the intruder. My eyes flutter open, and they instantly meet Ryan's concerned gaze as he kneels down beside my bed. "What's wrong, Whitney?" he says softly as he caresses my face.

I shake my head against the hotel duvet. He knows I'm lying.

"Come on. Sit up for me!" he commands.

I shake my head. "I can't. I'm scared I might throw up," I mutter, embarrassed.

"Why did you drink too much?" he questions me with concern in his voice.

A lump wells in my throat, but I don't answer.

"Whit," he prompts me again. He leans in close to me again, and I can feel his breath on my face. It is just as intoxicating as the wine.

I open my eyes, and Ryan is waiting for my response patiently. Tears well up in my eyes, but I am too intoxicated to fight them.

"Hey," he says softly.

I slowly raise my body up off the bed, into a sitting position, but look down at my hands while I desperately try to fight back the tears. I can feel Ryan's eyes on me. I can't look at him. What I thought would be a one-time event with Ryan has quickly become unexplainably more—much more. I can feel it down deep. For the life of me, I cannot figure out how Ryan and I went from borderline homicidal tendencies to this. These developing feelings that I have for Ryan are starting to scare me.

I raise my head slowly and meet Ryan's gaze. He is watching me intently like he is searching my face for answers.

"My nerves," I finally manage to mutter. "It's all too much. It is hard for me to be around you with other people because I am scared my feelings will show on my face."

Ryan lets out a sigh and looks away. My heart hits the floor. I continue, although he doesn't look at me.

"I am scared because if someone finds out, then I will be out of a job, and you will be on to someone new." There, I said it. You put alcohol in, and you get honesty out. I shrug my shoulders as Ryan finally turns back to face me. His look does not give anything away. I don't know how he feels or if he could feel the same way.

It's really only about the latter now. I know that I'm just a current conquest for Ryan, but it is hard for me to admit that I have let my feelings for him grow even though I know this could all end at any moment. Stupid, I know. But then again, I didn't take the time to think about this to begin with.

"I don't know how to make you understand or believe me, Whitney," Ryan says softly.

I shake my head because I don't believe him, based on his current track record—with women, that is. My stomach starts to roll, and my head spins. I raise my hand to my head to steady myself.

Ryan speaks softly again. "Lay back down." He runs both hands around my neck. His touch sends chills down my spine, and I close my eyes. He grasps each end of my necklace and unlocks the fastener. I watch his every move as he removes my necklace and places it on the nightstand.

Ryan looks around the room and spies my duffel bag on the floor. He rifles through it and comes up with a T-shirt. He returns to my side and kneels down. He hands the T-shirt to me as he proceeds to remove my shoes. While he is preoccupied with my sandals, I pull the T-shirt over my strapless dress, suddenly embarrassed by the way he is caring for me like a child.

Ryan helps me stand. He pulls my blue sundress down caressing my legs with his fingers. "I love this color on you, and the fact that it matches my car, too." I smile shyly although I am about to collapse from the sensation of his touch.

I step out of my dress and kick it to the side as Ryan pulls the hotel duvet back. I slide down into the cool sheets. It feels heavenly. Ryan steps back and removes his shoes and empties his pockets. *What is he doing?*

"Slide over," Ryan says softly.

I obey his command, and he slides down into the bed with me. I turn away from him, and he snuggles behind me. Ryan drapes his arms over me. I can feel his lips on my ear when he says, "I don't mind if you tell Brooke about us. I know how important she is to you."

I nod against his embrace and whisper, "She is only thing I have left."

"Not anymore," Ryan says, then softly kisses my neck below my ear and pulls me deeper into his arms. I smile into my pillow and am sated as I drift away.

* * *

I awake to the sound of my iPhone alarm. Oh no! My head pounds with each ring. I sit up, not even sure where my phone is, but quickly find it lying on the nightstand within arm's reach. Suddenly, I realize as I swipe the home screen to silence the alarm that I am alone. Ryan is gone. Or was he ever there? Did I dream it?

I try to process all these thoughts, but I am hit with a wave of nausea. I have to take something for my head. I turn back to the nightstand, and there is a glass of water waiting for me. *Strange!* Beside the glass is a note.

> I didn't want to leave you, but I had to get back before dawn. Drink this water, and eat your breakfast. You will feel better. See you at the track.

Gasp! He was here. My heart swells. Before I can process any thought in my brain, there is a slight knock on my door. My heart skips a beat.

"Room service!" I hear someone call out from the door.

I scamper to the door, still in my T-shirt, open it, and the attendant rolls though my door with a breakfast spread and a large vase of beautiful white roses. He hands me a small card as he sets up the feast. I am taken aback. I can't believe Ryan coordinated all this for me.

I hold the card tightly in my hand, then reach for my purse to find a tip.

"Oh, no, ma'am, please, it has already been taken care of."

Of course it has. I smile and nod as he leaves. Once the door clicks and I am safely alone, I remove the white card from a small envelope.

> Please don't worry. We will figure this out. RFC

I laugh out loud at his signature, RFC, and the memory it evokes. My Ryan Fucking Carter. I lie back on the bed with a million thoughts fluttering in my mind. Does he want to figure this out? Is there more to figure out? He must care, or he wouldn't have coordinated all this, this morning. Or does he know that he has already screwed me up and he feels sorry for me, as the end to this fling is near? My head continues to pound with each thought. I cannot do this to myself. This internal self-dialogue is taking its toll on me. I have to get control.

I sit up and look at the roses and breakfast again. He does care on some level, no matter what my subconscious might say. I stand up shakily and walk over to the table. The breakfast smells heavenly. Before I sit down, I reach out and finger the gorgeous white roses that grace the table. So soft. Hmmm, I wonder. *Why white?* Doesn't each color stand for something? I will have to ask him. *No, don't even go there, Whitney!* He probably doesn't even know himself. Just leave well enough alone.

* * *

Ryan was right. After a good breakfast, Advil, and a hot shower, I feel good as new. Plus, my anxieties from this morning seemed to have passed. As I approach the pedestrian tunnel, race adrenaline begins pumping carelessly through my veins. I am filled with exhilaration as I jump out of the Escalade and bid Max good-bye.

Today is a huge day, qualifying. This is as big, if not bigger, than the race itself since the time trial decides how each car will start the race. There are fifty cars on the docket today, but only forty-four will make the cut. Ryan has secured a morning qualifying position, while Garrett will take his turn in the afternoon.

We have events scattered throughout the day, as if qualifying wasn't enough. At lunch, we have a photo shoot with Ryan's car for the race. It has a special paint scheme to celebrate the Fourth of July. Then, we have a meet and greet in the Sprint Fan Zone at 1:00 p.m., and lastly, a ribbon cutting and cocktail reception for the new opening of the Carter Racing Legacy display in the Daytona 500 Experience. It makes me exhausted just thinking about it all, but I can't think about anyone or anything right now. I have a job to do.

The hauler is quiet. Everyone must be over in the garage. I place my duffel and my garment bag in my usual spot. Since today is so hectic, I won't have time to go back to the hotel to change before the reception. I will have to change into my cocktail dress here.

I set out to the garage to see how close we are to Ryan's qualifying slot. When I arrive, everyone is gathered around Ryan's car as he sits inside. Bobby is talking animatedly and waving his hands in the air, which I'm sure means he is giving Ryan a lecture. I laugh.

The sound of my laughter causes everyone to turn in my direction. I flush, then smile.

Bobby walks over to me. "It is almost his turn, and then he is all yours!"

I laugh at him. "So soon?"

Ryan interjects. "I can hear y'all, you know!"

I smile at Ryan. "I would be worried if you didn't," I snap, then turn back to Bobby. "How is the car?"

Bobby sighs, "It is good, real good, probably the best car we've had all season, but if hothead doesn't keep his britches on and learn to be patient, we are *all* screwed!"

I almost choke on Bobby's response. Ryan gives us both a disapproving look and then fires the engine to his number #62 Chevrolet. We watch and laugh at his expense as he backs his car out of the garage to proceed to pit road.

Bobby and I stand in the garage and watch the monitor as Ryan takes the track for his warm-up laps. I take a deep breath.

"It has gotten to you, hasn't it?"

Bobby's question takes me aback, and I blink rapidly, trying to process his question. Did he say "it" or "he"?

Bobby quickly clarifies. "Racing, the adrenaline?"

I take another deep breath, trying to steady my nerves. "Yes, it has." I smile.

"Ryan really does have a great car for Saturday, and I just hope he can keep a clear head about him. We need a win badly." Bobby sighs.

"I understand." I nod, then turn my attention back toward the monitor as Ryan gets the green flag for his qualifying lap.

Bobby is very tense, and I can't hear the words that he is muttering under his breath. Ryan is moving effortlessly through the turns and then fires down the back straightaway. The monitor displays his current speed versus cars that have already qualified. Unfortunately, I don't have a clue as to what they mean or how Ryan relates.

Ryan sticks the car down low, very close to the apron, as he navigates turn three, then turn four. He guns the car out of the last turn, then fires across the front stretch.

As Ryan crosses the start/finish line, Bobby lets out a throaty and exaggerated, "Yeeeaaahhh, baby! That's what I am talking about!"

Bobby fist pumps the air and sets off. I look back at the monitor, and Ryan has posted the fastest time trial so far, but there are still many more to go. It will be late afternoon before the final pole position is determined. So far, it looks good for Ryan. I turn to retreat back to the hauler, when a firm arm snakes around my waist. I step back, stunned by the touch, and am pulled into the arms of Colton Johnson.

My eyes are wide with surprise, which he laughs off. I try in vain to wriggle from his grasp, but he holds me tighter.

"You never texted me back last week," Colton says softly in my neck. He is very calm, but something about his statement is very menacing.

"I...I turned my phone off when I left Kentucky and didn't receive your message until the next day." I mumble the lie very unconvincingly. In the distance, I can hear a car making its way to the garage, and I fear its Ryan.

Colton's embrace makes my stomach roll with nausea. I fight off the urge to convulse because Ryan now owns my body, and any touch other than his is just repulsive. I try to pull away from Colton again, but he tightens his grip on me once more. This time it starts to hurt.

My pulse quickens as Colton leans over and whispers into my ear, "I don't take well to being ignored, and I have been waiting a long time, Whitney." I can feel his lips move against my skin, and his breath is hot on my face. Colton's words and his manner send fear radiating across my body.

I gasp, not knowing what to say, and the inevitable happens. Ryan pulls his car into the garage. I look away from Colton and meet Ryan's cold gaze. I can tell he is very angry from witnessing Colton's grip on me. I try again to step out of his reach, failing again.

"Colton, now is just not the right time," I say softly, looking at him and watching from the corner of my eye as Ryan climbs out of his car.

Colton plants a chaste kiss on my cheek, then releases me with such force it causes me to stumble backward. He smiles a curt smile, slightly turns his head to acknowledge Ryan, nods, then walks away just as Ryan reaches my side.

"What the fuck was that about?"

Ryan's tone stuns me. "I...I..." I fumble for the words, still in shock about the encounter with Colton. "It was nothing," I say, trying to defuse the situation.

"It sure as hell didn't look like nothing," Ryan snaps and walks away.

I can't breathe. *What just happened here?* Colton completely flipped the switch on me. What a terrible misjudgment of character on my part! I gasp in desperation from this exchange with Colton and now a very angry Ryan Carter. Here we go again...

* * *

I step back into the hauler. It is empty except for Ryan, who is perched on a stool with his head leaning back against the wall. He doesn't acknowledge my presence.

I wait for a few minutes, then say, "It's time for the meet and greet."

Ryan abruptly opens his eyes, and his expression tells me that he is still radiating anger. He jumps down from the stool and walks past me in a huff. I follow suit behind him silent but frustrated.

After we take a few hundred steps in silence to the Sprint Fan Zone, I finally say, "He was angry with me because I didn't text him back last week."

Ryan stops cold in his tracks. "I don't give a damn what it was about, but I don't like it. I don't want him near you, much less have his hands all over you. Do you understand me?"

I step back, shocked by his sudden outburst. *Whoa. Jealous much?*

Before I can respond, Ryan explodes again. "You know, I don't even care right now! I have too much on my plate and way too much at stake for this bullshit." He waves his hands in the air for effect, then turns and stalks away. My shoulders fall in defeat. He is so unbelievably stubborn, but he is right. I let him go.

There are cars still waiting to qualify as we take the final shots of Ryan with his Fourth of July–themed Chevrolet. I can tell he is still mad even though it has been several hours since the incident with Colton. I have tried to give him some space because I know he is anxious about the qualifying times. So far, he still has pole position.

As soon as the photographer wraps, I leave quietly to go to the hauler and get my clothes to change for the cocktail party at the Daytona 500 Experience. Brooke brought over a beautiful short black cocktail dress for the reception. I am excited to wear it. It is a fit and flare with layers of black ruffles that start at the waist. Oh! And let me not forget about the gorgeous black-and-silver Jimmy Choos that Brooke has let me borrow. I am surprised she didn't make me sign a waiver to wear them—or that she didn't come back to the apartment and take them back after our fight. I laugh to myself.

I take my bags and set off for the ladies' room in the VIP area to change. It is quiet, and I have the bathroom to myself. It would be so nice to have a shower to wash off the Florida humidity, but it wouldn't last for long since I am going right back out in it. I spread out my makeup and find a plug-in for my CHI iron. After washing my face, I hoist myself up on the counter, trying hard not to think about how wonderfully this day started and how it has progressed. What a disaster! I hope that I can salvage the evening at the Carter Legacy opening. I completely redo my makeup and try in vain to take the frizz out of my brown locks with not much luck. Reluctantly, I pull it back in a loose, high bun. A few short layers fall in tendrils around my face thanks to the heat. This is the best I can do for now. I step into one of the stalls and strip down. The cool air feels good on my naked body, and I lean against the cool metal stall door to steady myself and my nerves. I have half a mind to just hide in here for the rest of the night. Wouldn't that be nice? Would anyone even notice?

I slide into the black dress, and it fits me perfectly. I take out my flip-flops for now. I still have to walk back to the hauler, then over to the Experience. While the Jimmy Choos look good, they are hell on the feet, and I wouldn't dream about ruining Brooke's shoes. Our friendship is a different story. It seems like I'm doing a great job of jeopardizing it these days. I sigh. I take out my cell phone to send her a quick text.

Can we have dinner next week? I need to talk to you.

I hesitate over the send button, but only for a moment. Ryan said that I could tell her. I want to tell her. Maybe she can help me sort this all out. I hit send. I gather up my belongings and steal a glance at my phone for the time. I am right on schedule.

I step out of the hauler and take a deep breath. I have a long walk in these heels, but here goes nothing. Before I can take a step, a blue GCR golf cart flies up beside me and screeches to a halt. The driver lets out a long whistle.

"Hey Whitney, you clean up good!"

I laugh. It is Justin, a young, sandy-haired crew member who can't even be eighteen years old.

"Thank you!" I say politely. "Can you give me a lift?"

"Of course, let's go!"

I sit down in the golf cart, and Justin takes off with a jolt. I have to hold on to the side to steady myself.

"Sorry!" Justin smiles apologetically. "Can you believe we could possibly have pole position for Saturday?" he says excitedly.

"I know! It is exciting!" I reply as we pull up to the museum. I take a few seconds to gather my senses before I get out of the golf cart.

"Have fun tonight! We didn't get the invite," Justin says, referencing some of the other crew members. He is basically a gofer, but I can tell he loves his job. Surely, he is happy to do whatever they tell him to do just to be a part of this race team. I can now relate to what a privilege it is to work for a NASCAR organization.

I smile sweetly at him as I step off the golf cart. "Well, if I had known that, you could have come as my date!"

Justin flushes about twenty shades of red. I wave good-bye, and he gives me a wink as he takes off.

Chapter 25

I walk into the Daytona 500 Experience a few minutes early. I produce my team credentials and am ushered quickly through the door. I have only taken a few steps into the museum when I am thrust a glass of champagne from a passing waiter. Scared to tell the overexuberant server no, I take a glass. I wonder if it would be impolite to take two. I shake my head. *Remember last night, Whitney. We don't need a repeat*, I chastise myself.

There are a few early partygoers milling around the exhibition hall. I can see the area that holds the Carter Racing Legacy display, but it is covered by a cobalt-blue cape and a huge red ribbon. I take a moment to look at the other displays and am captivated by the rich family history and legacy that NASCAR is enthralled in. It is amazing.

I am distracted from my reverie by the entrance of a large group of people. I look up from the Daytona display to see Garrett and a beautiful brown-haired woman in her midfifties who I assume is Ryan's mother, Laura. They make their way into the museum, and a throng of people flock to them. Garrett and Laura greet each one of them warmly and fondly. It makes me feel very comfortable. Garrett makes eye contact with me and smiles curtly. Then, he proceeds to lead

Laura over, and my anxiety level is back on the rise. I take a deep breath as he approaches.

"Whitney," Garrett says formally, "I would like for you to meet my wife, Ryan's mother, Laura." He pauses. "Laura, this is Whitney Parker, Ryan's new public relations manager."

I smile and offer my hand, which she takes and smiles grandly, making me comfortable in their presence. Laura is beautiful and says kindly, "Whitney! I have heard so much about you and how you are making a huge difference with Ryan." *Really?*

I smile, although I'm confused. "Thank you, though it is more than a full-time job." Both Garrett and Laura look at one another and laugh out loud at my joke. I am sure they can relate.

Our conversation is interrupted by another beautiful middle-aged woman who steals Laura away into another conversation. I turn back to Garrett, who says, "Speaking of the devil, where is Ryan?"

"I'm not sure," I say timidly.

Garrett nods. "Whitney, it is your job to know where Ryan is at all times, and I expect you to find him now. He is late!"

I step back, stunned at Garrett's son-of-a-bitch tone. *Whoa!* I know now where Ryan gets his tendencies. I nod my head to let him know that I understand, then quickly walk to the exit.

I walk past several people as they enter the venue. When I am safely outside, I take my phone out of my clutch to call Ryan. I pace as I ring his cell phone. It rings and rings and rings, then goes into his voice mail. *Damn it!* I turn to walk toward the infield area and walk right into Ryan.

I step back and stumble. Ryan reaches out and grabs my arm gently to keep me from falling. The sight of him takes my breath away, eases my anxiety, and raises my blood pressure all with one look. Ryan is gorgeous. He is dressed in a black tuxedo. His hair is styled and gelled in a way I have never seen. He looks as though he is about to walk the red carpet at the Academy Awards. I smile, relieved. Ryan looks anxious but relieved now too. Our looks seem to mirror each other.

"Is my tie straight? I hate this shit!" he confesses, fiddling with his suit.

He looks flawless, but I touch his tie to add my personal touch. "Your dad is asking for you—no, I should say demanding was more like it!"

"I bet he is. He hates these events too," Ryan laughs. "Let's go." He leads me back into the venue with his hand on the small of my back, which sends shivers down my spine. As we walk through the door, Ryan leans into the back of my neck and says, "You look gorgeous in that dress. I hope I get the chance to take it off of you later."

I smile. Actually, I grin like a jackass because I know that he can't see my reaction. I am so relieved that the tension from earlier today has passed.

The moment we walk through the door, Garrett is standing impatiently, waiting for us. I flush scarlet because he has just witnessed our intimate exchange. He eyes us warily but grabs Ryan immediately and steals him away from me. I sigh as I watch him approach his mother and lovingly embrace her. It warms my heart seeing a softer and gentler side to him. I've always heard that you can tell a lot about a man by the way he treats his mother. Maybe that's just a southern thing, but his action gives me hope that it is true.

The event is in full swing with a few hundred people in attendance. I mill around the exhibits and stop to talk to the few people I know who from our team. After a few short speeches, Garrett, Laura, and Ryan are called to the small stage to cut the ribbon on the Carter Racing Legacy display. It is beautiful. Immediately, I recognize some of the photographs from Garrett's collection.

After awhile, Garrett steps back up to the microphone. "Sorry to interrupt your evening, folks, but I have a very important announcement to make." He pauses momentarily and raises his champagne glass. "Despite my best efforts this afternoon on the track, I am pleased to announce that my son, Ryan, has secured pole position for Saturday night's race here at Daytona International Speedway with a *new* track record of 45.98 seconds! I am proud of you, Ryan!" Garrett looks around the room and raises his glass higher to salute Ryan, who is nowhere to be found—again!

A round of cheers and applause goes up throughout the crowd. I can even hear Bobby's loud roar from the back of the room, which causes me to laugh. I scan the room, looking for Ryan, as does everyone else. I am desperate to see his reaction, but I don't see him. I have lost Ryan again. I meet Garrett's firm gaze again. *Damn!* He nods at me from across the room, which reiterates his earlier command to find him.

I raise my half-empty glass of champagne at Garrett, signaling that I am on the case of Ryan Carter yet again. I hastily make my way to the door, downing the last of my bubbly in one gulp. I drop the glass on a table as I hit the exit door. The Florida humidity has decreased noticeably since the sun has gone down, but the heat is still thick in the air. It is like walking into a brick wall.

My feet are screaming, but I am going to have to find him on foot nevertheless. Since Justin is nowhere to be found, it would probably be frowned upon to take one of the golf carts parked outside. I lean against the building and take off the beautiful but painful Jimmy

Choos. I hook the straps together and set out in pursuit barefoot. Then it hits me—I have no idea of where to even start looking for Ryan. He could be anywhere at this point.

I reach Ryan's team hauler first, and it's empty. I take my iPhone out of my clutch. Then, I throw my purse and the shoes into my duffel bag. Before I walk any further, I call Ryan's cell phone. It doesn't even ring. The call immediately rolls into his voice mail, which means he either ignored my call or his phone is turned off. Both are good possibilities. I groan.

I decide to try Ryan's luxury motor coach next. I knock warily, not sure of what I might find. I wait, but no answer there either. I pull the door handle anxiously. It's locked. *Damn it!* I stand back. *Think, Whitney. Think!* The garage is locked up. Ryan's car is locked up. Maybe he left altogether, but with whom? Max and his security team are at the reception. He never leaves the track during race weekend, unless he is breaking into my hotel room, that is. I laugh to myself.

My last resort is our pit box, but those haven't been set up yet. I walk listlessly down pit road. I walk over to the infield and run my bare feet over the cool grass. It feels heavenly on my swollen and sore feet. I sit down on the edge of pit lane and sink my feet into the grass. I sigh, defeated. The event is almost over by now. Garrett is going to be ticked, but I can't find Ryan. Maybe we need to install a tracking device on him. I inwardly roll my eyes at myself.

I am broken from my reverie by an incoming text alert on my phone. I swipe the home screen to read the message.

Looking for someone?

It's Ryan. A huge sigh erupts from my lungs. I text him back.

Yes, namely you. I am in trouble for letting you disappear again.

Where are you?

As I hit send on the text message, I look around. He must see me.
Then, I hear a loud crash that comes from the grandstands. I raise my
head quickly to look through the seats, but I don't see anyone. The
overhead lights are blinding, and I have to shield my eyes from their
brightness. Another text comes through from Ryan.

Up!

I look into the stands again and see nothing. Another text prompts
me.

Higher

I look higher into the stands and up into the press box. Nothing.
Then another loud crash that sounds like glass breaking makes me
jump. I look up higher. Then, I see him. I can barely make him out
as he waves his beer to me from high atop of the spotter's perch
that overlooks the front straightaway. *Sweet Jesus!* How did he get
up there? I hope he doesn't expect me to come up there because it
ain't happening!

My phone beeps again.

Coming down

Thank God. I walk across the grass as I wait for him. I find myself walking across the start/finish line and into turn one. I am surprised at the embankment and the degree of the corner. I can barely walk up it. I had no idea it was so steep.

As I patiently wait on Ryan to come down, I walk back over to pit road and sit on the makeshift barrier wall. I feel him approach me from behind long before he reaches out to caress my bare back. I take a deep breath to stand up and steady myself, but goose bumps run down the length of my spine. Ryan pulls me into an embrace with my back resting on his chest. His breath is hot on my neck, and it's intoxicating as ever. I close my eyes, very aware of the fact that we are intimately standing together in the middle of this huge super-speedway where anyone could be watching us. And with that thought, the large overhead lights go out on the track. It is completely dark.

I spin around and gasp, "Ryan!" He immediately envelops me in a passionate embrace and kisses me deeply. I lean into his feverous grasp and smell/taste the beer on his breath.

Then suddenly, Ryan pulls back. "I am still pissed about earlier!"

I step back, stunned from the change of tack. I open my mouth, but he puts his hand up to silence me. I am taken aback by his confession and not sure what to say, but Ryan starts to speak again.

"I am not good with this...this feeling." From his stuttering speech, I can tell Ryan is drunk. "It is something that I am not used to, and I don't handle it very well."

"What feeling?" I mutter.

"Jealousy," Ryan says flat out. "If Colton so much as lays another hand on you, so help me God, I *will* kill him!" he whispers through gritted teeth.

Oh!

With that statement, Ryan reaches out and pulls me back into a heated embrace. "But...right now...all I can think about is ripping that dress off you!" he mutters against my lips.

I can't breathe, but before he kisses me again, I manage to protest, "Ryan! You're drunk! We can't do this here!"

"I can and I will make love to you on this track or any other place I damn well please!" Ryan exclaims determinedly as he lifts me off my feet, carries me effortlessly across the infield grass, and lays me down across the start/finish line of the Daytona International Speedway.

Chapter 26

The green flag falls on Saturday night. Finally! I take a deep breath and settle into my seat. The sun is going down, but it is still dreadfully hot. I am sweating from every orifice, it seems. Ryan leads forty-four cars across the start/finish line to start tonight's race in Daytona. I laugh to myself as I watch the cars fire across the starting mark as I recall my intimate experience on this racetrack. The race is just starting, and we have almost 160 laps to go, but I can't sit back. The atmosphere at the racetrack and the fact that we have the pole position makes this race more exciting than usual.

I listen closely to my headset at the communications between Ryan, Bobby, and Mike. Everything sounds to be running smoothly. Let's see how long Ryan can keep the lead. The more laps we lead, the more points we accumulate, and even though Ryan had a rocky start to the season, I am hoping that he is making a turnaround. He seems to finish better each week, and that means he is rising higher in the points standings.

The cars fly around the track at speeds ranging from 160 to over 200 miles per hour. With these speeds, I can't sit still. The adrenaline is too much for me to fight tonight. I stand up and decide to go check on Jake, our Make-A-Wish patient, who is Ryan's guest tonight at the track. He was scheduled to sit with me over pit road, but decided to sit with his parents instead after he heard the starting of the engines. I could tell he was getting tired after having his picture taken with Ryan, the crew, and several of the other NASCAR drivers, including Garrett. Jake is on cloud nine, though, and it gives me so much pleasure that I was able to make it all happen for this precious little boy.

I walk up into the spectator box, and I can tell Jake is exhausted as he lays his head in his mother's lap. His mother smiles warmly at me. "I don't know how much longer he will last."

I smile. "Can I take him for one more event?"

Jake raises his head, curious.

"Sure," she responds.

I hold out my hand to him. "The first pit stop is coming up. Are you interested?"

Jake nods enthusiastically.

As he takes my hand, I hoist him up onto my back, which is effortless for me because he weighs about fifty pounds soaking wet. His terminal illness is taking a toll on his little body. We descend down the stairs and then back up the small ladder onto the top of the crew pit box. I remain standing so Jake can get a good view as the cars start filing down pit road for their first scheduled pit stop.

Ryan slides his #62 Chevrolet into his pit box, screeching the tires. The smell of gas and burned tire rubber fills my lungs. These smells and the sounds are all exhilarating. They ignite my excitement all over again. Jake shouts and waves exuberantly to Ryan, but it is quick, loud chaos, and within 14.5 seconds, Ryan squalls the tires and is gone again. After his pit stop, Ryan maintains the lead.

There are one hundred laps down and still sixty more to go. I have gotten Jake settled into Ryan's luxury motor coach with his mother to rest, but I had to promise that I would wake him up before the end of the race.

When I reach the pit box, I find out that Ryan has fallen back a few spots but is still in good position. Garrett is running in the middle of the pack around twelfth position, but he is famous for a last-minute attack, so we won't know what he may have up his sleeve until later on the race.

As the laps wind down, I adjust my headset as I hear team communications start to pick up. Ryan has pushed back up to third, but his car is still strong. I hear Ryan call out, "I need some help up here! How far back is Dad? I need a drafting partner!"

Help? What does he mean by that?

I take my headset off and look over to Ben. "What is he talking about?"

Ben laughs and starts to explain, "This track is governed by restrictor plates because of the high speeds and the draft. You have to have a good drafting partner to maintain position."

I hold up my hand. "You lost me!"

Ben takes his headset off. "Here's the deal. Because of the length of the track and its dynamics, like thirty-one degrees of banking into the turns, this is considered a super-speedway because of the speeds that the cars can achieve, which could be two hundred miles per hour or more. A few years back, NASCAR implemented a device called a restrictor plate. This device confines the intake of power to an engine, and each car is required to have one because it limits speed and provides another level of safety for all drivers." He pauses for a breath.

"Now, since those plates restrict the speed and downforce on the car and the car's spoiler, drafting helps the drivers get some of that power back." Ben lifts his hands to demonstrate his point. "If Ryan runs nose to tail with another driver, he can push him through the high pressure faster and reduce the aerodynamic resistance on the car's rear spoiler."

I wave my hands candidly at Ben and exclaim, "Too much information!"

Ben laughs at me. "OK, the annotated version is, two cars are better and faster than one!"

I laugh and point at him. "Why didn't you just say that? I can understand that!"

Ben shakes his head at me as he finishes his explanation. "If Ryan doesn't have someone behind him to push him, or if the car that is behind him shifts his line to follow another driver, Ryan will drop positions like a brick in the water."

Oh wow! I nod enthusiastically at Ben because I finally understand. "Gotcha. I am on the bus now!" I exclaim as Ben mockingly rolls his eyes at me and slides his headset back on.

Now that I can make sense of what is happening on the track, I can understand what the cars are doing. There are two draft lines that are trading the lead back and forth. Ryan leads the outside, and another Ford stock car driver leads the inside line. The laps are whittling down now. According to Ben, the race doesn't get interesting until the last lap.

With twenty laps to go, I walk over to Ryan's bus to grab Jake so that he can watch the end of the race. I enter the bus to find him and his mom both asleep on Ryan's couch. They both look too peaceful to wake, but I did promise Jake. I softly nudge his mother, who opens her eyes wearily. She is just as exhausted as little Jake. She acknowledges me and begins to wake him up.

I slip back out of the bus and literally run back over to the pit box. As I climb up the ladder, Ben yells, "Come on!"

I sit back down in my seat next to him and slide on my headset just in time to hear Garrett say over the radio, "Did someone call for help?" I laugh. Garrett has advanced his position to sixth and has fallen in line about two cars behind Ryan. This is getting good.

The radio crackles as Ryan says, "Come on, old man, let's do this!"

Garrett remains quiet on the radio while he manages to negotiate another position through turn one. He is now directly behind Ryan, pushing him through the draft. Ryan holds his line and advances into first place with his dad's help. *Yes!* I jump up with excitement. Ben stands on his feet too.

Ten laps to go. I continue to stand as I watch the monitor closely. Garrett continues to push Ryan around the track, and cars pile up behind them, but they are both battling the inside draft line. With the constant change in positions, there have been about twenty different race leaders today—and there could be twenty more before it is all over.

As both lines navigate turn four, NASCAR safety throws a caution flag for debris on the back straightaway.

"Damn it!" Ben shouts. The pace car comes out to slow the speed of the cars while the safety officials clear fragments from a damaged

241

car off the track. There are only six more laps to go. Ben is starting to get antsy and paces the pit box. "It's going to be a drag race to the finish!" Again, I don't know what he means, but then again, I don't think I want to know.

As the cars slowly make their way around the track, each stock car weaves back and forth in the current line to keep debris from sticking to their tires and also to keep those tires warm for the restart.

The radio crackles with Garrett's voice. "Son, you ready for this? You better hang on!" I laugh out loud at their exchange. I know Garrett has something up his sleeve, and I can't wait to see what it is.

As the lineup navigates into turn four, NASCAR pulls the caution flag and exchanges it for the green flag. The pace car dives down onto pit road and out of the way as the stock cars roar back to life across the start/finish line. The sound of the acceleration ignites the fire back in my heart, and my adrenaline level spreads throughout my blood. Into turn one, Garrett abruptly dives down low and joins the inside drafting line, leaving Ryan high and dry.

"Oh No!" I gasp. Ryan drops positions like he is dead in the water, just like Ben described. Garrett is now pushing the inside line in second place.

The radio crackles. "What the hell is he doing?" Ryan fumes. Though he falters a few positions, another driver in a Dodge stock car comes to his rescue and picks up the slack. He begins pushing Ryan back through turn two.

The radio crackles again as the cars fire down the back straightaway. "You didn't think I was going to just push you over the finish line, did you?" Garrett is joking but serious. Ryan remains quiet.

I watch the monitor intently as Ryan picks up positions thanks to the help of his new drafting partner. The inside and outside lines are still battling it out with only four laps to go. By the time Ryan hits turn three, he is pushing 192 miles per hour. He accelerates over 200 onto the back straightaway, taking back his lead position for the outside line of cars.

I hear the radio crackle again, and this time it's Ryan. "I hope you want to finish third because there is no way you're gonna get around Matt." Matt must be the lead driver that Garrett is behind.

The radio crackles again, but it's Mike. "Ryan keep calm. Hold your line."

The cars circle around with two laps to go. I realize that I am barely breathing, and the humidity, mixed with an eighty-five-degree temperature at night, isn't helping matters. I watch as the inside and outside lines still battle back and forth. I really have no idea how this will play out. I am almost shaking. Ben and I now stand in silence as we watch the final laps unfold. As the cars race down the back of the track again, Ryan has the lead, but only by a fraction of a second. It's too close to tell even on the monitor. And then there is Garrett. I know he is going to make a last-minute move. I guess this is why Ben says that this race doesn't get interesting until the last lap.

As I think those thoughts, NASCAR throws out the white flag signaling one lap to go. The cars are coming down to cross the start/finish line, to begin the last lap of the race. I want to jump down onto pit road with the rest of the crew, but I'm scared I will miss something. This is so intense.

Ryan maintains his fraction of a lead through turn one, then turn two. The cars come down the back field one last time, sparkling under the bright lights of Daytona International Speedway. It's anyone's race at this point. I watch the monitor intently as the cars speed into turn three. Garrett gets a run on Matt, the driver on the inside draft lane. Matt checks up, and Garrett plows him from behind but keeps on moving, never missing a beat. Matt's Ford stock car makes a hard left turn off the track and spins into the grass, but no caution flag is thrown.

Ryan and Garrett are now racing nose to nose within a matter of seconds. The dueling Carter cars throttle out of turn four and drag race to the finish line. Both cars have solid drafting partners, and it's like a train wreck—I can't take my eyes off of what is happening, but the intense action is about to send me into heart failure. I don't even look at Ben; I focus on the monitor. Come on, Ryan! Come on!

The crowd is going absolutely crazy and have been standing on their feet for these last spectacular laps. Ryan and Garrett barrel down to the finish line. The checkered flag is waving, and Garrett takes the win by only a fraction of a second. *Oh my God!* I don't know whether to laugh or cry. Technically, I work for them both, so a win is a win either way, but I desperately wanted Ryan to win.

"Son of a bitch!" Ben exclaims, breaking me from my reverie. "Come on, let's go down! I knew that bastard had something up his sleeve."

I can hear the radio crackle with banter between Bobby, Mike, Garrett, and Ryan, but there are too many people talking to keep up with the conversation. I hope Ryan isn't pissed. I take off my headset and jump down off the pit box as Garrett and Ryan bring their cars down across the finish line again. Both Chevrolets accelerate and spin simultaneously across the Daytona International Speedway logo imbedded in the infield grass. The crowd roars!

The cars stop, and I can see both drivers removing their safety gear to exit the cars. Both of our teams rush out to meet them, and I walk with Ben out to the madness. Ryan rushes over to Garrett, and they embrace. *He isn't mad!* The Carter boys wave to the crowd in celebration. What a wonderful moment between father and son, a duel to the end resulting in a one-two finish for GCR Racing at Daytona.

Behind us, I hear a sudden commotion. I turn away quickly to see Matt, the driver Garrett wrecked, angrily approaching us. He shouts loudly and incoherently, but in the midst of the celebration, all I can understand is that he is pissed. Maxwell appears out of nowhere and quickly intercedes with a throng of NASCAR officials. After Matt is removed, officials break up our teams' infield celebration and order us over to victory lane.

It is insanity. Garrett is actively arguing with some person I do not know but who appears to be in the NASCAR organization. Garrett says the race was way too close to call and insists to the NASCAR officials that Ryan share this victory with him! Since he is Garrett Ryan Carter Sr., they don't argue with him. With two cars, two teams, and a horde of media swarming the platform, I can't even get over to Ryan to congratulate him. I am stuck on Garrett's team's side as the awards ceremony begins.

Fireworks explode, and ticker tape erupts from sky. That's when the beer and champagne flies, even more so from Ryan's side. I am thankful now to be stuck with Garrett's team so that I don't get soaked. After the trophy presentation, the media descends. I manage to squirrel my way through the crowd to Ryan. Our eyes meet and he immediately reaches out for my hand to pull me through the crowd. In the midst of the madness, I believe he is about to draw me into his arms, but he stops himself. We stand stock-still in the middle of hundreds of excited people, locked in a heated gaze. The look on his face makes my stomach flip-flop. I raise my eyebrows to him in warning. I tighten my grip on his hand, then release it quickly.

"Congratulations!" I yell over the crowd.

"How fucking awesome was that?" Ryan says, grinning from ear to ear, and I desperately want to kiss him.

I laugh and nod. "Yes, it was great!"

And just like that, Ryan is pulled away from me and thrust back in front of a camera. And in the mass chaos, I lose him again. It's OK, though. My job is done for the day. Plus, I need to make my way to the airport.

It's almost midnight. I know the celebrations for Garrett's win will go well into the night, but I don't want to miss my plane. I want to be home to sleep in my own bed and enjoy my day off tomorrow, the rarity that it is.

Chapter 27

Luckily, the Daytona Beach International Airport is right next door to the super-speedway. Planes have been actively taking off for the last couple of hours carrying drivers and their families back to Charlotte. After the hat dance and a few hundred pictures, I arrive at the airport in plenty of time and easily waltz through security, probably because it's so late. When I get to the gate, I learn that my flight has been delayed for two hours. *Great!*

I locate a seat and attempt to make myself comfortable for the time being. I check my cell phone. There is a new message from Brooke.

Trial this week, maybe next Monday?

I nod to myself, though disheartened. But, I guess I have waited this long. Another week will not make a difference. I type back to Brooke:

ok☺

Thankfully, the plane ride home is a short one. I take out my iPod and secure my earbuds. I wonder what she has in store for me tonight as I hit shuffle. *Ahhh!* Norah Jones. She jazzily croons, "Come away with me in the night."

Nice, Norah. I laugh at the irony. It is night, and I am going away. However, I am alone. I laugh to myself. As Norah continues to sing in my ears with her sultry voice, I long for Ryan. It would be nice if he were here, but things are way more complicated between us than the simple journey Norah sings about.

I take out my iPad to pass the time. I start preparing a few press releases and sponsorship letters in conclusion to tonight's race, which means fewer things that I will have to do on Monday. I am fiercely typing out my thoughts when I am roughly tapped on the shoulder. Instinctively, I jump, almost dropping my iPad to the floor.

I look up and into the beautiful yet smug face of Ryan Carter. I scramble to gain my composure.

"Can't believe you just left like that!" he says suspiciously, but I am confused.

I mutter an apology. "I'm sorry. I didn't want to interfere. Plus, I didn't want to miss my plane."

He raises his eyebrows at me. "Why aren't you on the plane?"

I flush and stammer, "I...I just found out that it is delayed for two hours." I steal a glance at the time on my iPad. "Well...only by an hour now." I smile nervously. Since when does he make me nervous? *Since you started sleeping with him. Yes, that's when.*

Ryan reaches down to grab my rolling suitcase. "Let's go!"

Confused again, I ask, "Where?"

"My dad chartered a private plane, and it is about to pull out of the gate."

I exclaim, "Uh, no way! I am not gonna intrude, *and* your parents will be on the plane, and that would just be weird."

I can tell I have agitated Ryan, but he calmly says, "Whitney, cut the crap! Get on the damn plane!"

I raise my eyebrows at him and square my shoulders in preparation for another fight. Just as I am about to defend my position, I hear someone approach me from behind and say, "Get on the damn plane, Whitney!"

I whip my head around. It's Garrett!

Ryan and Garrett both laugh at my reaction. They don't give me the opportunity to argue. They trot off together through the private gate. I reach down to quickly gather my things and catch up with them, then walk through the gate and step out directly onto the tarmac. Ryan turns to make sure that I am following, but he is locked in a sideways embrace with his dad as they walk up to the private jet. It has been a wonderful night for them, and I am so glad they were able to share such a great experience.

As I climb up the stairs, I realize that I have never been on a private plane before. A girl could get used to this. I follow Ryan, and he directs me to a seat in the back of the plane. The plane is small, but it is incredibly comfortable. There is an empty seat beside mine, which I hope Ryan plans to take; although, I am not sure how to act in front of his dad. *Professional, Whitney! That's how you act*, I remind myself.

Several other people I recognize from Garrett's team get on the plane. I smile politely to them as they all congratulate Garrett and

Ryan. Ryan's mom follows shortly behind them, though she doesn't acknowledge my presence on the aircraft. Ryan slides into the empty seat next to mine. I beam up at him, relieved.

He motions to all those surrounding his dad and yells out, "I let him win, you know!"

I gawk at Ryan as a round of shouts and comments fly back to him. I know better. "Yeah right!"

He smiles smugly back at me and gives me a wink. *Bastard! My bastard!*

The plane takes off smoothly as we say our good-byes to the lights of the Daytona International Speedway. I have determined that night races are my favorite. Ryan and I continue to make small talk, but I am too tired to conversationally function. I lay my head back on the comfortable headrest and drift off.

It feels like I have just floated into a deep sleep when I feel Ryan rouse me from my slumber, "Hey," he says softly.

I groan quietly.

"We are about to land," he says.

As soon as he says those words, the landing gear pops out from underneath us, and immediately I am awake. That loud sound scares me senseless every time.

I am so unbelievably tired. It has been an emotionally, mentally, and physically exhausting week. Ryan helps me with my bags as the other passengers quickly leave the plane ahead of us.

"What lot is your car in?" Ryan asks as we walk across the tarmac alone.

I have to think a moment, but my brain won't function. Then I remember. "I took a cab here. I always take a cab to the airport. I'll just take a cab home," I say sleepily.

Ryan rolls his eyes at me. "If you think for one minute that I'm gonna let you take a cab alone at this hour, you are crazy! And, you're not going to your apartment."

What!

"Ryan," I whine, "it's so late! I am so tired, please! Where are we going?"

He simply replies, "Home."

At this point, I'm too tired to argue, and really, there is no place that I would rather be. I willingly follow Ryan to his car parked in the private lot.

Due to the time of night, or early morning, I should say, we arrive at Ryan's house about forty-five minutes later. I have never spent the night here, with the exception of sofa. I am not sure what he expects or where I should sleep, for that matter.

I must have a distressed look on my face because Ryan asks, "What's wrong?"

"I...I can just sleep on the couch," I stammer. I look back at Ryan, who looks pissed.

"Whitney, it is far too late for your shit!" he says angrily. "Get in the damn bed!"

I groan. "I...I need a shower, I think," I plead sleepily.

Ryan nods his head in agreement as he drops our bags to the floor. "So do I."

Oh my!

By the time we climb into Ryan's bed, it is almost 4:00 a.m. I am asleep before my head hits the pillow. Ryan nudges me, but I am still too groggy to move.

"Whitney, wake up!"

I open my eyes and can see light filtering through the closed blinds. "What time is it?" I ask drowsily.

"It's almost eleven a.m."

He is far too chipper after only seven hours of sleep. But they were glorious hours wrapped up in Ryan's embrace. I groan audibly. Ryan is awake and already dressed. *When did this happen?*

It takes me a minute to assimilate myself. Once I do, I close my eyes again, hoping he goes away and lets me sleep. I don't move. I am far too comfortable.

Ryan says, "Come on. I want you to go somewhere with me."

Whoa! Wait! What!

"Ryan!" I exclaim, now fully awake. I sit up automatically. "This is my only day off. Please let me sleep!"

He shakes his head and kneels down beside the bed. "Please don't argue with me. I need you to have an open mind. OK?"

"Where are we going?" I whine.

"Out!"

My heart falls to my feet. "Out! Where? What if someone sees us?"

"I don't give a shit anymore!" he exclaims. "All I wanted was to be able to hold you and have you celebrate with me, by my side. It was hard for me."

Oh!

"But Ryan," I whine at him, shaking off his heartfelt statement, "I don't think I have any clean clothes!"

He laughs. "We already solved that problem once, remember?"

I roll my sleepy blue eyes at him and fall back onto his pillow. "It is way too early for jokes!" I snap. "I cannot believe that you have just sprung this on me like it's no big deal."

He laughs at my distress. "Honestly, Whitney, it really isn't."

I put my head in my hands. I can't think. I am overacting as usual. *Get it together*, I scold myself.

Ryan turns around and strides out of the room. "You'll be fine! I made some coffee. I am going to get your other suitcase from the car."

I groan loudly again, but anxiety takes over. I have gone from sleeping soundly to majorly stressed out about going "out" to God knows where with Ryan. I get up from the bed and wander idly to the kitchen. Ryan has the best coffee. I make myself a steaming cup and sit at the bar trying to get my thoughts straight. The only thing my brain can recall is Ryan commanding me to his bed, but not before our *ahh!mazing* shower last night. I sigh loudly. I run my arm against the cool granite countertop and lay my head down on my arm wearily. There is a slight rain falling outside, and its overcast. Just like the last time I spent the night here. It is the perfect weather to sleep all day. *Ugh! Why did Ryan have to wake me up?* Maybe I can convince him to come back to bed with me. I sigh.

I have almost fallen back asleep with my head on the countertop when I am broken from my sweet recollections by a loud rapping on the back patio door. It scares me. I sit up on the barstool, but before I can process what is happening, I hear the doorknob rattle and the door crack. I jump up and fall backward off my barstool. *Shit!* I manage to stand upright on the floor, but the door swings open before I can hide.

I turn around suddenly and look into the eyes of Garrett Carter. I shriek! He is amused. I am quickly aware that I am wearing only a T-shirt that barely covers my bottom. I hop like a scared rabbit around the other side of the island to cover myself, and Garrett laughs at me. I am beyond mortified.

"Miss Parker," Garrett says, "Good morning!"

I flush. This is death by embarrassment. "I...uh...Hi...umm...Good morning!" I mutter.

About the same time, Ryan rounds the corner. "Whitney, I have your suitcase..." But he trails off when he sees me locked in an awkward moment with his father. He doesn't miss a beat. "Where did you come from?" Ryan looks back to me, then back to his dad and laughs. "What did you do? Scare the hell out of her?"

Garrett laughs. "I think that is a fair assessment."

I'm glad that they are both amused at my expense.

I smile sheepishly. Garrett doesn't seem surprised to see me here. *What is going on?*

"I just came down here to give you all a friendly warning." Garrett looks to Ryan. "Your mother is excited about Whitney coming to eat brunch with us today."

Brunch?

"She had me shining up the crystal at eight a.m. So, y'all better get your butts dressed and up to the house real quick." He chuckles as he spouts out his warning.

"Brunch!" I exclaim as I whip my head around to Ryan. He smiles cautiously at me because he knows I am about to erupt. He knows the signs. I throw up my hands in distress. "Well! I am so glad everyone knows about this but me!"

Garrett laughs out loud. "Well...I guess I will leave you two alone to sort that out! Don't be late!" With those words of caution, he is gone.

Ryan turns back to me and quips, "You heard the man. Get ready!"

I finally manage to breathe, then shout, "Ryan! I think I'm going into heart failure!" He laughs and shakes his head. "Brunch with your mom? This is just too much. And your dad, too? I am absolutely mortified. Why was he not surprised to see me here?"

Ryan rolls his eyes at me. "He knows about you. Both of them know."

What? My eyes open wide with surprise. *Since when?*

"I tell my dad everything, Whitney. He is my best friend. In fact, he told me that I was stupid if I didn't go for it with you, especially after you straightened my ass out that day in the boardroom." I am still at a loss for words, so Ryan continues, "He said you remind him of my mother!" He laughs as he recalls their conversation. I, however, I am not finding anything funny at the moment.

"Jesus, Ryan! When were you planning to tell me all of this?"

He laughs, "When we pulled up in their driveway!"

Chapter 28

Thankfully, we are not too late for his mother's brunch. My anxiety is at an all-time high. Apparently, Laura knows that Ryan's and my relationship goes further than the track, too, and she is very welcoming. She has cooked a delicious meal, and I must have been as hungry as I was tired. Their family dynamic is something to behold. I love it. From the inside, they look like your typical family. You would never know that they were racing royalty.

Garrett and Ryan talk actively about last night's race. While I help his mom clear the dishes, she asks me tons of questions related to my upbringing and my home in Georgia, no doubt in an attempt to give me a proper background check. *Who would blame her, though?*

After brunch, Ryan takes me on a golf cart tour of the Carter family farm, which is close to five hundred acres. The land is absolutely beautiful. The rain has let up but dark clouds still hang in the sky making this July day cooler than normal. He takes us on a trail that leads to what looks like a family cemetery plot embedded in the pine trees. I look up at Ryan inquisitively.

"This is my family's final resting place." He points to one gravestone. "That is my grandfather, Garrison." I nod to him, as I recognize the name on the headstone. Ryan looks at me funny. "How do you know about him?"

I smile. "The day that we had our argument in the boardroom, your dad took me into the museum to talk to me, and he told me about him."

"Really?" Ryan looks shocked. "My dad never speaks of him."

I shrug. "I asked him. I...I didn't know."

Ryan's eyes widen, and then he smiles. "Wow! You must have the same effect on everyone!"

I raise my eyebrow at him. "What do you mean?"

Ryan pulls me into an affectionate embrace, leaving soft kisses along my cheek. "You have this way about you, Whitney," he says. "You make people feel comfortable, I guess."

I smile at his compliment.

Ryan takes a step back and clears a few leaves off his grandfather's headstone. "He and my dad had a very strained relationship, but he was always desperate for his approval, even in his death. He was a very hard man, but a few days before he passed, he finally told my dad how much he loved him and how proud he was of him. I guess that is why my dad is the way he is with me." He shrugs.

I smile because I know. "It is a great relationship to have, Ryan. Don't ever take it for granted," I say, but I know Ryan knows that. He takes my hand and leads me back to the golf cart.

As I sit down, Ryan turns to face me and looks at me with some mixed emotion that I cannot understand. "Whitney, I...I meant what I said this morning." I watch his face intently as he looks like he is having some type of internal struggle. "It was hard for me last night, not being able to hold you and celebrate with you. And I don't know have any answers about what we should do, but I do know that I don't want to be conflicted with that decision again!"

What is he saying?

Does he mean he is ready to go public with us, our relationship? He may be, but I'm not so sure that I am. It has only been a few weeks. I shift uncomfortably in my seat, unsure of how I feel about of his declaration and his honesty, but Ryan doesn't give me a chance to respond. Without another word, he grabs the steering wheel, and we begin our journey back up to his home. I snuggle into Ryan's embrace as we drive. It is a tender moment between us, and I leave those questions alone in my head. It has been a great day, and I don't want to complicate things any further. If it ain't broke, eh?

"You wanna go back to sleep?" Ryan says, bringing me back from my deep thoughts.

"Yes, I would love an afternoon nap with you," I say softly as we pull back into his garage, but I know sleep is the farthest thing from his mind.

Chapter 29

This weekend is one of the toughest ovals in motor sports, Loudon. Ryan says it is an intense track, with high speeds exceeding 145 miles per hour and sharp corners all condensed into a one-mile radius, which has caused several racing tragedies at New Hampshire Motor Speedway. Remembering his stories of past accidents sends chills down my spine. Ryan will be rounding this short track about three hundred times today. That task in itself seems impossible to me.

The anticipation for today's race has been building since qualifying on Friday. Ryan secured pole with a qualifying time of 27.81 seconds, which means excellent field and pit position—not to mention the coup de grace of winning the pole position in back-to-back weekends. Word around the garage is that Ryan has the car to beat. I am so excited that I was not able to sleep at all last night, especially alone in my hotel room.

Overnight, it seems our relationship has advanced to the next level due to Ryan's recent revelations. And now his parents know, but that is all for now. I don't like to be away from Ryan, but I refuse to sleep in his million-dollar luxury bus that stays parked in the infield during race weekend. It is his haven away from the madness.

Ryan needs to be focused on the race and finishing well. The story of us complicates that, I am sure of it. Plus, I don't want anyone else to know about us yet. I am not comfortable with my job being under scrutiny from Jerri, or any of my other coworkers for that matter. After I pleaded my case late Sunday night after brunch with his parents, Ryan agreed, but only after I agreed to stay with him during the week. My heart swells at the memory because it is still hard to believe that he wants me around at all, not to mention sleeping in his bed.

I arrive at the track early, and Ryan and I attend all of the events together. It's hard for me not be affectionate with him, but I maintain a safe distance. At the morning devotional, which is much like a normal church service for the drivers at the track, I look up at Ryan as he listens intently to the speaker. All I want is to be able to hold his hand. He looks down at me and smiles, a gesture that makes me believe he feels the same way too. I look back to the speaker, trying to focus on his message, but I can't concentrate. I look around the room at all the drivers, their families, and team employees in attendance. My eyes immediately meet up with Colton's. I notice him watching me closely, and my stomach turns. I have not seen or spoken to Colton since our intense moment in the garage at Daytona. I smile cautiously at him. He gives me a look that I am suspicious of, a look that makes me think he knows about my relationship with Ryan. Then again, I could be paranoid.

After the national anthem and invocation, Ryan crawls into his #62 Chevrolet for three hundred miles at the New Hampshire Motor Speedway. I am about to make my way to my seat over pit road, when Ryan motions for me. I quickly return to his car and lean over into the window. He covers his speaker so Bobby, his crew chief, or Mike, his spotter, cannot hear our exchange.

"I changed my mind," Ryan says softly.

"Oh! What about?" I say, confused.

"I'm not sleeping without you anymore! I want you on the bus with me from now on," he commands almost in a whisper.

I know now is not the time to argue, so I smile smugly but feel like my heart is going to burst out of my chest with happiness. I don't have the strength or desire to tell him no. "Is that an order, Mr. Carter?" I question jokingly.

"Yes, it is!" Ryan snaps back at me.

I laugh, "Whatever you say, RFC!"

He winks at me as he closes his helmet shield! *Oh! I love that!*

Ryan secures his window net in place as a celebrity gives the traditional "start your engines" call. Forty-four stock car engines roar to life, as does the blood in my veins. Ryan was right about the adrenaline rush, which is still overwhelming to me, but I love it. It is addictive. I scramble up to my seat next to Ben in the pit box overlooking pit road. It is an absolutely gorgeous Sunday afternoon in New England. The temperature is about ninety degrees with a slight breeze, but that is nothing compared to the heat and humidity last week in Daytona.

I am giddy like an errant teenager, which must show on my face, because Ben asks, "Is everything okay, Whitney?"

I smile like I have a grand secret because, of course, I do. "Yes. Everything is perfect!" For once in my life, I truly believe that everything is.

The race begins and is fairly uneventful, mainly because Ryan is dominating the track. He is executing all the right moves. Plus, his pit crew is cranking out awesome times today. They are all still on a high from Daytona. It looks like Ryan will be making a trip to victory lane as the race laps quickly count down. It is exciting. I wonder how I am supposed to act if he wins. How will Ryan act?

I am broken from my daydreams of the winner's circle due to a scheduled pit stop. Ryan takes on four new tires and a full tank of gas. There are no other adjustments that need to be made. His Chevrolet is on time today. But before Ryan can speed away from his pit box, Colton comes from out of nowhere to beat him off pit road. *Where did he come from?* I hear Ryan ask the same question over his radio frequency. I look over to Ben, who only shakes his head at me in confusion.

There is no way Colton could have beaten Ryan off pit road because he qualified poorly and has a pit stall way in the back. I don't understand. I listen intently to the communications between Mike, Ryan, and Bobby. The radio correspondence that I am tuned in to helps me clear the air.

Apparently, Colton took on only two tires in that scheduled stop even though it called for four. Ryan takes the track back effortlessly from Colton, but he refuses to move his obviously slower car out of the way. Colton keeps shifting his car to block any pass attempts made by Ryan.

What is this about? Does it have something to do with the look Colton gave me in the service this morning? A pool of dread bottoms out in my stomach, making me nauseous.

I take a deep breath as I watch the monitor in disbelief. Ben steals a nervous glance over at me. He, too, is anxious.

Ryan explodes through the radio, "What the fuck is he doing? Mike! Tell him to get the hell out of my way!"

I cringe at his sharp words and frustration. Ryan is hot, literally. I need to caution Bobby about Ryan's language, but I know now is not the time.

I hear another series of conversations between Ryan, Mike, and Bobby. Mike is consulting with Colton's spotter as Bobby heads down pit road to speak to Colton's crew chief. What is happening? I don't understand. Even though Ryan and Colton don't get along, they are still teammates. I stand up and begin to pace the pit box, but it doesn't help my nerves, so I sit back down.

Ben and I sit in shocked silence as we watch the monitor. I hear a NASCAR official begin to get involved with Bobby. Hopefully, NASCAR will black-flag Colton. His actions are just unprofessional, not to mention out of character.

Finally, Ryan is able negotiate a pass high on the right side entering turn three. I can hear Mike guiding him through the turn. He almost clears the #58 Chevrolet, when Colton drifts up intentionally and rams into Ryan's stock car.

Oh No!

Ryan's car slams hard into the wall of turn three at 139 miles per hour. His car bounces off the wall, ricochets back down the track, and clips Colton's Chevrolet, which causes them both to spin violently into turn four. I jump to my feet instinctively. A million things flash through my mind, but the most prominent are Ryan's stories of the horrible accidents at this track. I am unable to stifle the sob in my throat.

"Oh my God!" I cover my mouth with my hand.

My reaction takes Ben by surprise. He reaches over to take my hand. "It's OK, Whitney," he says softly to reassure me even though he doesn't look as confident.

Ryan is silent over the radio even though he is prompted by Mike and Bobby to speak. He didn't hit head the curve head on, but I know it's bad. The impact alone, especially at that speed, could kill him. *Please God no!* I fight the thoughts away. I listen carefully over the frequency, willing Ryan to speak. I hear nothing from him. Again, both Bobby and Mike call out to Ryan, but still no response. His car rests in the infield grass out of turn four, smoking.

I feel like hours have passed, but it has been only a matter of seconds. Sweat is running down my back, a lump is suffocating me in my throat, and the blood in my veins is searing. If it was not for the adrenaline, I am sure tears would be flowing freely, too.

Finally, the radio crackles, and I hear Ryan's voice. "Sorry, guys, I thought I was clear."

Ryan! I fall back into my seat feeling dizzy and nauseous.

Ben looks ashen too. "Whew," he says as he releases my hand to rub his own head in relief.

Ryan is OK. However, this situation is not good. I can feel it in the air, like that Phil Collins song. I sit helplessly over pit road as Ryan pulls his battered car into his assigned box. The crew hastily begins working to repair the damage to Ryan's Chevrolet. It's bad and I know it. Within seconds, sheets of metal fly off, new tires go on, and a mallet loudly hammers out a dent in the front fender.

Ryan is unnervingly quiet over the radio. My instinct tells me that this must be the calm before the storm.

"Go! Go! Go!" the pit crew calls out, and Ryan pulls out to head back to the track. I and the rest of Ryan's management team sit in silence, intently listening to his radio transmissions.

My stomach churns with pure trepidation. Ryan's spotter guides him back onto the track, and I can hear the car accelerate. I watch the monitor as he negotiates the first turn. *So far so good!* Then the second turn. He comes out of it smoothly and hits the gas to thunder down the straightaway. We have lost precious positions, not to mention we are several laps down, but if anyone can turn this around, it's Ryan.

Within seconds, I hear a noise from inside the car, and Ryan sprays our ears with a stream of horrible expletives. "That motherfucking son of a bitch!"

I wince. That outburst is going to warrant a penalty from NASCAR, and I make a mental note to do damage control. I can hear Bobby speaking to Ryan in terms that, of course, I don't understand.

Bobby takes off his headset and slams it to the ground. "We're out! Something broke in back! Ryan isn't sure what!" He looks at me. "Whitney, you better get over to the garage quick!"

I know exactly what he means. I don't even think. I jump up and off the pit box. Ryan is mad as hell and guaranteed to make a scene. His language over the radio has already assured him a fine from NASCAR, but we definitely do not need a suspension to boot.

Adrenaline and anger fuel my pace as I run to the garage area. I make it over there in time to see Colton stopping his damaged car in the middle of the lane. I stop in front of his car and throw up my hands.

"What the hell?" I shout at him as he jumps out of his car, abandoning it in the middle of the roadway. Colton ignores me, so I hit the front hood of his car. "You clipped Ryan on purpose, Colton!"

Colton rips off his helmet and throws it angrily into his car. "I guess you decided to violate company policy after all."

I am confused, but then my internal light bulb goes off. *He knows. Shit! Deny! Deny! Deny!* "I don't know what you are talking about."

Colton is furious. He walks angrily toward me, scaring me. He jumps up in my face and grabs me by my left arm, above my elbow. "Why him? Why that son of bitch?"

I wince in pain from his grip on my arm. "Colton, I don't know what you are talking about!" I continue to lie and try to wriggle from his grasp, but he clamps down harder. Ryan's warning comes to my mind from Daytona. *"If he lays another hand on you..."* I shudder.

"Come on, Whitney! I saw you with him this morning at chapel. I saw the way you looked at him. I am not stupid."

I try in vain to come up with a believable story, but I am not good under pressure. Colton eyes me with utter contempt. I can't breathe, and panic has stricken my chest. "You are mistaken..." I say, but before I can respond any further to Colton's tirade, we both turn to acknowledge the sound of an injured car roaring into the garage area. *It's Ryan!* However, instead of slowing down, he guns the gas pedal to accelerate his engine, which is still in working order. The engine roars, and Ryan slams his car into the back of Colton's Chevrolet.

Colton instinctively jumps out of the way, but I am frozen where I stand. I can't move. The force of the collision causes Colton's car to advance forward, clipping me under the knee. I hear a sickening crack, but the impact throws me up into the air and a few feet away before I hit the concrete facedown with a thud. I look up in time to see the front of Colton's green stock car roll over the top of my shoulder, crushing me to the ground and suffocating me like a thick, heavy blanket.

The commotion is deafening to my ears, and I can't assimilate the aftermath. I hear many unfamiliar voices and incoherent shouts. I try to speak, cry out, but my voice fails me. I try to move, but my body does not obey my commands. I am pinned under Colton's car, wedged between the tire and the front spoiler, but strangely, I feel no pain.

I somehow manage to reach out my hand. Suddenly, it is grasped by a familiar touch. *Ryan!*

I recognize Colton's voice as he shouts out to Ryan, "Don't! Don't touch her! We don't know how badly hurt she is!"

Hurt! Am I hurt? The shock of the accident must be taking over. Ryan releases my hand. *No, please! Don't leave me!* I hear more commotion and shouts, then what sounds like a scuffle.

I begin to feel disoriented, and an intense panic starts to well up in my chest. I scream out in my head because my voice won't obey me. Then, the overwhelming smell of gasoline and burned tire rubber takes what's left of the air from my lungs. As I try to breathe, I hear a series of shouts, "One! Two! Three! Lift!" Suddenly, blinding light rips my eyes as the car is pulled away and the pain rages. There is a searing pain in my shoulder, neck, and back.

It hurts. Everywhere. Instantly, strong arms pull me up from the asphalt. Ryan is on the ground with me, pulling me into his arms. "Whitney!" he exclaims. "Look at me!" I recognize his voice, but am unable to focus on his face. I cry out in pain as hot tears flood my face.

"Whitney! Damn it! Please! Look at me!" I can hear the anguish in his voice

I manage to look up into Ryan's distressed blue eyes before the over-powering darkness takes over.

Chapter 30

I awake in a small, quiet hospital room. It is peaceful. The only sounds present are the hums and beeps of the medical equipment that keeps track of my vital signs. The sounds are welcome and soothing. After the horrible commotion in my ears at the track, this quietness is therapeutic.

It takes me a few minutes to adapt to my surroundings. The room is dark, but I can see Jerri sitting in a chair to my left. *How did she get here?* She looks frazzled, like she has aged in the last couple of hours. God bless her. She has looked after me like my mother since I started at GCR. Over in the right corner, Ryan sits hunched over with his head in his hands. He still has on his tracksuit, but I can't tell if he is asleep or awake. I begin to feel dizzy and nauseous.

I close my eyes to steady myself. Suddenly, the memory of being pinned under Colton's Chevrolet comes barreling through my mind. I can still smell the gasoline. A sob wells up in my throat. Why can't I be one of those people who forgets what happens in a traumatic accident? I am afraid to open my eyes to look at my wounds. If I am in the hospital, it must be bad.

Carefully, I open my eyes again. I slowly survey the damage on my body. I can't see my head or face, but I can feel a patch of cotton with tape over my left cheek. *I bet that's pretty!* My head...eww! It's throbbing! I look down. My arms are good, though marred with several scratches and bruises, but the small fingerprint marks above my left elbow bring tears to my eyes. Those purple bruises are from Colton, not from the accident. I close my eyes as I remember the fiery look in his eyes and how angry he was. I shudder at that memory.

I have an IV secured in my right arm that must be providing some type of medication or fluids. I'm not sure which, or maybe it's both. My eyes move to my legs. My left leg is propped up under several pillows and is cast from the thigh down. I gasp out and the sob escapes from my throat, "Oh no!"

My sudden outburst alarms Jerri and Ryan. They jump up, shocked that I am awake, and are both immediately by my side.

"Oh, honey, are you in pain?" Jerri offers with a pained look of concern on her face. I nod. "Let me get the nurse for you."

Ryan interjects softly. "No...I'll go." I can't bear to look at him. I am unsure of my emotions, and I pray not to make a scene in front of Jerri. I close my eyes and offer up that silent prayer.

Jerri begins to speak softly. "Your mother is on her way from Georgia, and I have released a statement."

"Thank you," I whisper. "What do you need me to do for damage control?"

Jerri gapes at me. "Oh honey! We will handle all this. It is being taken care of as we speak. Please don't worry! I need you to focus on getting better, which you will have plenty of time to do."

I am confused. I give her a questioning look.

Jerri proceeds to tell me that Ryan has been suspended from racing for six weeks because of the accident, and that Colton has been fired from GCR Racing altogether. *Oh God!* It is too much information for me to take in at the moment. I raise my hand, signaling her to stop. Jerri nods her head knowingly at me.

Before she can go into any more details, Ryan returns with my nurse. She goes through a series of vital checks.

"My head is throbbing," I say to her.

"That is to be expected," she responds sympathetically and shoots a very disapproving look to Ryan. "You took a nasty fall, not to mention the amount of fumes that you inhaled."

I notice Ryan running his hands through his disheveled hair and pacing the floor. Jerri is watching him warily. The nurse adjusts the oxygen tube under my nose, then steps away to retrieve a pain reliever for my head.

Jerri steps back to my side, and I remember what she said earlier about my parents. "My mom is on her way to New Hampshire?" I question.

Jerri smiles. "No...honey, I am sorry. You're back in Charlotte. Garrett had you airlifted from Loudon's infield care center to Carolinas Medical Center once you were stable enough."

Oh!

"Once we knew the extent of your injuries, he wanted you here with his doctors for the surgery."

Surgery!

"What day is it?" I ask, tears forming in my eyes.

Jerri smiles. "It is Monday."

"But..." I stammer because I don't understand. "Ryan still has on his fire suit."

Jerri looks over to Ryan, who is back to his perch in the corner, watching us intently. "He refused to leave you. He flew in the helicopter with you."

My eyes widen with shock.

"I have never seen him like this." She mumbles the last statement softly. "Oh, and your friend Brooke, she has been here since you arrived, but she had to leave to take a deposition. Ryan called her."

Oh no! Brooke and Ryan together. What did he tell her?

Jerri eyes the look of distress on my face. "Sweetheart, this is a lot of information right now. I will fill you in on all the details. You are going to be just fine. Please rest." She sighs and looks to the nurse as she reenters the room to administer my medication.

As soon as the nurse retreats again, Ryan is by my side and takes my hand. I steal a nervous look at Jerri, who is watching us intently. I turn back to Ryan, who I am forced to look at now. A huge sob wells up and out of my throat, cascading over my whole body.

"Hey," Ryan whispers as he tightens the grip on my hand. "It's OK." His words summon the tears from my eyes, and they spill out onto my cheeks. Ryan reaches up and gently caresses my face with his other hand.

Through my blurred vision, I look to Jerri. She looks to me, then back to Ryan, confused. Then, within an instant, I know she knows. She has just witnessed this intimate moment between us, and now she knows there is more between Ryan and me than work. Suddenly, I am embarrassed and ashamed of what I have done. I give Jerri a tearful apologetic look, then shift my gaze toward the ceiling as she quietly walks out of my room, leaving us alone.

The tears fall harder now. I believe they have been building from the time I moved to Charlotte over six weeks ago, and today's accident was the coup de grace. Ryan takes a seat in the chair beside my bed, but doesn't remove his tight grip on my hand. He tries to calm me.

"Shhh..."

I am glad that he doesn't say any more. There is too much to say, and I wouldn't even know where to begin. I am thankful for his silence, too, because I'm groggy from the medication. Trauma and tears take over my body, and I succumb to the darkness again.

* * *

When I awake again, I notice that Ryan has not moved, but is asleep in the chair. I shift slightly and release my hand from his. He moves somewhat, but doesn't wake up. He looks disheveled. I want to reach out to touch him, to comfort him, but I don't. He doesn't deserve it. His trademark attitude and arrogance are the reasons why I am lying in this hospital bed. It seems that I have awakened with some new determination. I have been slapped in the face with a new resolve. And now I know what I have to do.

Ryan shifts and opens his eyes. He looks at me intently when he finds my eyes fixed on him. "Are you OK?" He speaks softly.

I nod, stock still. "Ryan, it is probably best if you go," I say quickly and calmly while I have the strength.

A look of shocked horror washes over his face. "Whitney! Why? I'm not leaving you," he says firmly.

Tears spring to my eyes, and I look away. "I can't do this anymore," I say quietly. "Just please go."

"Whitney, please..." he pleads.

I hold up my IV-laced arm to stop him from speaking further.

Ryan fumbles, shocked from my dismissal. "Whit, please!"

I close my eyes to remove the hurt look on his face from my mind, but I can still hear his wounded voice.

Desperate, Ryan stammers, "I...I...I swear I never saw you..."

I shake my head at him, not wanting to hear what he has to say. I can't bear it.

Even though his actions, anger, and hot temper are the reasons that I lie in the hospital bed, my actions and my choices were the catalyst for it all. I recognize that now. Although I tried to do what was right with Colton, it all blew up in my face, literally. Now, Ryan is suspended, and Colton is out of a job, which completes the trifecta.

"I will turn in my resignation to Jerri tomorrow," I add quickly.

In frustration, Ryan paces the room. He is furious. He tries to meet my gaze, but I continue to stare into space. He quickly retreats to my side. "Whitney, look at me!"

I comply, and his eyes search mine.

"We can get through this. I know we can!" he exclaims.

The sobs creep back up into my throat, and I couldn't speak even if I wanted to, so I simply shake my head with my eyes closed.

I take a deep breath with the help of the oxygen tube under my nose, but my chest lurches in pain. "Ryan, I am sorry," I manage to say softly. What I am apologizing for is unknown to me at the moment.

Ryan stands firm and snaps, "No!"

The distress in his voice is enough to throw me over the edge. Tears flood my cheeks and burn the injury to my face. I am so embarrassed that I can't control them. Ryan walks to my other side so that I am forced to look up at him. I can't bear it. I can't look at him, or I know I will change my mind. I look up to the ceiling as tears steadily flow down my cheeks.

Ryan pleads with me once more, "Whitney! Why are you doing this?" And then suddenly it's quiet.

I feel him leave, and the small click of the hospital room door confirms that Ryan Carter has left the building. As the door closes, panic seizes my chest again, this time with ardent force. The tears that flow like a river down my face ignite a raging rapid of sobs that rack my body. I can't fight them. I can't even breathe. It took everything I had to make Ryan leave.

This emotional trauma is reflected in my physical vital signs because my monitors ring out in alarm. Within a moment, Jerri and a throng of nurses flood my room. I am surrounded by a circle of wide-eyed caregivers who are desperate and determined to find out the cause for alarm. Jerri must know, but she stands silent in the back with an anxious look all her own.

Several nurses frantically shout a series of incoherent questions at me while another one administers a drug into my IV. I hope whatever she slipped me takes the agonizing pain from my chest. The pain paired with the sobs make it impossible for me to speak or even breathe. I am able to make out the word "shock" from one nurse. Yes, shock would be right, but not from the trauma of the accident. It would be shock from the trauma of a broken heart. And those are my last thoughts as darkness consumes me again.

* * *

I don't know how long I have been sedated, but I begin to hear voices. I feel woozy and disoriented. Where am I? I stir around in my bed, willing my eyes to open. They feel like lead balloons that weigh a thousand pounds each. I finally manage to open them.

I look around and quickly remember that I am in the hospital. I only see Brooke and my mother talking candidly while Brooke flips through a magazine, *Cosmopolitan*, probably. My eyes sweep the room again, no Ryan. Finally, they notice that I am awake and immediately they are by my side.

The pain is still present in my chest, like a vise grip that is firmly placed over my heart. The only thing that is helping me breathe is the oxygen tube that runs under my nose. It must show on my face because Brooke looks concerned as she takes my hand.

"Hey!" she mumbles in a whisper.

I look at her with fresh tears in my eyes. "It wasn't a dream, was it?" And, I am not referring to the accident.

Tears spring to Brooke's eyes. She is unable to speak, so she only shakes her head no. *Wow!* Brooke at a loss for words. That is a first. On that note, I fall back into the depths of sedation.

Chapter 31

The hospital releases me to my mom the next day once they have determined that my blood pressure has stabilized. Jillian is in full caregiver mode, which I love. Her presence alone is comforting. I have missed my mother more than I realized. She is bustling around the apartment cooking and taking care of me, although my medication causes me to sleep throughout most of the day.

The pain in my leg is unbearable at times. I experienced a clean break in my upper fibula, but the force of the impact from Ryan and Colton's car, and the way that I fell onto the concrete, caused the fracture to rip the ligaments in between the knee and the bone, which is the reason I needed surgery and several pins to stabilize my leg. And that is also why I needed a fiberglass cast up to my thigh, hot pink—the cast, no less. Thanks to Brooke! The doctor said it must be kept stable, with no ability to move, in order to heal properly.

I attempt to contact Jerri several times during my lucid moments, but I don't get a response. I suspect Ryan told her that I was quitting and she is avoiding me. Sometime in the evening, I believe I hear a knock on my door, but I chalk it up to my pain medications. Then a conversation of other voices in my home confirms my suspicious. My heart skips a few beats. *Oh my God! Is it Ryan?*

I silently hope that it is Ryan. I briefly second-guess my decision to send him away from the hospital, but shake my head to fling those thoughts from my brain.

My mother nervously knocks on my bedroom door and peeks inside. "Darling, are you up for visitors?"

I smile anxiously and slowly sit up in bed as best as I can. Jillian has my leg propped up under a million pillows, to the point that you can only see my leg when you walk in the room. "Sure, Mom," I mumble.

I look up over the mountain of fluff and I am shocked to my core when Jerri and Garrett stoically make their way into my bedroom. What is this about? I smile warily at them both.

Jerri starts, "I am very sorry to drop in unannounced, but we wanted to visit you briefly to make sure that you were comfortable and that you have everything you need. I know you are in very capable hands, though." She smiles at my mom, who takes her leave from the room.

Garrett looks pained yet conflicted as he begins, "Whitney, I can't begin to tell you how sorry I am."

I nod, feeling a lump well up in my throat.

Jerri interjects. "We both are!"

"Thank you," I whisper. "And thank you for everything you did for me, getting me to Charlotte and all."

Garrett smiles, but looks tense. "Don't thank me. It was the least I could do after my son nearly killed you."

Gasp!

"And," Garrett continues warily, "I have made arrangements with our team physician to come to you for your follow-up appointments. I understand from Jim that you will need weekly visits and physical therapy, but, rest assured, I will make sure that you are accommodated for it all."

I nod in silent gratitude.

Jerri interjects softly, "I am working to extinguish the rumors and media reports that are swirling around the accident, and your involvement with Ryan." I flush. *Rumors?* I don't even want to know. I nod quietly again, mortified that Jerri knows about my relationship with Ryan.

"Whitney..." Garrett speaks again firmly, taking me by surprise. "I will get right to what I have to say because I know you need your rest. I understand you have intentions of resigning your position, but I need to discuss a few things with you before you make that decision."

I nod, but my decision has already been made. It is clear there is a specific reason for their visit. It is like some sort of sneak attack, which would explain why Jerri has been avoiding my calls today.

Garrett wastes no time getting to the issue at hand. "If you insist on leaving GCR, if you follow through with your resignation, that is, Ryan will be fired, effective immediately."

My medication must take over because I shout out, "That's not fair!" Tears flood my eyes. This is not happening. *He can't make me stay. Or can he?* My pain meds are making me crazy! I shake my head, making a desperate attempt to pay attention to what Garrett is saying. Surely, I must be dreaming.

Garrett shakes his head and stands firm. "What's not fair is that *I* have to come out of retirement to pick up the slack from this spectacle. So, let's not talk fair. I want to talk fact. Since you joined our team, Ryan has made noticeable improvements every week. He has been in a slump since the season began, but he has been rapidly improving in the last few weeks, since you have taken over as his PR manager."

I steal a "what the hell" glance at Jerri. She nods to me in agreement with Garrett. I knew Ryan was improving, but I had never, not once, attributed that turnaround to me, even when Bobby mentioned it to me in Kentucky.

Garrett continues to make his case. "I understand that you are upset with Ryan, as you should be, as we all are right now. The fact of the matter remains, you are good for my son."

Confused, I interrupt. "Did he put you up to this?"

Equally confused, Garrett responds by shaking his head. "No. Ryan has disappeared. He has absolutely no idea that I'm here. In fact, I would like to keep it that way."

I look back to Jerri for some type of guidance but receive none. She looks ashen.

"Whitney." Garrett beckons my eye contact. I turn my eyes back to him as he speaks sincerely. "I need you on this team. Ryan needs you. At least say you will stay on with us until the season is over. By then we may have an option to switch you to another driver. I am very pleased with what you have done in my organization thus far, and I don't want my foolish son to drive you away. Especially when we all need you!" He finishes his sermon with a heavy sigh.

I am stunned. I look down at my hands, and tears prick my eyes. I started out as a lowly receptionist, not knowing a thing about NASCAR, and somehow became a key player in the GCR organization. Something about this just doesn't seem right. *Could I be the cause of Ryan's turnaround?* Tears began to fall softly on my cheeks. Garrett sighs again and looks at Jerri, then back to me.

I try to speak. "I don't know if I can do this?"

Garrett shakes his head. "I'm sorry, Whitney, but this is how has to be!"

How can I do this? How can I continue working for Ryan, especially now, under these circumstances?

I know Garrett means business, and a light bulb goes off in my head. I quickly think back—Garrett is right! Since I have been working with Ryan, he has been on top of the leaderboard each week. I know that his career hangs in the balance. I cannot let my feelings for him or our relationship cause the decline of his career. I am a professional, and by God, I am going to do my job, the job I was hired to before Ryan got in the way. I can do this even if it kills me. And I cannot let Ryan lose his job with his father's organization. After all, I was a key player in all this. He shouldn't suffer because of my bad decisions.

Immediately, I agree to the terms and conditions, not thinking about the repercussions. "OK, I will stay until the end of the season."

Jerri lets out a long breath and a beaming smile. Garrett immediately looks relieved. "Thank you, Whitney!" He walks over closer to me and gently touches my arm. "You don't know how much I appreciate what you are doing."

Appreciate, hell! You backed me into a corner. I feel like I am working for Tony Damn Soprano. So, don't thank me just yet!

Chapter 32

Several days pass. I am beginning to get restless. Bed rest and being bound to my apartment is not my thing. Brooke has agreed to stay with me so that my mother can return to Georgia. I must admit that I am looking forward to Brooke's company. However, I am a little nervous because I know she is going to let me have it as soon as my mom leaves. I wonder what Ryan told her.

Brooke arrives on what I am told is a Saturday morning. The days are running together. She is dressed casually in sweats with her blonde hair pulled up into a ponytail. As always, she looks like she is ready to walk the runway even dressed down. Again, here I sit...a hot mess again. Brooke gives me a wry smile as she drops her bags onto the living room floor. Mom flutters around making sure she has collected all her belongings, but I can tell she is hesitant to leave.

"Now, girls..." Mom starts slowly, "are you absolutely sure that you will be OK? I can stay longer. Or better yet, you could just come back home with me, Whitney."

I raise my eyebrows at Brooke. She laughs out loud at my mom, knowing full well that Jillian would have to drag me kicking and screaming by my good leg back to Georgia. "We got this, Mrs. Parker. Please don't worry about a thing. I will be here for as long as she needs."

My heart swells with love. I am so blessed to have such great women in my life. I smile warmly at my mom to confirm Brooke's statement.

We say quick good-byes, and I listen as Brooke escorts her to the door. The soft click of the lock lets me know that I am finally alone with Brooke. Maybe this is what I need, girl therapy. But first, I am going to have to go through Brooke's Spanish Inquisition. And it is going to be brutal.

Brooke walks over to where I am semi-propped on the couch. "OK, let's see...I have your medicine schedule, which you are good to go for a few hours. Don't need any of those. Are you hungry? Do you need something to drink?"

I eye her suspiciously. I know she is leading up to something because nursing is not her thing. "I am OK for now," I say softly.

Brooke raises her eyebrows at me. "Are you sure? Please be sure because you are not moving from this living room until you tell me just what in the hell happened. And I mean *everything*, Whitney Elaine Parker!"

And...there it is!

I laugh out loud. I mean really laugh. It hurts my body, but feels good for my soul. I haven't laughed in some time. However, Brooke doesn't get my humor.

"OK...OK..." I acquiesce. "I am not even sure where to start, actually."

Brooke snaps giving me the stink eye, "You better starting figuring it out quick, sister!"

I can tell that she is not in a mood for my jokes today, but I under-stand her concern. It was Brooke's idea for me to move here. Then she basically got me the interview at the temporary employee agency that led to the job at GCR. I understand she feels responsible for me, not to mention the fact that I have been blowing her off since I became involved with Ryan. I knew she would figure me out sooner or later since we are more like sisters than friends.

I take a deep breath. "OK...you want the annotated version?" I laugh again. This is so not the time to aggravate her, but I can't help myself. I somewhat feel like me again, if that is possible. I can sense Brooke's impatience. I don't know what she knows, what Ryan told her, or if she knows anything at all, but I am going to lay it all out for her. "OK, OK, we both know that Colton was interested in me. I told you that, right?"

Brooke responds impatiently, "Yes, and it was very evident that night we had drinks."

"I talked with Colton to explain to him that I did like him but did not want to get involved for two reasons. Number one, because it was a direct violation of company policy and I did not want to jeopardize my job. Number two, I was not ready to begin another relationship. I gave him a little background information on my previous relationship, and he said he understood."

Brooke looks confused. "So, how does this all lead to your accident and these rumors about you being involved with both drivers?"

I hold up my hand. "I'm getting there. You wanted the complete version, right?"

She holds up her hands in defeat.

I continue, "Colton and I maintained what I thought was a friendship. We had very minimal contact, but I made a mistake."

"You changed your mind about Colton?"

I sigh, "No, I just violated company policy with someone else."

Brooke's eyes narrow like she is processing my statement, and then automatically her face lights up like she is about to explode. She mouths the name "Ryan" to me. I shake my head as tears begin to fall at the sheer mention of his name. I look away, embarrassed by my emotions.

"Shut up!" Brooke exclaims. Then, in a hushed whisper, she enunciates my name like it has ten syllables, "Whiitnee, no!"

I turn back to meet her shocked gaze and nod my head, unable to speak. Brooke opens her mouth to speak, then closes it again. She is wide-eyed with shock.

Brooke finally gathers her composure. "When?"

I take a deep breath. "About a month or so ago, I guess."

"A month!" she shrieks. "How could you not tell me?"

"I am sorry! Really, it all happened so fast, and I was so caught up in him and my job, but I knew...I knew if I talked to you that you would know. And I couldn't risk it. For the first time in my life, I finally felt like I was in the right place at the right time. I didn't want to say anything to anybody in fear of who might find out."

I continue to explain, "Ryan tried to explain it to me one night about how racing affects you. How it gets in your blood. How the adrenaline rush is addictive. I didn't understand him at all, but now I get it. And you know me, it's not like me to act first and worry about the repercussions later. I got so caught up in my job, traveling, and trying to understand this sport that I made a bad decision. But..." I stammer, "it felt so right, you know? I have never felt that intense connection with another person."

Brooke sits silently, taking in the overload of information. She looks up at me. "Where is he? Why isn't he here?"

Her words open a floodgate of tears that soak my cheeks. Brooke gets up and moves to sit on the end of the couch with me. I hold up my hand, signaling that I need a minute to regain my composure.

A few minutes pass, and I am able to speak again. "I broke it off with him."

Brooke gasps, "Why?"

I roll my eyes. "Wouldn't running me over constitute a good enough reason?"

Brooke shrugs her shoulders and laughs at me.

I try again to finish my story. "The day of the race, I noticed that Colton seemed upset with me. He gave me several disapproving looks that made me uneasy. I started to get the feeling that he might suspect that Ryan and I were now involved. I just chalked it up to paranoia. Ryan and I both agreed that no one should know about us until we figured out what 'us' was. I just never believed that it would be anything serious since Ryan changes women like he changes his underwear. I was just along for the ride, literally!" I laugh at my own bad joke.

"But..." Brooke doesn't get my humor, but begs me to continue.

"Apparently, Colton knew, somehow."

Brooke interrupts me. "Oh my God! So that is why Colton intentionally wrecked Ryan on the track that day."

I shake my head to confirm her statement. "Colton was furious that I had chosen Ryan over him."

Brooke sits up with new regard. "So that's where the rumors came from."

I raise my hand. "I have no idea who could have ever said anything. Unless it was Colton. Maybe the paparazzi were grasping at straws...I don't know. It is mortifying. But Jerri has officially silenced them. Thank God!"

Brooke shakes her head at me. "Well...don't be so sure. Just wait till you see all the magazines I have that are talking about it."

She reclines back on the couch like she has just run a marathon, then immediately sits back up with more questions. "OK...I understand all that now, but why would Ryan hit you with the car?"

I shake my head. "I don't know. I believe it was really a case of me being in the wrong place at the wrong time. Jerri told me in the hospital that Ryan didn't see me. So, I guess I was caught in the cross fire."

Brooke looks confused again. "What did Ryan say?"

I look at her and take a long pause. "Nothing, really." I shrug. "I didn't give him a chance to explain."

"Whitney!" Brooke exclaims again.

"Listen, Brooke, I screwed up. The majority of this is my fault."

"Like hell!" Brooke interjects.

I sigh, "Yes, it is. I told Colton that I didn't want to be involved with anyone, especially someone that worked for the team. Then what do I do? I go and get involved. See? All roads lead back to Whitney Parker." I point to myself for emphasis. "Now, one person is out of a job, and another's career hangs in the balance."

I continue, "I have made up my mind to go back to work and finish the season. I am not, nor have never been, a quitter. I have to be professional, put my feelings aside, and help Ryan get his career, what's left of it, back on track."

Brooke looks at me sympathetically. "How on earth will you be able to work for him?"

I shake my head and avoid eye contact with her as tears well up again. "I don't know, but I have to do it for his sake. It is the least I can do to repair the damage that I helped cause."

Brooke relents. "I have one more question. Then I will leave you alone—for today, that is. I am *so* not done with you, Whitney Parker!"

I laugh, "I would be afraid if you were!"

Brooke eyes me cautiously. "My question is this, how on earth can two people go from hating one another to being romantically involved?"

I throw my head back and laugh so hard pain shoots throughout my body. I grasp my leg to steady myself and stop the pain.

"What is so funny, Whitney?" Brooke looks pissed.

"Ryan and I had the same conversation that first night we were... uh...together," I stammer, embarrassed. "I hated him because he was so arrogant and rude, while he despised me because I was new and had absolutely no knowledge of NASCAR whatsoever. But we worked through all of that."

Brooke smiles at me and says sarcastically, "I would say so!"

We fall together and erupt into a fit of girlish giggles.

Chapter 33

I awake the following morning. Well, I guess it's morning since I have no window in my room, but I believe I can hear Brooke moving around in the kitchen. The pain in my chest is still present, but not as gripping. I guess the girl therapy worked after all. Between gossiping, reading some good fashion magazines, and blabbing the whole story, spending time with Brooke has helped alleviate some of the pain. I manage to sweep my legs up and off the bed. As they dangle over the side, I can tell that my leg pain has subsided as well. What a difference a week makes! And that thought reminds me that it is Sunday. There is a race today, and it is odd not being at the track.

I look over to my nightstand. My iPod sits quietly in the dock. Normally, my music device is my safe haven, my comfort in times of distress, but now I don't trust it. My iPhone, my connection to my job, sits just beside the dock. I reach out for it, but in one swift motion, I take the phone and sweep it into the drawer below. I can't be tempted by work or anyone I might want to call. I cannot second-guess my decision to send Ryan away.

I reach for my crutches and pull myself into a standing position. This is going to be tough. I amble into the bathroom. I look at myself for the first time in a week. I look like I've been in a war, but then again, I guess I have. My face is gaunt and pale. Dark circles line my eyes, and the stitches on my face are hidden by white 4x4 gauze. *Gorgeous!* I shake my head at my internal sarcasm. I don't look at the rest of me. It's just all too much!

I hobble on my crutches into the kitchen. Brooke has the small flat-screen television turned to Fox News, where a middle-aged man is discussing today's race.

"Ryan Carter will be noticeably absent from the lineup today in Indianapolis. After severely injuring his public relations manager in a bizarre garage accident in Loudon, he has been suspended for six weeks, and his future within NASCAR remains questionable at best. His father, legendary driver, Garrett Carter, will be picking up the slack for his two missing team members."

The reporter concludes, and I say, "Wow! World news, eh?"

I startle Brooke, who snatches up the remote and quickly turns off the news report. "Why didn't you call me? I would have helped you!"

I raise one eyebrow at her. "You can't babysit me forever. Besides, I need to be back to work tomorrow."

Brooke snorts into her coffee. "Bullshit!"

"Yes!" I exclaim. "I am going back to work tomorrow. If I lay up in this apartment one more day, I may be suicidal."

Brooke shakes her head at me. "I'm not even going to argue with you. If you can figure out the logistics, be my guest."

"Oh, I've got them figured out, all right."

Brooke eyes me warily, no doubt scared to ask what I have planned since I cannot drive myself to work—or since I am not "supposed" to drive for six weeks.

I sit down at the table with Brooke, who is browsing through the morning paper and eating a bowl of cereal. "Would you like something to eat?" she asks hesitantly.

I shake my head. I sit quietly watching her. I can tell by her actions that she is chewing on more than the granola in her cereal bowl. She notices my stare and raises an eyebrow at me.

"What?" she asks.

"That is exactly my question to you, Counselor." I raise my eyebrow back to her.

She lays her spoon down in her bowl. "There is something that I forgot to mention to you," she says warily. "Actually, I was not sure if I was going to tell you at all, but I don't want to keep it from you."

Brooke has my undivided attention now.

She takes a deep breath. "He called."

"He...who?" I exclaim. "Ryan?"

Brooke shakes her head softly. "No, him...the bastard that we don't speak of!"

I am shocked. Brooke's confession makes me want to jump from my seat. I have completely forgotten about him. I guess Ryan's plan worked after all.

"What did he say?" I question her.

She rolls her eyes at me. "Oh, just some bullshit about how he did still care for you and was concerned. I suppose he was curious, too, if the rumors were true about you being involved with Colton and Ryan. Jealous jerk!"

Brooke is right. He was only curious and wanted to spread that gossip around Georgia. "What did you say to him?" I ask hesitantly, not sure that I want to know.

"Well, frankly, to sum up, I told him that you did not need neither his care nor concern…but fuck you very much for calling, and I hung up on him!"

My mouth falls open, shocked. "Brooke!" I hiss at her audacity, then erupt into a fit of laughter.

"He should have known better than to call you anyway! What a dumb ass!" And Brooke laughs with me.

After a few moments of therapeutic laughter, Brooke sighs deeply. "I have been going over everything you have told me, and I have one more question."

"Just one? I'm disappointed!"

Brooke shakes her head at me. "Yesterday, you said you had feelings for Ryan. Do you love him?"

Her question catches me off guard and stops me dead in my tracks. I shoot her my best "are you freaking crazy" look.

She raises her hands up to me in defense. "I'm just saying, from what you've said about your relationship, both personal and professional, not to mention the fact that you met his parents."

I laugh in an attempt to throw her off. "I work for one, and the other was just incidental."

"Oh, come on, Whitney, you agreed to keep working for him so he wouldn't get fired."

I snap my head back to her. "Yes!" I exclaim. "So he wouldn't get fired because of me, remember?" I throw my hands up in frustration. "Did you not get that portion of the story?"

"I know, but Whitney, this is sooo unlike you. I mean, I have literally been up all night trying to figure this whole thing out because this is so out of character for you."

She's right. It's not me. I do what I am told, I abide by the rules, and I don't blur the lines of right and wrong. But I guess I shot that all to hell and back.

I shake my head at her. I lean over the kitchen table and rest my head in my right hand. "I don't know either. I feel like I am losing my damn mind. For the first time in my life, I finally felt like I belonged somewhere. And that I had found a career that I was passionate about. And those feelings carried over to Ryan. I have never had that intense emotional or physical connection with someone. You know? The electricity or charge between two people that says to hell with everything else. And I couldn't deny it. So, for once in my life, I was enjoying myself. And I didn't want to stack up any more regrets in my life. But look where it got me, a broken heart and a broken leg!"

Brooke looks at me warily like she is finally putting everything together. She smiles sympathetically at me. "I'm just so worried about you because of everything that you have been through prior to this and now this. I feel somewhat responsible for it."

I shake my head at her and reach across the table to clasp her hand. "Please don't! It's not your fault. I made my own choices, hasty ones at best. I guess it wasn't enough that I drove out of Georgia smoking and spinning, because I ran straight into the wall this time."

Brooke groans loudly, "Did you seriously just make a NASCAR analogy out of your life!"

I laugh again. "It's bad, I know. Sadly, I would do it all over, broken leg and all, just to feel those emotions with Ryan."

Brooke raises her eyebrows. "He loves you. You know that, right?"

Her statement turns my gut. *No!*

"As an outsider looking in, I'm just saying, is all." She shrugs. "Especially when I look back now, watching him with you in the hospital, the fact that he called me...you didn't see what I saw. I mean, he was really distraught, Whitney. I was so confused by it all. But now that I have put everything together, I can see it all clearly."

Her statement makes my stomach roll again. *Could it be true?* No. Hell no. If he did, he wouldn't have walked out so easily from the hospital. *But you made him leave, Whitney,* I chastise myself. The thought of him walking out shakes me to my core again and reopens the floodgates.

I shakily stand up from the table in a desperate attempt to flee this conversation. I am nauseous from Brooke's latest inquisition. This is too deep and way too early in the morning.

"If that were true," I snap with raw emotion, "where the hell is he? And why am I going through this alone?" I grab my crutches and hobble back to my bedroom as Brooke calls after me.

"Whitney...!"

I collapse onto my bed and begin to sob. Do I love him? Yes. Does he love me? All signs point to no. If he did, he wouldn't have walked away so easy. The anguish in my chest is too much, and no comparison to the pain in my broken leg. Is this what heartbreak feels like? Even with the Georgia bastard, I never experienced a pain of separation like this. With him, it was over in a second, and I moved on just like that. But this is different. I hurt more over Ryan than I did my own former fiancé of six years. Something is clearly wrong with this picture. My thoughts make me cry harder.

I hear Brooke make her way into my room, but she doesn't say anything else. She knows she has already said too much. She simply lies down beside me and holds me as I cry, like any best friend would do.

Chapter 34

Even though Garrett offered me the entire length of Ryan's suspension to recuperate, I get up early Monday morning, only a week after the accident, to get ready for work against Brooke's wishes, crutches and all. I had to cajole, threaten, and eventually blackmail her to get her to agree to drive me to the office. She was not happy, to say least.

I make a haphazard attempt to fix my makeup despite the new scar on my face. I take extra time with my long brown locks. I use my curling iron to create some waves around my face in hopes that it will help camouflage the cut on my cheek.

I hobble to my closet. As I stand trying to decide what to wear, the first thing I spy is Ryan's shirt hanging front and center. My stomach drops to the floor. I snatch it from the hanger and pull it up to my face. I take a deep breath through my nose, but his smell is gone. *How poignant and incredibly ironic is that?* The shirt that once represented the start of a new relationship, new career, and a promise of something more now hangs as a reminder of my bad decision. I take the shirt and fling into the bottom of the closet. I kick it into the back with my good foot. I don't need anything else to remind me of Ryan.

After strict instructions and threats of her own, Brooke drops me off at the office very early so I can avoid any chitchat from the other office employees. I went with my long cobalt-blue maxi dress that covers my leg. I don't want to draw any further attention to my injuries. I can't handle the sympathetic looks, probing questions, and overall small talk. It is just too much right now. I just want to work. I sneak to my desk in hopes that no one will realize that I am here.

I sit and stare blankly at my computer, not even knowing where to start on damage control. This morning, I have cast away all my feelings for Ryan so I can get back to the business at hand. *Yeah, I don't believe that either.* But I am in full business mode now, which is the way it started and the way it should have remained. Ryan's career hangs in the balance. With his suspension and almost termination from GCR, my number one goal is to get him back on track, literally, in good physical and mental condition. NASCAR has demanded that he attend a six-week anger management program that coincides with his suspension. I sincerely hope it is beneficial for him, but I know better.

I am broken from my new internal mission statement by a slight knock on my office door. *Here we go...*

I turn around slowly, almost afraid of who it might be. It's Josh. I let out a long breath and smile. He casually takes a seat at my desk.

"How's it going, kid?"

I just nod, afraid to speak, afraid the dam will break again. Josh must sense my reluctance.

"I have been thinking..." He pauses. "I know I have given you a wealth of information to process in an attempt to educate you on the great sport of NASCAR, but I guess I forgot one major point."

I eye him warily because I know this is leading up to something.

"You see, a stock car is much like a horse...You don't want to stand directly behind or in front of one." He sighs at his own joke. I laugh out loud.

"Yes, that little bit of information is say, oh..." I look at my watch. "About a week too late!" We both laugh, and I immediately feel better about coming into the office today.

"Seriously, though..." Josh trails off, concerned. "Are you OK?"

Ahhh! The question of the day. I simply shake my head from side to side, then nod from top to bottom in succession.

Josh smiles. "I understand. But I am here if you need me!" he offers as he leaves me to my work.

I smile and say quietly, "Thank you!"

Jerri calls me in for a meeting shortly after lunch. I have been dreading my first conversation with her. She knows about my relationship with Ryan. She witnessed our exchange at the hospital. And she has had to work damage control on the rumors swirling about our involvement. But we haven't spoken about it. A pool of anxiety is like lead in my stomach as I enter her office. She regards me with cool concern.

"Whitney, I really wish you would have taken off longer. You went through a very traumatic event," she says, sounding motherly.

I nod. "I need to work. I need the distraction," I am barely able to mutter due to the gigantic lump in my throat.

Jerri knowingly nods her head in return.

I know she is disappointed in me, so I feel the need to explain. "Jerri, I'm *so* sorry!" I exclaim.

She holds her hand up to stop me. "Don't apologize. For the life of me, I cannot figure out the power he has over women!" Jerri shakes her head. We both laugh, and my anxiety immediately eases.

I continue, "I don't even know how it happened. But it did. And again, I'm sorry."

"Have you spoken to Ryan?" Jerri asks cautiously.

I look away from Jerri and quietly shake my head no. Word around the water cooler is that Ryan is holed up at his home on Lake Norman, but that could just be idle gossip. I don't offer any information, nor do I ask Jerri about his whereabouts. I feel tears rim my eyes, and I violently fight them off. *No more of that!*

After a beat, I finally manage to say, "I made a very bad decision that was the catalyst for all this turmoil."

Jerri looks at me, confused.

"And Ryan's arrogance and quick temper are always gonna be a factor that we cannot overcome."

She nods her head in concurrence. This she understands because she, too, knows him all too well.

I look back to Jerri and catch her gaze. "I just want to do my job and salvage what's left of the season for Ryan and GCR. I let that aspect get away from me, but I am refocused and reorganized."

Jerri smiles proudly. "I am glad to hear it. Now, if you need to leave early or work only half days, I completely understand."

I nod my head knowing that schedule is a pipe dream. I laugh, "I wish! I have six weeks' worth of damage control to start on!"

Jerri laughs with me. There are so many events that are going to have to be rescheduled since Ryan cannot even go to the track. His sponsors are going to be livid, and I start sweating just thinking about it. I can handle it, though. I will handle it, for Ryan's sake.

Chapter 35

In the blink of an eye, a month of Sundays has passed. Literally, it seems. August has flown by despite the North Carolina heat. At the office, we are *all* in DEFCON five anxiously awaiting Ryan's return to the track, not to mention his return to the office. Each day, I am anxious that he will just waltz through the door like nothing ever happened, but he doesn't. Plus, the office chatter is at an all-time low. It's unnerving but evident that the whole office is on pins and needles waiting for him also. But day after day he doesn't show, which only increases the collective anxiety level of our team. All we can do is stay engrossed in our work and wait.

I have two weeks to prepare for Richmond, Virginia. All of Ryan's sponsors are clamoring for attention after his six-week hiatus. Unfortunately, most of them have made specific demands that must be met in order to keep the sponsorship intact. I am not surprised. I actually find it hard to believe that we didn't lose any sponsors. I am actively working to make sure they are all covered and given proper attention, which will hopefully prevent any lost contracts after the race season is over. Ryan is still in hot water with Nationwide after that fiasco in the event suite. I laugh to myself. Ryan and I have come a long way since then. I shake my head. Those thoughts and memories are done. I have to focus on the job at hand.

Ryan's return at Richmond is my main concern. It is a night race, which are my favorites, but I cannot get excited about it. Too much has happened since Loudon, and there is still too much to get through before the green flag falls, like my first, sure to be awkward encounter with Ryan. I realize now that it's not only my relationship with Ryan but the fear of being around the cars that is causing my anxiety. I shudder as goose bumps run down my spine. For the first time in my life, I am fearful, an emotion that does not sit well with me. I try to put those thoughts out of my mind in order to get my job done. I have to climb this mountain of trepidation that I hope will lead me back into the excitement and adrenaline of NASCAR.

Over the last four weeks, I have fallen into a routine of alternating work and sleep. It is the only thing that helps me to pass the days. I wake up each morning and get to work as quickly as I can. Since there is not much for me to do with Ryan, I have been assisting Jerri with Garrett's team and the search for Colton's replacement. Garrett has had to break out of semiretirement to pick up the slack for Ryan's and Colton's vacant driver's seats. He has been in a race car every weekend since Ryan's suspension, which is stressful for the whole organization, not to mention him. The few times he has been in the office, he didn't seem happy. I can't blame him.

I work as long as I can. Most evenings I am escorted out by Jerri or by the threatening calls from Brooke. When I get home, I shower and put myself into a wine-induced coma. The alcohol not only helps me sleep soundly, but I don't dream, not of Ryan, not about the accident. This is my routine. Terrible, I know, but it works!

Tonight at the office is one of those rare nights when I have slipped under the radar. It is around eight o'clock, and Ryan's warning about security immediately comes to my mind. Paparazzi have been crawling around Mooresville like crazy since the accident. It also reminds me of that late night Ryan practically dragged me out of the office.

I laugh. That night was the start of it all. Tears prick my eyes, and I force them back.

I stare blankly at my desk calendar. I cannot believe four weeks have already passed and Ryan has not shown his face in the office. The office gossip has not changed. Supposedly, Ryan is still up at the lake, avoiding everyone. The lake house, where he planned to take me during our next weekend off. Tears sting again. I bat them away again. Why is he hiding? Is it because of me? I can't take this apprehension anymore. The fear and anxiety that grip me every day are about to push me over the edge. I grab my things and purpose-fully head out of the building. By God, if Ryan won't come here, then I will go to him. Maybe, just maybe, he is at home now. I reach the parking lot to discover that my car is the only one in the lot. Shivers run down my spine as I carefully climb in, mindful of the cast on my leg.

Even though I am the only one left in the area, I make a right out of the parking lot to make the long circle around to Ryan's house. We have made it this far without anyone knowing, and I am certainly not going to screw it up now. I make the quick loop and pull down the short path to Ryan's gate. As I pull up, I take a deep breath to dis-cover that the gate is locked. I look past the gate to see that all the lights are dark in Ryan's house that sits high on the hill.

I hit the steering wheel in anger and cry out, "Damn it!" Where is he? I lay my head down on the steering wheel. What am I doing? I've got to get out of here.

I look up into the rearview mirror, and my breath catches in my throat. Another vehicle has pulled into the drive behind me and has me blocked in. *Oh no!* I peer into my rearview mirror again, but I can't see who is behind me because of the blinding headlights. A slight knock on my window causes me to jump and cry out again. I look through my window, into the night, to spy Garrett looking back at me cautiously. I press my automatic window button.

"Hey, it was not my intention to scare you. I was coming in from the farm and spotted your taillights. I thought it was more vultures, those damn paparazzi. And, for a second, I thought...I hoped it might be Ryan finally coming home. I didn't realize it was you."

I nod my head, not sure of what to say.

Garrett takes notice of my hesitation. "He must be still up at the lake."

I nod again, still unable to speak.

"Is everything OK, Whitney?" Garrett questions me.

"No...yes...yes sir, everything is fine. I..." I stammer. "I just wanted to speak to Ryan before Richmond."

Garrett steps back and sighs, thrusting his hands down into his jean pockets. "Well...good luck with that. I haven't spoken with him in over a month. He refuses to take my calls. To my knowledge, he has only had contact with his mother, and that has been brief. I think Bobby has been out to the lake to see him, but that is all I know."

I am shocked at Garrett's revelation. *What in the hell is going on?*

I nod again. "OK, well...I guess I should get out of here before anyone else sees me."

Garrett nods in agreement, but looks concerned. "Why don't you come up to the house? You look like you could use a good meal."

Anxiety grips me again. "No, I couldn't do that, and I really do need to get back to the city before it gets any later." I don't know how I would begin to face Ryan's mother, nor have a conversation with the both of them after so much has happened.

"OK, Whitney," Garrett says, disappointed. "Everything will work out. He is stubborn like his old man, but he will come around."

I nod to him and force down the new lump in my throat. "No, sir. It's not that. He..." I sputter. "He is just doing what I asked of him for once in his life."

Garrett cocks his head to one side, confused, "Oh, what's that?"

I take a deep breath. "To stay away."

* * *

I watch in my rearview mirror as Garrett pulls away. I take a deep breath and slowly back my Honda Accord out of the driveway with a million thoughts in my head. Why is Ryan hiding? Is he alone? Why won't he see his dad? All this shit is my fault. If I had stuck to my original plan, none of these events would have happened.

As I accelerate on Interstate 77 South, panic seizes my chest, and I feel that familiar sob rising in my throat. I am not going to do this. I cannot cry anymore. I pound the steering wheel physically trying to fight the tears. I lose. These feelings that I have been fighting and suppressing for the last six weeks violently erupt from my body in a huge sob. I can't breathe, but I can't compete with them anymore either.

Tears flood my face, and I cry, hard. My body is racked with sobs. I haven't cried this hard since that morning in the hospital when Ryan left. I thought this was over. Now I know that no matter how hard I try to fight these feelings, the pain will not go away. In fact, the pain is worse than it ever was.

Why, is the only other thought that will come to my head. Why does it hurt so much? Why did I agree to keep my job? Why didn't I just walk away altogether?

You know the answer, Whitney. Ryan.

As I take the exit to my apartment, my iPhone rings out. I have no plans to answer the call since I am a heaving, blubbering mess, but I fumble through my purse to find my cell. It is probably Brooke wondering where the hell I am. I grab my phone, and the number on the ID says, "blocked call." *Strange!*

I can barely speak due to my current emotional state, but curiosity gets the best of me. I hit accept and whisper, "Hello," doing my best to mask my distress. There is no answer. I can only hear dead silence. It must be a wrong number, but I have a sinking feeling in my gut. "Hello," I call out again. And then the call immediately goes dead.

The phone call managed to stop my tears, but now I feel nervous. I turn the radio up, hoping to drown out my thoughts and uneasiness. Before I realize that my iPod is plugged in, I hear the beginning of a horribly depressing Brian McKnight song. Instead of panic and fresh tears, anger takes over my body. I reach up with one swift movement to grab the auxiliary cord and rip it from the port in the dashboard. I can't keep doing this. I cannot afford another meltdown or its aftermath.

Chapter 36

Ryan's suspension is finally over. I can't believe this day is here. My plane leaves for Richmond, Virginia shortly after lunch. I hold Ryan's itinerary in my hands, and the paper shakes from my anxiousness.

Damn! I take a deep breath. *I can do this! Come on, Whitney! Get it together already.*

I don't know if I am more anxious about seeing Ryan for the first time in six weeks or being back at the track. I guess it could be a combination of both, but the former is the majority. It would be a hell of a lot easier if Ryan and I were able to talk before. However, it doesn't look like that is going to happen.

A soft knock on my office door breaks me away from my thoughts. "Whitney," Jerri says softly.

I can tell she is concerned. I smile to reassure her.

Jerri takes a step into my office and hands me a folder of documents. "Here is your travel itinerary. I have booked you at the Jefferson. It is a great hotel, but it is also off the radar. Since press has ramped up again now that Ryan's suspension is over, paparazzi will be crawling."

She sighs. "So...I hope you will be able to hide out there without the media bothering you."

I nod my head and look down.

"Are you sure you are ready to do this?" Jerri asks.

I look up and push down the lump in my throat. I nod. "No, really, Jerri, I can do this. I have to start back somewhere, right?"

She smiles at me reassuringly. "I have complete faith in you."

Jerri's words mean so much to me. I have come a long way in the last few months that I have been employed at GCR Racing. And we have all been through so much in these last few weeks. The stress and after-math of my accident still shows around Jerri's eyes. It makes me sad because I know I am the root cause of it all. It breaks my heart that I have let her down.

Jerri turns to leave, then turns back to me. "Still nothing?"

I know she is referring to Ryan. I shake my head. "I have e-mailed his schedule to him, but have not received a response."

Jerri nods. "He will come around. I am sure he is anxious about the weekend, too. We all are." A truer statement has never been spoken.

* * *

I arrive at the airport in record time. I have gotten to be a profes-sional at timing my travel just right so that I don't have to wait to board the plane. I hobble through security and walk into my gate just as the attendant gives the first boarding call. I can walk much easier these days since my cast was removed this week. I was able to ditch the crutches for a new walking boot. It is removable and will help me to readjust to using my leg again. It will make this weekend much easier on me, physically that is. I settle into my seat and take a deep breath. *Here we go...*

After four hours and a brief layover in Washington, I land in the historical town of Richmond, Virginia. I wish I had the time to tour, but sadly, that is the drawback of being in a different city each week. There is only time for one purpose, racing. Over the past few months, I couldn't give a shit less about anything else but watching Ryan drive his #62 Chevrolet around in circles. It has become my life. I desperately hope that thrill of my job is not lost because of the end of our relationship or my accident.

I check into the Jefferson Hotel under Jerri's name. The young girl at the reception desk eyes me intently. "Here is your key, Ms. Andrews." She smiles and asks hesitantly, "Do you work for a race team?"

I nod. "Yes, I do." The young girl watched me walk across the lobby with my impairment, so undoubtedly she has put two and two together thanks to my picture being blasted across every news media outlet in the country. She smiles back at me broadly.

When I insert my key into the lock, I open the door to a large room with a king-size bed. On the bedside table is a bottle of wine with a card beside it. I laugh, but wonder anxiously who it could be from. *Ryan, maybe?* My heart skips a beat. I rip open the envelope. Jerri. The note says,

You may need this.

I hope your weekend goes well.

Jerri

She is right. I do need it. I put the bottle into a bucket of ice, grab the room service menu, and desperately try to take my mind off tomorrow.

* * *

The alarm clock on my iPhone sings out at 7:00 a.m. Ugh! I cry out as the bottle of wine that I killed last night, courtesy of Jerri, hammers in my head. It was the only way that I could sleep though. I stagger to the mirror in the bathroom. I take a deep breath and recite to myself several times, *I can do this. I can do this.*

I shower and dress in record time. Track activities start early this morning and culminate tonight with the Nationwide Series race, which is the minor league to Sprint Cup Series. I start to get excited, but I can feel the anxiety creeping back in on me too. *What will Ryan say? How will he act?*

I meet the courier in the hotel lobby. He will take me over to the track. In each city, I get the opportunity to meet new people. GCR hires couriers and runners in each city to help transport staff and drivers around each area. In addition, they run errands and help with support during the race weekend.

My driver today is a middle-aged man named Charlie. He is sweet. He gives me a brief tour of the city and points out some historical areas on our way to the Richmond International Raceway. It takes my mind off the issue at hand and calms my nerves temporarily.

As we approach the track, I can feel a lump welling up in my throat. *No! No! No!* I try to fight it back, but it doesn't work. My chest starts to constrict. What the hell? As we approach the infield tunnel, it is hard for me to breathe. I try to take a deep breath, but my lungs seize and resist. I reach out to grab the door handle to steady myself.

318

Tears spring to my eyes. I look up at my driver, who is watching me intently in the rearview mirror. "Are you OK?" he asks warily.

I nod, unable to speak. Fact is, I don't know if I am or not. What the hell is happening to me? I manage to catch my breath. "I just realized that I left my schedule back at the hotel. Do you mind if we go back?" I manage to stutter.

"No...Absolutely not!" Charlie exclaims. He turns the car around en route back to the Jefferson.

Instantly, I can breathe better, but my chest is still heavy with pain. It feels like a hundred-pound elephant is sitting on me. Charlie parks the car outside of the Jefferson and turns back to face me.

"Are you sure you are OK, Whitney?" Charlie asks.

I nod again.

Charlie eyes me intently. "Now, I have strict instructions from Mr. Carter to look out for you this weekend."

I gasp, "Which Mr. Carter?"

He smiles. "Garrett, of course. I have been working for him for many years. I know what you have been through. If you need some time, I can come pick you up later." Charlie reaches down to pick up a card. He passes a business card to me with his cell phone number imprinted on it.

I take the card and shake my head, fighting a new lump in my throat. "Actually, I don't know if I can do this at all," I say. "But, I will call you if I think I can go back."

Charlie smiles at me. "I can be here quickly. Take all the time you need."

I text Jerri when I get back into my room.

I just had to leave the track.
Major panic attack.
I don't know if I can do this.

My phone rings instantly. It's Jerri. "Hi," I mutter.

"Whitney, are you OK?" she asks with quick concern.

"Yes," I reply hesitantly, "but I don't know if I can go back, or if I can go back at all."

Jerri sighs, "You can do this, and I have complete faith in you. Just take all the time you need, OK? Rest and try again tomorrow. And call me if you need anything."

I sigh deeply. "I will!" I hang up the phone and sink down deeper into my desperation.

Chapter 37

I arrive at the track early Saturday morning. Anxiety and trepidation rack my body again as I make my way through the infield tunnel, but I push through this time. There is no turning back now. I have to do this today no matter what. The fact that I have not seen or heard from Ryan during his suspension will only make our first encounter today a tense one, I am sure of it. But I can't avoid it anymore. I am stronger than this!

I make my way through the infield to Ryan's hauler. It is empty. There aren't any crew members milling around, which is strange. I put my backpack down in my spot and grab my two-way radio. As soon as I switch it on, it immediately comes to life.

"Whitney!" It's Ben. "It's great to be back, isn't it? Are you ready?"

"As I will ever be!" I respond dryly to his over enthusiam.

"OK, then, let me know when you have him! I know you know this, but we have to be on step today," Ben squawks through the radio.

No shit, Ben! That is the understatement of the century. I press the speaker button to simply reply, "Stand by." I am not in the mood for chitchat.

I walk through the maze of million-dollar luxury RVs to find Ryan's bus. Anxiety starts to well up in my throat as I spot it. I genuinely hope we can talk a few minutes before the start of the mandatory drivers' meeting. It will be better for both of us to get the awkwardness out so Ryan can get down to business in his race car.

I knock firmly on the bus door. The door opens slowly as my breath catches in my throat. Only, it isn't Ryan who stands to greet me. All I can see is a cascade of blonde hair and boobs. It's Annalise! *Son of a bitch!*

Taken aback, I quickly recover to give a polite but forced smile. "Is Ryan ready to go?"

"Ryan has already left for the drivers' meeting," she says sultrily, suggestively, and smugly. "I made sure he was awake early!" she finishes with a wink. *What a bitch!*

I don't even bother with a response. I turn sharply on my good heel as she closes the door. *Damn it!* I wish I was closer. I could have slapped her in the face with my ponytail as I left. That's it, I'm officially homicidal! The pain in my chest is back. But it is no longer anxiety; it is straight up anger. I am about to burst with rage.

I stride as best as I can, fuming, to the meeting. *How could he do this? Why her? Has he been with her the whole time he was suspended?* Then my thoughts stop me dead in my tracks. *Or is he doing this to piss me off?* If so, he more than succeeded.

My radio crackles with Ben's voice again. "Whitney, what's the status!"

Leave me alone! Damn it!

"No!" I shout into the radio. I take a deep breath to regain my composure. "No, apparently he is already at or en route to the meeting."

"OK, I will be on the lookout," Ben responds.

When I arrive at the drivers' meeting, I am greeted both fondly and sympathetically by those in attendance. It pisses me off even more. I quickly survey the room to find Ryan seated in the very front. I try to make eye contact with him but fail. He is looking everywhere but at me. David, head of NASCAR safety, leads the meeting with an invocation and politely welcomes Ryan back. He begins with garage safety, and I know it is pointedly toward Ryan, GCR, and my accident. The thoughts send goose bumps throughout my body, and I shudder. That frightening apprehension rises inside me and turns my stomach. *No!* I chatise myself.

The meeting concludes with the day's forecasted weather and a few other safety concerns regarding pit road. Then, we are off for morning track activities and sponsorship events.

I wait beside the door because Ryan will have to pass by me to get to the exit. He strides past me, completely ignoring me, much like our first race together. Anger fuels my resolve, and I immediately pick up his stride. I am grateful that I was able to trade in my crutches this week for a new walking boot; I can almost match his pace. But it is difficult, and I will no doubt pay the price for it tonight. He must know it is hard for me to keep up, but he continues at a strong pace. It only makes me angrier. *Bastard!*

Once we are out in the open air, I grab my radio and press the speaker to talk to Ben. "We're walking."

He replies, "Ten-four."

Ryan and I walk in continued silence. Either the silence or my radiating anger must get to him because Ryan finally steals a sideways glance over to me. I keep a stoic, face-forward expression. Ryan knows I'm mad as hell. He recognizes the signs. He has witnessed my rage on more than one occasion. I follow him into his assigned pit box, although I'm not sure why we are here. There is no one in the vicinity. His first event is across the infield. Ryan turns to face me full on. I know it is about to burn him up that I am so quiet, but it is taking all my determination to remain silent. *Calm, Whitney, calm.*

"Where the fuck were you yesterday?"

I roll my eyes behind my sunglasses and shake my head, trying to keep calm, but his curt words blow the lid right off my anger. I snap back, "Where the hell have you been for the last six damn weeks?"

Ryan takes a deep breath and gives me a cold stare that says, *I'm still waiting for your answer.*

"I missed my flight!" I exclaim with a lie.

"Oh bullshit!" Ryan hits me right back. "Charlie said he picked you up from airport Thursday night."

Thanks a lot, Charlie!

I explode. "Don't start this shit with me, Ryan! We have to work together, and I'll be damned if you're gonna treat me like this."

"It was your choice to keep your job," Ryan rebounds. "You could have quit. You said you were going to quit!"

I guffaw at Ryan, who looks hurt by my choice to stay. I am confused. "Number one, I was not gonna give you that satisfaction. And number two, I didn't have a choice."

He looks confused. *Oh no! I shouldn't have said that.* I quickly remember Garrett's instructions to me. The rage has blown my brain cells.

"Forget it!" I quip.

"What the hell are you talking about? What did you mean when you said you didn't have a choice?" he snaps.

"Nothing!" I snap back. "We both have jobs to do, so let's just do them," I say, trying to discourage him from the topic at hand.

"Damn it, Whitney, tell me what the hell you meant."

I falter looking into his wounded eyes. "I'm sorry. I thought you knew!" I lie.

"Knew what?" Ryan roars.

I sigh, "If I resigned as your PR manager, your dad was going to fire you!"

He sharply turns back to me, and I can tell this news has shocked him to his core. Ryan blinks rapidly as if he has been slapped.

I don't give him a chance to respond. "Yes, it's true. I only stayed to save your ass, so the very least you can do is show me some freaking respect. I think I deserve that much after what you did to me!" I shout as I look down at my broken leg.

Thankfully, the pit area is empty, and no one is around to witness our public meltdown. Ryan paces the pit box, his body is rigid with pure rage. He runs his hands through his hair, and I know exactly how he is feeling. He leans back on the pit wall with his head in his hands, still silent. I don't let him rest to process this information. I continue to release six weeks' worth of feelings and aggression off my chest.

"And for the record, your little stunt with Annalise this morning was complete and utter bullshit!"

He looks up at me quickly, scowling. His blue eyes turn gray and are smoldering. I continue pointing my finger at him.

"I know exactly what you're doing. But my question is this, does she know you're only fucking her to make me jealous!" My rage has given way to hurt, but it feels *so* good to yell at him.

Ryan gawks, "Why the hell do you care who I fuck? You made me leave, remember?"

Those words cut me to the core. I did. I made him go. Again, another fault that is all mine.

Ryan stands up to pace the pit box again, but remains silent.

"Why, Ryan? What are you trying to do to me? Haven't you hurt me enough?" I mutter.

He abruptly stops, but doesn't look at me, and I can tell he is hurt, too, by the desperate look on his face. I flash back to the morning in my hospital room, and I fire again. "I mean, you didn't even apologize for what happened to me."

Suddenly, Ryan leaps at me, and we are nose to nose. His vehemence causes me to jump back and almost trip over my disabled leg. Ryan reaches out, grabs my arm, and jerks me upright to keep me from falling backward. He tightens his grip on my arm.

I draw a sharp intake of breath as he roars through gritted teeth, "You didn't give me a fucking chance!"

Tears spring to my eyes. I swallow and fight them back, but Ryan realizes instantly that he has frightened me with his outburst and immediately softens his expression as he steps back and releases my arm.

I swallow the lump in my throat. "I can't do this, Ryan, not here, not now." My voice is wavering. I stumble back on my aching leg. A regretful look washes over Ryan's gorgeous face as he reaches out to steady me again, but softly this time. His touch resonates throughout my body and calms me instantly. It is amazing the power he still holds over me.

My radio interrupts. "Whitney!" Ben barks. "Whatever is going on over there, wrap it up now!"

Where the heck is he? I wonder as I look around. I sigh.

"Done," I reply back instantly.

"We have a lot of eyes on us today." Ben castigates us both knowing that Ryan can hear his reprimand too.

Ryan stalks away without even looking back at me. I feel as though he has punched me in the stomach. My shoulders fall in defeat because I know we won't be able to resolve this until after the race, or even at all.

Chapter 38

Tonight's race was very calm for lack of a better word. Ryan finished in the top twenty. He was very careful and cool on the track. Although we did not speak again after our early morning argument, I was very proud of him for advancing his qualifying position from twenty-sixth to finish twelfth. The team needed a good finish. Hopefully, this means we can all move forward and get back to work. I vow to maintain a safe distance from Ryan so that I can do my job. There are only a dozen or fewer races left in this season, and I sincerely hope that Garrett will transfer me to another driver in November. It would be the only way for me to get over Ryan.

It is nearly midnight when I arrive back at the Jefferson. I'm so tired that I can barely see straight. I set my bag down at the door of my hotel room to find my key. My leg aches severely from the overexertion today, but I have plenty of meds for that. I just need to lie down. I swipe my key card and slowly enter the room. As soon as I take a step into the small entrance, I see an embarrassing display of fresh-cut white flowers in a white wicker basket on the main table. *What!*

I blink my eyes to make sure that I am not hallucinating. I close the door, set my bags down, and turn back to retrieve the basket. I snap on the bedside lamp and rip open the card. *Ryan! Oh!*

Even though I never got the chance to tell you, you will never know how deeply sorry I am or how much I will forever regret what I did to you.

RFC

Tears fall instantly as a million thoughts run through my head. His words, they touch me deep down. So deep, it makes me long for Ryan. Why couldn't he have said those words six weeks ago? I want to call him badly, but have no idea what I would even say. Is he back in Charlotte? Is she with him?

My thoughts are interrupted by an incoming message alert on my iPhone. I grab my phone. *It's Ryan!*

> Are you back at the hotel?

I reply as I feel my blood rushing throughout my body.

> Yes. The flowers are beautiful, but I am most thankful for your words.

Ryan's response is instant.

> It's the least I could do. I really am sorry.

I take a deep breath before responding again.

> Me too! Good job today. Keep it up, and maybe we will both get to keep our jobs!

I try to keep the mood light. I don't want another repeat of this morning.

His response is clipped and short.

Yea. Maybe so.

I wait a few minutes to respond because I am not sure of what to say next, when another message from him comes through.

I need to see you!

A lump rises in my throat. *No!* But my fingers disobey my mind.

When? Tomorrow?

He pleads with me.

No, tonight.

Why? I can't deal with a replay from this morning.

It's so late, Ryan.

Ryan's next message reads.

I don't care. I need to see you now.

Tears begin to pool in my eyes again. Truth is...I need to see him too. The last six weeks have been pure hell. I can't fight him anymore. I don't want to fight him anymore. We need to talk this through so we can at least get past what happened.

I swallow the lump in my throat as I type.

OK.

He responds quickly.

OK what?

Duh!

You know where I am. My flight doesn't leave until the morning.

My iPhone sings out with a new message.

Open the door.

I am confused.

Text me when u arrive.

Ryan's last message takes my breath as I read.

I'm already here.

Whoa! Wait! Where!

I walk to the door, open it slowly, and peer out into the hallway. Ryan is sitting on the floor with his back propped up against the wall. He is his normal gorgeous, smoldering self. His hair is still damp from the shower, and he is dressed in jeans, T-shirt, and his leather jacket. He has one knee pulled up and his cell phone in his hand. His trademark smirk is replaced with a sad, dejected manner, emotions that I know too well.

I stand outside my door, lean against it, and fold my arms in front of my chest. "So...what would you have done if I had said no?" I say casually.

Ryan rises from the floor gracefully and is at my side within a blink of an eye. He bends down and lifts me off my feet, cradling me tightly against his chest. I hold on to him tightly and snuggle my face into his neck, breathing in his intoxicating scent.

"I was not gonna take no for an answer," he says as he crosses the threshold into my hotel room and kicks the door shut behind us. Ryan carries me back through the room and gently sets me down on the sofa. I must have a confused look on my face because he says, "We need to talk first." *Really? Do we?*

With that statement, the air around us has considerably changed from light to tense. Formerly, when Ryan would sweep me off my feet, we would go straight to the bedroom or nearest available surface.

Ryan begins to pace the little square area of my room. He looks nervous. "There are several things that I need to say that I should have said to you that morning. I...I..." he stammers, then stops. "Damn it!" He looks angry as he fishes his cell phone out of his back pocket.

It must have been on vibrate because I didn't hear it ring. "What?" Ryan snaps into the phone. "Yes, I am with her. No, everything is fine. I will take it from here. What? No...take my flight back to Charlotte. I will take care of her from here on out. Yes. OK. Oh! Max...thank you!" Ryan presses the power button on his cell phone, turning it off. *Max? What the hell?*

"What was that about?" I exclaim. Ryan shakes his head at me. I prompt him again. "Ryan..."

He throws his hands up in the air in frustration. "It was Max. I hired him to watch over you after the accident!" he says sheepishly.

"What?" I gasp as I put it all together.

Ryan shrugs. "You didn't want me around, but I had to know that you were OK! That you were protected from all this."

I sink down into the couch, overtaken by his confession. I cannot believe that he did that.

"So, Max has been what...following me for the past six weeks?" I blink at Ryan wildly, trying desperately to understand why.

"Yes, the media storm alone was crazy enough, not to mention Colton. And I didn't know what he was capable of." He shrugs again.

I take a sharp breath in. "So, you know that I was at your house last week." Ryan looks me dead in the eye and silently nods. I swallow the huge lump in my throat.

"I tried to call you, but when you answered, I knew...Your voice...I could tell that you were upset. And I couldn't handle it. So, I hung up."

All this information is too much for me to process, but one fact is evident: Ryan still cares for me. My chest swells with pride, but I am still so defeated.

As I sit in silent shock, Ryan takes the opportunity to start talking again about the accident. "Look, Whitney...there are several things that I want to say to you."

I hold my hand up to stop him because this revelation about Max is enough for me to process right now. "Ryan, please, there is no need to rehash it!"

"No!" he exclaims. "Don't you fucking dare! You kept me from this that morning, damn it, and I'm not gonna let you do it again! I have had to relive that moment every single day for the past six weeks. I have to get this off my chest!" He's angry now.

"OK, OK..." I hold up my hands in defeat to let him continue.

"You have no fucking clue, Whitney. I mean, I didn't even realize what had happened until I had gotten out of the car. I swear I never saw you! Colton was shouting your name. I couldn't even process what had happened. Then...there you were." He motions down to the floor as if we are standing back in the middle of the garage lane. "All I could see was your hair on the ground, sticking out from under Colton's car!" He pauses and runs his hands through his own hair in exasperation. "I lost it. I went out of my fucking mind! I had to get you out from under his car! I...I thought you were dead. I have never *ever* been that scared in my *life*. And I have been through some bad shit on the track. Do you understand me?" Ryan takes a ragged breath.

He is exhausted. I don't say anything. I let him continue, but I can't look at him, so I look down at my hands, tears pooling in my eyes. It has been such a long day, yet still he goes on.

"Everyone was shouting, and no one would let me move you. Then, I smelled the gas. It was pouring out of Colton's car. I guess I busted the fuel tank. I panicked, thinking the car would catch on fire with you under it. Several of the crew guys helped me lift and roll the car back over you. As soon as I saw your face, I-I just grabbed you in my arms and held you until the paramedics arrived."

Wow. This is too intense. I have never had anyone give me a play-by-play of what happened that day. I have really vague memories of the accident, thankfully. I do remember seeing Ryan's face, but I thought I had dreamed it.

I keep my head down. It's too painful to look at him. I understand now. While I felt and have had to deal with the physical and emotional pain, he has had to relive daily the repercussions of his actions. I feel a huge sob welling up in my throat.

"Whitney! Look at me!" Ryan snaps.

His sharp tone makes me shudder. I raise my head, and hot tears cascade down my cheeks, and a terrifying sob emits from my throat.

Ryan is beside me in a second. "Please, please don't cry," he pleads. "I don't want to upset you with all this, but I just needed you to know how I felt, is all. I wanted to die. Every night I am haunted not only by the accident, but you forcing me to leave you at the hospital. It's not only then, but now too. When I saw you for the first time today, it all came roaring back to me again. I just can't believe that this happened to you and that my anger and arrogance caused it. These bruises, this horrible scratch on your beautiful face, and your leg with that damn cast, I can't stand it. I can't stand myself!" He stands up with disgust.

It's a surprise. His words. His apology, especially! Ryan Carter does not apologize. I learned that early on. I don't know what to say, so I continue to cry softly. Ryan drops down to the floor in front of me. He positions himself in between my legs so that his face is peering up into mine. He softly caresses my cheek in the way that he does. It takes my breath away.

Ryan's touch still has the power to burn me. My breath hitches, and my tears momentarily stop.

"Whitney...I..." He falters. "I can't explain these feelings that I have for you. I don't understand them myself. All I know is that I need you so much. I lov—"

I immediately stop him. "No! Don't *you* fucking dare!" I jump up off the sofa and walk away to create some distance in between us. I rest my tired body against the wall. My leg is throbbing. With my back to him, I question, "How can you say that to me after you've slept with *her* last night?" It's too much to take. I know I love him. I've known it for some time. But I can't bear to hear him say the words after all that has happened.

"I didn't sleep with her, Whitney!" Ryan admits, still seated on floor.

I turn back to him sharply. I give him my best "don't think for one second that I believe you, Ryan Fucking Carter" look. He recoils. Mission accomplished.

"Whitney," he pleads, and I roll my red-rimmed eyes at him. "She came to my bus last night to talk to me about Colton. She confessed that he was pursuing her while she was with me. And that she continued the relationship after she quit as my public relations manager."

I cock my head to one side. "So, all that stuff that was delivered to my hotel room in Sonoma was from Colton?" I ask, but already know that it is true. My gut instincts are always right on.

Ryan nods his head. "She tried to tell me that she broke if off with him because of me. Then, she made a move on me, and I told her that she needed to leave. I went to the back and got into bed. I thought she left. But when I woke up this morning, there she was, asleep on my couch. I got dressed as quickly as I could and got out of there so I didn't have to deal with her. I didn't even think about you coming to the bus this morning," he says all in one breath.

I feel nauseous thinking about Colton and how I completely misjudged him—and subsequently how I got the wrong impression about Ryan, too.

I hear Ryan stand up and feel him as he approaches me. He slowly turns my body to face his. He intimately brushes my hair off my shoulder in that way he does, then runs his hand softly around my neck and back up into my hair. He angles my head back so that I am forced to look directly into his stunning blue eyes.

"I'm sorry for that, too," he whispers softly. His eyes search mine. Then he gently says, "I love you."

Tears fill my eyes again. I try to look down, but he is holding my head firmly in place. I nod my head in acceptance of his statement, then manage to say, "I...I have something that I need to tell you that might change your mind." I grab Ryan's hand and pull it down from my head, then step back as he eyes me warily.

"What is it? Or who is it, should I say?" Ryan asks, confused but scared.

"What do you mean?" I snap.

"I know he called after the accident," Ryan says, almost in a whisper. "Are you back with him?"

"What?" I shake my head, then remember that the bastard from Georgia called after my accident. *How did Ryan know about that, though?* "No, Brooke dealt with him. That is over. You know that! Now, sit down," I command through gritted teeth as I point him back to the small sofa. I take a deep breath. "There is a reason why I wanted you...no, needed you to leave the hospital that morning."

Ryan looks at me quizzically, then cocks his head to the side as if he doesn't understand.

I continue with my confession. "Colton."

The pure mention of his name sends Ryan's gorgeous face into a fit of rage that emits several shades of red across his cheeks. "What about him?" he demands.

This is gonna be harder than I thought. I should have just kept my damned mouth shut.

I take another breath to steal some courage. "Colton...umm..."

Ryan angrily injects, "Damn it, Whitney! Just say it, for God's sake!"

"OK...OK!" I take a deep breath to force down the lump in my throat. "Colton was pursuing me as well. I guess he was playing Annalise and I together."

Ryan rolls his eyes at me. "Yes, I know he was." I am surprised that he knew. I stop in shock, but Ryan begs me to continue. "Go on."

"After the first race that I attended as your PR manager, Colton and I met for drinks, but it wasn't anything. I mean...Brooke was there, so it wasn't like a date or anything. I think I really did it just to piss you off initially. Not that you would have known."

Ryan raises an eyebrow at me. "I knew. Even before you told me in Kentucky."

I stand, shocked again. "How?" I mouth quietly.

"Whitney, I know a lot of things. Stop changing the subject," Ryan demands.

"After a couple rounds of drinks, he asked me to walk him out. I did. We talked in his car for a few minutes. He made it clear to me that he wanted a relationship with me, quite clear. But I told him that I was not about to jeopardize my new job by getting involved with him." Ryan smiles proudly at me. I hold up my hand. "But..."

Ryan's face falls. "But what?"

I look down, not sure I can tell him the rest because I know he is going to go ballistic.

"Whitney, so help me God. Spit it out!" I take a deep breath, but before I can speak, Ryan asks me quietly, "Were you seeing him too?"

His statement takes the breath out of my lungs. I am shocked he would ask me that. "No!" I almost scream at him.

"Then what?" Ryan loses it.

"I'm...I...I'm not sure," I stutter. Ryan's anger makes it hard for me to concentrate, but I manage to continue, "I guess Colton was watching us closely at Loudon, maybe even Daytona. I don't know. Maybe he saw an exchange between us or something. Again...I don't know, but he somehow knew that we had become involved."

"So what?" Ryan barks.

Then suddenly I can see the light bulb go off in his head as I say the words to him. "Colton wrecked you intentionally because of me, because I got involved with you and not him."

Whew! There, I said it. I cover my eyes with my hands, waiting for Ryan's rage to blow off the roof.

"That son of a bitch!" Ryan exclaims as he jumps off the couch. He begins to pace the floor. "I am glad that I broke his damn jaw now. Shit!"

I collapse on his vacant seat on the couch, exhausted from my own declaration. *What?*

"You broke Colton's jaw? How did I miss that?"

Ryan rolls his eyes at me. "See? You see?" he shouts, angry as hell, ignoring my question. "I have been trying for weeks to work this all out in my head. Why? Why would he purposefully sabotage me on the track? We have never really gotten along, but we have always been teammates. This is why I have never liked that bastard!" Ryan shakes his head, still radiating rage. I peer up at him, scared.

I try to fill in the gaps for Ryan. "I ran over to the garage to stop you from making a scene, but Colton stopped in the middle of the lane. He jumped out of his car, and we began to argue. That is why I was in the middle of the garage lane. He was angry with me because I was with you and not him. This all could have been avoided had it not been for me. My choices were the catalyst for all of this chaos. It really is entirely my fault," I say firmly.

Ryan turns back to face me. "Whitney! Are you kidding me? This is not your fault. Colton made a choice to do what he did. It is *none* of his damn business what you do. You obviously didn't care enough about him to get involved with him in the first place."

I shake my head and look away.

"Look at me, Whitney!" Ryan demands as he drops to the floor in front of me again. I look back into his eyes. "This is not your fault! Do you understand me?"

More tears flow down my cheeks, carrying weeks and weeks' worth of guilt and anxiety for what I have caused to two people's careers. I try to stifle a sob. "If I had just said no to you or made you leave my apartment that night, none of this would have ever happened!"

Ryan takes me in his arms as I cry fresh tears. "Whitney, you know what we had...how we feel about each other. You couldn't deny that if you tried." I nod because I know it's true.

I finally manage to say, "In the beginning, I thought you were doing a fine job of ruining your own career, but I never in a million years dreamed it would have been me that helped you to accomplish that feat. I just felt like the best thing was to take myself out of the equation altogether, which is why I made you leave."

Ryan nods, finally putting all the pieces together. "Whitney, why?" he questions me desperately. "Why couldn't you have told me this in the hospital?" He pauses, conflicted. "I could have been there for you. I would have helped you recover." Then he shakes his head and looks down in defeat.

He is silent for what feels like forever, then looks at me with those beautiful blue eyes. "The hardest thing..." Ryan trails off as he chokes up. "Goddamn it!" he exclaims, pumping his fist to fight back the sob in his throat. "The hardest thing I have ever had to do was leave you in that hospital."

I gasp.

He continues, "I swear I will never leave you again!" Ryan leans up and grabs me in an all-consuming embrace with tears on his own face. *Oh no!*

My handsome, arrogant bastard in tears. It breaks what's left of my heart. In this moment, I am lost to him. No matter how Ryan has hurt me, emotionally, mentally or physically, wild horses couldn't drag me away from him.

Ryan pulls out of our embrace and looks at me with intense anticipation. He searches my face. "You haven't forgotten, have you?"

I am not sure what he means, and I raise my eyebrow in question.

"Us..." he whispers. "What it was like between us?"

I shake my head at him, afraid to speak. "I tried...to forget."

Ryan smiles warily as he tightens his grip around my body and whispers against my ear, "I have never felt this way in my life. I swear I will never let you go again!"

Watching him, I realize that this is our moment, our moment to hold on to what we had, hold on to us. I can't deny what we had was good—complicated, but amazing. I don't want to fight him anymore, and I no longer give a damn who knows that I have fallen under his spell.

Instead of making my own proclamation, I launch myself at him, wrapping my body around his. Ryan responds by engulfing me into a desperate embrace. I run my hands around his neck and up into his hair. He leans in and softly presses his lips to mine. The kiss ignites that feeling between us, and the softness leads to desperation as the floodgates to our emotions burst.

There is a delicious ache deep within my body that I know only Ryan can alleviate. Our bodies are gloriously intertwined by lips, legs, and arms.

Suddenly, Ryan pulls back from our embrace. He says breathlessly, "Say it!"

I am dumbfounded. "Say what?"

He looks at me warily. "I want to hear you say the words...tell me that you love me," he says desperately.

I look deeply into his beautiful blue eyes. "I love you, Ryan."

My profession renews our passion, and we are entangled again. I am lost. I am so overcome with relief, desire, and love that I am nauseous. I feel like I'm going to pass out from the intensity.

I cry out, "Oh!" Ryan immediately stops. I steady myself against him.

Ryan looks at me, concerned. "Am I hurting you?" he says, no doubt because of my accident.

I am so overwhelmed by the last six weeks, today, and tonight that I am overtaken by the emotions of the elapsed time period. My body cascades with a loud sob, and instantly tears pour from my eyes yet again.

Ryan holds me as I cry and makes no attempt to stop me. He silently consoles me, stroking my hair as we stay locked in a tight embrace.

Finally, he sincerely says, "I will never, ever hurt you again." With that promise, he sweeps me off my feet and softly lays my war-torn body down on the hotel bed.

Delicious memories of our first night together flash through my mind. We have come so far, and so much has happened since then. Ryan gently lays down beside me, careful of my healing leg. I watch him so intently, blinking rapidly to make sure that I am not dreaming, to make sure that he doesn't disappear. I ache for him to touch me, but he doesn't. He just looks at me. It makes me uneasy.

Finally, Ryan gently strokes the upper thigh of my broken leg. "How bad does it hurt?" he asks warily.

I shake my head because I don't want to answer that. I am scared it will open the floodgates again. Instead I say, "It's almost healed now. You can remove this cast." I point to the straps of my walking boot, then pop the Velcro tabs and slowly remove it. My leg, foot, and toes are grossly swollen. Ryan shakes his head and looks away like he is distressed. "Hey..." I say softly. "I can take the physical pain over the emotional pain any day."

Ryan looks back to me. "Whitney..."

I grasp his chin and angle his face so that he is looking at me in the eye. "We already rehashed this, remember?"

Ryan nods his head in agreement and places his hand over mine. We stare at each other in silence, not sure of the next move.

I move my hand from his chin to his cheek. "What did you tell me earlier?"

He looks at me, dumbfounded. "I'm sorry."

I shake my head, signaling a wrong answer.

He tries again. "I love you?"

"Did you mean it?"

Ryan gets defensive. "Yes, I did!"

I smile at him wryly. "Then show me, damn it!"

Ryan obeys my request. We come together, and it feels so good. The rhythm of our bodies picks up like they never missed a beat. Ryan is careful and attentive of my healing body. He gently removes my clothes. I can feel the grime of the short track on my body, and there is tire rubber in my long brown locks, but I couldn't care less. We are together. I remember it all: the attraction that pulled us together, the emotions and anger, and our physical chemistry when we made love. I let these feelings and sensations I had banished rush over my body. I writhe against Ryan's skin with desire and desperate need.

Ryan takes his time like he is savoring every inch of my body and memorizing my curves. I am cloaked by his attentiveness, and his smell overtakes my senses, that glorious smell that is so intoxicating to my body.

I cry out, "Ryan," and he pulls back and looks at me with concern. "I can't take it. Please...I need you now." My body is on fire with desire.

Ryan swiftly but gently obeys my command as he enters my body. We are one. A feeling of sudden relief comes over me. The relief of being able to reconnect to these feelings that I was scared were lost. I close my eyes and totally experience every kiss, every movement, every thrust. Ryan picks up his pace as if our inner emotions are the same. It is a heady, mixed feeling to be this intertwined with another person, body and soul.

Ryan's hands caress my breasts, then move softly up and down my midsection. I feel my body quickening. I want to savor this moment completely filled up by him. I want to give him everything that I have. And now I know that I can't live without him. With that inner confession, my body unloads with an intense orgasm that erupts over my entire body. Ryan follows immediately, calling out my name in desperation and reprieve.

* * *

In the back of my mind, I am broken from a calm and comforted contentment. I stir to the noise that has awakened me from a sweet sleep free from anxiety, guilt, pain, alcohol, and so many other variables that have taken over my body for the last six weeks. I realize it is my iPhone alarm that sounds out the time. I try to move to silence the aggravating disturbance, but I am trapped, gloriously trapped, under Ryan Carter.

Last night, Ryan said he would never let me go. I guess he meant it literally, too. I smile and breathe a sigh of relief.

Ryan stirs. "What the hell?"

It is way too early, I know. We have been asleep for only a few hours, but I have a plane to catch at 7:00 a.m. "My plane..." I say blearily as I grab my phone to switch the alarm off.

"Forget it! We will get home later," Ryan responds sleepily.

I don't even argue with him. I have no doubts that he will take care of our return to Charlotte. I snuggle back down into Ryan's embrace.

My mind, body, and soul are overtaken by feelings of relief and happiness. I am confident and sated in the fact that Ryan will take care of me.

Chapter 39

Even though it is early Monday morning, I am all smiles. I shift and turn over in bed to face a peaceful, sleeping Ryan Carter. My movement stirs him slightly, but he doesn't wake. I'm glad. I know he is exhausted, as am I. These last six weeks have taken a toll on us both. Not to mention our reconciliation in the early hours of the morning was a shocking eye-opener that left us both worn out.

Ryan loves me. Or so he says. It is a lot to take in, but I can't think about that now. I don't want to think about it now. I want to focus on my job and being happy with him. Forget the specifics.

Speaking of my job, I know I am late. Thankfully, we came to Ryan's after we landed in Charlotte, so I don't have far to drive to work. I lean over to softly kiss his shoulder, being careful not to wake him. I move to rise from the bed, and a strong arm reaches out for me. Ryan grabs my side and pulls me back into an embrace against his body. *Oh!*

Ryan groans softly. It is early, but I can feel that he wants me. "Don't get up," he says groggily.

I sigh. I don't want to leave this secure spot either, but I have to get to the office.

"I have to get to work, or my boss will fire my ass," I quip.

"I will fire your ass if you get up! Now, come here," he says seductively.

And I am lost to him once again. There is no need to argue.

* * *

Despite Ryan's distraction, I manage to make it to the office at a decent time. I am in an unusually good mood. I know everyone knows it from the looks I have been getting, but I smile, keeping my little secret to myself. Lunchtime finally arrives, and I am famished. With our ongoing backlog from Ryan's suspension, I don't have the luxury of taking an actual break to eat. I take a bite of my turkey sandwich that I brought from Ryan's, when I hear a commotion outside my office door.

A distraught Jerri sticks her head through my office door. "Whitney! Get your things! It's Garrett! We have to go *now*!" she yells.

I don't think. I grab my bag and choke down the mouthful of my sandwich.

I stand up to go and am quickly reminded that I am not working on all cylinders, but I manage to catch up to Jerri in the hallway. It is hard for me to keep up with her because of the "boot," but I scale down the stairs effortlessly on one foot. She remains silent, but the look on her face speaks volumes. We make it outside, quickly jump into her Mercedes SUV, and speed away.

On the drive, Jerri finally explains what I feared. With a sob in her throat, she says, "Garrett has had a heart attack! Or at least that is what they think! Ryan just found him out in the field."

Ryan!

"Is he...?" I manage to mutter. Jerri shakes her head as if she doesn't know.

I grab my purse and fumble for my iPhone. I scroll quickly to find Ryan's number and press send. It goes straight to voice mail. *Damn!* I switch to text.

Ryan, I am on my way.

I am shaking with fear. Jerri and I sit in silence as we make our way to the Carolinas Medical Center. Jerri's words come back to haunt me, *"This situation is stressful for all of us, especially for Garrett since he has to come out of retirement to pick up the slack."*

Please don't let this be the cause of his heart attack, I plead to myself.

We reach the emergency room in record time. Jerri pulls up at the entrance to drop me at the door. I grab my iPhone, leave my bag, and hoist myself up and out of the SUV. I hobble to the desk as quickly as I can and flash my GCR Racing Team credentials.

With an attitude, the nurse at the desk rolls her eyes at me. "That ain't gonna get you through these doors, honey!" Then she laughs at herself like she is some kind of comedian. I lose it.

I go off on her with my uncouth no-brain-to-mouth-filter attitude that is normally reserved for Ryan only. "Excuse me, but I know you know the severity of this situation. My question is, why in the hell has the facility not been locked down?"

She blinks at me, dumbfounded. *I got her attention. Good.*

I continue my rampage. "It is only a matter of time before every paparazzo this side of the Mason-Dixon Line is crawling in this reception area with some type of false ailment to try to get back through these doors. So, I strongly advise that you get your supervisor in here to speak with me immediately."

With that statement, I turn as I hear Jerri's voice from behind me. "Whitney, I have the hospital CEO on the line now."

I turn back to the smug nurse, who has quickly changed her attitude and is cowering back. I smile and raise my eyebrows at her. *Take that!*

Jerri is irreverently speaking to the CEO. Then, I hear instructions come over the loudspeaker about locking down the emergency room. I hear a buzzing sound, and we are ushered through the door into the treatment area.

Jerri presses the end button on her BlackBerry and turns to the nurse. "You will be getting further instructions from your supervisor. I suggest that you follow them to the letter!" she exclaims.

The nurse concedes like a scolded dog. *Go Jerri!*

We are ushered into a small waiting area by another nurse. Jerri says, "We have to wait here."

I blink rapidly at her. "Like hell," I snap. I stalk off from her to the nurses' station, "Where is the restroom?" I ask a triage nurse.

She eyes me carefully, and I know she is on to me. I hold my ground and smile politely. She grants me a pass and directs me down the hallway toward the restroom.

I find the ladies' room and duck in momentarily in case she is watching me. After a beat, I stick my head into the hallway. *All clear!* I make my way down a back corridor as quickly as I can. I look to my left and right, nothing. I walk quickly to the next corridor. Down the right wing at the very end, I see Ryan sitting on the floor.

Ryan is sitting outside a door with his knees pulled up to his chest. His head is in his arms. He looks so young. The closer I get, I realize that he is sobbing. I cry out, and my audible gasp grabs his attention. I break out in a full-on run to him. The pain in my leg is no match for heartbreak I am feeling for Ryan right now.

Ryan flies up from the floor and envelops me in a desperate embrace. I begin to cry with him as we sink back down to the floor. He sobs into my hair, and I let him. I don't know what to say or how to comfort him. This is something that I have never had to deal with.

After a few minutes that seem like hours, Ryan begins to speak. "Whitney...I...I was too late! He's dead!" he exclaims like he has been bulldozed.

"Oh my God, no!" I exclaim. I am desperate for words, but I am devastated, too. This cannot be happening. Garrett had so much faith in me.

Ryan and I sit on the floor of the hallway in silence. "I thought you were watching the race highlights with him this morning?" I question, remembering our conversation this morning as I left for the office. Ryan was supposed to have breakfast with his dad and go over the race. This is their ritual every Monday morning.

Ryan sighs. "I called him this morning. We had breakfast, but he said there was no need to watch the film. He said to me, 'Son, there is nothing that I can tell you that you don't already know. I am so proud of you and how you have turned this season around despite the accident.'" Ryan pauses. "Then, he said he had work to do out in the field before the rain came in today." He shakes his head. "It was strange for him because we do this every week, but I didn't realize it at the time."

I reach out to grasp his hand.

"Mom called me when he didn't come in for lunch. So, I set out to where he was working on constructing a dam for the pond." He pauses again, and my chest constricts with pain for him. "He was sitting on the tractor, limp and not moving. But, I...I was too late." He shakes his head, and tears fall anew.

Fighting back my own tears, I stand up with new determination. I have to be strong for Ryan and for our organization. Then it hits me. "Ryan, your mom?"

He looks toward the door. "She is inside with him. She wanted to be alone with him."

As he utters those words, Ryan's mom opens the door and walks out to us. She has no life in her eyes, but manages to give me a weak smile. Ryan lets go of me to grab her because she looks like she is about to fall over. He looks at me, grief stricken, like he doesn't know what to do next either. Instantly, I know what I have to do!

I take hold of them both and usher them back to the waiting area where Jerri sits. She looks distraught as we enter the small, dimly lit room. I know she knows.

I take charge of the situation. My first call is to Max. I take out my iPhone and select his personal cell phone from my contact list. The phone rings once, and Max says, "Hey Whitney!"

I sigh into the phone remembering how Ryan contracted with him to watch over me after my accident. "Hi," I murmur.

"Everything OK...?"

"No...I need you. Can you come to Carolinas Medical Center now?" And I reveal to him the most heartbreaking news of my life. Even Max is choked up. I can hear it in his voice.

I secure his staff immediately. He reassures me that he is on his way to the hospital for a private escort back to Mooresville. Then, I coordinate with the hospital staff, prepare a small public statement requesting privacy, and secure a back exit. I have to get us all out of here, and quickly, before the paparazzi descend on us yet again.

Chapter 40

It is late. I am grateful that Ryan wanted to come home tonight. We have not left his parents' home since Monday. I follow Ryan into his house down the corridor that is lined with racing photos of him and Garrett. Normally, I look at the photos because each time I see something different, but tonight, I can't look at them. Ryan is unnervingly quiet, which is the way he has been for the last few days. I can't blame him. He has been through one of the most traumatic events a person can face, the loss of a parent. I have no idea of how to console him, but I have not left his side.

Ryan turns on the kitchen light and walks over to the refrigerator. I stand watching him sympathetically. Even after these few days, I still have no earthly idea of what to say. My heart aches for him. He jerks the sub-zero door open and grabs a beer. His sudden movement takes me by surprise. Exhausted, I slowly step out of my one black heel and lean over to unlatch the straps on my walking boot.

To say this week has been exhausting would be the understatement of the century. Since Garrett's death on Monday, I have been solely working public relations for the family at Laura's request. The office has been completely shut down, and the GCR teams will not compete this weekend at Chicagoland due to bereavement. There has been a horde of people in and out of Ryan's family home, not to mention private services for the family, including a wake, and another public memorial service for Garrett's fans.

It exhausts me to replay it all in my mind. And the mere fact that I planned it all for Laura and Ryan is inconceivable. But there was no way they could have done it alone. The shock and grief are more than anyone can bear right now. I have been by Ryan's side, but have kept a close distance due to prying eyes. No one else knows that Ryan and I have reconciled except for his mother and, sadly, Garrett.

I had planned to take some time to rest this afternoon, but Ryan insisted that I attend the private interment, for immediate family only, on the Carter plot on the farm. He was extremely adamant about me going, which was confusing. It should have been a private time for Ryan and his mother. I could not figure out why he wanted me there so badly. I guess it was mainly for moral support. My thoughts remind me that even my brain is too tired to function right now.

I look over at Ryan to tell him that I am going to bed, but before I can utter those words, he loses it. He howls a low, guttural wail that sends chills down my spine. The sound is a battle cry as he tosses the bottle up, grabs it by the neck, and then slings it with unnatural force across the room. I cry out watching the events in slow motion. *Oh, Ryan!*

The bottle slams into the opposing kitchen wall. I stumble backward and throw up my arms to shield my eyes from the spray of glass and hops. My reaction must remind him that I, too, am in the room. Ryan's head snaps in my direction, making sure that I'm OK and not hurt from his outburst. I look back at him with sympathetic shock. He stands stock-still, staring at me, not realizing what he has done. Ryan slides down the length of the stainless steel refrigerator door to the floor. He buries his head in his hands and weeps.

I move quickly and take a seat on the floor next to him. Ryan has been amazingly strong for his mother. The only tears I have witnessed, aside from these, were at the hospital. Certainly, he is allowed his own meltdown after what he has been through.

I put my arms around him tightly and rest my head against his. After what seems like a lifetime, Ryan says, "Damn... you know... there was so much I didn't say to him. I...I wanted him to be proud of me. And lately, all I have done is show out like a pubescent teenager."

I laugh out loud at his confession.

Ryan snaps his face around to mine. "What's so funny?"

I raise my eyebrow at his anger and shake my head at him. "The way you made that statement, for one. It was a very accurate assessment."

Ryan is still not amused.

"And two, your dad was insanely proud of you."

Ryan gapes at me. I give him a look that says, *I can't believe that you don't know this.*

"Yes, he was. He told me so. That morning after I let you have it in the boardroom. He said, and I quote, *'Ryan will be an even better race car driver than I ever thought I could be.'*" I relive the conversation for him.

Ryan looks at me with relieved shock. "I can't believe he said that." He stands from his bereaved position on the floor.

"Well...believe it!" I quip.

Ryan helps me up from the floor and looks at me achingly. He is so hurt. He runs his fingers through his hair in exasperation and walks over to the kitchen counter. "After the accident, Dad said he was extremely disappointed in me. And those words cut me to the core. That conversation is on constant repeat in my mind. And the fact that I lost six weeks with him because of my stubbornness..."

He leans into the granite and steadies his body with his hands. My heart hurts to see him this broken. I move to his side and place my hand on his back softly. If I can't find the right words, maybe my touch will be enough. I have been hesitant to be affectionate with him because of so many people from the team, media, and general public around us these last few days. I run my hand slowly up his back, and he turns around suddenly, grasping my hand in his as if he wants me to stop.

My breath hitches in my throat. Ryan gives me a desperate look, and I can see several emotions wash over his gorgeous, rebellious face. The depth of his emotions are starting to scare me, though. Ryan intently searches my face. Then, he instantly runs his hand up into my hair and jerks it free from the rubber band that holds it neatly back away from my face in a bun. My brown hair cascades down my back, and I cry out to him in surprise, "Ryan!"

My stomach somersaults in my body much like the very first time I laid eyes on him. Ryan takes my face in my hands. "I need you! I need you so bad!" he says breathlessly.

Before I can respond, he fervently presses his lips to mine. His passionate kiss instantly takes my breath away. I fall into his body as he envelops me. This is home.

Ryan instantly sweeps my languid body up into his arms. He strides purposefully to his bedroom and doesn't bother with the lights. He lays me down gently on his bed in the darkness. "I feel like I'm losing my mind, and you...you are the only thing that is keeping me sane," he mutters intensely.

Tears begin to fall down my cheeks from the intense pain that we have been through, not just the death of Garrett and my accident, but the last six weeks, too.

"Hey," Ryan says softly. "Please, Whitney, please don't cry."

I know he has seen enough tears, but I am overcome with emotion. I have tried to be strong for him this week, but I have lost the battle tonight in his arms. The moon is full. It is casting a glow throughout the room that makes it just possible to see his face. I try in vain to fight back the tears, but they continue to flow freely.

Ryan is now looking at me sympathetically. "You have been great this week, but you don't have to be strong all the time. You can't be everything for everybody, Whitney."

I shake my head, not able to mutter a single syllable. Then suddenly, I know what I need. "Make it go away. This week, these past six weeks, make it all go away...Love me," I say breathlessly.

Ryan obeys my command. He softly wipes away the last of my tears. Then, he kisses me so fiercely that my back arches up from the mattress. Ryan cries out from his gut. It is hot. It's working too. I am forgetting already. Our bodies move together in that delicious rhythm that only they know. Ryan removes my little black dress effortlessly, and I help him with his white dress shirt and slacks. I have no idea what happened to his tie. It disappeared hours ago.

Ryan trails soft kisses over my body; each one burns and sends a delicious heat over my body. *Oh, I love this! I love him*, I think as Ryan enters me abruptly in desperation. I cry out. He stills for a moment, then begins an arduous rhythm. He, too, is trying to forget.

Ryan and I make love for what seems like hours. We are in a constant roll of positions. I don't want to stop. I beg my body to enjoy and fight off my orgasm at every turn. I'm not ready for it. I want to lose myself in Ryan. I don't want this moment to end.

"Whitney," Ryan mutters against my lips. I know what he means.

"No! Please...don't stop!" I shout breathlessly.

Ryan pulls back and looks at me questioningly. "I don't want to hurt you."

I shake my head to let him know that he is not. "I want to forget everything...everything but us," I say anxiously.

Ryan doesn't miss a beat. He continues at a much slower and gentler rhythm. I trail soft kisses down his neck and behind his ear. I bury my head into his shoulder, taking in his scent.

Ryan cries out like he is in pain. "I don't know how much more I can take, Whitney!" he exclaims.

"Then let go," I say.

He snaps back, "Not without you!" *Oh!*

I look up at him as our rhythm picks up again mercilessly, for a purpose now. I feel my body building, and I cannot fight the overwhelming burst of pleasure that barrels over my body and throughout my soul. Ryan cries out in response to my victory, but continues his stride until he crosses his own finish line. He falls over my body with a series of harsh expletives that are barely coherent. Our bodies heave together with exhaustion. Sleep inevitably follows.

Chapter 41

I awake sometime during the night, or maybe it is early morning. I am not sure. It's Friday, I believe. Instantly, I know that I am alone. I reach out for Ryan even though I already know that he is not there. As my hand comes up empty, I abruptly sit up in the bed. I have a sinking feeling in my gut that something is wrong. I jump onto my good foot. I grab Ryan's T-shirt from the floor and pull it on as I hobble out of the bedroom to find him.

Panic seizes in my chest the closer I get to the main part of the house. I begin to hear Ryan's harsh, arrogant voice.

"I don't give a shit what time it is!" His tone is firm, but in a forced whisper. "Just get my fucking car to the track! Do you understand me? No, I will handle that. Just get my damn car there." He slams his phone down without an audible good-bye to the recipient of his tirade, which I now assume was Josh.

I stand shocked in the entryway of the great room as I process Ryan's conversation. I feel like I'm going to throw up as I put two and two together. He wants to race. Ryan turns back toward the bed-room, but stops cold in his tracks when he spies me intruding on his conversation. He regards me cautiously. I blink rapidly. I can't believe it. He wants to race.

"I'm sorry," he apologizes no doubt unsure of my reaction. "I didn't mean to wake you."

I shake my head. "I woke up because you weren't there."

He strides over to me and puts his hands on either side of my face. "I have to do this, Whit. I have to do this for him. Please tell me that you understand?"

I nod nervously. There is no need for me to argue with Ryan, nor to question him. "Can Josh get the car there in time for qualifying?"

Ryan nods.

"OK, then, I will handle the rest," I offer anxiously. I am not sure how he is going to pull this off, but getting the car to the track is a start.

Ryan lets out a huge sigh of relief. I guess he was expecting a fight. He runs his hand from my face around my neck and pulls me into a fierce embrace. He pulls back and looks at me with a heated gaze. "I love you!"

And with that confession, he envelops me in a passionate kiss that leaves me breathless.

Ryan pulls back and looks deep into my eyes. "Do you need some time?"

I cock my head to the side, unsure of where he is headed with this question.

"What I meant was, do you want some time off to go see your parents? I know you haven't been home in a while, and now...I know how important that is."

I take a deep breath. I miss my parents, but I can't go back there.

Ryan must sense my conflict, and he offers, "I could go with you."

I laugh. "No, but thanks. I will figure something out when the season is over. I just want to focus on my job and getting you back where you need to be."

He smiles warmly. "Whitney, I really appreciate everything you do for me. And thank you for understanding that I need to race on Sunday."

I nod.

Ryan leans in and kisses me deeply again. "I need to do this as much as I need you."

I smile against his lips and gently pull away. "Let's get to work then!" I smirk and turn sharply on my good heel, but not before he smacks me softly on my behind. I laugh and kick up my good leg. "Ha!" I start to limp away, but Ryan sweeps me up into his arms and takes me back to his bed.

* * *

I wake up early despite the midnight disruption. I have work to do. Within an hour, I have secured a late qualifying spot for Ryan and a private charter flight for us to Chicago. I also made hotel reservations. It's too late in the game to get Ryan's bus to the infield. He barely got his race car there. No one will be expecting Ryan at the track today. I place a call to Jerri to inform her of his plans. Our team doesn't need anymore surprises.

While I have been steadily making arrangements, Ryan has gone back over to his parents' house to tell his mom that he plans to race on Sunday at Chicagoland. The thought sends chills down my spine. I can't even imagine that conversation. I know his mom will be devastated. I know she wanted Ryan to have some downtime to grieve. That is not going to happen. Then I suddenly realize that this is how he is grieving, doing what his dad taught him and what they loved doing together. My thoughts instantly go back to Daytona, now only a bittersweet memory, but I am so thankful to have been a part of it.

I glance at my iPhone to check the time. The plane will be fueled up and ready to leave Charlotte Douglas International in two hours. I text Ryan.

Plane leaving in two hours.

As soon as the text is sent, I hear the back door close, and Ryan shouts, "I'm here!"

He walks through the kitchen and eyes me sitting at his kitchen island. I am still wearing only his T-shirt. I know that look on his face.

"Oh no!" I gasp. "I have to take a shower!"

Ryan gives me that smug son-of-a-bitch smile. "I can do two things at one time."

I roll my eyes at him as he flings me over his shoulder and strides purposefully to the bathroom. *Bastard!*

* * *

Somehow, we make it to the airport on time. We board the private plane and take our seats. The flight is a good three hours long, and as soon as it lands, Ryan will barely have enough time to get to the track to qualify his car. The time schedule for the afternoon is hectic, but it takes my mind off the past few days and keeps me focused on the task at hand.

"How did it go with your Mom?" I ask warily.

Ryan takes a deep breath, "A lot better than I expected, but she was very upset." I nod quietly not wanting to press him for more details. I turn to look out the cabin window as our plane ascends into the sky.

I realize midflight that I have not a damn clue about the track we are headed to. I normally research the track and surrounding area during my race preparations. I look over to Ryan to ask him a few questions, but he is reclined back in his seat, with his earbuds in place, and his eyes closed. For the first time in a week, he looks peaceful. Whatever he is listening to, I need to download. I choose not to bother him. I guess I will figure out Chicagoland when we arrive.

Chapter 42

Our plane touches down at a private airfield outside of Chicago around three o'clock. I steal a glance at Ryan. He is back in tense mode. The emotion radiates across his face and body. Since we are alone on the plane, I reach over and gingerly grasp his hand. Ryan smiles at me, and I can feel his whole body relax. It worked.

A car is waiting to take us directly to the track for qualifying, but we have to fight through a gang of paparazzi at the airport entrance. Evidently, our arrival in Chicago was leaked. Ryan effectively ignores the shouts of invasive questions from the unsympathetic media. He takes my hand and calmly pushes a way for us through the madness to the waiting courier, a gesture that will no doubt incite a gossip riot before Sunday.

Finally, we arrive in Joliet, Illinois, which is about forty-five minutes outside of Chicago. Tension radiates throughout the car and the silence is unsettling.

"You don't have to do this, you know?" I say, trying to reassure him.

"Yes, I do!" he snaps back, but apologizes quickly. "I'm sorry, Whit. But this is the only way that I know how to deal." I nod as he looks despondently out of the window.

As we approach the speedway, my stomach is in nervous knots. I actually want to hyperventilate, but I try to breathe deeply for Ryan's sake. He is about to jump directly into his car to qualify, and he doesn't need my anxiety on top of his. Ryan reaches over and takes my hand as we make our way through the infield tunnel. I look over at him and smile despite my anxiousness.

The car slows to a stop. Ryan leans over and gives me a chaste kiss before jumping out. He heads off to his hauler to gear up. I grab our bags and start over to pit road, hoping that Bobby and the crew have had ample time to arrive. A big sigh of relief washes over me when I find Bobby in the garage.

"Hey kid," he says softly. I can still see the pain in his eyes, too. Our whole organization is bruised. Bobby worked alongside Garrett for over thirty years.

I smile sweetly. "Hey yourself! Can we pull this off?" I ask, trying to lighten the mood.

He smiles back at me and shakes his head. "I don't know, but we are gonna give it one hell of a try."

Ryan rounds the corner all suited up in his racing gear. He embraces Bobby with an all-consuming fatherly hug. This team is all family. I realize this now, and it has taken a tragic event to remind them all. Suddenly, I am extremely grateful for becoming a part of this wonderful organization.

Ryan apologizes to Bobby. "I'm sorry I threw this on y'all at the last minute."

Bobby smiles. "Your daddy would have kicked your ass if you missed a race!"

We all laugh. True story.

Ryan climbs into his car and sets out for pit road. I pull out my iPad to do some quick research on the track. Chicagoland Speedway is a one-and-a-half mile D-shaped oval with varying speeds averaging 145 miles per hour. It's fast, but not super-speedway fast.

Ryan takes the track effortlessly as I watch the monitor. He takes a warm-up lap, then proceeds across the start/finish line for the timed trial. Ryan fires his car into turn one, accelerating around 180 miles per hour. I can tell he is being extremely careful in an attempt not to screw up the lap, or maybe in anxiety. I am not sure. He roars down the back straightaway, into turns three then four.

I hear Bobby muttering under his breath, "Come on. Come on!"

Ryan slides his car over the start/finish line in 29.78 seconds, landing him around nineteenth position. I let out a long breath that I didn't realize I had been holding. That was intense!

Ryan pulls his car back into the garage. He slides out stealthily, and damn, he is so hot in that racing uniform. He peels it back, and I feel like I'm about to melt.

Ryan looks at me, concerned. "Everything OK?"

I smile wryly. "Yes." All my anxiety is definitely gone now. He takes notice, but still looks confused.

Ryan walks over to Bobby. "The car is awesome, but it's me that's the problem." He is radiating tension again. "I just can't get into the groove. I can't focus."

"Ryan," Bobby responds, "get in some practice laps. You have been through a lot lately. It will come back to you. Don't force it. Now, go get some rest. You're gonna need it for Sunday!"

The car is waiting to take us back to Chicago. The Joliet area was booked solid because of the race weekend. Plus, with the media coverage surrounding my accident and Garrett's death, I felt like Ryan needed to be away from the madness and paparazzi. In fact, I even made a reservation under a false name, which I am grateful for now since the incident at the airport.

Ryan is very quiet in the car. I can tell he is in race mode, but the atmosphere is still tense during the drive. I fidget uncomfortably, and Ryan notices.

"Are you sure everything is OK?"

I smile. "Yes, just a lot on my mind. This all happened so fast. I booked at the Ritz. I hope that's OK?" I say fast.

"I have no idea. I am sure it's fine, though. One room?"

"Umm...yes. Since we are away from the track, I thought it would be okay." I'm glad I was right. He smiles and takes my hand. I steal a nervous glance at the driver. Ryan firmly grips my hand so hard that I have to look back at him.

"I told you, I don't care who knows anymore," he whispers firmly as he pulls me in close to his side, erasing the distance between us. "Everyone will know on Sunday anyway."

What? I raise my eyebrows in confused silence.

* * *

We make it though hotel check-in unnoticed. Ryan collapses onto the bed as the bellman brings up our luggage.

"Do you want to go out to dinner?" This is our first time together during a race weekend, so I have no clue what is customary. He is lying facedown on the bed, but I can see him shaking his head no. "OK... well, I'm gonna take a shower." Ryan doesn't move or respond.

I grab my cosmetic case and head to the shower. The bathroom is glorious, and the shower is therapeutic. I take my time soaking up the scalding water. I can feel my muscles relax almost instantly. I hate to step out from the oasis, but my fingers are pruning. And unfortunately, I have work to do.

When I emerge from the bathroom, Ryan is pacing the floor of the hotel room. He is on the phone, but his voice is not audible. The curtain on the expansive glass window has been opened, exposing the breathtaking vista of Chicago at night. The combined scenery is breathtaking.

Ryan immediately stills when he senses my presence. He turns back sharply to me. "I will call you back!" Ryan abruptly hangs up the phone.

I raise my eyebrows at him. He looks like a kid caught with his hand in the candy jar. *Strange!*

Ryan walks over to me, and I realize he has changed clothes. He is dressed up. I look him over, confused. He has on jeans, a button-down shirt, and his leather jacket. He is gorgeous. *But where is he going?*

"I thought you didn't want to go out?"

Ryan looks uncomfortable and shifts his weight from his left to right foot.

"Is something wrong?" I ask.

"I...I need to go out for a bit. Is that OK?" Ryan says.

I am unsure of what is happening or where he is going, but I don't question him. "OK." I look down at my hands. "I have work to do anyway," I mumble.

Ryan laughs and pulls my chin up to meet his gaze. "No, you don't. I will bring back some dinner for us." With that statement, he caresses my face, and I lay my head in his hand. "Whit, you're tired. You haven't fully recovered from the accident. Please rest until I get back."

"OK," I whisper.

Ryan gently kisses my lips, and the heat radiates through my body. He shakes his head and leans his forehand against mine. "I have to go now, or I will never leave." He smiles against my lips.

"Then don't go," I say in a hushed whisper.

"I won't be long, baby. Get some rest."

Ryan leaves the room, and I feel a pool of dread in my stomach and a huge lump in my throat. I fight back tears because I have no idea why he left. I sincerely hope that it's not because of me. I shake my head to rid my brain of these thoughts.

I pile up in the super-luxurious bed and take out my laptop. I have a few e-mails to send in regard to Sunday and Ryan's last-minute decision to race. Plus, I need to inform Jerri of a few pre-race details. I fire off a few e-mails and feel my eyes getting heavy. I don't realize it, but I fall asleep in the middle of updating Ryan's fan page on Facebook.

I am gloriously sleeping when an intoxicating smell overtakes my senses. Without opening my eyes, I know it's Ryan. I feel him slide my laptop out from under me.

I open my eyes sleepily. "What time is it?"

"It's late. It took a little longer than I expected."

What took longer than expected?

"I'm sorry. I brought you some food, though."

"I'm too tired to eat," I moan. I can hear Ryan emptying his pockets and the sound of his clothes coming off. He slides into the bed and wraps his body around mine, spooning me. It's heavenly. He nuzzles my neck and hair, and that is all I need to push me back into sleeping bliss, regardless of where he's been or what he has been doing.

I awake for the second time, and the room is dark with a small hint of light coming from under the now-drawn curtain. *When did those get closed?* I wonder. I lie still as I wake up. I don't want to bother Ryan. I turn my head slowly to find that he is already wide-awake, staring at the ceiling.

Ryan turns his head slowly to face me. He smiles, but I can tell something is wrong. A wave of nausea creeps over my body. *What the hell is going on with him?*

He notices my concern. "Whitney, are you okay?"

I roll my eyes. "I should be asking you that question."

He turns his face away from mine and fixes his gaze back on the ceiling. Since we left the track yesterday, Ryan has been radiating several emotions that I don't understand. I am confused and worried.

Without looking at me, Ryan says, "I need you to arrange a press conference on Sunday, a short one for me to thank fans, sponsors, et cetera. Let the media know, also, I don't want to be interviewed before or after the race. Got it?" His tone is rude, clipped, and makes my skin crawl. It reminds me of how he treated me when I first started working for GCR.

"Sure," I say quietly. "You don't have to do this, you know. I can see how stressed and tense you are. It makes me nervous."

Ryan doesn't offer a response. His silence and disregard tick me off. I sit up in the bed sharply. My gesture takes him by surprise, and he mirrors my movement.

"Ryan, for God's sake!" I plead. "What is going on? I know you are under immense pressure, not to mention still grieving the loss of your father, which carries a myriad of emotions in itself, but, please help me understand what you're feeling or something! I can't stand it when you are like this!" I shout breathlessly.

Ryan falls back on the bed and covers his eyes with his arm, still silent. I want to scream at him! I cannot stand the silence. I lean over Ryan and pull his arm from his face with quick force. It takes him by surprise.

"Whitney!" he gasps.

I look angrily into his eyes, with tension radiating off my face and a huge lump in my throat. "Is it me?"

Ryan gives me his best "don't be stupid" look, and the tension evaporates from my body before he can say a word.

"Fine!" I say in my best pouty teenager voice. Then I quickly devise a plan. Ryan is still staring up at the ceiling. I slowly pull the down duvet back from his body and move in close to him. He notices my movements from the corner of his eye, but doesn't look at me or say a word.

I lift my body over his and place my knees on the bed on either side of his body. I am straddling him. This gesture gets his attention.

"Whitney! What the hell? Your leg!"

I place my hand over his mouth. "Oh no, you don't want to talk remember?" I say sarcastically. He gives me a funny look. Before he can speak, I peel off my pajama top. "If you don't want to talk, I know of several other things we can do!"

With that, Ryan sits up in the bed and grabs me with a cosmic force. His fierce and sudden contact takes my breath away. His lips are on mine, possessing me. I cry out with surprise. He pulls me down on top of him, but his lips never leave mine. His hands are in my hair, grabbing and pulling. This may not have been a good idea after all. It feels like he is taking out some unknown aggression on me.

Ryan runs his arm around my waist, and in one swift move, he flips me over to my back. He is on top of me now. *Oh my God!* This is so intense. Ryan stares me down with a look of desperation or anxiety; I'm not sure which emotion it is. He peels off my pajama bottoms and my panties with one quick motion. I cry out again, this time with desire, as he takes control over me.

Ryan continues his dark stare into my eyes while he plunges inside me. I cry out from the sudden fullness. It's heavenly. Ryan's body moves, and together we pick up the rhythm that only our bodies know. He is focused and forceful, not taking any pity on me or my body.

It takes only a few moments before I start to feel my body building in response to his. I don't want to stop it, but I couldn't even if I tried.

My body reaches its peak, and I shatter into pieces. Ryan rams his body into mine and quickly stills, calling my name. I am almost dizzy. I can't believe that just happened, and so fast.

Ryan collapses on top of me, but quickly rolls over, pulling me on top of his chest. I lay out across him, sweaty, with my limbs feeling like Jell-O. *Holy hell!*

"I'm sorry," Ryan mutters. And I giggle.

"I guess my plan backfired on me."

He pulls my chin to his face and smiles. "Yes, it did!"

Ryan shakes his head. "I'm sorry, but I just have a lot on my mind, you know."

"Yes, I know you do. But please don't shut me out. It drives me insane." He nods his head as if he understands. "Where did you go last night?" I finally ask him.

"I...I..." he stammers. "I just needed some time. I wanted to get some air to try to clear my mind, but that didn't work."

For some reason, I still believe he is lying to me. I try to shake it off. I feel like I'm fighting a losing battle. I slide off Ryan's chest and move to the other side of the bed. I lay silent for a moment, then decide to leave the bed altogether.

"Where are you going now?" Ryan asks.

"Shower," is all I can manage as I disappear into the bathroom. Two can play at this game.

Chapter 43

I shower quickly. I know we have to get to the track for practice. Ryan needs it. I focus on getting myself ready and not whatever is bothering Ryan. I pull on my favorite jeans, #62 polo shirt, and my matching Asics tennis shoe. Then, I strap on my walking boot. My hair looks like hell, and I don't even attempt to brush it. I throw on some basic makeup and pull my curly brown locks through my GCR Racing hat, thankful that we don't have any PR or sponsor events today. I can dress down. I check my look in the mirror. *Done. Let's do this.*

I walk back into the bedroom area. Ryan is sitting on the edge of the bed, waiting for me to come out. "We need to go, Whit," he says as he rolls his eyes at me.

I smile sweetly and say sarcastically, "I'm ready!"

He waltzes into the bathroom and slams the door. *Seriously! What is his deal?*

We arrive at the track after forty-five minutes of virtual weirdness, although he does hold my hand in the car. So, that does reassure me some. I hang out in the hauler and work on my laptop while he practices. I schedule the press conference, as Ryan requested, and have sent out a blanket e-mail to all media outlets. I want everything to run smoothly for him tomorrow since tensions are so high.

I take a break from my work in the hauler to watch a few of Ryan's practice laps. The car looks great. By watching him bring the car effortlessly through the corners, I can tell he has found his groove. It is a huge relief. I hope this changes Ryan's mood.

I am finishing up a series of e-mails to sponsors about upcoming races when I am accosted from behind. Two strong arms wrap around my body, and I am overwhelmed by that scent. The scent of my man.

Ryan nuzzles my hair and the back of my neck. "Are you ready to go?" he asks.

It is late in the afternoon, but I am not sure of the time. I smile, completely sated from his embrace and no longer conscious of who may see. "Whenever you are."

Slowly, Ryan turns me around so that I am facing him. He looks at me appreciatively and lovingly. "Thank you. Thank you for everything you did to help me make this happen." And with that statement, he folds me into a firm embrace. All of my anxiety evaporates with his touch.

I take everything in, Ryan's sincerity, his appreciation for my work, his kindness, and his strong arms that envelop my small body. I am enjoying this moment, and like him, I no longer give a damn who knows. Ryan pulls back and leans down to gently kiss me.

"Let's go," I murmur against his lips.

* * *

By the time we arrive back at the hotel, we are both exhausted. "Room service?" Ryan asks coyly.

"Best idea you've had all day," I say.

Ryan shakes his head, watching me warily as I strip off my clothes. I am beyond tired, and we still have the main event tomorrow. I drag on my pj's and climb into bed.

"Whitney, it's still light out!" Ryan snaps.

"Yes, it is. But, that is one of the many perks of room service. Wake me when it gets here!"

Ryan moves swiftly across the room and slides into bed with me, clothes and all. "Who says that I am going to let you sleep?" he says sexily as he pulls me into his arms. *Ahh!* There is no point in arguing now.

After another glorious round of lovemaking, our room service arrives. Ryan ordered a variety off the menu, and I am thankful because I am starving now, too. We take our time as we enjoy the food and each other's company. We eat in front of the large window looking out into the beautiful Chicago nightlife. The twinkling lights dance on the skyline. It's romantic. And, it reminds me that Ryan and I have never really had a first date! *Oh well!*

We talk much like the first night in my apartment. I love these long talks. It helps me to know Ryan better. Even though we have been through so much, we still know very little about each other. Tonight, he talks animatedly about Garrett. He shares stories from his childhood, racing memories, and the like. I know it must be helpful for him. Ryan chuckles to himself.

"What is it?" I ask.

"Nothing. I just remembered what my Dad said when he told me that he had given you the job as my PR manager."

"Oh! I was wondering who delivered that good news to you." I laugh recalling the first days of us working together.

Ryan raises his eyebrows, *"Son, you met your match! And I can't wait to see how ya'll duke it out."* A wave of sadness washes over his face and my heart drops. Because, we both know that he won't get to see how our relationship progresses.

Chapter 44

The alarm clock on my iPhone sings in my ears. I will the sound away and try to block it out. I am far too comfortable. I must get up. I must get up. It's race day! I finally reconcile myself internally to get up from my slumber. I sit up in the bed and instantly see Ryan sitting across the room at the table by the large window. He is already dressed and ready for the track. I can tell he is in deep thought. A chill runs down my spine as I think about the weight that must be on his shoulders.

My movement from across the room stirs Ryan from his deep reverie. He turns his beautiful face to meet my concerned gaze and smiles his glorious megawatt smile that turns my body into Jell-O. *Oh my!*

"Good morning, beautiful!" he says. I smile, relieved that he is in a good mood. Ryan moves quickly from his perch across the room and is by my side instantly. He leans over and caresses my cheek. "I love waking up with you on race day and every other day for that matter."

I smile and rest my head in his hand.

* * *

When we arrive at Chicagoland, it is pure madness. The news of Ryan's arrival and intent to race has gone viral despite my attempts to keep the news on the down low. The moment Ryan and I climb out of the car, we are surrounded by a sea of media, paparazzi, and a throng of wild fans. Ryan takes my hand to lead me through the crowd. The cameras snap, and I am aware of each flash that pops in my eyes.

Ryan effectively ignores a series of questions and harsh invasions of privacy as the crowd follows us en route to the mandatory morning drivers' meeting. I feel my chest begin to seize with panic. Ryan must sense my nervousness because he lets go of my hand to snake his arm tightly around my waist, pulling me in close.

When we reach the building, I stop short of the threshold. Ryan looks at me nervously, and I smile. "Let me handle this. Go inside."

Ryan's eyes are wide with shock. "You don't have to do this."

I smile, "Yes, I do. It's my job."

Ryan nods stoically, but I can tell he is thankful. He quickly disappears inside as I turn to face the mob. I hold up my hands for them to give me some space as I speak. I take a deep breath and shift my weight, so that I stand firm despite my leg.

"Ryan will be giving a brief press conference about ten minutes before driver introductions. He will not answer any questions nor give any pre- or post-race interviews. Ryan appreciates your concern and your sympathy. Please respect his privacy during this difficult time. Thank you!"

I smile warily, but before I can step inside for the meeting, an arrogant paparazzo shouts, "Does your relationship with Ryan go beyond the track?"

Then another. "So the rumors were true about you being involved with both Colton and Ryan?"

Before I can respond, another one hits me. "Are you and Ryan a couple?"

I feel panic rise in my chest again, but I stand my ground. I hold up my hands in defense this time. "Please just back off!" I say sternly catching myself off guard. "This is a very difficult time for Ryan and for GCR. If Ryan has any comments, you will be the first to know!" And I step through the door of the building. I gasp for air as Ryan grabs me.

"You didn't have to do that! Are you OK?"

I take a deep breath. "If I hadn't told them to back off, the whole day would have been chaos. And I don't want that for you today."

Ryan envelops me in his all-consuming embrace. I lose myself in his arms, my safe haven. I hold him tightly as if my life depended on it. We can do this. We can do this together.

Ryan pulls back. "The meeting is about to start."

I step back sharply. His words bring me back to reality. And, suddenly I am aware that we are being watched by everyone in attendance. I feel like a thousand eyes are on me, and my face burns with embarrassment.

Ryan gives me a reassuring look and takes my hand again to lead me to our seats "Come on."

I follow behind him. I can't look up or make eye contact with anyone. Ryan and I are under intense scrutiny, and I am well aware that going public with our relationship doesn't help matters.

Pre-race activities fly by, and before I know it, Jason Luke, country music superstar, gives the starting engine call. I stand by Ryan's #62 Chevrolet as long as I can. I clasp my hand firmly over his through the window of his race car. Throughout the ceremony, I hear cameras snapping and flashing. Each pop feels like a bullet in my back. I can't even imagine how the headlines will read in the morning.

Far too soon, Ryan pulls his hand away to secure his window net. He gives me his signature bad-boy wink as he slides the eye guard down on his helmet, and I desperately want to crawl into the car with him to get away from all these prying eyes. *Lucky bastard!*

Forty-three stock cars proceed down pit road for the starting laps as I make my way to my seat next to Ben on top of our team's pit box. Ben smiles to me knowingly as I sit down, but doesn't offer up anything. I know he witnessed the moment between Ryan and me in the drivers' meeting, but he doesn't acknowledge it or ask me any questions. *Thank God!*

Ryan will have to make 267 laps around the mile-and-a-half intermediate speedway today. As the cars take the green flag, I whisper a silent prayer for Ryan, a prayer for safety and a clear determination to finish. With everything that has gone on these last few months, it is clear that we all need a higher power to get through this race, races to come, and our daily lives. I raise my head from my prayer as Ryan's car roars down the front stretch.

The laps tick off one by one in an uneventful manner. Ryan maintains his qualifying position and runs in the middle of the pack. I notice that his racing style is significantly different today. He is not as aggressive or impatient. Ryan's car must be good and accurate because his radio frequency is eerily quiet, too. The only words that come through are Mike's commands from the spotter's tower. He keeps to his line and is driving the car safe, keeping his nose clean, literally.

With fifty laps to go, the lead lap cars come in for a final pit stop. Ryan's car roars into his pit box and comes to an abrupt stop. His pit crew hops over the wall to crank out a mind-blowing pit stop, including fresh tires and a full tank of gas. No other adjustments are needed. Ryan pulls out of his box in what seems like a whirlwind. The crew is super excited and fist pumping the air as Ryan advances ten spots thanks to the awesome pit stop. I can feel the excitement and adrenaline begin to flow through my body again. *Thank God!*

Banter among Ryan, Bobby, and Mike has picked up significantly since Ryan has considerably advanced his position on the track. He is now running in twelfth position with forty-odd laps to go.

I can hear the excitement in Ryan's voice as he fires down the backstretch into turn four. "Awesome job, guys!"

Ryan negotiates turn four and picks up another position as he crosses the start/finish line. "Watch your line, Ryan. Don't screw this up at the last minute now," I hear Mike say through the radio.

Screw what up? I wonder.

Next, Bobby comes through. "Is the car OK since the last stop? How are the tires?"

I hear the squawk of the radio as Ryan fires back, "Car is fine. Let me concentrate!" *Whoa!*

Suddenly, I realize from the arrogance in his voice that Ryan is back to his old self in the race car. I study the monitor closely as he speeds around the track and begins to pick off more positions. According to the race commentators, Ryan's car is the fastest on the track at 143.5 miles per hour; however, we are down to fewer than twenty-five laps to go.

I start to get anxious and shift nervously in my seat. In fact, the adrenaline gets to be so much that I stand up. My blood is roaring through my veins. It is the same rush I get when Ryan and I are alone together. I can't get enough of it. I feel like I am about to burst from my skin. I want to scream from the intensity. And at the same time, I am so thankful these feelings were not lost after all Ryan and I have been through.

Ben looks at over me with the same trepidation and rises from his seat, too. We stand together in silence. I watch the monitor as Ryan continues to stealthily pick off drivers on the track. He gracefully fires through turn three and picks up another position, sliding past a Ford stock car. Ryan is now up to eighth.

There are fifteen laps to go. I know a win is not possible, because Ryan is running out of racetrack. There are not enough laps left for him to negotiate to first position. Hell, I'm just proud of a top-ten finish. Ryan just has to hold on. I repeat that mantra in my mind. *Hold on, Ryan. Hold on.* Anything can change with at a second's notice in this sport. We all know that.

The radio crackles again, and I hear Ryan's voice. "I feel him. He is with me in this car."

I know exactly what he means, and I realize within a moment what Ryan is doing. I choke back a sob in my throat and grasp my mouth with my hands. Overnight, he has adopted Garrett's style of racing. He has played it cool throughout the race and now is making his move. A move for the win.

Neither Mike nor Bobby responds to Ryan's comment. No doubt they are choked up like me. Finally, Mike speaks in a strained voice. "Hold your line. You have a lapped car to pass. You're clear." Then he shouts with excitement, "Go! Go!"

Excitement, tension, and adrenaline are all radiating through our pit area. Bobby talks over the radio. "You got this, Ryan...Hold tight, buddy. Hold tight."

My thoughts exactly. I begin to pace the pit box. Ryan fires back around turn three and accelerates down the backstretch with eight more laps to go. Through turn four, he easily picks up another spot. Clearly, he has the fastest car because he is picking off drivers left and right. Down the backstretch, a stock car in fourth position blows a tire and slams into the wall off turn one. NASCAR immediately throws a caution flag. *Damn!*

Ryan slows the car to caution speed as the pace car takes to the track to lead the drivers. After the car involved in the accident is cleared, it takes Ryan up to fifth position. Thankfully, the track is cleared of debris quickly, and the caution is limited to only one lap with six laps left to go. The pace car drops off the track back to pit road, and the cars accelerate full throttle. My heart pounds with each drop of the hammer. Ryan picks off two cars from the restart. He is up to third, but is running out of time.

Despite the cool, fall breeze; I am sweating as I pick up my pace on top of the pit box. I steal a glance at Ben, who is intently watching the monitor. I turn up the radio frequency in my ear. It is quiet as Ryan rounds turn four and pushes through, remaining in third position. He runs the car mercilessly past the start/finish line with five laps to go.

I can't take it anymore. I jump down off the pit box and rush over to Bobby's side. He smiles nervously at me but doesn't say a word. Neither do I. I continue to listen intently to the radio banter and watch the coverage monitor. I feel like my heart is going to implode as Ryan easily rolls through turn two and pushes out onto the backstretch.

I can see on the monitor that Ryan is attempting to pass, but the driver is not making it easy. Mike squeaks through the radio, "Clear high," as Ryan is making an attempt to pass the second-place car.

Ryan approaches the right side of the #34 Dodge and attempts to pass. However, the driver blocks him. He can't get by. *Damn!* Ryan holds down the throttle, and they go two wide out of turn three, then back through turn four and down across the start/finish line. Four laps to go.

Into turn one again, Ryan successfully completes the pass on the #34 stock car and gains second position. I can't breathe. Then, suddenly, it hits me. This is what he was so uptight about. He and Bobby had a plan this whole time. A sneak attack, just like Garrett was famous for. He must have been anxious, wondering if he could pull it off. And he has almost successfully followed it through. I steal a glance at Bobby, hoping for some clues, but he watches the monitor, stock-still, giving nothing away.

Two more laps to go. The first-place car isn't going to give up easily to Ryan. They battle into each turn as Ryan fights to take the top position from the #17 Chevrolet. Ryan gets a nose on him in turn two, but is blocked by the driver. They roar, two wide, down the backstretch, neck and neck.

Ryan pulls down dangerously low on the apron close to black flag territory. If he crosses that boundary line, NASCAR will send him down pit road, which will put him a lap down. My heart catches in my throat as Ryan pulls past the #17 stock car and into first place. He slides past the car as the flagman throws out the white flag and crosses the start/finish line with only one more lap to go.

I scream. The pit crew roars out! Ben jumps down from the pit box to join us. We all stand together, united in shocked silence, as Ryan pulls the car into turn one.

Mike speaks dryly into Ryan's ear. "You got him. Hold your line. Only two more turns."

I can't believe this. Ryan is going to...*No. Don't say it!* I watch the monitor as he successfully negotiates turn two and fires down the backstretch.

Mike sounds off again to Ryan. "Steady...You walked off on him. You have the strongest car. Just hold on."

I jump up and down as I will him. *Come on! Come on!* I lock arms with Bobby and Ben as Ryan takes the last turn into four and smoothly guides his car through the corner. I look up, and the flagman begins waving the checkered flag as Ryan crosses the start/finish for the last time—in first place. *Oh my God! He won!*

An explosion of cheers go up from the seventy-five-thousand-plus crowd in attendance as tears stream down my face. Whether you love Ryan or hate him, today of all days, you couldn't be anything but happy that he won, especially after the death of his father. I can't believe what's happened. *What a week!*

The remaining cars on the lead lap slow through the finish line and head back to pit road. Ryan is yelling over his radio, but I can't understand him for all the commotion. Our pit box is mass hysteria. I take off the headset and flip my eyes back to the monitor. Ryan brings his car back across the start/finish line in a celebratory burnout typical of most drivers. What a happy day! After Ryan burns out what is left of his tires, he roars his car across the infield and turns up the grass. We all watch, so excited for him and for our team.

The entire pit crew rushes out to congratulate him right where his car comes to rest in the infield. I hobble along with them. Ryan climbs out of his car, stands on the window opening, and fist pumps the air in front of the crowd. He turns around to acknowledge us when we all arrive and jumps down into a sea of pit crew members, media, and NASCAR officials. I watch as he pushes through the crowd with purpose-driven force effectively ignoring the mob. He looks angry. I don't understand why.

As we make eye contact, Ryan strides up to me with vehemence and says, "Your ass is fired!"

I laugh out loud, taking his statement as a joke. *What is this about?*

"No...I'm serious. I don't want you to be my public relations manager anymore."

My heart flip-flops in my chest. More people and camera crews rush out to our place in the infield. My face burns with embarrassment because I know this could all be on live TV. I glance around at them nervously, not sure where this conversation is going. I am shocked at Ryan's declaration. The lump in my throat makes it hard to speak.

"Why?" I ask simply. *What could I have possibly done?*

Out of the corner of my eye, I watch as Ryan sticks his hand up to catch a small object that is tossed to him from behind me. Our eyes are locked in a heated stare, but Ryan doesn't break it. He grabs the object, drops to one knee, and proudly says, "Because...I want you to be my wife instead."

The air rushes out of my lungs, and I feel like I am going to throw up as the world around me stops. Very slowly, I look down, trying to make sense of what is happening in the midst of all this commotion. *Could he be serious? Did I hear him right?*

I look down at Ryan as he slowly opens the pale blue Tiffany box. Then, in front of God and everybody, he says, "Marry me!"

Another loud round of cheers goes up from the crowd around us and from the grandstands. I hear the snap of cameras and commentary from journalists crackling in the background. I look around, stunned, trying to assimilate the situation.

Ryan takes my hand to garner my attention. "Whitney, you know that I love you, and I never want to be away from you again!"

Suddenly, tears flood my eyes unexpectedly. I never want to be away from him either, but this means I must make another choice. I quickly think back through the last three months, which is a very short amount of time to be with someone, especially after we spent six weeks apart. I made some bad decisions trying to do the right thing, trying to get my life back on track; however, all those decisions led me to Ryan, to this moment. I love him. I would do anything for him—not only him, but for this sport, which is now my life. The adrenaline, the addiction, it all flows through my veins. This dangerous combination of Ryan and racing is what I need, and I never want to be without either one of them. Suddenly, this decision seems not so hard after all.

I look into Ryan's eyes, which causes a look of sheer panic to come across his face, no doubt because I have yet to give him an answer. I nod and smile through my tears.

Ryan's lips quirk up in a half smile. "Say it then!"

"Yes!" I exclaim as another loud roar goes up from the crowd.

"No," Ryan chastises me. "Yes, what?"

I throw my head back laughing. "Yes, I will marry you!"

Ryan leaps from the ground and sweeps me off my feet, cradling me in his arms. He twirls me around the infield as I become insanely aware of the media speculation we are causing. I hear the audacious and prying cameras snap and pop. *Oh, who cares?*

Ryan sets me down to the ground and slides an incredibly gorgeous and large diamond ring on my left hand. After he secures the sparkler on my finger, he runs his hand up my neck and into my hair, in his way, then softly places his lips against mine.

Despite the thousands of people in attendance, and millions most likely watching on television, I feel like Ryan and I are the only two people on this planet. He pulls back all too soon and slowly turns me around to face the crowd that stands behind us. I am dazed, but I manage to look out and into the eyes of my parents, Laura, and Brooke, who are huddled together!

"Oh!" I gasp, and the tears flow again. I look back to Ryan and instantly put everything together. This is the reason he was so quiet and troubled. He pulls me into his chest, embracing me from behind and nuzzles my neck, "Surprise."

He smiles and whispers, "I love you," into my ear. I know that whatever consequences this decision may lead to will be worth every second that I spend wrapped up in Ryan and the adrenaline and excitement that is NASCAR. I will gladly slam into the wall, smoking and spinning, if it means spending the rest of my life with him.

www.ingramcontent.com/pod-product-compliance
Lightning Source LLC
Chambersburg PA
CBHW072300020726
47501CB00002B/335